D1355633

A PAGEANT OF VICTORY

BY THE SAME AUTHOR

THE AMATEUR GENTLEMAN
THE MONEY MOON
THE BROAD HIGHWAY
THE HONOURABLE MR. TAWNISH
THE GESTE OF DUKE JOCELYN
THE CHRONICLES OF THE IMP
THE DEFINITE OBJECT
BELTANE THE SMITH
OUR ADMIRABLE BETTY
BLACK BARTLEMY'S TREASURE
MARTIN CONISBY'S VENGEANCE
PEREGRINE'S PROGRESS
THE LORING MYSTERY
THE QUEST OF YOUTH
THE HIGH ADVENTURE
SIR JOHN DERING
GYFFORD OF WEARE
THE SHADOW AND OTHER STORIES
ANOTHER DAY
OVER THE HILLS
THE JADE OF DESTINY
CHARMIAN, LADY VIBART
THE WAY BEYOND
THE WINDS OF FORTUNE
JOHN O' THE GREEN
A PAGEANT OF VICTORY
THE CROOKED FURROW
THE LONELY ROAD
THE HAPPY HARVEST
A MATTER OF BUSINESS AND OTHER STORIES
ADAM PENFEATHER, BUCCANEER
MURDER BY NAIL
THE KING LIVETH

EPICS OF THE FANCY
A BOOK FOR JANE
A NEW BOOK FOR JANE

A PAGEANT OF VICTORY

BY
JEFFERY FARNOL

LONDON
SAMPSON LOW, MARSTON & CO., LTD.

MADE AND PRINTED IN GREAT BRITAIN BY PURNELL AND SONS, LTD.
PAULTON (SOMERSET) AND LONDON

CONTENTS

BOOK ONE

BOOK TWO

BOOK THREE

BOOK ONE

CHAPTER I

INTRODUCES TWO IMPORTANT PEOPLE

BLODWEN stood where she might watch the road and the river, this river of her dreams, flowing down towards her from the wonders of the North to lose itself in the deep, leafy solitudes of the vast wilderness; this straight road, a great highway that through leagues of forest, led on and ever on across the wild, skirting mountains, fording rivers, piercing the awful silence of plain, desert and savannah, past struggling settlements and desolate outposts, to the unknown wonders of town and cities; Philadelphia, Boston, New York and the mighty ocean beyond which lay a far country, of which she had heard and read so much, called England.

Before her the road and the river, leading to this world of vivid life and action, behind her my lord George Charteris' great House of Wrybourne, throned upon its three terraces, builded sixty odd years ago by my lord's noble sire and like as possible to his ancestral home in England; a stately house beyond which clustered the thatched cottages and huts of his many retainers and negro slaves.

But it was towards the road and silent river that Blodwen's long-lashed, sombre eyes were turned in dreamy contemplation until, startled by a faint sound, she turned with the lithe quickness of some shy forest creature and thus beheld the earl's son and heir, my lord Charles, with his boon companion, the young Marquis de Vaucelles.

And both young gentlemen were gazing at her and in the eyes of both she read that which deepened the dusky bloom in her cheek and set her vivid full-lipped mouth to sudden bitterness: she glanced from the French nobleman to the English aristocrat, then veiled the fire of her eyes, as lord Charles addressed her.

"Aha, Blodwen!" cried he gaily but with no courtesy of bow or flourished hat. "Why so early? Will you go a-hunting with us? I've been boasting to the Marquis of your marvellous skill with the rifle . . . but faith now I protest you grow handsomer every day, by the very hour and minute! How sayst thou, Gaspard?"

"*Pardi!*" answered the Marquis, "thou'rt right, my Charles, she is of a beauty so compelling—ah, ravishing! Here for me is better sport than in your so damp woods yonder. Go thou and hunt, my old one. I have flushed my lovely game!" So saying the Marquis set by the light fowling piece he carried and approached her with all the smiling, joyous assurance of the fine gentleman and accomplished gallant he was.

"My lord," said she in her soft, rich voice, "I am no man's sport . . . take warning." The Marquis laughed gaily, and before she might prevent, had set arm about her slender waist; but with a supple ease she broke his hold and threw him off so strongly that he staggered and all but fell.

"*Mordieu!*" he exclaimed, straightening hat and wig, "but this is of the most appetizing! She is to tame and gentle, this one! Regard now and I—"

"No no," said Charles interposing, "let be, Gaspard, she's a sullen baggage shall scratch and bite; 'stead o' being grateful for a gentlemanly proffer she's apt to flash steel."

"Sayst thou, my old one, my dear Charles?"

"Ay faith, she's done it ere now. Cut young Wimperis in the arm with her knife scarce a month ago. Damme! You'd think her the proudest fine madam of 'em all, must be sued and wooed 'stead of a mere . . ."

"What, sir?" she demanded, as he hesitated. "Oh, pray what . . . what am I?" Here, seeing the look of pain in her eyes, the quiver of her sensitive mouth,

Charles had the grace to flush and was dumb; wherefore the Marquis smiling as gaily, though eyeing her more warily, made a sly pace towards her, saying:

"I protest thou art a goddess, a thing of joy, a creature of delight—"

But once again Charles interposed, and slipping hand in his friend's arm drew him away.

"No no, Gaspard," said he scowling, but a little shame-faced, "'tis a bitter prude and a most peevish shrew. Come, I'll shew thee better sport, man, howso you will. Come let us go."

"*Hélas!*" sighed the Marquis, with exaggerated woe. "*Adieu* thou dark and tempting Venus! . . . Another time we are alone and you shall be more kind . . . *au revoir!*" And saluting her with profound obeisance, he caught up his fowling piece, laughed, kissed his white bejewelled hand, and so, the one laughing, the other frowning, off they went together, gallant figures in their hunting gear; while Blodwen watched them, arms crossed upon her resurgent bosom, nor stirred she or suffered herself to wipe the slow, painful tears that blinded her, until these gay gentlemen were out of sight. Then, striving to check the sobs that shook her, she turned and leaning against a tree, hid her face and wept awhile with strange passion.

And when the fit had spent itself, she dried her eyes heedfully lest they be reddened, and went slow-footed down to the river.

Reaching the margin where the water ran deep and still beneath the bank, she knelt and stooped down to look at herself in this pellucid mirror, viewing her image with a strange and fearful intensity, scanning her every feature with a close scrutiny, in which was an eager questioning, a deep and anxious care; this darkly oval face, glowing of cheek, ruddy of lip and framed in sweeping curtains of night black hair in such startling contrast with these black-lashed tawny eyes that were gazing up at her in such wistful, troubled speculation.

Now as she crouched thus, came old Gideon Ash, rod on shoulder and in his hand a string of gleaming fish, new-caught; and roused by his familiar step she glanced up and beckoned him near.

"Aha," quoth he, obeying her imperious gesture, "be tha' admiring at thy beauty, lass?"

"No!" cried she fiercely. "No! I look to find the evil of me. Oh, Gideon, I think there is a curse on me that turns men into beasts!"

"Eh? Beasts, lass—?"

"Brute beasts!" said she between white teeth "More especially my lord's fine friends. Oh, these gentlemen o' quality! Why must I forever wake the evil in them? I that do so hate men! How old am I, Gideon?"

"Why . . . lemme see, now," he answered, rasping stubbly chin thoughtfully between finger and thumb, "'twere all o' twenty year ago as I found ee, and on just such another morning as this, afloat on the river here in a fine Injun canoe and yourself lapped in a buffler-robe, also very fine, and under that a silk petticut, like-wise mighty fine and round your li'l neck on a golden chain, a Injun charm o' wampum—"

"This!" said she, drawing from her bosom a small pouch of exquisite Indian work and frowning at it.

"Ah, that same," nodded Gideon, "and in it a ruby ring and a writing with the word 'Blodwen.' So Blodwen us called ee. And then my lord's lady having lost her own li'l darter, 'dopted of ee, had ee eddicated like a lady until she died, and then—"

"Then I was allowed to run wild," said Blodwen, bitterly, "the stables, the river, the forest, and to-day . . . Oh, Gideon, who am I? What am I—?"

"A mighty handsome critter as few women can ekal for looks and fewer men match wi' musket or rifle! Ah, 'twas me as larned ee how! Lord love ee," said the old hunter, looking down into her troubled face with eyes of deep affection, "'twas me and old Chacomeeco, the Muskogee, as larned ee all manner o' woodcraft, and you so wonnerful quick, took to it you did like . . . like . . ."

"An Indian!" said she, and with the word was afoot, had grasped him in compelling hands, searching his face with that same wild look of fearful questioning. "An Indian!" she repeated. "Can this be the reason? Is this the answer? Oh, Gideon, is my blood . . . am I an Indian?"

"No, no, lass . . . not you, Blodwen!"

"But are you sure?" she pleaded, clutching him the tighter. "Oh, are you quite sure?"

"Sarten sure!" he answered, stoutly, though his honest old eyes quailed before her eager regard. "But Lord love us all!" he exclaimed cheerily, "here be me idling and to-day my lord's birthday and the great house full o' grand company and more a-coming . . . nigh all the gentry o' Virginny and Maryland. 'Tis bustle, lass, bustle I tell ee! So leggo o' me, dear maid, and lemme to my work, do ee now!" Mutely she obeyed, and nodding cheerily, old Gideon went his way.

Then Blodwen turned and with head bowed in troubled thought went on beside this river that twenty odd years ago had borne her on its broad, gentle bosom out of the unknown. Reaching a favourite place where trees and dense-growing, flowery thickets made a green bower, she sank down and, clasping arms about her rounded limbs, crouched to watch the murmurous waters with her strange golden eyes.

Here, remote from the stir and bustle of the great house and busy village, she sat in a primeval stillness broken only by the soft rustle of leaves about her and the rippling murmur of these ever-flowing waters.

But after some while her quick ear caught the faint, rhythmic beat of paddles and, glancing through the leafage, she espied a long, birch-bark canoe approaching and in it two Indians, but as they drew nearer she saw one of these was a white man, though clad in the Indian fashion, who, throwing up his paddle, said something to his companion, whereupon the canoe, turning in its own length, came gliding smoothly to the bank nearby and Blodwen, hidden in her bower, saw the white man step lightly ashore.

And now a strange thing happened; for scarcely had his moccasined foot touched land than, as if she had called to him, he turned swiftly, looked, and saw her golden eyes peering at him through the leaves—these and no more. Catching up his long rifle, he came striding through the brushwood and parting the leaves, stood looking down at her, and off came his silver fox-skin cap.

A slender, shapely, quick-moving man of no great height though powerfully built and clad like an Indian from throat to ankle in close-fitting garments of native deerskin beautifully worked with coloured porcupine quills, belted with wampum and armed with knife and tomahawk; a youngish man, bronzed and hardened by travel in wild places and yet whose grey eyes smiled down on her from a lean and comely face; silent thus and motionless stood he, one sinewy hand grasping his long-barrelled rifle, his fur cap in the other.

"Why do you bare your head to me?" she demanded ungraciously, and making no effort to rise.

"Because you are a lady," he answered in tone gentle as his look.

"No!" she answered frowning, "I am Blodwen."

"Why then," said he, smiling and bowing with a courtly grace, "I salute you because you are a woman, which is better."

Now because in his frank, well-opened eyes she read a sincerity that matched his words, her frown vanished and when she spoke now, her tone was softly wistful:

"I think you must be my lord's nephew, Mr. Anthony."

"Yes," he answered, drawing a pace nearer, "I'm Anthony Falconbridge. But pray how should you know this?"

"Because I am Blodwen and because I saw you here twelve years ago. But in those days you went very splendid in velvets and laces and 'stead of Indian tomahawk, carried the sword of a gentleman."

"Twelve years ago?" he mused, rubbing smooth shaven chin. "This was when I had but newly come from England, the university of Oxford. You must have been a very small person in those days . . . very young. . . . And Blodwen? A strange, pretty name! Early British I think. . . . Aha, I begin to remember! There was a lovely child my Aunt Anthea doated on, and very pampered and petted by that extremely stately, overwhelming personage, my uncle George . . . Well?"

"Yes, Mr. Anthony, I was that spoiled child. But you now, being my lord's nephew, are a great gentleman despite your Indian trappings, why must you steal ashore thus and so far from the Great House?"

"Faith, Mistress Blodwen," he answered, smiling a little ruefully "this is because I'm in no little doubt how my lordly uncle shall receive me, for he is so preposterously stately and Tory and English, and a great power here in Virginia."

"Yes," she nodded, "everything hereabout is English, the house, the park, even the country for miles around he has altered and planted and made as much like his England as possible,—or so they say, for I have never seen England . . . to my knowledge. But my lord would have everything and everybody English, even his black slaves bear English names and are called after towns and villages in England."

"Ay, I remember," smiled Anthony. "There was old Pevensey Sussex, his black butler, and Wilmington Alfriston, and Chailey Arundel. Yes, Uncle George was always himself and too proud to be anything but an Englishman."

"But you, Mr. Anthony, are just as much an Englishman as your uncle."

"Why yes, I am, or rather, I was. But to-day I am a Colonial. America is my home and shall be, so to-day I am an American and proud of it."

"And to-day you are here for your uncle's birthday, Mr. Anthony?"

"I came because I was especially summoned. There is to be a family reunion, it seems. And considering Great Britain's new repressive acts and General Gage's cursed folly in Massachusetts, I can guess why."

"You mean the late rioting in Boston? But my lord says this is no more than the foolish clamours of a drunken mob soon to be hushed."

"Ah," sighed Anthony, shaking his head, "would to God it were! Here is smoke shall grow to a quenchless fire, I guess!"

At this moment from beyond flowery thicket, a deep voice hailed softly in the Indian dialect, whereto Anthony answered in the same musical speech; then turning to Blodwen, "Lady," said he, flushing and somewhat abashed it seemed by her cold, dark scrutiny, "my good friend the Sagamore yonder has prepared breakfast, grilled trout, and now I'm wondering if . . . perhaps you are hungry . . . perhaps you will honour us? Would you eat with us, Mistress Blodwen?" He said this with such diffidence and in his look such boyish shyness that Blodwen's woeful heart swelled and, though her eyes were misted with sudden tears, her sullen features were transfigured by such smile that Anthony caught his breath at this revelation of her warm and radiant loveliness. Then with an effortless ease, she rose, saying with a check in her voice that was something between laugh and sob:

"Oh, Mr. Anthony, I . . . shall be very happy to join you." Then she reached out a hand, shapely, though brown almost as his own. So Anthony grasped this hand in warm clasp, and, with the courtesy of the time, bowed his head and kissed it.

He brought her where, close beside the river and screened well from all chance observation, an Indian was busied over a small fire that gave forth much heat but little or no betraying smoke. Espying them, the Indian rose and stood with all the reposeful dignity of his race, watching their approach; a stately man and taller for the three eagles' feathers above his brow; about his neck a string of bears' claws, his deerskin tunic and leggings rich with embroidery, their broad seams fringed and adorned by the many scalp locks of his slain foes.

"Mistress Blodwen," said Anthony, "here is my comrade and blood brother, Mahtocheega, Sagamore of the Tuscaroras, a great warrior and chief." The Indian saluted her with grave courtesy to whom Anthony now spoke in his own dialect. Once again the Indian saluted her, then taking a buffalo robe from the canoe, spread it upon the ground to her comfort.

And thus, throned between the white man and the red, Blodwen talked and ate, questioned and listened in such communion as she had never known. But presently the Sagamore, having ended his frugal meal, rose and saluting them like the natural aristocrat he was, went down to busy himself with the travel-worn canoe, leaving them together.

"Has your Indian Sagamore any English?"

"Why yes indeed, when he chooses."

"And you, Mr. Anthony, you live alone in the great wilderness?"

"Near the Lake Country, but not alone," he answered, his grey eyes a-dream. "I've built a log house there . . . in a very earthly paradise. And I live with my three men Tom Laurie, Nat Joyce, Nick Brewer and his wife. Also I have founded a little settlement not far away. Then Mahtocheega and his people have their village hardby, so I'm not lonely."

"Then you do not . . . despise the Indians?"

"No, no, not I!" he answered warmly. "These are the natural lords of the forest and prairie, and in their native innocence is a nobility, a strict universal code of honour hard to find in our own great cities and vaunted civilization."

"And yet," she demurred, "we are forever hearing tales of their merciless ferocity, their terrible tortures, their treachery and massacres of helpless folk and lonely settlers."

"And alas, with some truth. For after all the redskin, like the white, is good and bad, but I'm bold to say, the worst of them is not so vilely evil as the worst of us. The red man is proud and vengeful and, God forgive us, has suffered many bitter harms and wrongs. Yet I have found that the Indian in his native state is clean, body and mind, and as truly honourable as any gentleman should be. But Lord!" he broke off with self-deprecating laugh, "I fear my tediousness wearies you?"

"No," she answered, with quick shake of the head, "I am interested. Pray go on, tell me of your Indians and your life in the wilderness."

So they talked together until the sun was high and a powerful contralto voice was heard calling:

"Missie Blodwen, oh Missie Blodwen, where is you, now?"

"There is Marileena, my old nurse," said Blodwen, then called in answer:

"Here I am, Leena."

Ensued a prodigious crackling of twigs, rustling of leaves and, forth of the underbrush stepped a gigantic negress being large every way, her black, good-natured face surmounted by a vivid turban.

"Well, foh de Lord's sake!" she exclaimed, setting hands on ample hips and shaking her head. "De lady Ann done say foh me to find you dis minute and I done go looking everywhar and heah yoh is long of a lot o' pooh Injun trash! I 'lows youse de bad chile! Come 'long now, come 'long and be dressed. De lady Ann she done say you is to make yo'self into lak what is a dairymaid and oversee dem lazy niggah-wenches in serving de great ladies wid de syllabubs, so come 'long now dis minute."

"Very well!" said Blodwen rising. "Go you before, Leena, I'll follow." But after the tall negress, grumbling good-naturedly, had departed, Blodwen stood some while motionless and silent, her sombre eyes upon the river again. Then turning where Anthony stood beside her, she spoke softly, though without looking at him:

"Twenty odd years ago, a baby in an Indian canoe came drifting down this river and round her neck . . . this!" Here with swift gesture she did off the golden neckchain.

"Why, this is a Sachem's medicine bag!" said he. "And of very splendid workmanship . . . Blackfoot work I think."

"Or Cree," she sighed. "In it you will find a scrap of paper with the one word 'Blodwen.' There is also a plain ruby ring with the graven words '*Semper Eadem.*' Pray look at them." So Anthony took out these treasured relics with reverent fingers, viewing them with profound interest,

"*Semper Eadem!*" he murmured thoughtfully. "Ever the same . . . a splendid motto, and one I remember having seen while at Oxford in England and . . . yes, by heavens I believe in just such another ring as this, though whose and under what circumstances, I can't for the life of me recall."

"Not even if you . . . think very hard?" she enquired breathlessly.

"No!" he answered, staring down at the ring beneath knit brows, "it is but the vaguest recollection."

"Why then," she sighed, "Mr. Anthony, pray look at me."

"Indeed I am!" he answered. And now at last she raised her strange, golden eyes to his, and drawing comb from her hair, shook down her blue-black glossy tresses.

"See now, Mr. Anthony," said she in the same breathless way, "my skin . . . so dark! My hair so black and straight as . . . any Indian! Well, Mr. Anthony, you that know so much about Indian peoples, think you that I . . . am an Indian?"

"God love you, no!" he answered awed more by the pleading intensity of her gaze than by the dark and yet vital beauty of her. "No . . . indeed!"

"Yet, sir . . . my history . . . this Indian medicine bag . . . my looks and bearing! Remembering all this, can you . . . dare you be certain there is no strain of the Indian in my blood? Ah . . . you cannot!" she gasped, "you cannot! I see it in your eyes"—and snatching the Indian talisman from his lax fingers she set it about her creamy throat with a swift, wild gesture and turned to be gone, but he stayed her with outflung arm.

"Mistress Blodwen," he protested very earnestly, "who is there might answer such question, surely not I—"

"Oh, sir," cried she with mirthless laugh, "your eyes be truer than your tongue, I think."

"Howbeit," he answered, "my lips tell you that you are as God made you, and my eyes tell me you have a beauty might lift a man up to heaven—"

"Or lure him down to hell!" she retorted and, with another laugh evil to hear, she sped away.

CHAPTER II

WHICH GIVES TWO SIDES OF A VERY VEXED QUESTION

GEORGE CHARTERIS, fourth earl of Wrybourne, lived in an almost royal estate and medieval splendour, with a staff of gentlemen-in-waiting, each the scion of a noble house; with an army of liveried servants to his behest, and numberless black slaves to till his wide lands and tend his rich plantations. His Steward of the Household was a stately personage, his Clerk of the Kitchen, his Bailiff of Husbandry, his Brewer of Beer, these all were personages and esteemed themselves as such.

To-day proudest gentlemen and humblest slaves were in full force and glory; jewels glittered, gracious ladies curtseyed in billowing satins, gentlemen bowed gallantly with swirl of embroidered coat-skirts, while soft-footed servants went to and fro to their refreshment, for the day was warm, ranks of negro slaves rolled great eyes and flashed white teeth.

Here to-day was gathered the quality of Virginia and Maryland, and more constantly arriving, grand folk all, blue-blooded aristocrats, offshoots from noble English stock, and though so far from their ancestral halls, English one and all and Tory to the very core, and, every one of them, journeying hither, to this England out of England, to grace my lord's sixtieth birthday and take counsel with this right potent and very noble Englishman how best to stem the rising tide of unrest in the North and keep these English Colonies as English and law-abiding as of yore.

Just at present my lord's many visitors were congregated upon the wide lawns, sitting or strolling across this soft, thick turf that was eloquent of ceaseless care and labour, a brilliant assemblage waited upon by lacqueys in my lord's rich liveries, while the sunny air was joyful with the babble of merry voices and happy laughter.

Hitherwards about noon came Anthony, the Sagamore stalking at his heels, but, in the shade of a lofty tree remote from the throng, he paused to gaze upon the bright and animated scene, a pageant of vivid colours that moved in splendour against the wide frontage of the Great House.

Now as he stood seeking among this assemblage for the face of friend or acquaintance, out from a pleached walk hardby sped a vision of fluttering, silken loveliness, a small, dainty creature who catching sight of Anthony and the Sagamore, checked in full career, threw up small, jewelled hands, screamed prettily and stood gazing at him with wide blue eyes, an exquisite creature from dainty shoe to powdered hair and perfectly aware of it.

"An—thony!" she gasped. "Is it . . . can this be twooly you?"

"None other," he laughed, bowing cap in hand. "And you, I perceive are your own radiant self as ever, Priscilla."

"But . . . oh Anthony! Why these fwightful twappings? . . . so savage! Is it a jest to tease your wuncle?"

"No no, I assure you, Priscilla. You see his message reached me far in the wilderness and I had to come as I was, or not at all."

"But why oh why dwess yourself like a howid Wedskin?"

"Because leather garments are best suited to travel in thorny places and—"

"Then why twavel in thorny places, Anthony?" But as she spoke from the shadowy pleached walk a baritone voice called:

"Priscilla!"

"Oh," she laughed, "there's your nice cousin Fwank Wilding looking for me." At this moment rose another voice, somewhat further afield, a flutey tenor wailing: "Oh, Priscilla!"

"And there's your wich cousin, lord Charles. And they're both twying to pwopose to me, and I'm in a dweadful quandawy for Charles is so wich and a lord, and Fwank is so handsome but only a lawyer, and you, Anthony, that I pwomised to mawwy when we were children, are gwown into such a fwightful wild man."

"Ho—Priscilla!" "Priscilla—hoy!" cried tenor and baritone in unison. And forth together from shadowy yew walks, though from different directions, emerged two resplendent young gentlemen who, beholding their lovely quarry hanging on the arm of this outlandish leather-clad anomaly, halted to stare, then came striding amain.

"By God, it's Anthony!" exclaimed Mr. Wilding pausing again in very evident surprise. "It's Cousin Falconbridge!"

"Demme if it isn't!" quoth lord Charles, pausing also. Thus for a long moment the three cousins surveyed each other speechlessly; all three were young, comely and marked with that same indefinable air of high breeding, yet each the other's opposite. Anthony in his travel-worn deerskins, lord Charles magnificent in brocade and silk from glossy wig to sparkling shoe-buckles, Francis Wilding, who wore his own brown hair unpowdered and tied in a queue, as elegant though more soberly clad in dark blue and silver.

"Well," exclaimed his lordship at last, "Tony, I'm glad to see thee, but why, oh demme why in such outlandish rig—?"

"Nay now," said Priscilla, "I pwotest it becomes him extwemely, Charles!"

"Ay but," said my lord, shaking his head, "Gad's life, Tony, my honoured sire will like as not fall into convulsions at mere sight o' thee!"

"Why then, Charles, I'll bide here out o' sight."

"But han't you any civilized clothes, Tony?"

"Alas not a stitch . . . and yonder I think is one of your father's gentlemen, seeking you." Even as he spoke the gentleman in question ventured to approach breathless with haste to bow, and, glancing askance at Anthony, begged to announce that my lord the Earl was about to make his appearance and demanded his son's instant attendance. So perforce away went lord Charles and with him Priscilla and Francis.

"See you anon, Tony!" smiled Priscilla, blowing a kiss.

"I'd like a word with you later, Anthony, anent these troubles in Boston," said Francis Wilding.

Anthony smiled and doffed his cap and leaning back to the mighty tree-bole, gazed dreamily upon the scene before him, yet saw little of it for before the eyes of his mind was a sullen beautiful face lit by black-lashed, tawny eyes . . . the strange wild passion of her . . . good or evil . . .?"

So lost was he that he started at a touch on his arm and the Sagamore's soft spoken words.

"My brother . . . behold he comes, this great one!"

Anthony glanced up as forth into the sunshine, his son Charles upon his right hand, his gentlemen behind him, stepped George Charteris, fourth Earl of Wrybourne.

My lord walked leisurely, toes delicately pointed, hat in one hand, laced handkerchief in the other, glancing serenely this way and that, until he had reached a horse-block covered with an Oriental rug whereon he mounted the better to see and be seen.

A quaint and imposing figure was my lord the Earl, bedight in the stately magnificence of a bygone generation; upon his head a lofty, full-bottomed, curling peruke (none o' your scratch, tie or bob wigs for him); his velvet coat, of royal purple, was full skirted and enriched with gold braid and jewelled buttons; jewels sparkled in the snowy lace at his throat, they gleamed in his shoe-buckles and in the gold hilt of his sword, that famous weapon wherewith his grandfather (the wild

Charteris and boon companion of the Merry Monarch) had killed his best friend on a point of honour (when gentlemen were gentlemen, demme! and a gentleman's honour very precious and delicate as his garments). Thus as my lord the earl stood looking down upon his many guests, so superbly sure of himself and his world, he might have just stepped from the bygone splendour of the Great Louis' Court, nay indeed he might almost have been a reincarnation of the Grand Monarch, *Le Roi Soleil* himself.

"My lords," said he in rich, full-throated tones, "ladies and gentlemen, good friends all, be welcome. This, as you know, is my sixtieth birthday. But it is with a graver and I think even a worthier object that I have convoked you here this day. I allude to the growing spirit of lawlessness displayed by certain ignorant mobs fostered and fomented by the irreconcilable Irish, those haters of England and all law and order. I have summoned you here then that you, and I, being gentlemen of Virginia and Maryland, are first and always gentlemen of England and loyal subjects of his Majesty the King, that we may take counsel together how best to check this wave of lawlessness and stem this tide of rebellion. But this shall be later; for the present my pleasure is to greet you, one and all, personally and to make joyous festival on this my birthday."

So saying, my lord descended from his pedestal, whereat unseen musicians struck up, filling the air with melodious strains now sweetly plaintive, now gay and heartening, but each and every songs of Old England, while my lord went to and fro among his guests bowing, smiling, kissing the hands of noble ladies, grasping the hands of noble gentlemen, talking and laughing with everyone until four gigantic negroes in gorgeous livery marched forth, two and two, and summoned the company to the banquet with flourish and fanfare of trumpets.

The great banqueting hall of Wrybourne, modelled exactly on my lord's ancestral hall in England, was lofty and spacious, its panelled walls hung with antique arms and armour, its mighty roof-beams richly carven, and, with a minstrel's gallery whence my lord's musicians were discoursing sweet melodies. Here were long tables covered with snowy damask whereon gold and silver gleamed and cut glass sparkled; and at these tables my lord's guests were seated according to rank, that is to say, the humbler their degree the further were they from that lofty table where sat their noble host.

Thus Anthony presently found himself placed very far from his stately uncle, which, under the circumstances, he deemed fortunate, the more so indeed when he espied Blodwen seated opposite to him. But his smiling bow she hardly noticed and, despite her finery of silks, patches and powder, he thought her more sullen and ungracious than ever, and was seized of a cold wonderment that he could ever have thought her beautiful.

Seeing himself thus disdainfully ignored, and for no imaginable reason, he felt hurt, then angry; and becoming aware of his many neighbours' curious or supercilious glances, he kept his frowning gaze on his plate, grew morose, and when any ventured to address him, answered only in monosyllables; so that he was presently shunned altogether; then being painfully aware he must seem the veriest boor, became only the more angry.

So this birthday feast progressed, courses came and went, glasses were emptied only to be instantly refilled, voices waxed louder and laughter more strident until this very festive babblement was suddenly hushed and all eyes turned where stood the Earl, wine-glass aloft.

"Ladies," said he, "my lords and gentlemen, I give you his Majesty the King!"

The toast was drunk standing and with vociferous acclaim, during which my lord mounted his chair and stood, jewelled hand upraised until once again came an expectant silence. Quoth he:

"Good friends all, we have pledged and honoured the toast to His Majesty the King, presently I shall call on you all to drink confusion to his enemies. But first I demand who are the King's enemies? Sirs, His Majesty's enemies are all such as break his peace and show themselves inimical to established law and order, and, being the King's enemies, they are and must be ours also. Gentlemen, there hath been trouble in the North, rioting and bloodshed, at first 'twas a small matter but one that hath grown daily, fomented by such evil-disposed wretches as John Hancock and Samuel Adams, nursed and encouraged by rebellious and loud-voiced demagogues, in particular a certain Patrick Henry and many other of those Irish that are known the world over as natural breeders of strife and bitter faction, and passionate haters of England. It is such as these that are, even now, endeavouring to widen the breach between these our colonies and our beloved England, to open the rift in the lute, whereby, 'stead of sweet harmony shall be hateful discord; to inflame and keep open the wound in our body politic whereby shall come present suffering and possibly a future dissolution. But, sirs, we gentlemen of England though here resident far from that blessed isle, yet carry, ay each one of us, England within our hearts—" Here my lord's voice was drowned in such shouts of fervent acclaim that the lofty roof rang, until my lord's white hand once again imposed silence on his eager auditory.

"Therefore I am persuaded, my good lords and gentlemen of England, should this braggart talk of arms and war ever materialize into open rebellion, sure am I that no man in whose veins leaps the unconquerable blood of the true Anglo-Saxon, but will himself leap, sword in hand, for the preservation of law and order and to bind these great colonies yet closer to that small yet mighty country whence the best of us came. For this, gentlemen, if needs be, we will fight to make of these United Colonies an England of the West, which, though severed by ocean, yet still undivided in soul and spirit, shall together be one mighty England, one heart, one hand, one set of laws, to bring peace and order into this troubled world and be the salvation of Mankind—"

Here there went up a universal shout, gentlemen rose the better to cheer, ladies wept or fluttered scarves and handkerchiefs, until once again the Earl's upraised hand quelled this wild enthusiasm.

"And now, my lords, ladies and gentlemen," said he in his clear, dominating tones, "I ask you to charge your glasses, bumpers all! I ask you—" My lord's voice seemed to fail him suddenly, his lips, parted for speech, were dumb, for his eyes, rolling in the fervour of his oratory, had lighted upon a vision that seemed to freeze him to momentary silence; and this the leather-clad form of Anthony and the eagle feathers of Mahtocheega the Sagamore standing motionless behind his chair.

His lordship choked, glared and thus fixing Anthony with terrible eye, at last became articulate.

"You, sir, that, despite redskin fripperies, show the features of a civilized white man, be so good to stand forth and be so obliging to permit myself and these my friends, better sight of you."

Meekly Anthony obeyed, and being conscious of the many hostile and scornful faces all about him, frowned and bowed his head.

"Now, God . . . bless . . . my . . . soul!" exclaimed the Earl with a dreadful deliberation. "Ladies and gentlemen I am astounded! I am amazed, nay I am indeed almost shamed to recognize in this . . . anomaly, one who should be of ourselves, my own only sister's only child and therefore a gentleman of noble birth and breeding, my nephew, Anthony Falconbridge."

Here from the staring company went up a murmur very like a groan above which rose a woman's hysterical laugh that ended in a gasp as my lord proceeded:

"Nephew Anthony we demand why you, a gentleman born, present yourself before us like a Redskin savage?"

"My lord," answered Anthony in voice meek as his look, "I am but lately from the Indian country."

"Nephew Anthony," pursued my lord inexorably, "we demand of you why, since you stoop to garb yourself as a mere Indian savage, why you are not daubed as Indian savage should be? Where, sir, is your warpaint? Where your reeking scalp-locks?"

Then Anthony raised his head and beneath their thick, black brows, his flashing eyes showed anything but meek. He glanced round about upon the many intent and stormy faces, he looked at his stately uncle, he bowed and spoke.

"My lords and ladies, since an explanation is demanded, I will answer the best I may. Uncle George, I have travelled nearly a thousand miles by wild ways, and at shortest notice, merely because you summoned me as one of the family. Then I wear these garments because, though my blood is purely English as that of any here, I am an American—"

"Hold, nephew!" cried the Earl, rising. "Hold there! You must know there are no Americans save your redskin savages,—these only are Americans. You and we, thank God, are English!"

"Nay, sir," retorted Anthony, "I maintain, with all due submission, that we are none of us gentlemen of England, but rather English gentlemen of America, and this is surely a very different matter. England should be our inspiration and beloved memory, but America, this land whereof we are now part, should be a loved and cherished reality. Again, sir, these men whom you scornfully dismiss as mere demagogues are men indeed, and most of them as English as ourselves, men, sir, who have thus identified themselves with this great country of America and are spokesmen of the many, voicing grievances which, to them as Americans, are very real—"

"I protest!" cried a choleric gentleman in scarlet and gold, his face almost red as his coat, "I protest, my lord—"

"Nay, sir," said the Earl, motioning Anthony to go on, "let us hear him."

"My lord," said Anthony, very earnestly, "I protest there is no one here that, knowing England, her noble traditions and all that she has stood for in the past, can love that little, mighty island more than I. But when her Government becomes oppressive, when the King, his guiding hand a merciless fist, becomes a tyrant—"

"My lord," roared the scarlet gentleman, "here's vile blasphemy!"

"True, sir, alas!" nodded the Earl, "yet we permit him speech, praying he shall contrive to excuse himself."

"Uncle George," continued Anthony, "I do but voice a truth which I implore you and these gentlemen to heed well. You have spoken of our Anglo-Saxon blood that brooks no injustice, sir, it is the blood of most of us colonials. It was men of this blood that battled through the ages to be free men, that for the sake of liberty suffered and were not dismayed, it was such men that later fought and endured and at last struck off a kingly head at Whitehall."

"Ha—sacrilege!" screamed the scarlet gentleman, above the sudden shocked and angry clamour.

"Enough!" cried my lord, both hands upraised. "Nephew Falconbridge, you have said too . . . too much; ha, by God, sir, it was to save that same kingly head, to prevent that bloody martyrdom that our ancestors, yours and mine, died in battle or were beggared. . . . Anthony Falconbridge I, as a loyal subject of His Majesty King George and lover of England, disown you henceforth, disclaim all kinship and here denounce you as rebel and traitor—"

The awful words were caught up and shouted on every side; glancing about him Anthony beheld faces direly transfigured, this polite assemblage, forgetting all its affectations and restraint, was raving against him; these dainty ladies and courtly fine gentlemen had given place to that primeval savagery which despite man's long ascent from the dark, ever lies so near the surface; fists were shaken, steel flickered to menace him and, foremost of all, smiling and debonair as ever, the young Marquis.

"Pray, oh pray," cried he, "let one so kind friend oblige the gentleman with a sword."

A weapon was thrust into Anthony's hand, but instantly he bent and snapped it across his knee.

"No!" he cried, tossing the broken pieces to the Marquis' feet, "not here! If we are to meet, if blood is to spill, as I fear it must, it shall be on the battlefield. And so I—"

His words were drowned in sudden tumult at the door, struggling servants were hurled aside, a great voice roared:

"Mr. Anthony—Mist' Anthony!" And in upon the astonished company strode a long-haired, bearded giant in garments of leather who flourished a long rifle and, heedless of all others, strode towards Anthony, crying:

"It's war, Mist' Tony. It's bloody war! Red coats and minute men before Boston! Bunker Hill, sir. But, what's worse for the likes o' you and me, Mist' Anthony—the Ottawas are up! The Cagugas and Mohawks are out . . . painted for battle and on the war-trail. They ha' massacred the settlement at Naylor's Forks. We ran into a party on 'em at the Crossing and fought through 'em. Here's proof lookee!" And he pointed to new scalps that dangled at his girdle.

Women screamed, men shouted, swords glittered everywhere and all was confusion and uproar until the Earl, mounting upon the table, sword high above his head, commanded them to silence.

"If it is war, so be it!" he cried. "It shall be England and America for England against these damned rebels. God save the King!"

So, with fierce cheering and warlike clamour all about him, Anthony turned and went forth of the noble hall that he was never to see again.

CHAPTER III

DESCRIBES FAREWELLS AND—A PROMISE

COMING forth into the open air Anthony drew a deep breath, mopped damp brow and looked up and around him, upon the peaceful landscape, like one a little dazed.

"Lord love me!" he ejaculated, then turned as the gigantic frontiersman came striding, rifle on shoulder.

"Ha, Mist' Anthony, you missed it!" he cried. "Bunker Hill! You missed it . . . and them redcoats! But I were there, along wi' my old 'Blastem' here!" And he patted the stock of his rifle lovingly. "By heck, but there's a purty good few o' them British soldiers won't fight never no more, seein' as they'm buried nice and quiet on Bunker Hill!"

"Tell me of it, Septimus. Was it a hard fight?"

"While it lasted 'twas purty hot. And why them soldiers must march close and in red coats wi' white crossbelts and brass buckles as no man couldn't help but hit, I dunno."

"Was it a very bloody business, Sep?"

"Ay, for these bloodybacks it shore was! Twice they come up at us nice and reg'lar like they was on parade, Mist' Anthony, and twice we druv 'em back, they was laying dead in their ranks all the way 'long the hill! Twice we licked 'em, Mr. Anthony, druv 'em down that bloody slope, trippin' over their own dead they was, and scarce a man of us teched, snug in our trenches we was. They give us a volley or so, but heck! what's a smooth-bore musket agin a frontier rifle? All their shot, purty nigh, flew wide! And it's—'Hold y'r fire, boys! Wait for the word an' aim low—at their belts!' On they came, up and over their dead, cheerin', bay'nets twinklin', up an' up till we could see the very whites o' their eyes. Then: Fire's the word! Aha, our rifles cracked all along the trenches an' when the smoke cleared there was mighty few o' them on their feet an' them staring about wild-like, ah, like lost children . . . and down the hill they went again. And we thought they was licked for good. But no, by heck! They throws off their packs, ay, an' ca'tridge belts, they forms up shoulder to shoulder and up they come again at the double, but nary a cheer now, savin' their breath this time d'ye see. Up they comes at us, bay'nets at the charge, nary a shot from 'em now! We waits till we can see their eyes, we fires into 'em point-blank and then, afore our smoke clears, they're at us—all that's left on 'em—on us and into us with their bay'nets. And 'twas then as we had our losses, for a bay'net's quicker nor a clubbed rifle! And so, because we'd no time to reload, we give way at last and left 'em to it. But, by the Lord, Mist' Anthony, we made 'em pay cruel dear for it. Aha, we showed 'em the old Brown Bess as won for 'em so many battle-fields ain't no manner o' good agin a Yankee rifle, we did!"

"But," said Anthony, "they won the hill and trenches."

"Well . . . ye see, Mist' Anthony, our shot was nigh all spent."

"Still, they captured the position at the point of the bayonet, eh, Sep?"

"Which I ain't denyin', Mist' Anthony. But it cost 'em precious dear, it did, so sure as my name be Septimus Tutt."

"And what now, Sep? What shall you do?"

"Well, over the border in Caroliny I got six brothers as can line a rifle as good as me, or purty nigh, and I'm going to 'list 'em all, ah and others like 'em, and we're a-goin' to hunt them redcoats till we've buried 'em all or drove 'em back where they belongs. And what o' yourself, Mist' Anthony?"

"Oh I shall be deep in this bloody business . . . somehow, somewhere . . . sooner or later, I suppose. Though, instead, I would to God we were off on another hunting trip, you and I, Sep."

"Why so we be!" laughed Tutt, patting his rifle again. "The finest hunting as ever was, we're a-going to hunt them sojers into the sea. Redcoats is better sport than bufflers or moose and jest as easy to kill. And you know as my ol' Blastem here don't never miss. S'long, Mist' Anthony, and good luck!"

"Good-bye, old friend!" said Anthony grasping the great hand Septimus held forth to him. "May we meet again soon."

"Amen, Mist' Anthony! Maybe I'll show ye some English hair along o' these yer Injun scalps. Good-bye and good huntin'!"

So saying this young giant grinned, nodded, shouldered Old Blastem and went striding away, his hunter's feet soundless in their moccasins.

And now beckoning the Sagamore beside him, Anthony went wandering on very pensively a while.

"War!" sighed he at last, in the soft Indian dialect. "War is a vile and terrible thing, Mahtocheega!"

"My brother speaketh truly!" answered the Sagamore. "Verily war is ever a very bad thing for cowards and those that are captured or conquered."

"Nay, my friend," said Anthony smiling somewhat ruefully, "war is an evil for both victor and vanquished, I think. To spill and waste this precious thing we call life, to kill a man is ever an awful business, Mahtocheega."

"Truly, brother, except that man be an enemy. To kill an enemy is good! And a man that is a man must ever have enemies!"

"Ay, faith it would seem so!" nodded Anthony despondently. Then, hearing a sound behind him, he turned, to behold Priscilla Worth speeding across the lawn towards him.

"Oh, Anthony," she gasped, "they say you are a

webel, but I don't care! I couldn't let you go without telling you that . . . that you are my dear fwend and that I shall always love you . . . as a fwend. And, oh Tony, dear . . . Charles has positively pwoposed to me, yes while they were all shouting and cheering so fuwiously . . . and I said 'yes.'"

"Why then, God bless you, Priscilla! Congratulations, my dear, and may you both be very happy."

"Thank you, Anthony. But oh, my dear, I . . . I was thinking . . . if you are twooly a webel and go to battle . . . you and my Charles may have to fight each other—"

"God forbid!" said Anthony, very fervently.

"Yes, God forbid!" said she, clasping her hands about his arm. "But oh, dear Anthony, I want you to pwomise me you would never, never hurt him . . . even if you had to. Pwomise me, Anthony!"

"I do promise, with all my heart!" he answered, taking her small hand to kiss it very solemnly.

"Thank you!" she sighed. "And God bless you, dear Wanthony. Now I must fly back or Charles will be looking for me and . . . oh dwat it, there he is now!" Glancing whither she looked, Anthony saw his cousin approaching, very stately, very youthful but extremely grave.

"Priscilla," he demanded, never so much as glancing at Anthony, "what do you in company with this . . . this . . . gentleman?"

"Thank you!" said Anthony. "I had expected a less kind epithet, Charles."

"And pon my life, sir, you deserve one!" quoth my lord. "Yes ye do, demme if ye don't. For, as my father said, you are a demd rebel and . . . so forth."

"No, Charles, I am an American! So are you and all the rest of us. Any man who lives in and by this rich land of America, is and must be an American. But enough o' this. Pray believe, Charles, that I am heartily sorry to have grieved the earl, I beg you will tell him this. . . . And whatever may chance in the future, know that in my heart I am as much your friend as ever I was in our boyhood days, indeed even more so. Therefore, Charles, if you . . . care to have it, here's my hand, old fellow."

Lord Charles frowned, hesitated, then grasped his cousin's outstretched hand very suddenly.

"Right, Tony!" he muttered. "If we must be enemies well . . . blood's thicker than water . . . old schooldays and . . . oh demme, you know what I mean!"

"And just for this," cried Priscilla, slipping a hand within the arm of each, "just for this, Charles, I shall kiss you, because you are my generous man and a weal nobleman; and then I shall kiss Anthony, because he is my fwend and such a lonely soul." So she kissed them both and thereafter they stood viewing each other very wistfully in a silence more eloquent than any speech.

"Oh," she whispered at last, "may God be kind and keep you safe both . . . both of you! Good-bye, Anthony, and oh wemember your pwomise."

"Bless you, I'll not forget!" answered Anthony, little guessing the cruel tricks this bloody war was to play him.

CHAPTER IV

TELLS HOW THREE WENT NORTH

DAY was waning yet it was with a strange reluctance that Anthony turned his back on the Great House and began to descend towards the river, that smooth highway that was to bear him so many hundreds of miles into the troublous North. He went very slowly, often glancing back over his shoulder, and once he halted as if greatly minded to return, whereat the Sagamore, halting also, questioned him in his own dialect.

"What holdeth my brother, making his swift feet heavy and slow, is it passion of anger or love,—hate for yon old, great man or desire for the golden-eyed maiden?"

Anthony started, his sunburnt cheek flushed, his dark brows knit themselves and, glancing askance on the Sagamore, he strode forward again, saying over his shoulder:

"Mahtocheega, how shall you ever learn English as I would have you, if we speak in your own tongue? Let us talk English. As for hatred and anger, no,—there is nobody I have the least cause to hate, thank God, and . . . as for love—"

Once more he halted suddenly and stood dumb, glancing about keen-eyed and poised for swift action, for here was the place where they had landed that morning, but the canoe was gone.

"Well, comrade," he demanded, "what say you now?"

"If I speak the English, my brother, now it is I say damblast cursem!" quoth the Sagamore gravely. Then, laying by his rifle, he unslung the powerful three foot bow he carried and strung it, for his quick eye had discerned some movement in the dense leafage on the other side of the river.

"Enemy!" he nodded and drew an arrow from his quiver, as, out from that same hanging foliage, glided the canoe impelled by a figure at sight of which, Anthony grasped the Sagamore's bow in restraining hand, for, though clad in leather like himself, this lithe, shapely youth was looking at him with tawny eyes beneath the dark serenity of low-arching brows.

"Mistress Blodwen," he cried, coming to the river's margin, "what does this mean?"

With slow, graceful strokes, she urged the canoe nearer, nor troubled to answer until, being come within easy speaking distance, she checked and turned up-stream, keeping thus stationary against the current with dexterous paddle.

"Mr. Anthony," said she in her smooth soft voice, "I am travelling North, do you go with me or must I steal your canoe and go alone?"

"Gad's life!" exclaimed Anthony, looking his astonishment, "is this a jest, madame?"

"It is deadly earnest," she answered, setting her chin at him and frowning.

"But," said he, beckoning her nearer, "this is positive sheer madness—"

"However, will you come, Mr. Anthony, or do I go alone?"

"Go?" he repeated. "But whither, where to, child?"

"Philadelphia."

"Lord love you, but this is many hundreds of miles, and desperate hard travel."

"Well, I am strong."

"And a woman!" said he.

"This shall never trouble you!" she retorted. "Do you go or stay?"

"Impossible!" he answered, very decidedly. "Out of the question. The wilderness is no place for any woman these days."

"Then," said she softly, edging the canoe further away, "I must go alone."

"Now damme!" he exclaimed.

"And also Good-bye!" she retorted.

"No, wait—wait!" cried he for already she was heading up stream. "Blodwen, for God's sake, wait,—Blodwen!"

"Well?" she demanded, watching him beneath level brows.

"It is the most difficult journey . . . through a trackless wilderness and what's more—"

"Well, I love the wilderness, Mr. Anthony, so no matter."

"You will be lost and perish."

"Not while I have powder and shot, so 'tis no matter for this either!" she answered serenely.

"But I tell you there are worse dangers than hunger and thirst. . . . Wild beasts, girl, roving Indians . . . war parties, the forests will be full of them!"

"Well, but these shall nowise fright me!" she answered bitterly. "Maybe these shall prove my kith and kin. And should death come, none shall grieve for me, surely not myself."

"Wait! I implore you . . . Blodwen!"

"And so, for the second time, Good-bye, Mr. Anthony!"

"Oh, child, why . . . why will you run such desperate hazard?"

"Because," she answered, with sudden strange passion, "oh because I will find myself, to know what manner of creature I really am . . . all the good and all the evil of me, yes, though it prove my death!" In her flashing eyes, her vivid cheek, the quick surge of her bosom, he read such deep emotion, that for a long moment he was silent, gazing down into these wonderful eyes that gazed back unflinching into his; and when they had thus mutely questioned and answered each other, Anthony's frown vanished and he held forth his hand.

"To find our real selves!" said he. "To prove to ourselves and to each other our true worth! So be it!"

"You will go with me?" she questioned in the same passionless voice, turning the canoe inshore, "both of you?"

"We will go, both of us."

"You will promise me," said she urging the canoe nearer yet, "on your faith as a gentleman you shall suffer me to share all work and every peril, forgetting I am a woman?"

"We promise!" Her long-lashed eyes grew suddenly gentle, the vivid mouth curved to smile very tender, and once again he was amazed at this swift, beautifying change.

Then the canoe touched shore and Blodwen, taking Anthony's proffered hand, grasped and shook it very warmly even as a man might have done.

"So we are to be comrades, Mr. Anthony?"

"Yes," he answered, "yes indeed, so you must not mister me any more."

"Very well, Anthony, then you must let me take my turn at the paddle!"

Thus presently with the Sagamore paddling at the prow, with Blodwen astern and Anthony amidships upon the buffalo robes, they were off and away upstream upon this long and perilous journey.

Lying thus at such unwonted ease, Anthony glanced at Blodwen, the broad-winding river, at Blodwen, at the tree-shaded shore and at Blodwen, watching the graceful swing and balance of her as she plied the paddle, her vivid lips just apart to show small white teeth, her well opened eyes fixed on the vague distances ahead.

"Your hair!" said he suddenly. "What have you done to your hair?"

"Cut it off!" she answered, her gaze still on the distance.

"This was great pity!"

"Oh? Why?" she demanded.

"Well, it was so long . . . silky—'dark as a starless night'—"

"Like an Indian's!" she nodded.

"It was beautiful," said he.

"This was why I cut it off."

"But what need was there?"

"To save the labour of it. And lest I show too womanish."

"My child," said he, gravely but with a laugh in his grey eyes, "were that head of yours shaven like an Indian brave's you would still look a woman, the manly hunting shirt and long leggings you are wearing also proclaim this fact most eloquently."

"My hateful womanhood!" said she between snapping teeth. "Well, you will be pleased to forget it while we company together."

"I shall do my best," he answered, smiling. "Though why you should so hate your womanhood passes my understanding." At this she merely frowned at him, then fixed her gaze upon the distance again.

"This is your rifle, I think," said he, laying his hand on the splendid weapon that lay beside him, "may I look at it?"

"Of course!"

"It is a fine piece," said he, handling it, "and beautifully balanced. Can you use it?"

"Oh yes, I should not trouble to bring it else."

"You have a bow and arrows also, I see."

"For hunting in a hostile country," she nodded, "an arrow cannot be heard, as maybe you are possibly aware."

"You are well instructed, it seems."

"Very well."

"But how comes this? Who taught you, pray?"

"Two famous hunters, one a white man and one a red. These were my playfellows as a child and my friends always."

"Miss Blodwen," said he, after a pause, "I am still wondering why you are running away to Philadelphia?"

"Oh enough of me, talk of yourself," she demanded. "How you have lived since leaving your Oxford University. And why you chose to settle in America. And if you are truly a rebel, as my lord says. And if so —why? Now," said she, keeping exact time to the Sagamore's long, easy paddle-strokes, "while I work and you idle—talk to me."

"Well," he answered, settling himself more comfortably, "I left Oxford after my father died. I'd lost my mother long and long ago. And being thus solitary, when Cousin Charles left Cambridge and crossed home to America I came with him. England was at war with France, there was some sharp fighting in Canada, so to Canada went I."

"You must have been very young."

"About twenty I was then and a sizeable infant. I marched with Forbes' regiment against Fort Duquesne in 'Fifty-eight, in the advanced guard commanded by Captain Washington, a wealthy neighbour of my Uncle George's and one time friend. After this I was in the campaign that ended in the victory at the Heights of Abraham. When the war ended I turned hunter, became a landowner and built a loghouse in the wilderness. And there is your humble servant's history in a nutshell, Miss Blodwen."

"You have been in many battles, then?"

"Enough to abominate war."

"Yet would fight again."

"I wonder?" he sighed. "Yes, I suppose so, if needs must."

"And your loghouse in the wilderness, is it strong? Is it . . . cosy?"

"Very!" said he, sitting up with a sudden eagerness. "These two hands helped to build it. Yes, it is a good house, roomy and comfortable, yet strong as a fort, nothing like Uncle George's stately edifice, of course, but very homelike and set in an earthly paradise of forest and mountain, river and lake. . . . And in a clearing between forest and lake the Tuscarora village. Yes, there shall be my home someday, God willing."

Here Anthony was silent awhile, his musing gaze upon the bright waters, and Blodwen, silent also, swaying to her paddle, viewed him furtively,—this man who must be her companion for so many weeks. Was he to become as the many others whose avid wooing had so shamed and angered her, varying as it had from the lustful brutality of Sir Joseph Wimperis to the cynical gallantries of such fine gentlemen and accomplished libertines as the Marquis de Vaucelles. Well, this Anthony was a man also, but was she, like Circe (but despite herself) to change him to a beast also? Thus, she viewed him with a dreadful speculation; his lofty brow, keen eyes and tender mouth, this bold line of nose with aggressive jut of chin and masterful carriage of head; so she watched him, striving to read the weakness and strength, the latent evil and good of him.

Now suddenly meeting this searching look, Anthony smiled and in this moment, her dark mistrust forgotten, into her face came such radiance that his voice was not quite steady as he questioned her:

"Why do you look so? . . . What are you thinking of me?"

"That you are a man," she answered impulsively; "strong and clean like this great wilderness. And yet also," sighed she, "you are a . . . fine gentleman."

"No no," he answered, smiling a little ruefully, "you heard them disown me. *Je suis declassé*. Henceforth I am what you say . . . just a man of the wilderness. But surely this is as good and honourable, at least I think so—"

"It is better!" said she in soft, rich voice like a caress. "Better and far nobler, for in His Wilderness the Lord God walks."

"Yes," said Anthony, watching her with quickening interest, "yes indeed. But here also fierce beasts lurk and death in many shapes to catch the unwary."

"Yet are not these of God?" she murmured. "However, Mr. Anthony, I had rather fight any beast on four legs than beasts with two and, when I die, breathe back my soul to God here in these clean wide solitudes, 'stead of airless sick chamber."

And now she questioned him concerning the long journey before them, the perils and difficulties of this great north-western country that she had so often imagined but never seen. And very frankly he told her how cruel the wild could be and how pitiless to the weak and stricken. He spoke of foaming rapids and roaring cataracts, of weary portages where they must carry canoe and gear from river to lake and lake to river until cacheing it at last, they must plunge deep into the hush of the forest, going silently by run-ways and narrow trails made by the Indians or wild animals of these primeval woodlands, long since.

"And of these Indians, Mr. Anthony. Pray do not fear to tell me."

"Yes," he answered, looking at her with troubled eyes. "The Cagugas, so long our friends and allies, have been goaded till they have risen at last and, with them, the Mohawks."

"How, pray, how have they been goaded?"

"In a thousand devilish ways. Our pioneer traders make them drunk, then trick and cheat them, and once you break faith with an Indian he neither forgets nor forgives. They were wont to be a clean, honourable people these red children of the forests, but now . . . ! Ah well, their raiding parties are far to the North and West of us, so you may sleep secure to-night and for many—ha, what now?" And speaking he caught up his rifle and cocked it; for round a distant bend of the river shot a canoe coming down upon them with the current very swiftly, paddled by four savages whose heads were shaven and adorned with black feathers white tipped.

"How think you of them, Sagamore?"

"Senecas."

"Ay, three chiefs and a sachem." As he spoke, Anthony laid down his rifle and lifted his right arm high above his head palm outwards, as did the Sagamore also, whereupon the Senecas answered this peace sign, and, as the canoes drifted close, called out harshly and with fierce gestures, showing their war axes new burnished while one held up belts of wampum and all of these red, at sight of which, Anthony called out very urgently gesturing now with both hands out-turned. The Senecas frowned, shook their heads pointing again to their glittering hatchets; then lifting their hands in farewell, bent to their paddles and shot away downstream, while Anthony stared in frowning dismay at the Sagamore whose lean hand was fumbling at the tomahawk in his girdle.

"They brought evil tidings, I think," said Blodwen softly, "news of death, Mr. Anthony?"

"News of murder!" he answered, between shut teeth. "The head chief of the Cagugas mourns his family, his whole family, women and little children . . . murdered by white men. The Long House is astir, those Senecas are away to preach war and bloody vengeance to the Indians of the South and along the Ohio . . . the whole Six Nations will be up! And so God have mercy on this poor country!"

CHAPTER V

DESCRIBES DIVERS INCIDENTS AND IN ESPECIAL —ONE

THREE days have elapsed and the travellers have journeyed far. All day long the tinkling plash of their paddles and the rippling murmur at the prow, as the long canoe glides against the stream ever north-westerly, is broken only when they land to eat or stretch their limbs.

Halcyon days of ceaseless yet joyous effort; nights of murmurous talk beside the camp fire and dreamless sleep beneath whispering leaves or starry heaven. A time this of ever-growing intimacy; for Anthony, putting aside future cares, is merry as a boy, while Mahtocheega, the Tuscarora chief, becoming less taciturn, is much readier of speech and grave smile and all because of Blodwen; for she, forgetting all past doubts and fears, laughs often and sometimes falls to singing in her soft, rich voice as she is doing now, while Anthony watches her unconscious form with eyes that miss nothing of its lissom shapeliness, its sweetly tender curves, until, as if suddenly aware of this, she turned and meeting his look frowned and hushed her singing.

"Pray go on," said he.

"No!" she answered almost sullenly. "No. Besides I forget the rest."

"However it is very strange to hear 'The Bailiff's daughter of Islington' in this American wilderness. It is a song of old England."

"And yet I seem to have known it all my life."

"And this is stranger yet," he nodded thoughtfully.

"Like my ring," said she bitterly, "my ruby ring

that you half recognize yet cannot remember how or why. And so here again is the old mystery that none can ever answer—who am I and what?" She sighed. "All I can be sure of is that this—this is the river that bore me out of the unknown past so many years ago, and to-day is bearing me into the unknown future. . . . And to what? Oh God of mercy—to what?" Now though her voice was gentle as ever, there was that in her look so altogether unexpected that Anthony almost dropped his paddle.

"Lord!" he exclaimed, "Lord love you, child, you go to find happiness I hope and pray."

"I wonder!" she whispered.

"Why then, at least to the welcome and loving care of your friends in Philadelphia."

"I have no friends in Philadelphia."

"No . . . friends?" he echoed.

"Not one in all the world."

"But," he stammered, "why then . . . ? Then why go to Philadelphia?"

"As well there as anywhere else," she answered wearily.

"But this . . . this is preposterous, unthinkable! How shall you live?" he demanded viewing her in such stark dismay that her vivid, sensitive lips quivered.

"Indeed, but I am not so useless as you think, sir. I can sew as well as I shoot—almost. And you've never seen me really shoot yet, Anthony. And then I can cook besides. Oh, I am quite an accomplished person! But, talking of cooking, I'm ravenous! See, it's sunset already! When do we camp?"

"When you will, Blodwen. Here if you wish, though I know a little creek some miles ahead, a very excellent place, if you can wait."

"To be sure," she answered, looking bright-eyed at the radiant West, "let us go to your creek."

"Oh, Mahtocheega," said Anthony to their silent companion, "our last camping place coming down, can we reach it ere dark, think you?"

"Assuredly," answered the Sagamore, glancing back across swaying shoulder, "if my brother plieth paddle nimbly as his tongue."

"Ay, faith!" laughed Anthony.

Down went the sun in splendour, making the river a flaming highway winding between sombre woodlands where purple shadows crept, as this glory waned, and evening grew to a glimmering dusk lit by faint stars whose radiance waxed as night closed down.

And now they journeyed through a vast and silent immensity, a star-spangled firmament above them, a mystery of waters below, fretted with starry gleams that came and went, and no sound but the rippling whisper of their going, the rhythmic dip and tinkle of their paddles. And presently Anthony spoke softly:

"A wonderful world, Blodwen."

"Yes!" she sighed. "Ah yes! Do you wonder I so love it all, I that am a waif of the wilderness?"

And after some while up rose the moon to pale the stars and fill the world about them with a magic radiance; and the river now a broad path of rippling silver.

"Yonder it is, my brother!" said the Sagamore, his deep voice strangely loud in the pervading stillness.

"True enough, Cheega! I was dreaming, egad, and should have missed it."

The canoe turned inshore, coasted a line of shadowy trees, swung between bush-grown banks, followed a narrow channel and was finally beached where a little spring bubbled.

"Well," said Anthony when they had landed and drawn up the canoe, "here we are, comrade!" And he glanced where stood Blodwen, a strange, lovely shape in the bright moonlight, looking about her glad-eyed.

"Oh, a paradise!" she murmured.

"The question is," said he gathering an armful of twigs, "do you cook to-night or shall I?"

"I will, of course!" she answered very decidedly, but with such smile and so joyously eager that he smiled also.

"Why, then, the Sagamore and I will build you a wickiup."

"Why trouble?" said she, busied with the tinder-box. "My bed shall be a buffalo robe beneath this tree. Pray, sir, remember I am no finical fine lady."

"However," said he, in his gentle though dogged fashion, watching how deftly she set and lit the fire, "you shall sleep in a bower to your comfort—see, the Sagamore is busy at it already." So saying, Anthony unslung his tomahawk and fell to work beside the Sagamore, though more than once he must pause to watch and listen where Blodwen sang softly sweet as she prepared their meal. And after some while comes the stately Tuscarora to take her hand and lead her to see the leafy bower their woodman's skill has wrought for her.

"Wigwam!" quoth he, with his slow, grave smile. "Sleep so, very good, my daughter!"

Smiling, she thanked him, and coming back to the fire, found Anthony in the act of dishing their supper. So down they sat and ate, and laughed and talked like the good friends they had become.

The meal ended, Anthony gave her his hand, leading her away to walk beside the little creek; and now they spoke seldom but paused very often, listening to the murmur of the stream, the rippling of the spring, or to gaze up at the radiant moon.

"Lord!" he murmured at last, "but you are marvellous changed, Blodwen! You can laugh and sing. Is this because you are happy?"

"Yes," she answered, glancing up and round about them, "yes, Anthony, for this is God's great wilderness, unspoilt and new from His hand, clean with new life and . . . infinite possibilities. In this deep silence a great, still voice speaks, to such as may hear, of what was and shall be. Here is triumph and failure, hope and final achievement. And here I think I shall find happiness or death. . . . And I suppose," said she, turning to look at his intent face, "all of this sounds very strange and wild to you?"

"Strange . . . yes!" he answered, struck anew by her vital, glowing beauty. "But I also love the wilderness, this was why I built my house deep in the forest. Perhaps . . . someday you . . . you might care . . . to see it."

"Yes," she answered, turning to go back, "someday . . . perhaps."

"Well, here is your lodge, Blodwen . . . and yonder lies the Sagamore asleep already. No need to keep watch to-night, you may slumber sound."

"Then Good night!" said she, reaching him both her hands with impulsive, half-shy gesture. "Sleep well, friend Anthony!"

"Good night!" he murmured and took her hands and kissed them, then drew and seized her in sudden, compelling arms to clasp her to his heart, kissing her fragrant hair, her eyes, her quivering mouth until, warned and chilled by her passionless compliance, her dumb resignation, he freed her, stepped back and blenched as from a blow, at the hate he read in her look.

"Oh . . . God!" said she, in voice more dreadful because it whispered. "You too! So all men are the same, even . . . Anthony Falconbridge. Now for this I could kill you . . . and myself!"

"But . . . but Blodwen," he stammered, "I . . . oh upon my life I meant nothing evil."

"No!" sighed she, with miserable, hopeless gesture, "No, I waked the beast in you."

"Never think it," he pleaded, "you do but insult your own womanhood."

"Well, why not? I hate it!"

"You also insult me,—ah bitterly!"

"Very well," she answered, turning from him, "now you may go and sleep."

"Not till you believe that I . . . oh, Blodwen, I had no least thought of hurting or offending you, I vow . . . I swear it!"

"And now, Mr. Anthony, I beg you'll leave me . . . or must I stay and be kissed and kissed until you weary and are sated?"

"Blodwen—!" said he, and choked, and stood for a moment quite confounded.

"Mr. Anthony, will you leave me?"

"Yes," said he in strangled tone, "and for your wilful, cruel misjudgement of me let God forgive you, for I will not!" And so he turned and went striding away in a cold fury to scowl from placid moon to the placid waters of this little creek and to heap curses on the whole universe and all women therein.

And when at last he lay beside the Sagamore who slept placid as the night itself, he tossed and turned, watched the dying fire until it was dead and the moon until it was down, and when sleep took him at last, scowled in his slumber.

CHAPTER VI

TELLS OF LIFE, DEATH AND A GREATER THING

THE days have multiplied to weeks and the weeks to a month and more. In these British Colonies, north and south, a thousand miles or thereabouts, is a ceaseless stir, an ominous, never-ending hum that shall presently wax and swell to thunder of desperate strife, screams of sharp agony, cries and moans of despair, wild cheers and triumphant shouts,—an elemental tumult to herald the advent of a mighty nation, a great, new people that out from the smoke and roar, the bloody confusion of battle, shall come marching, resolute to meet its destiny.

In city, town and village is roll and ruffle of drums, hoarse commands and tramp of feet where once-peaceful citizens are transforming themselves by the thousand into soldiers eager for war.

In the wilderness, far amid the dark aisles of primeval forest, stealthy shapes, painted for war, flit unheard, unseen, yet to desperate purpose; Indian raiding parties these, thirsting for bloody vengeance upon all and any invaders of their lands and spoilers of their hunting grounds, be they white men or red; tomahawks and scalping knives glitter amid the green.

In Cambridge town, Ensign Francis Wilding, handsomer than ever in his new regimentals, glances dubiously at the ragged files of his Colonial riflemen, dismayed by their unsoldierly bearing until, noting their resolute faces and the unconsciously purposeful handling of their rifles that is eloquent of habit and long usage, his doubts, of these slack-seeming, homely fellows, gives place to hope and a resolution keen as their own.

In New York, this polite hotbed of loyalty and

Toryism, Captain lord Charles Charteris, very gallant in his King's uniform, glances proudly along the serried ranks of his redcoated infantry, this smart-moving company of picked men with their shakoes, white cross-belts and heavy muskets topped with glittering bayonets, these many that move as one, this crack, white-gaitered company of a crack English regiment that is become the joy of his heart, second only to the small, lovely creature whose bright eyes meet his so often across the wide parade-ground, where she stands forgetful (almost) of the gay throng about her; thus, Charles glances proudly at his smart company, gazes adoringly at Priscilla as she at him, and no wonder, for in a few hours they are to be wed.

And here also, astride noble charger, is the Earl himself, a soldierly figure from plume to spurs, in scarlet and gold, and upright as his son, riding stately at the head of his newly enlisted troop of gentlemen volunteers, each of these superbly armed, mounted and accoutred, one and all of them pertinaciously drilling and joyfully eager for a 'brush with these demd Yankee rebels.' So, at word of command, this splendid troop wheels to right, to left, splits itself into sections, transforms itself into a long line of tossing plumes, rearing horses and flashing sabres; it trots, gallops and charges, in mimic fury, with rolling thunder of hoofs, recovers and halts with jingling clash; and every man of them very conscious of the lovely eyes that watch their efforts, even as my lord the Earl himself who now, smoothing the glossy neck of his charger, bows to the ladies and turns to the very ornate officer beside him, saying:

"Extreme pretty women here this morning, eh, Marquis? Now what I say is, my dear fellow, I say there is no time more apt for love and weddings and so forth than the eve of war. I say,—let us make sure of the next generation ere we peril this."

"*Parfaitement!*" exclaims the Marquis, kissing his sabre hilt towards the many fluttering scarves and petticoats in a kind of ecstasy. "Here is *par example, le mot juste*, milord! It is indeed the duty we owe to ourselves and Nature! Su-perb! My own thought precisely milord, *mordieu*—oh, yes!"

And thus in due course, forth into the glad sunshine comes lord Charles Charteris, his small lady and beauteous wife upon his arm, walking from church door beneath a long arch of glittering swords that soon shall be dimmed by more awful stain than rust; but little reck they of this, since their thoughts are for, and their eyes behold, only each other.

Meantime in a narrow boulder-strewn defile amid the green gloom of the forest, Anthony sat crouched lonely beside a small fire, scowling at the blackened cooking pot thereon though it gave forth very appetising savour. He sat in the shade of a great boulder, close beside the opening of a little cave that gaped in the rocky bush-grown steep above him, a gaunt, haggard, travel-worn figure his left forearm swathed in a bloody bandage where a Mohawk arrow had smitten him a week ago; and though he muttered frequent curses on the throbbing smart of this wound, his scowl was for the absent Blodwen who, avoiding him as usual, was away with the Sagamore somewhere on the wooded heights above, watching lest their stealthy foes should surprise them again, for this was the heart of the Indian territory.

Now being thus lonely and a little fevered with his wound, Anthony's bitter reflections ran on this wise:

'Avoiding him as she always did now! And why? Simply because he had once kissed the little prudish fool. Since when she had shown for him a passionless contempt, a placid disregard beyond all reason and not to be endured. Even when the arrow had transfixed his arm she had evinced little or no concern. A hard, unlovely creature! True she had broken and extracted the shaft neatly enough, and dressed and bound up the ugly wound and tended it regularly ever since, but—with not so much show of compassion as she would have bestowed on a dog. A bitterly unforgiving creature, not that she had anything to forgive,—and therefore callous, vindictive and more implacable than any man, and all because of a momentary folly! Weeks of ceaseless travel and constant peril, wherein she had borne her share unflinching, had made her but the more sullen, a sexless creature who could fight like any man and shoot far better than most . . . a round-limbed, deep-bosomed anomaly he would be mighty glad to part from, and would to God Philadelphia were nearer. As it was, he must be patient and endure, coldly remote as she—'

A rustle in the bush-grown ledge behind him and, reaching instinctively for his rifle, he glanced up, saw a black shape in the air above him and was smitten headlong. Death was on him as he knew for, though his powerful fingers gripped and held its furry throat, death was glaring at him, stifling him with hot and foetid reek. Yes, here was his end, and an evil one . . . claws and fangs to rip him, tear him! An instant's wild flurry of despairing effort, a momentary stillness . . . then, above wild-beast snarl and human gasping, was the loud report of a rifle. The puma snarled again, whimpered and rolling away, writhed convulsively and was still.

Then Anthony rose to quaking knees and saw Blodwen high on the steep above, grasping her smoking rifle.

"Blodwen!" cried he, breathelessly, "Oh, girl, it . . . was you saved my life . . . ?"

"Yes," she nodded, "and what pity to kill such beautiful creature!" So saying she descended the precipitious slope, her moccasined feet very swift and sure, and leaned on her rifle to look from dead animal to living man with her serene, golden eyes. "Are you anyways hurt, Mr. Anthony?" she enquired, gently.

"Oh, what matter?" said he, bitterly. "Cherish your damned puma." And turning from her he took up his rifle with a hand that dripped blood.

"Surely," said she, recharging and priming her own weapon with quick, dexterous fingers, "it is strange to find puma so far north."

"We are west also. And your grief for killing this

murderous beast . . . ha, by God madam, I believe you have heart of stone!"

"Also a true eye and trigger-finger, Mr. Anthony."

"Yes," said he, frowning, "it was marvellous shot!"

"It had to be!" she nodded. "Oh, poor, proud man, is it such shame to owe your life to me because I am a woman?"

"No, merely because you are Blodwen!"

"However," sighed she, setting down her rifle, "I see your arm is bleeding again, let me tend it while I may—come!"

"Thank you, I'll contrive it myself."

"Oh foolishness!" she exclaimed, gently scornful. "You act like silly child. If the Indians heard my shot and come down on us again, we may be fighting for our lives very soon and you will do better with that arm properly bandaged."

Very unwillingly he suffered her ministrations, watching her dexterous fingers and intent, too-placid face, this firm mouth, these long-lashed eyes that showed no least quiver, no least sign of a tear.

"Indeed," said he at last bitterly as he might, "you should have been a man!"

"A man?" she repeated, flashing a quick look up at him while her fingers yet soothed and cherished his smart. "Is this compliment or reproach, I wonder?"

Anthony merely shrugged his shoulders.

"Do you commend me, sir, because I have never troubled you with any least complaint in all these weary, weary days—?"

"Have they seemed so very wearisome, Blodwen?"

"Do you honour me," she demanded, "because I have hidden my fears of battle and horror for bloodshed, or . . . do you upbraid and sneer at me because I despise kisses lightly given and love that is no more than sport and pastime? Tell me your true thoughts, if you dare."

"Very well!" said he, leaning back against the great boulder. "I think you are a proud, blind, self-deluding little fool that will not see the so obvious thing. And mighty glad am I that Nature framed you so womanly because, Madam Folly, if ever we win out of this to safety, I am determined to make you the mother of my children . . . my wife. Yes, by God even though I must compel you to it by—"

"Wife?" she repeated, like one amazed. "Oh, but—"

"There are no buts between us henceforth, there shall be none!"

"Your . . . wife!" she murmured again. "So this . . . this is how you love me!"

"I have not said so, Mistress Fool! No, by heavens, I'd marry you now even though I hated you, ay I would, if but to avenge all your vile misconception of me. Do I show such a damned loose fish, such libertine, such lecherous satyr you must forever keep me at arm's length and avoid me all these weeks? Is it my Manhood shames your sickly prudery that you must abhor me for but once touching your lips with mine? Well, my lady, we'll change all this . . . what now do you fear already?"

"No, Anthony."

"Then why must you tremble? You that shoot better than ever I saw, that are bold in fight as any man, why must you shiver and shake now?"

"Not with . . . fear, Anthony," she answered softly, and though she met his look unquailing, her rich colour deepened to painful flush. Then Anthony laughed, though very unconvincingly, and reaching out his arms, beckoned with imperious hand.

"Blodwen," said he, "little fool that has flouted love and me all these weeks, you that are mine and know it even better than I, come now and kiss me."

"Anthony," she murmured, brokenly, "Oh Anthony . . . if . . . if you can say you . . . truly love me—"

"No!" he answered, "I name you 'wife' instead. Shall not this suffice?" Speechlessly she turned from him,—then from the height above them a rifle cracked answered by shrill and dreadful screaming.

The feathered head of a Mohwak warrior hideous with warpaint, a gleaming axe! These Anthony glimpsed as the Indian leapt . . . and Blodwen was down, inert and lying at her assailant's mercy: a deadly tomahawk glittered above her defenceless head, flashed down and was met by the stock of Anthony's rifle, biting deep, then he and this Mohawk warrior were locked in mortal grapple, the Indian striving desperately to draw his knife, Anthony waiting and watching for chance of disabling blow with fist or knee. To and fro they reeled, panting, straining, breast to breast, sinewy bodies quivering with unceasing effort; but as they stood thus rigid, Anthony glimpsed Blodwen's motionless form and tightened his grip, heard his antagonist gasp, saw the painted face, so near his own, all suddenly convulsed with agony . . . blood spouted and as the Mohawk fell, Anthony saw him transfixed by a long, tufted shaft that he knew for one of the Sagamore's war arrows.

Then Blodwen's body was in his arms and so like death that he groaned as he bore her to the comparative safety of the little cave. Catching up their two rifles he wrenched the tomahawk from his own, reprimed it and crouching behind the great boulder, waited for the sudden fury of attack that he knew must follow, while his keen eyes quested the steep slope to his left for some sign of the Sagamore.

Heat, and an utter stillness, for the afternoon sun was ablaze and no wind stirred: an ominous quiet that, as the moments dragged, became more threatening; the hands grasping his rifle grew moist but were steady as ever, sweat trickled on brow and cheek, yet the grey eyes beneath this brow were wide and resolute, eyes that narrowed suddenly to shining slits, for his quick senses had warned him, he crouched lower. . . . A stealthy rustling and this narrow defile was athrong with his ferocious assailants ghastly with warpaint green and yellow and scarlet; the air rang with their dreadful quavering battle cries . . . arrows whizzed about him, muskets roared, bullets spattered and chipped splinters from the sheltering rocks while, crouched behind his great boulder, Anthony fired twice and with deadly precision. But on they came, these Mohawk warriors, to be met by a madman whose long clubbed rifle, swung by powerful arms, checked and drove them back upon each other in howling confusion for in this narrow ravine their very numbers hampered them; and in this moment, before they might loose shaft or hurl tomahawk, Anthony was among them smiting amain with heavy rifle-butt.

Then from the steep above, rose the Sagamore's deep and terrible war whoop, the killing shout of the Tuscaroras of the Lynx; a Mohawk tossed up his arms and fell clutching at the arrow in his throat. Thus while the mighty sweep of Anthony's clubbed rifle held them, the Sagamore's long war-arrows smote them from above until these Mohawks, valiant though they were, gave way at last, broke and scattered and were gone.

Breathless and spent, Anthony leaned on his rifle and presently glancing about, saw he was alone save for their fallen assailants who writhed feebly or lay very still, and gasping he called:

"Ho, Mah—tocheega!"

"Here am I!" And down the tree clad slope came the Tuscarora, bow in one hand, gleaming scalping knife in the other.

"Good, my friend," panted Anthony in the dialect, "now but for thee dead were I . . . and hairless . . ."

"Oh my brother," smiled the Sagamore happily, "Warriors great and mighty are we! Seven, my brother, seven have we slain, wherefore do I love and honour thee oh my An—to—nee." So saying, he slung his deadly bow and descending into this place of battle, proceeded to dispatch the wounded and scalp these fallen Mohawks very methodically while Anthony, having recharged and primed the rifles, brought water into the cave and did what he might to rouse Blodwen from her swoon.

He bathed the purple bruise that marred her brow, he kissed it tenderly with reverent lips, he called her name: but she still lying like one dead, fear seized him and a great despair. Sitting down he took this soft, inert body in his arms, her pale cheek upon his breast, and strove desperately to woo her back to life; holding her close upon his heart, touching her pallid cheek with trembling hand, smoothing back her raven hair and, with every caress, staining her with the blood of his reopened wound.

"Blodwen," he whispered breathlessly, "Don't die, girl! Oh my dear . . . don't leave me! Brave, true comrade that you were . . . without you I am lost, for you . . . you are my very life! Blodwen, if you die now, by God I'll die too . . . follow you out . . . out into the unknown, into the dark or light . . . to find you again. Blodwen come back . . . live for me. Ah, d'you hear me, d'you hear?"

Lying thus in the despairing passion of his embrace, stirring not and scarce breathing, she spoke at last, whispering:

"Oh, Anthony . . . say you . . . love me."

"God knows I do!" he answered passionately. "I love you more than life and beyond death, Blodwen. I love you with my every breath, I . . . I think I always have and I know I always shall."

Slowly her arms crept up to clasp about his neck.

CHAPTER VII

TELLS HOW, AMID THE WILDERNESS, IN A PLACE OF DEATH, THEY WERE WED

THE sun, veering westward, made of this little cave a place of shadow, it was also a very poor thing as caves go, but for these two it was become a hallowed spot, a place they were to remember all their days.

The Sagamore meanwhile having completed his task upon all seven of their foes with his usual dexterity, having stretched these reeking trophies on pliant twigs and set them to dry, glanced up at the declining sun to judge the hour, listened to the happy voices in the cave, and set himself to reclaim as many of his deadly arrows as he might together with such weapons of the dead Mohawks as pleased him. This done, he glanced again at the sun and coming to the cave, spoke softly.

"An—to—nee, oh my brother, it were wise, I think, that we now take counsel together what presently we shall do. Ha, but the eyes of my brother dance now, the heart of him singeth—"

"Ay, by heaven!" exclaimed Anthony. "Gladness such as mine comes but seldom to any man, Mahtocheega!"

"Why, truly," answered the Sagamore, with his slow grave smile, "so thought I upon a time, so think all that truly love."

"See now, Mahtocheega, here is my wife that is to be. . . . Lord, to think of it!" he exclaimed, viewing Blodwen radiant-eyed. "Oh surely none ever loved as we, tush it were impossible!"

At this she, conscious only of Anthony, caught his hand to fondle it. "Ah, Blodwen," sighed he, "I did not build my house in vain, soon, pray God, you shall rule there, the log house of yesterday is become a home to-day, and there's a blessed thought, dear heart o' me! We must have servants for you, we must plant flowers . . . what, d'you weep, child?"

"A little!" she murmured, leaning pain-racked head against him. "For oh, my Anthony, I that have been so desperately lonely am . . . coming home at last . . .!"

"Yes, home!" said he, drawing her close. "And soon as may be. And how say you to this, Sagamore old friend?"

"That my brother's happiness is my joy. And may the Great Spirit Manitou make her fruitful to bear such men as yourself, oh my An—to—nee."

"Pray God!" whispered Blodwen, nestling closer.

"But now to our council," quoth the Tuscarora, his keen gaze forever questing gorge and slope, bush and tree. "Is it to-night that we shall follow the trails north that are to us known, or go we by the water?"

"The water," answered Anthony. "Let us follow the river for, though it take us something too westerly, it shall be safer, I guess. Besides after this day's work we are none of us fit for hard travel afoot."

So it was agreed. And thus as evening fell they stole forth of this rocky gorge that had been their defence; first the Sagamore with his great pack and trophies of war, next Blodwen with her rifle, then Anthony, heavy laden but so skilfully that in a moment he might cast off his burdens and be free for action. Like three shadows and as soundless, went they amid a world of shadows ever deepening until they moved in a close darkness where no ray of star might reach them, for above and all around them was the gloom of these mighty forests.

Through this darkness the Sagamore led them never faltering, his soundless feet treading an unseen trail, following it as by instinct until, all at once, he halted and coming beside him they were aware how he stood, head thrown-back and turning this way and that to snuff the spicey air.

"Watchfire! Mohawk!" he whispered and strung his bow; then he flitted on again, and they after him. And, presently upon the darkness to their right was a ruddy, palpitant glow, a red spark that grew to a fire.

But still the Sagamore led them on until they could discern four blanketed shapes outstretched in slumber about this fire while a fifth, seated cross-legged thereby, nodded drowsily.

The Sagamore hissed softly, halted his companions with compelling gesture and was gone, silent as a ghost. Now pressing close within Anthony's sheltering arms, Blodwen shuddered violently and whispered:

"Oh . . . what now?"

"Hush!" he breathed, folding her to his breast. These Mohawks are camped too near where we hid the canoe . . . close your eyes, beloved!" The sharp twang of powerful bowstring and the sleepy sentinel started to his knees, clawed the air and sank a shapeless huddle; then into the firelight stole Death; the Tuscarora's war-axe smote four times; a busy knife flashed and flickered; quick feet stamped out the fire. And presently the Sagamore was back again, saying in his deep, soft tones:

"Come, my brother, our enemies sleep and shall not hear us now!"

So they went on again, but quicker now, until the dense gloom thinned and before them was the gleam of water.

Unhesitating, the Sagamore brought them to that place beside the river where they had hidden the canoe and, soundlessly as possible, they launched it; then with Blodwen couched between them on bed of buffalo robes, they pushed out upon this dark river, dim forms in a dim world whose very silence was a menace.

Dip and ripple of stealthy paddles, bubbling murmur at the prow and presently above this, Blodwen's whispering, happy voice:

"Good night, my Anthony!"

"Sleep well, dear love!"

All night long they drave the swift canoe northwards, and all night long Anthony watched the pale glimmer of this loved face so near him, joying now in her sleeping as he would do in her waking, and musing fondly on all that was to be . . . until came daybreak at last to show him this same face all rosy with the dawn, and then up rose the glad sun to steal his level beams beneath her curling lashes and wake her; and she, starting to this warm caress, turned and looking up at Anthony happy-eyed, smiled and reached up her arms to him. And so they kissed.

"Another day, thank God!" sighed she. "Another day to live and . . . love you better."

"And so much nearer home!" he answered.

"Are you not tired, my Anthony?" And your arm, does it pain—?"

"Lord, I haven't thought of it!" he laughed. "And as for pain, you are my counter-irritant,—come and kiss me again! Ha, but your head, your poor, lovely, adorable head."

Instead of answering, she reached his rifle whence it lay to look at the deep cleft made in the stock by the Mohawk war-axe.

"Here," said she, laying her slim brown finger in this broad groove, "here, but for you, was my death."

"Yes," he nodded, "thanks to my rifle and the Sagamore's arrows, here you sit beautiful with life, thank God, and more lovely for the love in your eyes. And here am I, Blodwen, worshipping you with my every breath. And so we are quits, dear heart."

"And so, Anthony, having saved each other from death we are more each other's own than ever."

"And for ever!" he added, fervently. "Through life and beyond death." As he uttered this word the Sagamore ceased paddling and with hawk nose aloft began again to snuff the air, his thin, sensitive nostrils a-quiver.

"What now, old friend?" questioned Anthony, reaching for his rifle.

"Smoke, my brother, bad smoke! I think many people they die."

The paddles dipped and went on again, eyes scanning the dense leafage right and left, hands ready to snatch weapons; and presently they reached a place where the waters divided, one channel trending northwesterly, the other curving away almost due east and it was this narrower stream they followed.

And now the fume of smoke was plain and strong, an acrid reek that stung the nostrils, an evil smell that was in itself a warning. The paddles dipped slower, and turning a bend they saw—

A wide clearing in the forest, but this now no more than a fire-blackened waste surrounded by smouldering heaps of what had been cabins and hutments, and, in the midst of this desolation a group of people, men, women and children, clustered about an open grave; at sight of the canoe and the Sagamore's fierce aspect, they snatched musket and firelock and drawing together, fronted the newcomers, like the fearful, desperate creatures they were.

But turning in to the bank Anthony made the peace sign, calling out to them such words of kindly welcome and sympathy as he might, and with Blodwen's hand in his, stepped ashore, whereat these poor folk came thronging to greet them, and foremost of all a small, gaunt, haggard man who grasped a musket in one hand, an open Bible in the other.

"Oh friends . . . oh friends," he gasped and choked, "this was our village, we called it Sharon because we had made this wilderness to blossom like the rose . . . I am John Billing, a minister of the Gospel and shepherd of this little flock. Thirty-two were we, but now a third of our number lie dead and buried . . . indeed we have been burying our loved dead all this day . . . yonder is the last, come, sir, and pray with us for the brave soul of him."

Now while Anthony followed mutely whither John Billing led, Blodwen went aside where stood the women and children, a hushed and woeful company, and did what she might to comfort them, kissing the little, pale faces of these very small pioneers, questioning these sad-eyed mothers as to their names and ages, thus rousing them from their brooding, silent grief, while the Sagamore, remote, an impassive and stately figure, leaned on his long rifle and watched all things with his calm, bright eyes.

"This sir," said Mr. Billing, gesturing to the open grave with the Bible he still held, "was our leader, Amos Billing, a bold man yet godly. He was also my brother. But alas, there is no one of us but hath lost brother, father or son."

"Sir," enquired Anthony gently, "when did this evil befall you?"

"Yesterday, sir, at sunset, and we all unprepared. For we loved the Indians and they us. I strove to teach them of the gentle Christ, and now . . . this!"

"And the work of a Mohawk war party, I think sir?"

"Mohawks and Senecas . . . these that once made me welcome to their lodges."

"And now," questioned Anthony, looking round upon this small and sorrowful community, "what shall you do, what is your purpose?"

"To build our village again, sir, and replant our fields to the glory of God and those our beloved dead. Someday perchance, on this devastation, dedicated by our blood and suffering, here upon our dust shall rise a city where another generation shall praise the everliving God. . . . So come now all ye that are His children, come and let us pray His blessing upon this our brother that is risen above all pain and every sorrow—and then upon ourselves yet in life, that we may live worthily, enduring all things steadfastly to the end, for the glory of the Lord and for the sake of those coming after us. . . ." Then lifting his tearful gaze heavenward, "Lord God," he cried, "look down on us and let the memory of these our dead, newrisen to life in Thee, oh let their memory abide and dwell with us to be our inspiration that we may live or die in Thy service humbly yet valiantly as they."

This prayer ended and the grave filled in, the little minister thrust the small, much-worn Bible into his breast and instead of musket, took up an axe.

"And now, friend," said he, pointing to the tomahawk in Anthony's belt, "if you be so minded, I beg you help us cut saplings to make a shelter for our women and children against the night."

"Sir," answered Anthony, drawing Blodwen's hand within his arm, "with all my heart. But first I would have you bless and make us man and wife."

Now looking from one to the other with his gentle, tear-dimmed eyes, the little minister smiled; then down went the axe and out came his thumbed Bible again.

"This will I right joyfully!" said he. "For in such place of death it were well to sow seeds of new life. Come then, kneel ye beside this grave of a worthy man whose soul perchance looks down even now to bless us from the mercy seat of our God."

So thus in the wilderness, beside this new made grave, with these sad folks kneeling humbly amid this desolation to pray a blessing on them, Anthony and Blodwen were wed.

CHAPTER VIII

TELLS HOW BLODWEN MADE DECISION

A new young Nation has come into being at last and is battling desperately to live, is struggling for a place in this grim, old world.

These British Colonies, welding themselves into a very Brotherhood of Freedom, have declared themselves One Indivisible, the United States of America, and are proclaiming to this same old, weary, world a gospel of equality for all men and their God-given right to life, liberty and the pursuit of happiness.

Beneath a flag never seen before, they have risen to front their own kith and kin on the battlefield, despite the common blood and because of it, and are locked in desperate strife.

Thus stand they embattled against each other, these people of the same blood, loyal English-Americans with soldiers of England against Englishmen of the New America with their fellow colonists Dutch, Irish, German and Scot, fighting races and passionate lovers of freedom all, and willing to perish, if they must, but as freemen of this new race, now first known as the United States of America.

So the young Nation is fighting for life. Its people have already known the fierce triumph of brief victory, they have suffered bitter hardships, have become acquainted with grief and the terrors and despair of loss and defeat, and are to learn much of the bloody hatefulness of war ere they have proved themselves and win a place among the nations of the earth, with a mighty power that shall endure.

But as they face each other, these white men that

are to do and die, upon the flanks of both their armies hang clouds of painted savages to carry death and merciless destruction far beyond the common usages of war and to work such atrocities as may scarce be told. Yankee rifle, British musket and bayonet, with blasting artillery, are at their usual deadly work; so also the stealthy arrow, the merciless tomahawk and ghastly scalping knife, sparing neither age nor sex nor babe in cradle.

At the belts of Indian warriors hang the long tresses of women, the silky curls of children, the white locks of aged and feeble; by lonely rivers and in desolate valleys are trampled wastes and smoking ruins of village, settlement and farmstead.

Vague whispers of all this had reached Anthony, from time to time, in his forest home, making his present happiness only the more precious, yet filling him with dreadful apprehension and the ever recurring question,—how long was he to be so blessed?

Since his marriage and home-coming, all had gone well; to-day his fields were teeming to harvest; beyond the river the little settlement was thriving; by reason of his friendship with Mahtocheega and influence with his tribe, the Tuscaroras hereabouts were peaceful and content; but, ever and anon, came faint echoes of that tremendous strife afar.

To-day therefore as he rode across his wide lands between Tom Laurie his bailiff, and Nick Brewer his chief forester, though each of these was full of cheery talk concerning bumper crops and the new road they were cutting through the forest beyond their flourishing settlement of Falconbridge, Anthony, being lost in troublous thought, paid scant heed until said Tom:

"And yonder's your lady, sir, waiting for you in the oak grove as usual. Jee—hoshaphat, 'tis wonderful what changes she's worked among us all! Carries joy wherever she goes."

"Ay so!" quoth Nick. "An' white-skin or red, she knows the names of all the children in the settlement, and there a'n't a Tuscarora, warrior, squaw or papoose as a'n't glad of her. 'Happiness'—that's your lady's second name, I reckon, Mr. Anthony, ah and with a capital aitch!" But even as he spoke Anthony spurred his horse to a gallop and was away; and now as they watched him, quoth Tom:

"But what I can't mek out, Nick, is why he'll get so 'tarnation dismal all at once, laughing and cheery one minute but gloomy as Old Scrat the next."

"Ah!" nodded Tom. "And 'tes growing on him, he's been a sight worse o' late."

Meanwhile Anthony, reaching her who waited him in the shade of the oaks, leapt from the saddle and leaving his horse to trot away stablewards, caught Blodwen in his yearning arms. And presently, looking deep within each other's eyes, they went on side by side, their hands clasped and very close together, walking in a communion too deep for expression and far beyond words. But ever and anon her fingers would tighten on his, and in her golden eyes he saw a light that set him wondering, until he paused at last and, lifting her head with finger beneath her rounded chin, saw these same lovely eyes misted with sudden tears.

"Why, Blodwen," said he, drawing her near, "sweetheart, what is your trouble?"

"Oh, Anthony!" she whispered. "Oh my dear love!" And clinging to him she was silent awhile and he wondering the more.

"Dear heart o' me," he murmured, smoothing her glossy, night-black hair, "what's amiss?" And now, feeling how she trembled, he chilled with the old dread of parting and farewell. "Blodwen," said he, hoarsely, "is there . . . have you news of the war . . . ill tidings?"

"Ah no, no!" she murmured. "It is . . . something shall make you very glad . . . I hope."

"Good news?" he questioned. "Then why are your dear eyes so large . . . so wistful? Are you afraid?"

"No, my dearest, blindest man, only a little, just a little . . . anxious. For . . . oh my own love, soon . . . I think . . . we shall be . . . three. And I have been praying God He will give us a . . . little Anthony—"

Then his loving arms were fast about her, and he so mute that presently she raised her head and uttered a little choking cry of gladness to see him looking at her through sparkle of tears and with such reverent, adoring eyes; yet all he said was:

"Oh, my Blodwen!"

Thus then they wandered on, heedless of direction and all else save each other, talking in rapt murmurs of the wonder that was to be,—and of that dark vale a woman must tread alone to come back crowned and glorified with Motherhood, bringing up from the very shadow of death a little, helpless creature for their cherishing, to be in time their blessing or their bane. . . . And now thinking on all this, Anthony grew tremulous with fearful anxiety for her, and she, clinging to kiss him, all radiant with gratitude and joy. So they talked together of this young life coming to them out of the mysterious Infinitude.

"And if, oh if I should give you a son, my Anthony, he must needs be like his father, nay, he will be, for your dear image is surely printed deep on my heart."

"And if a daughter," said he, kissing her with a new reverence, "then I pray God she may look at me with your glorious golden eyes and, like you, be, one day, some man's joy and inspiration—" He checked suddenly and felt again that same dreadful premonition, for striding towards them came a very tall man clad in the green-fringed shirt and fur cap of a rifleman. Now, glancing from this ominous, warlike figure to Blodwen he saw her very pale and trembling.

"Oh, my Anthony!" she whispered.

"My dear," said he, as the big rifleman halted to salute them, "this is Septimus Tutt, an old hunting friend of mine."

"But now a sergeant of rifles, Mist' Anthony," quoth Septimus with flash of white teeth, a Ranger, sir."

"And what brings you here, Sep?"

"Dooty, sir. I come to guide your cousin, Cap'n Wilding, sir, wi' letters for ye from the General."

And presently they saw the house and, before its wide portico, their servants, men and women, grouped about jaded horses and their weary riders and one of these, a slender person in blue and buff regimentals, at sight of which Anthony halted again, feeling Blodwen's fingers tighten on his, heard her shuddering breath and broken whisper:

"Dear God . . . has it come . . . so very soon?"

"Heaven forbid!" he muttered and drawing her tremulous hand close within his arm, went on to meet his destiny.

Aware of their approach the little, eager crowd opened as Captain Wilding dismounting stiffly, came to meet them hat in hand, though walking like a man very weary. His once smart uniform showed worn and stained by hard service, his handsome face thin and haggard; but he bowed gallantly to Blodwen and reached forth an eager hand to Anthony, his left, for his right was in a sling.

"It seems, cousin Anthony, that I am to congratulate you," said he, smiling on them rather sadly, "and indeed I do from my heart. . . . Though I fear your lady will think me a bird of ill-omen."

"Meaning, cousin?" enquired Anthony, dry-lipped.

"I bear you a letter from General Washington and a colonel's commission. He tells me how you and he are old comrades of the French campaign in Canada."

"Yes," nodded Anthony. "I was a lieutenant in his company."

"But," said Blodwen, "you are wounded, Mr. Francis. Come indoors and let me look to it."

"A Hessian bayonet in the affair at Brooklyn, madam, and no great matter. But I am happy you have not quite forgot me, Mistress Blodwen—"

"Come in, Frank, and refresh yourself, come in and let us talk," said Anthony. "Let us hear your news and see this momentous epistle."

They brought him into the house, where servants came with wine and cold meats, then, while he ate and drank, talking aside with Blodwen, who questioned him of the war in a tremulous soft anxiety, Anthony broke the seal of this most unwelcome letter and having read it, sat staring before him with troubled eyes.

"Frank," said he suddenly, "Washington writes here that the army is in full retreat . . . things seem going none too well, cousin."

Mr. Wilding set down his wineglass and shook his head.

"My dear Anthony," he sighed, "things are going very ill, though considering our raw levies, and especially the militia, it could have been much worse, our men are splendid individually but as troops they lack discipline and to-day, what with wounded, captured, and deserters, we are in a something desperate plight."

"So I gather," said Anthony, frowning at the open letter before him, "George Washington was always very blunt and outspoken and never more so than in this letter."

"Ah, and with reason!" exclaimed Captain Wilding. "Our needs are many and very pressing. Anthony, if our new Federation, this United States, is to live we must be prepared to die . . . we must have unswerving devotion and—men and more men, but specially officers and, above all, veteran officers such as yourself, able and used to command."

"Indeed," said Anthony, still frowning at the letter, "Washington writes very ill of the new militia, for instance listen to this: 'Their want of discipline, the indulgencies they claim and have been allowed, their unwillingness and, I may add, their refusal to submit to that regularity and order essential in every army, occasioned a great deal of confusion and disorder.' And here again he writes of: 'abominable desertions,' adding that 'fifty thousand pounds would not induce me again to undergo what I have done.' And lastly of the militia he says this: 'If I was called upon to declare upon oath whether the militia have been most serviceable or hurtful upon the whole, I should subscribe to the latter.' Well, so writes George Washington!"

"And all but too true!" sighed Captain Wilding. "And thus it is that, knowing I am your cousin, he sends me with this plain statement of affairs that you may know how desperate is the need of this young nation for such men as yourself, cousin."

"However," said Anthony, folding the letter and dropping it on the desk before him, "I cannot go."

Captain Wilding sat up in his chair and nearly gaped.

"Cannot?" he repeated in tone of amazed disbelief. "You, Anthony—? You . . . actually mean—?"

"That I cannot and will not!"

Now here Blodwen, watching her husband's so loved face, his frowning brow, grimly determined mouth and averted gaze, closed her own eyes and clenched her hands, like one in quick anguish.

"Then am I to understand," said Captain Wilding in the same incredulous tone, "you refuse this commission . . . that Washington summons you in vain?"

"Perfectly, Frank."

Frowning now in his turn, Captain Wilding rose.

"You can wilfully close your ears to this distressful cry of your country?" he demanded.

"By no means!" answered Anthony, his dark gaze still averted. "Be good enough to step to this window." Wondering, and a little stiffly, his cousin obeyed.

"Look yonder," said Anthony, pointing, "away there between the river and forest! What do you see?"

"An Indian village."

"Precisely. And there at this moment, Frank, are some five hundred Tuscaroras, warriors of the Lynx, living content and at peace with all men, and, while I am here, so will they remain."

"Can you be sure of this?"

"I can. As sure as I am of anything in this changing world."

"Yet these are but so many savages . . . but America, this young nation, is ready to die almost before it has lived. I tell you, cousin Anthony, if it is not to perish from the earth, it needs all our strength and every man of us. Well, you are a man, Anthony, of honourable name and past achievement. And God knows you are wanted, waited for . . . so think man, think how you shall answer. . . ."

The eager voice seemed to shake with the speaker's passionate sincerity, his eyes glowed, his pale cheek flushed, he reached out his one arm in gesture of eloquent entreaty. But Anthony still kept his frowning gaze averted and made no attempt to answer; so for a long painful moment they stood thus, each of them silent and very still; then both started to Blodwen's smooth, soft voice:

"Pray Mr. Francis, when do you return to your duty?"

"Madam, I start for General Washington's headquarters to-morrow at dawn."

"Then . . . to-morrow at dawn my husband will surely go with you."

CHAPTER IX

TELLS OF BATTLE AND AN OATH

FIVE hundred strong marched they, by Indian trails deeptrodden in the wild, picked men of the Ranger Corps and veterans all, because their mission was hazardous and very desperate. And they sang, they laughed and talked as they marched, for their courage was high; only the man they followed was mute, this lonely man who had proved his wise leadership often of late, for there had been much fighting, and won their faith and respect by his indomitable will and cold, passionless valour.

Thus of his chosen Five Hundred only Anthony was silent, thinking of and yearning for his home, his brave, gentle wife and the child he might never live to see.

Now as he went with his long, tireless stride, brooding unhappily thus, Francis Wilding came beside him and heeding his troubled look, questioned him softly:

"Does anything trouble you, Anthony? Is aught amiss?"

"Many things, Frank, and mostly—this war. Also I'm afraid, damnably afraid!"

"Eh—you, Anthony? Of what?"

"Death, man!"

"Well but you have outfaced it often enough o' late, God knows."

"Ay, but life might be so wonderful, Frank! There is such happiness waiting me that may be snatched from me by any chance bullet. . . . Frank, we never go into action but I'm cold with dread. There was a time I had no care or fear of dying but . . . since then I have found such deep content that life is become so very precious I dread to lose it. Happiness has turned me craven . . . a poltroon. . . ." Francis clasped an arm about his cousin's drooping shoulders.

"And here," said he, laughing, "here is the man whose cool courage and stark audacity is a byword, indeed sometimes I think you are positively foolhardy."

"Perhaps because I so dread to die, Francis."

"Then would to God such dread might inspire us all—though, b'Gad, 'twould but mean even harder service. . . . For here's the reason Washington chose you for this particularly ugly business,—to cut off a convoy double our strength and with dragoons and infantry of the line, seems asking the impossible—even of us."

"Choice of ground, Frank, and surprise is our only chance. Well, I know the ground and my plans are made, but it will be an ugly business sure enough and must mean . . . some loss."

Here they strode on pensively awhile, but suddenly taking his cousin's arm, Anthony spoke softer than ever.

"You've heard tell how that some men have a premonition of approaching death, well, I have sometimes felt that I shall not make old bones and . . . so, Frank, I've a message—"

"Yes, old fellow?" But instead of answering at once, Anthony glanced up and around him with a strange, yearning gaze.

"Such waste of time and life!" he muttered bitterly. "All this marching and fighting when I might have been with my Blodwen . . . my message is to her, Frank, and, I've never told you, but she is . . . a mother by now! And . . . not to know how she is . . . all these cursed leagues of forest between us! An hour or less, Frank, and we shall be in action, and if it should happen . . . if this should be my last fight, you . . . will find a letter for her stitched in the lining of my shirt . . . here, Frank, it must reach her somehow."

"It shall, Anthony, it shall, I vow. But oh, damme, you've borne a charmed life thus far—"

"And I'm thankful, Frank, ay, God knows it! However, if to-day be my last, should you ever see my wife, pray tell how I . . . spoke of her. Say also that if . . . if our child is a boy I would have her name him after me, and if a girl—oh God to think of it—she must be christened Blodwen. . . . And yonder comes Sergeant Tutt to warn us we are near the road, I guess. Order silence in the ranks, cousin."

At word of command the cheery talk and singing died away and all voices were hushed till no sound was there to hear but the muffled padding of those so purposeful, moccasined feet.

"Cunnle," quoth Sergeant Septimus Tutt, saluting, "yonder, ayont they thickets scarce a rifle shot, lays the road and, afore us three mile, the ford. An' no place couldn't be better for it, I reckon."

"This is why I chose it, Sep. The road thereabout runs between high banks thick with tree and brush, eh, Sergeant?"

"Shore do, sir, and wot's more, it narrers."

"Well, that is the place. Captain Wilding, halt the company and summon here every officer."

Silently they came to group themselves about Anthony who, seating himself upon a fallen tree, unsheathed his long hunting-knife and beckoning them close around him, drew a rough diagram on the hard-packed earth of the trail before him.

"Major Dunstan and gentlemen," said he, "our duty, as you know, is to intercept supplies and a battery of heavy guns intended for General Burgoyne's army. This convoy is strongly guarded by a troop of dragoons and infantry of the line. My orders are to destroy these stores or, if possible, bring them off for the comfort of our own armies, and I propose to attempt this at a place called Dana's Crossing, which is a ford some three miles in our front. See now—here is the road between high banks thick with brush and backed by the forest, here the river and the ford. I with two hundred men shall post myself in ambush on this side the road. You,

Major Dunstan, with another two hundred, will occupy the opposite side. Captain Clemmons, you with fifty men, will take post here to the south of Major Dunstan's position. You, Captain Wilding, will lie to the north of me. Thus, gentlemen, we shall enfilade them front, flanks and rear. I trust this meets with your approval, sirs."

"It cannot fail!" cried Captain Clemmons, eagerly.

"Unless they march with flanking parties," said the Major, "how then, sir?"

"Why then," sighed Anthony, "our task will be the harder. But frankly I can scheme no better plan."

"Nor I, sir," quoth the Major.

"So, gentlemen, we can but hope—and fight our best. I need scarce impress on you all, sirs, the necessity for absolute silence. And now pray number off your companies and let us advance on our several positions."

Thud and scuffle of cautious feet as the one company became four, and the four marched away to take up their appointed stations.

Prone with his men Anthony looked through a screen of leafage down into this narrow, sunken road bright with the genial sun, with steep, green banks where flowers grew, a pleasant, quiet place soon to be made a horror of blood and pain and slaughter; and looking from this peaceful spot to the placid river and the vista of serene, blue heaven beyond, Anthony sighed again and closed his eyes.

"By heck, they'm a comin'!" whispered Sergeant Tutt fiercely, propping himself on an elbow beside Anthony. "D'ye hear 'em, sir, d'ye hear 'em?"

"Yes . . . yes, I hear."

"Jee-rusalem! But ye couldn't of chose a better place, Mist' Anthony. Think jest what our first volley 'll do to 'em!"

"I am thinking, Sep. It will be very like cold murder!"

"There wun't be many o' they red-coats, them bloody-backs, win out o' this yer, I'll lay. Easier nor shootin' pigeons. Though as for these yer bay'nets, sir, I don't—"

"Be silent, man—listen!"

A faint murmur growing louder to a hum . . . a confused medley of sound; a far, rolling dust-cloud rising against the placid heaven, growing thicker, denser and in this rolling cloud, jingle of harness, thud of horsehoofs, trampling of men, creak and rattle of heavy wheels.

The rolling dust-cloud drew nearer until in it could be seen the tossing crests of plodding horses, the plumed heads of their riders, and beyond these, the white belts and crossbelts of the redcoated infantry, and beyond these again, the long train of guns, limbers, and heavy-laden, lumbering transport waggons. . . . This much Anthony had glimpsed when rose sudden clamour with the booming discharge of muskets answered by a crashing volley of rifle-fire.

Anthony started to his knees; the sergeant cursed bitterly.

"Their skirmishers ha' seen us, sir! What now?" he cried.

"Wait!" said Anthony.

Shouts and hoarse commands from the crowded road; the dragoons came on at furious gallop. Then Anthony raised his hand; a trumpet blared, and, down from the banks of this sunken road, death roared; horses reared and went down kicking; men screamed and fell to be trampled and all was wild confusion.

Now all at once the rifle slipped from Anthony's grip and he stared with horrified eyes, for there, amid all this red havoc, rode the Earl of Wrybourne. His face was streaked with blood, but his sword glittered aloft and, resolute as ever, he called on his own troop of gentlemen volunteers. And gallantly they responded, spurring their chargers at these precipitous slopes, striving desperately to come at their unseen slayers, with their sabres. But hemmed in on every side, smitten through and through by raking, deadly rifle fire, this splendid troop, for all its valour, was helpless, horses and men went down in bloody, tangled heaps. . . .

"Grenadiers . . . stand! Soldiers o' the Guard rally on me!" Through swirling dust and smoke Anthony caught a glimpse of his cousin, Lord Charles, leading his redcoats to attempt these deadly slopes; clambering on and over the dead, up they came only to be met and hurled back by goring bayonet or clubbed rifle-butt. . . .

Dust and smoke and furious uproar gradually subsiding, groans and wailing of stricken men and wounded horses, for the ghastly business was done at last and the Rangers, such as remained, were cheering and loudest, fiercest of all, Sergeant Septimus Tutt.

But stumbling down into this place of slaughter went Anthony, his pitiful eyes questing dreadfully among these ghastly twisted shapes until he paused at last, his anxious search ended, for he was gazing at a still form that, so short a time ago, had been his friend and cousin, Francis Wilding . . . this handsome face now frightfully marred by the sabre that had cut him down; close by sprawled a dead Indian and, between these two, mingling his proud blood with theirs, lay George Charteris, Earl of Wrybourne, his dying body propped against his dead charger.

Now looking up into Anthony's eyes, the Earl smiled and beckoned feebly.

"I'm passing, nephew Anthony," he gasped, "dying for my England and . . . King, so I nothing . . . repine. Nay, Death shows me a . . . vision of Truth. See you . . . here lie my enemies . . . an Indian brave and . . . a rebel officer blending their . . . life-blood with mine in . . . one pool. 'Tis the blood of the . . . new America and it is . . . a noble blood . . . shall achieve greatly. So . . . now—"

The gasping voice failed, the fumbling hand reached down to this awful pool and dipping finger therein, my lord crossed himself upon the brow; then leaning back against his dead horse, he sighed deeply, and so the indomitable soul of him passed.

While Anthony yet stood there awed and grieving, he

heard a fierce, inarticulate cry and glancing vaguely round about, saw his cousin Charles wounded and prisoner and with him the Marquis de Vaucelles.

"Dead!" cried Charles, wildly. "My father . . .! And you, Anthony . . . ha, God's curse on you . . . this is your doing!"

"No, Charles, this is—war!"

"You led these damned rebels . . . and so is my father dead . . . and so for this I swear to kill you someday . . . if I live . . .!"

"And if not, my Charles, my old one," said the Marquis, "I also make oath,—this shall be my duty if it is that I am not also dead. To achieve such vengeance shall be my joy and honour."

"Hey, what's here?" roared a fierce voice, and in thrust the mighty Sergeant Tutt, elbowing the prisoners aside, "Do these yer bloody-backs dare to threat ye, cunnle? Shall we string 'em up, sir? Shall we shoot a few on 'em to teach and larn 'em? Say the word, cunnle—"

Anthony looked at him and the tall sergeant saluted and was dumb; then turning on these two captives:

"Cousin Charles," said he, "I dare to say I grieve for this as deeply, as sincerely as ever you can. . . . If we should live to meet when this hateful war is over and done, I hope . . . pray . . . that it may be at the least without rancour . . . *Monsieur le Marquis*, you should be sufficiently a soldier to free me of all and any responsibility for any man's death in such close and desperate an action as this hath been. . . . And now, gentlemen, you are free to go, I cannot be burdened with you. . . . Sergeant, where is Major Dunstan?"

"Lays dead over yonder, Cunnle."

"So is poor Stockley!" cried young Captain Clemmons, limping forward to salute, "Ay and half my company, sir, and my young brother—"

"Are you fit for duty, sir?" Anthony demanded harshly.

"Yes, Colonel . . . this is only a flesh-wound . . . but oh God, my brother John is—"

"Captain Clemmons, muster our company . . . disarm all prisoners . . . set them digging graves—go! Sergeant Tutt, come you with me, this convoy must be on the move for General Washington's head-quarters before dark,—come!"

So, when the moon rose, this sunken road lay deserted and very silent, with nothing to show what had been, the fury of valiant effort and pain of dying, except a broken weapon here and there, a shapeless huddle of dead horses, dark pools and splotches that stained white dust and trampled grass, soaking into the thirsty ground soon to be forgotten; and the long mound of new-turned earth that hid the shattered clay of those who, dying so manfully in their duty, had risen above death together in a great, new fellowship.

CHAPTER X

TELLS OF REUNION AND DEATH

It was night of Autumn; and in a draughty, weather-beaten tent dim-lit by guttering candles, a man in general's uniform sat warming himself at an inadequate fire, for the night was chill. He was a very tall man extremely precise and neat as to person for though his coat of blue and buff was faded, its gold braid and epaulettes tarnished, his wig was trimly curled and the rich lace at throat and wrists showed spotless.

All about this little tent were many others, vague in the uncertain light of watchfires, with rough shelters and hutments row upon row, where a host lay sleeping and no sound to hear but the muffled tramp of sentries.

Thus then sat His Excellency General George Washington gazing thoughtfully upon the figure beyond the fire, a lean, haggard shape that, crouched upon a stool, stared into the flame with eyes of such stark, speechless suffering and face contorted by such mental agony that his own stern, somewhat grim features softened wonderfully, and rising, he stood to lay his hands on this mute sufferer's shoulders, large hands yet very gentle, hands that held and were to mould the fate of a nation; and presently when he spoke, his voice was gentle also:

"Now God comfort thee, Anthony, old comrade!"

The heavy head was lifted, the haggard eyes looked up, the quivering lips found speech at last:

"Seven months and never a word! Seven months, George, and now—this! The whole frontier in ashes! Blood and devastation and . . . my wife, George, my wife and child somewhere amid it all!"

"I humbly pray you shall find matters better than report speaks them. Howbeit, God strengthen you, friend Anthony!"

"Then you'll grant me leave, George? You'll let me go . . . give me men no matter how few . . .? For go I must, to know the truth of it or I . . . I shall run mad."

"Take your Rangers, Anthony. Things are at a deadlock here until the enemy moves as move he must and shall, soon or late. So take what power you will, —go through the Seneca country like a cleansing fire . . . hang me these blue-eyed Indians, these mock savages, ay and these Colonial gentlemen, these fanatic loyalists that are become so lost to honour as to rouse the Five Nations and loose these once friendly tribes against us. Take such force as you will and God speed you, sir."

Then Anthony rose and was silent for a long moment staring blindly on the fire.

"George," said he at last, "I'm grateful! I'll take no more men than I must! This has been a bitter war, but I believe the tide has turned for us at last . . . I believe that while George Washington lives, so will live our new America, certain of victory now, and to flourish mightily when this generation of ours has passed away. So may God long spare your Excellency! And now farewell, sir."

"Shall you march to-night?"

"This hour, sir."

They grasped each other's hands, they saluted each other; and so these two old brothers in arms who years ago had marched and fought side by side for England, now took leave of each other, the one to mount eager horse and ride away like a whirlwind, the other to seat himself at littered travelling desk to write out dispatches, pore over maps and sign orders while the great camp slumbered around him and no sound to break the pervading quiet except the busy squeak of his tireless quill and the sentries calling their posts.

But afar in the shadow of the forest where the Rangers had their bivouac, all was orderly stir and bustle; lantern light flickered and gleamed on fringed shirt and leggings, on rifle-barrel, powder-horn and belted knife and tomahawk, as the Ranger Corps stood mustered to hearken while their grim-faced Anthony spoke:

". . . We must be a quenchless fire, comrades, to sweep the country clean 'twixt here and the Iroquois border. We go to hunt down and exterminate that bloody regiment called 'The Greens,' with MacDonald's sham Indians and renegades and their allies the Senecas and Mohawks. We are to make an end of these slayers of innocents, these murderers of women and little children. And we can only do this by sudden onfalls, surprise of attack, meeting their greater numbers by the unexpected and tactics of time and place. We must be stealthy as any Indian war party but quicker and more deadly. Comrades all, you are men well-tried and hardy, as I know, but this raid shall tax even your endurance, it will be a cruel march, we go forward, stopping for nothing, fighting all and any odds, with mercy on none and least of all, upon ourselves. If any man, by reason of wounds or weakness, cannot keep up, he must be left behind, and this will mean death at his own hands or torture by our foes. Well, men of the Rangers, my company shall be four hundred, who volunteers?"

Even as he spoke, and as one man, forward stepped the whole corps. Anthony's haggard features twitched, his sombre eyes brightened.

"Now God love you all!" cried he. "Proud am I to be a Ranger! Captain Clemmons and you, Sergeant Sep, choose me my company. We march in half an hour."

And so, towards dawn, four hundred men filed off silently into the misty forest, bound upon this forced march, this bold irruption into a hostile country swarming with ferocious savages and defended by regiments of white men yet more merciless, to smite them in their very stronghold; a feat that was to make history.

Day and night they marched, eating as they went, halting only to snatch a few brief hours of sleep; following Indian trails, fording rivers, scaling mountains, clambering steeps where only wild creatures and such men as these might go. Twice they surprised and smote powerful Indian war parties; once their deadly rifles cleared them a way through a prowling company of irregulars. But on they sped, seeking this hated regiment of the 'Greens' and renegade whites masked in paint and feathers, who had out-done the very Indians in their atrocities, tracking them by ruined farmsteads, devastated villages, black desolation and death in horrid shapes. As upon a certain morning when, hard upon the heels of their unsuspecting quarry, they came on the site of a camp so lately vacated that the ground felt still warm beneath the scattered ashes of the cooking fires . . . and upon the pervading stillness, for the day was hot and windless, an awful whimpering voice cried on God. Now following this voice, they presently beheld something pinned to a tree, an eyeless, contorted, mutilated thing that had been human and that even now, despite long hours of torture and painful dying, yet had strength for speech:

"Oh if . . . ye be . . . Christian men . . . shoot me . . . for love of Christ!" Anthony looked and beckoned to the Sergeant.

"Steel!" said he. "A shot may betray us."

And, after a little while they went on again, silent as ever, but at even swifter gait.

So this devoted company fought its way, giving and expecting no quarter of savage foe or relentless wilderness; and some of these Four Hundred died in battle, others were lost fording rivers and some few weakening, fell behind and shot themselves to escape deaths more evil.

Three hundred and eighty-one they numbered when, in a certain dawn, Anthony halted suddenly to lean on his rifle like one smitten faint and sick, for in his nostrils once again was the acrid reek of smoke . . . and this was country dearly familiar, the earth he now trod was his own . . . beyond the wooded curve of the river yonder should be his new village, the little settlement called after his own name, and, beyond this again, throned above park-like meadow, his home, set in the wide gardens he had caused to be made and planted for Blodwen's pleasure, the garden she had afterwards tended with such loving care.

They went on, they climbed a tree-girt hill whence he might see. . . . The little settlement of Falconbridge was gone . . . beyond rose a hideous blackened ruin that had been his house.

The rifle slipped from his nerveless grasp and, raising both arms, he strove to hide the horror with tremulous clutching hands; behind him fierce voices muttered and whispered, but no man spoke aloud until came young Captain Clemmons and ventured to touch him.

"Colonel . . . oh sir," said he, recoiling before the face Anthony turned on him, "pray is . . . is this—was that—"

"My home, sir!" answered Anthony, hoarsely. "There was my wife . . . my child that I have never seen! And now . . . what is there for me? Rangers, fall in! Let us go down and look on . . . what we must. Forward!"

Silently they followed whither he led, down the hill, across the level and into the ravaged garden trampled and desecrated by many feet. . . . But here his courage failed and sinking down upon a rustic seat beneath a certain tree where Blodwen had often sat with him of an evening, he gestured wildly towards the blackened fire-swept ruin of his home, saying:

"Comrades, I . . . dare not! Go for me and seek . . . amid the ashes."

So, while he crouched there in shuddering horror of what they might find, his men turned over these dreadful ashes, peering beneath charred timbers and fallen beams. After some time becoming aware the sergeant stood beside him, he questioned with face bowed between his shaking hands.

"Anything . . . Sep?"

"Only . . . bones, Cunnle. And they ain't nothing to go by, so tek comfort, sir, p'raps your dear lady—" he paused suddenly and turned, rifle at hip, for softly, clearly, a bird seemed calling from the shady oak-grove hard by. Anthony lifted his head, he got to his feet and stood motionless, breath arrested, listening:

"Sep, did you . . . did you hear it?" he gasped brokenly. "Did you hear it too?"

"Ay, sir, a whippoorwill called from the live oaks yonder and I—"

Snatching up his rifle, Anthony began to run, and the sergeant with him until Anthony's voice and gesture checked him:

"Back, Sergeant! See the men are alert . . . watch the forest yonder." Then he sped on again, running with long strides; and suddenly from behind a great, gnarled tree stepped a tall, stately figure.

"Mahtocheega!" he gasped. "Oh, friend—?" The Sagamore smiled, pointed; and then he beheld Blodwen. She was pale, her garments stained and torn, but Anthony saw only her golden eyes, the quiver of her lips, her arms outstretched to him.

"Oh, my Anthony . . . at last!"

Dumbly he gazed on her and, speechless still, leapt and clasped her to his heart in joy too deep for any words, or even kisses as yet. Now presently she drew him behind the tree and showed him, cradled between its thick, massive roots, a small, shapeless bundle.

"Our little son, Anthony."

Down they knelt together and though Anthony's lean cheeks were wet, his eyes were radiant as he stooped and, with shaking hand, very gently put back the Indian blanket . . . a little, pink face topped by auburn curls.

And thus it was that he first looked upon his little son. Now presently with this slumbering precious atomy between them, Blodwen told how two days ago death and horror had leapt upon them from the forest, how the Tuscaroras, overwhelmed by numbers, had died or been scattered, and of how, but for the Sagamore's valiant devotion, his craft and cunning, she and the child must have perished.

Then up rose Anthony and strode where, remote and solitary, stood this Indian chief, this nobleman of the Wilderness, and cast his arms about his most desolate figure and clasped his hands, uttering such broken words of gratitude as he might, until speech quite failed him and they stood gazing into each other's eyes, like the good friends they were.

"Oh, Mahtocheega, my brother, you have given back to me more than life . . . much more, and I have no words, I . . . I cannot tell you—" But now the Sagamore, seeing Anthony thus moved indeed beyond words, smiled his slow, grave smile, saying:

"But, my An—to—nee, these were thy wife and child, and thou art my brother, therefore no need to tell thy gratitude, this is all known and understood betwixt such as we. And now would I find me comfort in thy happiness for my heart is woeful, An—to—nee! My people of the Lynx are no more . . . dead, my brother, or scattered to the eight winds by these mock Indians that shame us, and dogs of Senecas that do shame themselves. So now, brother, if all is well with thee, I would begone into the Land of Shadows wherebe others I have loved—" He checked suddenly, hissing softly between his teeth and quick to heed this danger-signal, Anthony looked whither he directed and saw an Indian peering at them from the forest verge. Then Anthony lifted his rifle aloft, at which well-known summons his watchful men came running in scattered groups until every tree, every gnarled root and tussock, screened a waiting marksman.

"Captain Clemmons, Sergeant Tutt, let no man fire till I command. Pass the order, then come you nearer," called Anthony softly, and turning for speech with Blodwen, saw only the Sagamore and starting to his knees stared wildly about until her voice spoke close beside him.

"We are here, my Anthony and oh my heart . . . take care . . . !"

"In the tree here, brother," quoth the Sagamore, stringing his powerful bow. "It was here she hid when death sought her before and found her not."

"Thank God!" sighed Anthony, his keen gaze watching the line of forest again; and thus presently he saw it alive with men, furtive shapes that crept amid the underbrush or crouched behind tree and thicket, a great company of men, red and white, feathered heads hideous with warpaint, green uniforms and glitter of bayonets, at sight of which last, a hoarse murmur went up from these hidden Rangers, a sound of bitter execration, lost in the sudden explosion of many rifles and muskets, and then these stealthy forms, the forest itself was blotted out in billowing clouds of smoke.

"May we loose a volley at the scum now, sir?" pleaded Captain Clemmons, eagerly.

"No no, not yet, man. Let them puzzle over us. I would have them think us fewer than we are, to draw their attack. I want them in the open. See, they are growing bolder!"

"Ay by heck!" growled the sergeant, "I can count over twenty o' the varments, Cunnle."

"You shall see them all presently, I hope. Now hearkee, Sergeant Sep, they are waiting our return volley to judge our numbers. Well, we'll give them no more than four shots in rapid succession as men few and desperate would fire, first yourself, next Petersen, Hans Kraus and last Sam Lloyd. Then reload and fire again in the same order. Repeat this three times. Is it understood?"

"Shore is, Cunnle."

"Then pass the word and fire when I lift my hand."

Thrice in rapid succession, one after the other these four picked marksmen discharged their unerring pieces and with deadly effect, for, upon the ensuing quiet rose shrill voices growing louder, fiercer, where crouched their dim-seen foes.

"Jee-hoshaphat! You are right, cunnle, they're

a-comin'," whispered the sergeant, cuddling his rifle-stock closer.

The vengeful hubbub abated suddenly, steel glittered amid the green,—then forth of the sheltering forest leapt the attack, men in green uniform, men in garments of deer-skin, flanked by Indians, painted, stripped and oiled for close battle.

"Wait the word, Rangers!" cried Anthony.

On came the enemy, the Indians shrilling their terrible scalping cry, the 'Greens' cheering or grimly silent, nearer, nearer yet; then at Anthony's word three hundred and eighty odd rifles volleyed and crashed.

"Now!" cried he and, before the smoke could clear, he and his company were up and leaping to hurl themselves upon the shattered ranks of their dismayed assailants. Hand to hand they fought, stabbing, hurling back their stricken foes in such reeling confusion that they broke, scattered and fled, only to be smitten down the easier by men who, with every thrust and blow avenged some deed of outrage or torture.

Now, Blodwen, hearing the battle roar afar, crept from her refuge and clasping the child to her bosom, strained anxious eyes for some glimpse of her husband's beloved form in that wild confusion of pursuit, slaughter and panic where fleeing men were smitten down by their merciless conquerors while some few, wriggling aside, fled for their lives. Thus she was presently aware of two Indians speeding towards her though she scarcely heeded, all her thought being for Anthony; but these, being terrified and beaten men, were but the more savage therefore and so turned aside to wreak their hate and vengeance on her helplessness. And now she heard and, turning, saw them and screamed and sank face down to shield the babe with her defenceless body, for the scalp-lock of one of these seeming Indians was red, the fierce eyes of the other showed grey blue.

And thus crying on God's mercy Blodwen waited for death; she heard the twang of a bowstring and venturing to glance up, saw the red-haired Indian reel back, clutching at the arrow that was his death; she saw the blue-eyed Indian turn, cursing in English, to meet the leap of the Sagamore who, casting aside his bow had snatched his deadly tomahawk. . . . A flicker of thrown steel and she saw her deliverer sway, recover and strike. And the Tuscarora war hatchet smote true as ever, for the Sagamore stood alone. But slowly, as if unwilling, he sank to his knees, staring down at the haft of the knife that was buried so deeply in his side. Then up sprang Blodwen and ran to him and, heedless of her wailing babe, set herself to cherish this stricken man who smiled on her, pointed to the knife and shook his head, saying breathlessly:

"Touch it not . . . little sister, for with it . . . goeth my life and I would . . . bid our An—to—nee farewell. . . ."

And at last Anthony came hasting with divers of his Rangers and these jubilant with victory, but seeing this stricken man and kneeling woman they stood dumb, only the Sagamore spoke, faintly:

"An—to—nee, my brother now . . . is farewell until . . . a better meeting in the Land of Shadows. . . . Lift me now, my brother . . . lift me. . . ."

Strong arms raised and supported the dying chieftain on his feet and now, standing thus, he looked up at the serene heaven.

"Manitou," he gasped, "Master of Life. Great Spirit of my fathers . . . I come!"

So died this Tuscarora Sagamore, Mahtocheega of the Lynx.

They dug his grave in the shady oak-grove and there, with his axe beside him and mighty warbow between his folded hands, they laid him to await the Great Awakening.

And towards evening, with his wife and little son thus miraculously alive, Anthony marched away to fulfil his destiny.

CHAPTER XI

WHICH RECORDS A DEATH, A GIFT, AND ENDS THIS FIRST BOOK

A PLEASANT town was New York in those days, with goodly houses set within fair gardens or shady orchards where, on such peaceful, sunny afternoon as this, one might breathe an air sweet with the sea and sit to watch the distant sails of passing ships, or busy one's self with spade or shears; for the war was ended and this new Republic, vital with youth and flushed with triumph, already a power among the nations, was binding up its wounds and girding itself to mighty purpose.

And Blodwen, seated in shady garden busied with her needle, was watching her husband's close-cropped head where he stood clipping and trimming a hedge with great nicety and precision; a bronzed, happy-faced Anthony who whistled cheerily while ex-sergeant Septimus Tutt, delving in the vegetable garden hard by, joined in every now and then, extremely loud and shrill. Thus master and man working together, whistled so resoundingly that Blodwen must needs bid Anthony hush lest he wake his small son and heir, but, even as she spoke, from the open lattice of the bedroom above, rose young Master Anthony's lusty wail and thereafter at this same window appeared Amalia, his dusky nurse, with this small gentleman on her ample bosom, to berate these the disturbers of his slumbers.

"Fo' shame now on de bofe o' yo'!" quoth she. "Yo' done go wake dis sweet chile! Dere now my li'l honey man nebber yo' min'!"

"Lord!" exclaimed Anthony. "I'm always forgetting."

"Me too!" quoth the ex-sergeant. "By Jiminy, Cunnle, but thet yer infant's got the sharpest years in the hull o' Tryon Country, I reckon!"

"Bring him down," called Blodwen, smiling happily as she laid by her sewing; "bring him down to his father, Amalia."

So this small personage duly made his appearance in the garden, to be kissed by his mother and thrust upon his father who took and handled him as if he had been made of extremely delicate china.

"Oh, Anthony, isn't he wonderful! See how big he's growing! And so strong, bless him! And such lots of hair!"

"Why yes," answered Anthony, glancing slyly at his young wife's beautiful face aglow with pride of motherhood. "Though he feels remarkably brief . . . he ends so suddenly and his robes so long . . . at least, his legs don't come down very far, do they, and——"

"Gracious goodness!" exclaimed his mother, indignantly. "His legs are just perfect, you know they are!"

"Li'l angel's laigs, dat's what dey is!" affirmed his nurse passionately.

"However," said Anthony, winking furtively at the grinning ex-sergeant, "there's not . . . no, there is not a great deal of him—as yet, eh, Sweetheart?"

"Why, Anthony, he is immense for his age."

"Lawd in hebben!" wailed Amalia, "dese yer men is nebber satisfied! Oh, Massa Ant'ny, does yo' 'spect him fo' to be growed all so sudden, wid hair on him chest so soon, an' great, big monstroolius laigs? Cunnle, I'se 'sprised at yo'! I sho' is! Him's jest a sweet, li'l wonder chile——"

"Not a doubt of it!" quoth Anthony, holding his kicking crowing son and heir high aloft. "Ha, little man," said he fondly. "Oh, Mr. Anthony Falconbridge the Second, I salute you, sir! May you prove a better man than your father and handsome as your lovely mother, sir. And, Mr. Anthony, though such a very small gentleman at present, you shall be a man of substance, one day, with property in old England and, what's better, wide lands here in our new America. . . . And this reminds me, dearest, I promised to see lawyer Torrence at three o'clock to go through those deeds with him."

"Den, Cunnle, jes' yo' gib me dis precious lamb fo' yo' drops him."

"And, my dear," said Blodwen, rising, "it is nearly three now. And you must change your coat, you shall wear the plum-coloured velvet, so hurry now!"

"Nay the inn is but a step across the green, sweetheart."

"And this time, sir, I'll take care you do not go abroad without your wig! Come and be dressed."

"Lord, I hate the things."

"But wigs are still modish, and a wig becomes you . . . and you must change those shoes. . . ." Thus presently, thanks to her care, he stood, a comely, well-beseen figure from well-curled wig to gleaming shoe-buckles, while her busy, loving hands patted and smoothed the plum-coloured coat and arranged the fine lace of his jabot. Then he kissed her gaily and went forth into the sunny air, smiling back at her, hat in hand, a goodly man happy in his strength.

Walking leisurely, he reached the inn, there to be greeted by divers of the neighbouring gentry, and had turned to salute Mr. Torrence when a slender cane interposed, and turning sharply, Anthony beheld a very elegant gentleman who smiled, bowing with graceful elaboration. Said he:

"It is, I think, my happiness to behold at last Mr. Anthony Falconbridge."

"And you, sir, are the Marquis de Vaucelles."

"Entirely and humbly at your service!" smiled the Marquis. "Sir, I have to inform you how that your cousin and my friend Charles, Earl of Wrybourne, lies sick of his wounds and is like to leave his so charming

Countess a widow and his new born son an orphan, alas! In these so distressing circumstances you behold me here in his stead, to demand of you that satisfaction which honour cannot refuse. Meanwhile, I beg you to defend yourself either here or outside as you shall prefer."

"This is damned nonsense, sir!" answered downright Anthony. "The war is over, thank God, and I have no quarrel with cousin Charles, or yourself." The Marquis smiled, bowed and smote his hat into Anthony's face and was instantly knocked down by Anthony's fist.

"Ah, perfect!" he murmured, rising. "But, sir, I perceive you wear no sword . . . will some gentleman pray oblige monsieur?"

And now, as upon another occasion, some meddling hothead thrust a sword into Anthony's reluctant grasp; instantly the Marquis's blade flashed up in swift salute, then flickered in a sudden lunge that Anthony instinctively strove to parry; thus for a breathless moment the narrow blades writhed about each other, then Anthony recoiled until stayed by the panelled wall and leaned there a moment, one hand outspread upon his breast. Presently uttering no word and while all spectators stood dumbstruck by the suddenness of it, he crossed to the door and reaching there, seemed to falter oddly; Mr. Torrence ran to him and seeing Anthony's fingers drip red and the widening stain they could no longer hide, called in shrill, breathless voice:

"Help here! Someone, for God's sake, run for a surgeon."

"No. . . . no!" said Anthony. "It is not so bad as that. . . . Pray lend me your arm to my house, it . . . is not very far." Then friends were about him and leaning on their arms Anthony went forth with both hands now tight clenched upon his pulsing hurt, that ever widening stain, leaving behind a hubbub of excited voices, some questioning, others loudly denouncing the murderous irregularity of it all.

So they brought Anthony home to a wife who wasted

no time in vain lament, but choking back the dread horror that sickened her, grew strong to aid as his weakness increased, doing all she might to his comfort, smiling brave encouragement through blinding tears, hoping against hope even when Mr. Purdee, the young surgeon, shook his head. . . .

Came evening with radiant sunset and Anthony so weak his voice was but a whisper:

"Dear Heart, show me . . . our little man." So the child was brought to be kissed by pallid lips and touched by failing hand.

"Hold him near that . . . I may see . . . your two faces together . . . for Beloved, I'm going . . . but this is not . . . the end! . . . The Sagamore's Land of Shadows . . . to wait for you. But I shall live in our son . . . this other Anthony . . . and he is part of our new America and this shall never die. . . . Beloved teach him to live for . . . America. My Blodwen . . . give him, pledge him now to . . . our America."

Then Blodwen lifted this little Anthony high against the radiant West where the sun was going down in splendour.

"Take him, then, America!" she sobbed; and in this moment sank upon her knees, uttering a heartbroken cry for she saw that her big Anthony was dead.

But the child upon her bosom, vigorous with life, crowed joyfully and reached forth little, eager hands to that glory in the West.

BOOK TWO

CHAPTER I

WHICH INTRODUCES ANOTHER ANTHONY

For almost a hundred years this young Nation, these United States of America, journeyed onwards and up, achieving mightily, growing ever richer and more powerful until came a day when, from within itself, rose that which threatened its destruction.

But this people, ever strangely fortunate, found to its salvation one who came forth of the great wilderness, a son of the backwoods; a rugged man with no graces of form or feature, a strangely humble, honest man all untutored in the polite arts of pleasing and therefore viewed askance by the cultured and wholly unwanted by the professional politicians. Yet this was a man indeed whose simplicity was such and whose faith in himself, his fellow man, and his God was so deeply sincere that, rising with a godlike strength, he reached forth mighty arms to the proud and desperate South and sternly implacable North, drawing them, knitting them together, fusing them at last into one and sealing this union with his very life blood.

And it was at a portrait of Abraham Lincoln, ill-drawn and worse printed, that Mr. Anthony Falconbridge, called The Master, chanced to be gazing with such lofty disparagement as he sat in the luxuriously appointed library of his great New York mansion on a certain spring afternoon in this very fateful year of Grace 1861.

And Mr. Falconbridge matched his surroundings, being himself richly though soberly clad and of a stately presence; for the years had made him a man of wealth with resources so many, so far reaching and powerful that he had become the master of men; and he knew it.

A lean, upright, commanding figure, quick with vigorous life but with hair already grey though he numbered hardly forty years; his aquiline features, clean shaven in this age of whiskers, showed leanly vital, arrogance was in the arch of his delicate nose, a prideful will in the jutting curve of his chin, but his shapely mouth had a humorous lift, and his eyes, deep-set, well-opened and black-lashed, these eyes were of a strange golden hue.

Still gazing down upon this blotted portrait, Mr. Falconbridge reached for and tinkled the small silver bell on the desk before him, in answer to which summons a knuckle rapped, a door opened and into 'the presence' stepped a tallish, powerfully-built young man, neatly though almost too sombrely attired, whose square and somewhat rugged features, framed in modishly trimmed whisker, showed a little grim as, with quick, perfunctory bow, he stood waiting.

"Marchdale," said his employer without glancing up from the paper before him, "have the goodness to bid my son to me."

"Mr. Anthony is out, sir."

"Out where, pray?"

"Trying the new horse you bought for . . . for Miss . . . Miss Leigh, sir."

"Ah! And she, I suppose, is out with him?"

"No, sir."

Mr. Falconbridge sat up, his thick, black brows knit themselves and he became 'The Master.'

"And where," he demanded, "where is Miss Leigh?"

"She was . . . is . . . she . . . the ladies are in the garden, sir."

"Hum!" quoth The Master, flashing a keen up-glance at his young secretary. "I notice lately that you are afflicted with a remarkable stammer, Marchdale, a quite peculiar stutter. . . ." Mr. Marchdale, very conscious of the speaker's keen, quick eyes that saw so much and so deep beneath the obvious, flushed guiltily, stared hard at nothing and groped rather awkwardly for his neatly trimmed right hand side whisker.

"How do you account for this, Thomas Marchdale?"

"I . . . don't, sir."

"Miss Leigh, you tell me, is in the garden, with whom?"

"Your sister, Miss Adela, sir, and . . . Mr. Lawrence de Witt."

"That puppy!"

"Exactly, sir! Precisely!" answered Mr. Marchdale, with such extreme fervour that his hearer's shapely mouth twitched.

"Speaking, Marchdale, of Miss Leigh, I observed you sitting with her in the garden last evening, you appeared to be reading aloud to her from a book."

"I was, sir."

"May I enquire the subject of your reading?"

"The poems of Walt Whitman, sir."

"Good God!" murmured Mr. Falconbridge and rising to his feet, became so very stately that his young secretary showed the more awkward by contrast, though his square face looked more grimly rugged than ever.

"Marchdale," said The Master, "I deplore your taste! Whether this indecently outspoken Whitman person writes poetry or doggerel is no matter, but, considering the pernicious licence he permits himself, I take strong exception to your reading his effusions to the young lady in question. I can but hope you were careful in your selection—"

"To doubt it, sir, is an affront!"

"Affront?" repeated The Master, and, having frowned upon the word, sat down again. "Then I will not doubt it," said he more affably. "Pray, how old are you, Marchdale?"

"Twenty-six, sir."

"Seven years older than my son. . . . And you have . . . hum . . . favoured me with your services how long?"

"Two years and four months, sir."

"And being my personal secretary, living here in my house, you are therefore, to some extent, in my confidence, and must consequently be very well aware that Miss Leigh is an extremely wealthy heiress and that my earnest desire and settled purpose is that she and my son should espouse each other. You are aware of this, I presume?"

"Certainly, sir."

"Then I trust you will not permit yourself to forget."

"Sir, it . . . it is never . . . out of my mind."

"That is well!" nodded The Master, grimly. "I should be sorry to part with you, Marchdale."

The young secretary bowed and turned away, but not quick enough to hide from those keen eyes the painful flush that swept from chin to brow.

"This being understood, Thomas, pray find my sister Adela and say I wish to speak with her,—no, first look at this!" And Mr. Falconbridge gestured, rather contemptuously, to the paper on the desk.

"I noticed it this morning, sir," said Mr. Marchdale, glancing whither he was directed. "It is an extremely bad likeness of our new President, Mr. Lincoln."

"Bad or no—look at it! This is the person who has been foisted upon us at such a crisis when if ever our country needed a man, God knows it does now! The Southern States seceding one after another and ready for open rebellion! The Union threatened with disruption—and we must have this backwoods nobody thrust into power, a raw-boned nonentity from Illinois! Only a strong, wise, clean-souled superman could handle this tragic situation adequately—and we must have this raw, half-educated, uncouth country-lawyer person! Well?" demanded The Master, for his secretary was gazing silently down at this inky portrait rather oddly, "Well?"

"Yes indeed, sir!" nodded Mr. Marchdale.

"Now pray what might you mean by 'yes indeed, sir'?"

"That I fancy Mr. Abraham Lincoln may do well enough, sir."

"But I say we need a statesman, a leader, a strong, clean man."

"This portrait, sir, makes him look extremely dingy, and is very little like him as I remember."

"What then, you know him?"

"Very well, sir, years ago. He was our neighbour and my father's friend when we lived in Springfield."

"I thought you were an Englishman, Marchdale."

"My father is, sir, but I am an American."

"Sit down, Thomas, and let me hear of this man."

Mr. Marchdale took a chair and a handful of whisker and staring down at the toe of his polished boot, glanced thence to the keen, golden eyes opposite and spoke:

"Mr. Lincoln is a character so various and of such extreme opposites that I find him very hard to describe, sir. He is very tall . . . a sad, great, bony man with wonderful eyes in an ugly face. His hair is black and coarse and usually on end, his hands like his feet, are very large and look clumsy, his gestures are awkward and his voice sometimes harsh. He is a man very gentle with children and kind to all animals, he was a child of poverty born in the wilderness and knew much of hardship, and this perhaps taught him a strange humility and gentleness. But then he has also roughed it in brutal company and in lawless places where strife was fierce and instant and this made him a mighty wrestler and fighting man, and being so powerful he was usually the victor and a kindly one. He—I trust I do not weary you, sir?"

"On the contrary. Pray go on."

"He can tell a story to set a bar-room roaring or a tale for children that can hold them spellbound, as well I know, for though his speech is very simple and direct, his words frame vital thoughts. He is a courageous man, very unpretentious, of tremendous determination yet patient . . . yes, he is of an immense patience. . . . And they call him 'Old Abe' . . . even as a young man everyone called him 'Old Abe' . . ." Here grasping whisker again, Mr. Marchdale twisted it gently, much as if he turned himself off, and glanced at his stately hearer rather wistfully, saying:

"I think, perhaps, I have said enough, sir, or too much."

"My dear Marchdale, I had no idea you could be so eloquent."

"Sir, I have an inspiring subject."

"Is Mr. Lincoln a wealthy man?"

"Far from it, I believe. But then he never seemed to care for money. I heard him say once that 'wealth was a superfluity of what we don't need.'"

"You paint me a very remarkable character, my dear Thomas, and one of whom—" Mr. Falconbridge started, frowned, and turned to the unwonted sound of contentious voices in the wide hall without, then rose at the more unusual sight of the door swinging wide, and stood thus, very tall and dignified, every inch the stately arrogant Master, as in upon his chaste seclusion strode two vociferous gentlemen, and each the other's opposite, for one was a large and ponderous personage who flourished a tall, silk hat much as if it were a weapon of offence; the other, a small gentleman, thin-voiced and slight, who crushed a wideawake to his narrow bosom and bowed meekly.

"Well, sir! Ha, Falconbridge!" boomed the massive gentleman, hat a-flourish, "It's happened! The dread thing is on us! I have it by the telegraph—"

"Neighbour," piped the small gentleman advancing before his ponderous companion, "what our friend Washam means to tell you is—"

"That the South has begun it—!" roared Mr. Washam.

"Yes!" cried the little gentleman. "These Confederates, curse 'em, these damned rebels, blast 'em, have dared commence hostilities."

"Positively fired on Fort Sumter, sir!" thundered Mr. Washam, smiting invisible foes to earth with his hat.

"Ah!" sighed The Master, and leaning back in his chair, turned to glance up at an old, long-barrelled rifle that hung in the panelled recess designed for it, "So, it will be war, you think."

"Alas, nothing less, I fear!" groaned Mr. Washam.

"And sooner the better!" shrilled his small companion.

"Then, gentlemen," said The Master, "I suggest refreshment. Pray be seated. Marchdale, give Mr. Doughty a chair and then ring for the butler."

Little Mr. Doughty, bowing humbly, seated himself meekly and piped ferociously:

"War? Yes, Falconbridge! War and bloodshed must soon become our duty, our constant—"

"Heaven forbid!" bellowed Mr. Washam.

"Why not, Cyrus, why not?" demanded Mr. Doughty, mild of eye but fierce of voice. "These hell-benders in the South are asking for it. What said Jefferson Davis only the other day? 'We must sprinkle 'em with blood,' says he, 'or these seceding states will be back in the Union! If war comes,' says he, 'it shall be on North not Southern ground,—in the North,' says he, 'where there are plenty of towns to loot and burn!' That's the spirit of these Southern rebels, curse their proud hides! They're a blot, gentlemen, a foul blot with their accursed slavery! They're a wart, a wen on the fair face of our vaunted civilization! Slavery must go, must be stamped out root and branch, say I, even though we must needs wade in blood—"

"Hold there, Henry!" boomed Mr. Washam. "Friend Falconbridge, you'll bear me out, sir, I'm sure,—this question of slavery is no concern of ours here in the North, no sir! Remember, Henry, the people of the South are our own kith and kin, a noble people, sir, deeprooted in a proud ancestry and heroic tradition—Falconbridge, I ask you—"

"Flapdoodle, sir!" piped Mr. Doughty, bounding in his chair. "Cyrus, I will rise to maintain with my last breath that slavery is against Nature and our noble Constitution! I say it shames and mocks us! It robs our Declaration of Independence of all its power, making it a lie, sir, a foul lie! Neighbour Falconbridge, who shall dare gainsay this? As slave masters, gentlemen, we are to ourselves and the whole wide world a nation of hypocrites and humbugs! You agree, Falconbridge? Yes, sir, I see you do! These poor, oppressed black folk being equal in the sight of the Almighty should therefore enjoy equal rights—"

"Hold again, Henry! Remember the Dred Scott case and how Chief Justice Taney's judgement therein was that at the time of the Declaration of Independence negroes were considered by general opinion to be so immeasurably inferior that they had no rights that the white man was in any way bound to respect. Then again as regards the Repeal of the Missouri Compromise—"

"Outrageous!" screamed Mr. Doughty, "A most foul injustice on both white folk and black, as Falconbridge must certainly agree. The negro, Cyrus, is our poor, defenceless black brother—"

"Yours perhaps, Henry, but surely not mine!"

"Sir, he is formed in the Almighty's image—"

"I've only your word for it, Henry—"

"And now, gentlemen," said their host as Erastus, his tall negro butler, entered bearing a large silver tray whereon were glasses and many bottles of divers shapes, "let us take a sociable glass or so, fill up and drink, I beg. And while you do, permit me as one who troubled too little about politics, to ask your opinions of our new President, this Mr. Lincoln—"

Mr. Washam very nearly dropped his glass.

"A huckster!" he boomed, "A mere political huckster! A slavehound of Illinois! A—"

"A rail splitter!" piped Mr. Doughty. "A hewer of wood and ought instantly to be sent back to his axe—"

"Agreed, Henry! Judge Douglas should have been—"

"Bosh, Cyrus, bosh, sir! Our President should have been Seward, he only might hope to—"

"But by your leaves, gentlemen," said The Master in tone dominating as his look, "tell me of Mr. Lincoln and what you have against him?"

"Everything, sir!" bellowed Mr. Washam, "Everything and more besi—"

"Neighbour Falconbridge," cried Mr. Doughty, "allow me to tell you, from actual experience, he is no more than a crass commoner with no sense of dignity or deportment, no least idea of the majesty of the high office thrust upon him, or its vast responsibilities. When I tell you, sir, that he received a most important deputation, myself being one, with his waistcoat entirely unbuttoned, his linen exposed and . . . in carpet slippers very much down at heel, you may judge him. When I further inform you that he interrupted our spokesman in the very middle of his exordium to tell us some idle story of three niggers and a crow, you may form some estimation of the person into whose woefully inept hands is placed the fate and lofty traditions of our noble country. Hearing this, my dear Falconbridge, I know you will deplore as—"

"Nay but, Henry," vociferated his portly companion, splashing him with flourishing glass, "if this man Lincoln can but keep us from war, from spilling the precious blood of our brethren, I am persuaded that Falconbridge must heartily agree with me that—"

"Never, sir!" shrilled Mr. Doughty, setting down empty glass very tenderly. "No, Cyrus, on the contrary our neighbour Falconbridge, though man o' the world, is first and foremost a citizen and lover of this his own fair country and, as such, must be for Abolition absolutely, at all and any cost, and . . . by Jingo, it's past three o'clock!" exclaimed Mr. Doughty leaping from his chair. "Alas, neighbour, I must tear myself hence, for it behoves all true patriots to be spry, sir, spry—"

"Alert, Henry! I should rather say—alert!" quoth Mr. Washam, heaving himself ponderously to his legs. "Falconbridge, my hand, sir! I am truly grateful to you for the many valuable and eloquent expressions of your opinion with which you have—ah—favoured us. Good afternoon!"

"Indeed," piped Mr. Doughty. "It has been a joy to hear you, neighbour, your remarks I shall cherish, sir, cherish. Falconbridge, good day!"

So, having shaken and wrung their host's hand, these very disputatious gentlemen departed, still engaged in loud debate; nor did Mr. Falconbridge speak until their wrangling voices had died away. Then sinking into his chair, he smiled and, glancing at his secretary, nodded.

"Upon my soul, Marchdale," said he, "I begin to have some faint hope of your Mr. Lincoln. . . . Ah, but this business at Fort Sumter! How should Washam hear of this before me?"

"Well, sir, Mr. Washam being a member of Congress and head of a great business organization—"

"I know, I know! Yet my interests are far wider, here and in the South. . . . Eight secretaries, beside yourself and each with his own staff . . . a host of correspondents throughout the country yet I receive no word of this most vital news! You will presently ride down to the Bureau, summon the whole staff and demand in my name the explanation of this laxity. Say I shall myself be there to-morrow at nine o'clock. Tell them I shall expect a full statement prepared of all my holdings and properties in the South. . . . For if this war should come . . . if war must come indeed . . ." Up rose this Master of Labour and Wealth, this potent aristocrat whose will directed the lives of so very many of his fellow creatures, and began to pace back and forth, scheming how best to preserve and add to this precious wealth that was his power, and with no thought above it, until his cold, musing gaze coming upon the old rifle where it hung so brightly burnished in its place of honour upon the panelled wall, he halted, his golden eyes kindled, his grimly prideful look softened and, when he spoke again, his clear voice seemed awed to unwonted humility:

"War is always hateful folly, Marchdale, ah, but such war as this . . . this fratricidal strife would be most terrible! Civil wars are always bloodiest! How many thousands now so full of life and the joy of it must die? What agonies of broken hearts and stricken bodies! Ah, and what a harvest of vengeful hate will be sown,—what bitter and dreadful aftermath! . . . Yet it is only by suffering and hardship that character is formed . . . it is not in rich and slothful ease that nations are made. Our forefathers suffered and endured much for us, and we must now endure our best for those that shall be. A strange, cruel world for poor Humanity! . . . Bring me my cleaning rags and oil."

So saying, Mr. Falconbridge drew off his close-fitting, full-skirted frock coat, turned up the delicate wristbands of his shirt and taking a large apron from a drawer in the desk, tied it about his nether man.

Thus equipped, he crossed to the panelled recess and took down the ancient rifle, handling it reverently like the honoured and treasured relic it was.

He smoothed its long, bright-polished barrel, caressed the satiny patina of its battered stock; he cocked it, swung it to his shoulder, levelled it at the broad hearthstone and touched off the well-oiled trigger, smiling, very boylike, as the flint sparked. And now, meeting the wistful gaze of Mr. Marchdale, he nodded, saying:

"They knew a thing or so, our ancestors. There's no modern weapon in the world to-day with sweeter balance or finer action. . . . My rags and polishers? So, well now be off. Bring back the estimates for my new railroad, ha, yes, with the plans and drawings for my new clipper ships."

"There is also the business concerning your mills in Chicago, the extension, sir, and—"

"That can wait, Thomas. If war comes we must think of transport, railroads and ships. Bring me the new designs for the ships . . . a finer sheer fore and aft . . . more tumblehome amidships . . . perhaps . . . should give another knot or so. Bid them send me the model of the *Foam Nymph* at once. And you may take one of the horses."

"Thank you, sir!" said Mr. Marchdale, his deep-set eyes aglow, "Which horse may I ride?"

"Any of them except my mare. Now away with you."

Mr. Marchdale bowed and departed, striding like a heavy cavalryman.

Then Mr. Anthony Falconbridge, The Master, sat down and began to scour, to rub and polish the ancient rifle of that other Anthony who had lived and loved, suffered and passed, so many years ago.

CHAPTER II

TELLS, AMONG MANY OTHER FATEFUL MATTERS, OF A PARTING

WITH handsome grey head bowed above the old weapon, Mr. Falconbridge sat so busily engaged that he was quite unaware the door behind him had opened until, roused by a small, soft mysterious plopping sound, he looked up and about to know what this might be and, his roving glance wandering at last in the right direction, beheld the face of one who, peeping round the door, was wafting him kisses from rosy-pouting lip by means of a slim, white finger.

"Why—Bethulia Ann!" said he, in glad surprise, "come you here, madam, and do it properly as you should."

And surely nowhere in these wide states of America, North or South, East or West, was more bewitching vision than she who now came obedient on slender, twinkling feet to bend a golden head with such demure grace and kiss him on grey hair, brow and cheek, and then stand away to clasp shapely hands, slant lovely head at him and exclaim:

"For Goodness . . . gracious . . . sake! The Great Mr. F. . . . the stately Master all tied up in a pinafore! Oh, Mr. Anthony senior, sir, whatever are you doing?"

"Come here, child, and I'll tell you. Sit beside me, so! Now look at this old rifle, it belonged to my grandfather, Anthony Falconbridge, a gentleman of England who became a loyal American and colonel of the Ranger Corps; he was also one of George Washington's few close friends. And this is the weapon he used, a beautiful piece, twenty-six riflings, my child, and wonderfully accurate still, for I have tried it."

"How interesting!" said she, glancing at the rifle but gazing at the speaker. "So he was named Anthony, too?"

"My dear, the eldest son of every Falconbridge is always named Anthony, and the eldest daughter, Blodwen, after the First Anthony's noble wife."

"And what a strange name, Master!"

"It was the name of an old time British Princess, I believe, one of the unfortunate daughters of that proud, tragic lady Boadicea, Queen of the Iceni, who defeated the Romans and burned London. . . . But now about this old rifle, look at it! No one ever touches it except myself, and I keep it clean and bright, as my father did before me, and as my son, Anthony, will do after me, because—look at it, my dear, see how it shines! And we honour and cherish it because this splendid old thing of steel and wood with its silver mountings, its scars and bruises, is—us! Yes, open those lovely eyes, Bethulia Ann, but it is perfectly true! Let me show you,—see here! This great, ugly cleft in the stock! Lay your pretty finger in it, so—this was made by an Indian tomahawk that would have killed my Grandmother Blodwen but for my fighting grandfather's quickness. So here, child, here in this cleft was her life and consequently the life of my father, of me, of my son Anthony,—yes and every Falconbridge that is yet to be."

"But how . . . wonderful!" cried Bethulia Ann. "So he saved her life, then—"

"And she saved him, shot a mountain lion that would have killed him. She would often tell me of it all when I was a very small person, and would pray over me that God would make me grow up as brave and honourable a gentleman as her loved Anthony who died so young."

"Oh, was he killed in the war?"

"No, my dear. After fighting unscathed through

many battles, he was killed on a sunny afternoon, within a stone's throw of his house, practically murdered, in a duel."

"A duel?" cried Bethulia Ann, ecstatic. "How . . . perfectly romantic . . . but terrible of course, so dreadfully tragic! Who killed him, Master, please?"

"He was stabbed by a Frenchman, a Marquis de Vaucelles, at the instigation of his cousin, lord Wrybourne of Virginia."

"Why then I know it!" cried Bethulia Ann. "Wrybourne is a little, old tumble-down village, a very sleepy place, but I never heard of any lords there."

"No, I believe they dropped the title years ago. The family is quite impoverished, I've heard, which does not particularly grieve me, for since my noble grandfather's killing, the families of Falconbridge and Charteris have naturally borne a very hearty dislike for each other. My father, when a young man and before he married, went South and hunted up the Charteris family, with the result that he and his cousin Charles 'went out' together. My father took a pistol ball in the arm, but hit his cousin in the knee, crippling him. If Charles Charteris is alive to-day, he will be hobbling still."

"Well now tell me of your Grandmother Blodwen, what was she like?"

"But, my dear, you must have seen her picture in the ante-room—"

"Oh,—you mean that picture of the beautiful girl with those wonderful golden—why, of course, your eyes are golden too! Though yours, Master, are not so gentle nor so sweetly sad as hers."

"Why, you see, my dear, I have never known such grief as she, thank God! Hers was a sad life despite her valiant heart. She mourned her young husband to the day of her death, and never married again, the dear, faithful soul! And, what's more, she managed her husband's money and estates so wisely, so marvellously well, that my father was a very rich man."

"And such a beautiful woman, too!"

"But so sweetly gentle, dear child. So kindly patient that everyone loved her, especially myself as a little lad . . . indeed she is a very fragrant memory to me, even now."

"Yes and now, my dear," murmured Bethulia Ann, leaning nearer, "now, in this moment, your golden eyes look sad and gentle and beautiful as hers . . . almost!"

"And my Anthony," sighed he, "my only child has blue eyes . . . a mistake there!"

"Why are you called 'The Master'?" she demanded, quite irrelevantly.

"Oh, some fool started it," he answered, frowning, "others copied and, well, it stuck, heaven only knows why."

"Well, I know also!" she nodded. "It's because you are such a very he-full man and seem so overbearing and dreadfully dominating and hard, and cold, like a rock, like a dash of ice water, which means you show too frightfully stately and superbly aloof, Mr. Falconbridge, sir!"

"Am I so indeed?" he questioned with strange humility, looking at her very wistfully.

"Oh no!" she answered, shaking her lovely head, "I say you merely seem so, to everyone but me."

"God bless you, child!" said he, taking and kissing her hand on sudden impulse. "Truly and indeed I do only seem so, for I am a very lonely soul, if you but knew."

"But I do . . . I do!" she murmured. "This is why I have always felt so . . . so cosy with you that I begin to wish they had named me Blodwen."

Mr. Falconbridge very nearly dropped this precious, old rifle; and now, glancing at this so bewitching speaker, he saw her eyes, usually so very serenely frank and direct, were veiled beneath down-sweeping lashes.

"Why . . . Bethulia Ann, what . . . my child, what do you mean?" he questioned; but she neither answering nor even glancing at him, he fell to work again, rubbing and polishing at the ancient rifle with quite unnecessary vigour.

"My dear," said he suddenly at last, "precisely how old are you?"

"Sir," she answered demurely, "I number twenty-two years, two months, a week and a day or so, and growing more aged every second."

"Why then, talking of my son Anthony—"

"No!" she said, very firmly. "Now you shall tell me more of the First Anthony and his Blodwen. Have you no picture of him, your Anthony the First?"

"Only a miniature his wife insisted on having painted before he left her on one of his desperate missions, and this unfinished. But she told me the likeness was excellent, and she wore it to the very hour of her dying. Come, and I'll show it to you." Laying down the rifle, he rose and crossed the spacious chamber to a certain cabinet and took thence a large gold locket which he opened and placed in her eager hand. "He is painted in his buckskins and with long hair."

Now, looking upon this comely, pictured face, Bethulia Ann uttered a little, murmurous cry:

"Oh . . . this might be you!"

"Yes, my dear, we are supposed to be greatly alike."

"Only his face looks . . . so much . . . kinder—"

"Oh, indeed, madam!"

"Or yours so much colder and sterner!" she nodded. "And then, of course, you have your golden eyes instead of his beautiful, gentle grey."

"Grey, yes, child,—like my hair that will so soon be white!"

"Yes, his hair is nice and brown and curly . . . yours would be much the same if you would let it."

"Men wore their hair much longer in those days, my child."

"And such a dear, kissable mouth!" she murmured. Mr. Falconbridge turned back to the cabinet:

"Now look at this," said he gently, "this little ring with its balas ruby . . . not worth very much intrinsically but priceless to me because this was Blodwen's ring and bears perhaps the secret of her parentage, but which, despite the exhaustive search I have instituted both here and in England, must remain an everlasting mystery, I fear. If you look closely you will see it is inscribed with the words 'Semper Eadem,' and nothing could have been more apt, for with the changing years her brave, gentle heart was indeed ever the same. So, here's her ring! The gold is a little worn and battered, yet bright and shining, the ruby glows redly as ever, while the lovely hand that wore it is withered and gone. . . . Yes, here they are together, his rifle and her ring, both serviceable as ever, yet they themselves, this man and woman who endured so much and loved each other so greatly . . . where are now the valiant, faithful souls of them? It is a sad and pitiful thought, my dear, that senseless objects such as these may still exist while this poor Humanity fades and passes so soon away. . . . Yet I dare to think, yes, I am persuaded there is a part lives on. . . ."

"Yes," murmured Bethulia Ann, replacing these honoured relics with gentle, reverent fingers, "there is the soul . . . this you and me . . . that may come back to live and love again."

"Bethulia Ann," said he, viewing her with growing wonder, "you are, I think, a very odd young lady."

At this she slanted her head at him and gurgled with laughter.

"I think I will call you Anthony the Third!" she nodded, whereat his tawny eyes widened at her.

"Bless my soul!" he murmured.

"And I regret you find me odd, Anthony Three, because odd young ladies are such horrors—"

"I did not say so," quoth he, rather hastily.

"Especially, sir, to ordinary and young gentlemen. But I suppose my oddness is because I have travelled too much, read too much, talked and thought too much, lived too long in England. I bought an old, old house there, the dearest, loveliest old place all gables and cosy corners, your First Anthony's Blodwen would have loved it."

"No, I think not, my dear. She loved the great wilderness, it was in her blood, she used to tell me the wonders of it, she told me how she herself was a waif of the wild, because she came out of the wilderness floating in an Indian canoe, and was married in the wilderness and lived and bore her child there and eventually died there too."

"Oh, but how . . .?"

"Why you see, child, my father rebuilt the old house that had been destroyed, and when she felt her end approaching, she had herself taken there, yes all those weary miles, and died out of doors in the old oak grove where she had so often walked with her Anthony."

"Oh, but I should have loved her!" cried Bethulia Ann.

"I'm sure you would," he nodded, "for she was indeed a noble lady. And to-day, my dear child, I would have just such another noble lady honour my family as my son's wife. . . . I have been hoping very earnestly that I might love you as my daughter."

"Your . . . daughter?" she murmured.

"Surely, my dear, surely you must have guessed how very much I desire that you and Anthony—"

"Indeed I have!" she nodded, her eyes full of laughing roguery. "But alas, your fond hope is vain, my poor, dear Anthony Three. Your Anthony will never marry me, and I—"

"Not . not marry you? Ridiculous! Preposterous—"

"Isn't it!" she sighed. "And how sublimely audacious in poor me to defy The Master and thwart his will! But, alas, Anthony Three, even you cannot order Love to arrest us and march us off to wedlock. Anyway," said she, rising and crossing lightly to the door, "now you know that I can never, never be your . . . daughter!"

"But . . . Ann child, oh my dear what . . . surely you can never mean . . . ha, what in the world do you mean?"

"Well," she answered, opening the door and pausing

to smile back at him over her shoulder, "I mean . . . perhaps . . . that I have no wish to become your daughter . . . or perhaps just because I don't love your Anthony that way—"

"Not . . . not love him? But I . . . I thought . . . hoped that you . . . he—" The Master for once was actually stammering. "May I ask if he . . . what it is . . . if you have anything against him?"

"Oh, nothing," she answered, viewing him laughingly askance, "except . . . perhaps . . . just because . . . his eyes are . . . blue." Having said which, she wafted him a final kiss and vanished, leaving him to stare at the closed door in a deep and troubled perplexity.

Even when he sat again with the old rifle across his knees, he did no more than stare idly down at it in the same profound abstraction until hearing a sound he started, glanced up and beheld a young gentleman who, propped upon a gold-mounted cane, was staring fixedly not so much at Mr. Falconbridge as the large apron that swathed him. A polished young gentleman this, for his elegant boots glistened like his sleek, pomatumed, black hair; a sparkling young gentleman particularly as to eyes, teeth and jewels; a perfectly assured young gentleman who, despite The Master's ominous frown, lounged gracefully on his cane, crossed his slim legs in their tight-fitting, pearl-grey strapped trousers and murmured, drawling in modish languor:

"Bai Jove . . . I say, y'know . . . 'xtraordinary!"

"That is the word!" nodded The Master. "For if you are indeed Lawrence de Witt, you are changed in a manner quite extraordinary. The raw American lad I remember is altered almost beyond recognition."

"I should hope so, bai George!" said Mr. de Witt complacently, caressing the small moustache that curled beneath his somewhat predatory nose and fingering the small, silky tuft that graced his somewhat proturberant nether lip. "One cannot live and mingle with the—ah—*beau monde* of Paris, Rome, Vienna and London without acquiring—ah—*bon ton.*"

"And pray which particular brand of it may you be supposed to represent at the moment, French, Italian, English or—what?" Something in the speaker's look and tone seemed to strip Mr. de Witt of his modish affectation so that he forgot to lounge, while his eyes, beneath their heavy lids, glittered brighter than his jewels, his mouth, despite foppish whisker, became strangely and quite unexpectedly formidable; but now, and before he could frame adequate retort, Mr. Falconbridge questioned him again:

"Do not trouble to answer, tell me rather why, after all your travelling, why must you favour my house with your presence?"

"Sir," answered this young dandy but in voice now changed as his look, "I understand that you and my father have quarrelled and—"

"No, no," said Mr. Falconbridge, gently, "I have simply ceased to permit him to transact business with any of the concerns in which I am interested. And now be so good as to answer my question."

"Mr. Falconbridge, I hope you will not be so extremely unjust as to make me share my father's disfavour—"

"Certainly not. And so, if you be here to see my son—"

"Tony's out, sir, I know. I saw him in the park across a dev'lish fine bit o' blood though dem fiery and skittish—"

"Why, then," said Mr. Falconbridge, taking up the old rifle again, "since I will not flatter myself that you came to see me, pray why are you here?"

"Well, sir, t' tell th' truth I was merely . . . looking around."

"Then allow me to suggest that you pursue your researches elsewhere,—no, wait! Tell me for whom or what are you seeking?"

Mr. de Witt lounged upon his cane again, caressed his small moustache, smiled again, struck an attitude and answered:

"Beauty, sir, the bewitching loadstone, the power irresistible, the feminine enticement that, as the—ah

—poet says, 'draws us with a single hair.' I allude of course to Miss Leigh, the one and only Bethulia Ann."

"Astonishing! Can you possibly be an acquaintance of this lady?"

"Acquaintance?" repeated Mr. de Witt and laughed, gently yet with such heartiness that he drooped upon his cane. "Acquaintance, I should hope so! Ah, sir, I'm happy to inform you that I am quite *persona grata* in that quarter, oh yes! In France her *cher ami*, in Italy her *cavaliere servante*, in London her extremely devoted, and home here in New York, her very pertinacious adorer and most determined suitor for her hand. And this may well astonish you sir, I venture to think." He paused as for reply, but, his hearer remaining silent, he laughed again, quite happily, and there was veiled derision in his narrowed eyes, as he continued:

"Since you have known me, sir, from my—ah—tenderest years, I expected from you some show of surprise to learn that I propose to become a—ah—Benedict, a tame thing called 'husband,' for I must confess I have been a rover in Joy's fair garden, sipping fugitive sweetness, flitting lightly from flower to flower, —indeed no lesser beauties have had the power to hold me for long—" Mr. Falconbridge positively snorted.

"Did you speak, sir?"

"Not yet, Lawrence. Pray continue."

"However at last, sir, my errant fancy has centred itself upon this most captivating she, this delicious creature and Matrimony, once abhorrent, no longer affrights or repels me. More especially as my Governor, who has long desired me to marry and settle down, has promised to place a round million dollars to my account as a wedding present." Here, once again, he paused to regard his silent hearer's frowning visage with very evident pleasure and, when next he spoke, there was in his voice a scarcely veiled taunt:

"I am perfectly aware, Mr. Falconbridge, sir, from hints dropped by your sister, Miss Adela, that you, alas, have cherished some idea of uniting Bethulia

Ann with your Anthony though he is a mere boy of nineteen. . . . This is so, sir, is it not?"

"This is so, Lawrence."

"Why then, sir, in wooing and endeavouring to win her for myself, though it grieves me to thwart you, yet I can assure you I do no disfavour to Anthony. As for our bewitching Bethulia Ann, should she bless my arms, pray believe she shall find in me a particularly loving, indeed a very uxorious husband, for I—"

But here The Master rose and, for all his shirt sleeves and ridiculous apron, there was in his lean face and erect, youthful figure, in yellow eyes and jut of chin, something so extremely unexpected and menacing that Mr. de Witt recoiled instinctively.

"You have reminded me, Lawrence, that I have known you since your childhood,—indeed yes, I remember you very well as a too plump and pampered boy for whom I had a pitying disgust; as a spoiled and spotted youth with too much money and no manners, and I thought you then sufficiently abhorrent; but to-day as a young man, I find you so altogether detestable that should I find you on my property again or venturing to inflict yourself upon Miss Leigh's notice, here or elsewhere, I shall give myself the extreme felicity of caning you very soundly and the greater satisfaction of shooting you afterwards, should you find the spirit to demand it. Now you may go. Out of my sight, sir! And not another word,—you hear me?"

Somehow Mr. de Witt found himself at the door and, having opened it, halted there to flourish defiantly; he caressed his little moustache, he cleared his throat as if about to retort, but, sensing all the latent ferocity of that quiet figure that yet seemed quivering for swift and furious action, strode away, swinging his cane quite jauntily.

"Dear me!" sighed Mr. Falconbridge and glancing down at his clenched fists, shook his head at them. "Quite preposterous! Perfectly ridiculous! A man of my age!"

Crossing to a mirror, he studied his reflection as he had never done before, feature by feature and with an almost painful intentness; he smoothed his thick, close curling, iron grey hair; he peered closely at his smooth skin, unmarked as yet by any wrinkle except between black brows and the corners of his sensitive, shapely mouth that, as he thus viewed it, curled in smile of bitter, self contempt.

"'Anthony Three!'" he muttered, "you are, for your age, a much greater fool than I deemed you . . . Anthony Three!" Turning suddenly, he hung the old rifle in its niche, tugged off his apron, bundled it into a drawer, got into his coat, all in as many moments, and strode hastily out of the room, much as if he fled from that which angered and shamed him.

Hurrying across the wide hall he surprised a young footman reading a paper who, leaping afoot in no little trepidation, found himself entirely disregarded and was stooping for the fallen newspaper when he sprang erect again at sound of The Master's voice:

"Mr. Anthony, is he in yet?"

"N—no, sir."

"Then so soon as he returns say I desire instant speech with him." So saying, Mr. Falconbridge went out into the wide gardens where were trim, winding walks and glory of flowers, broad lily pool and bowery arbours. But for once The Master seemed blind to it all, walking listlessly, head bowed and sombre gaze turned earthward. Pacing thus slowly, he reached a shady corner where stood a little bower half hidden in flowering vines, and stepping into this fragrant shade he sat down, arms folded and chin on breast, and so very still that he might have been asleep but that his eyes, beneath puckered brows, were so very bright and wakeful.

And thus, he suddenly beheld one who came flitting amid the flowers, herself as fresh and lovely as they, for her poor, plain dress moulded the gracious lines of a form whose native splendour matched the vivid yet gentle beauty of her face; a lovely, stealthy, timid creature who glanced fearfully this way and that, pausing now and then to listen and then speeding on again until she reached a great, old tree, gnarled with age, a relic perhaps of the forests that had clothed this Island of Manhattan long before the White Man's heavy foot had trampled its silent trails into roaring busy thoroughfares; here then, beside this solitary old tree, this furtive, lovely creature paused to listen again and to glance nervously round about all unaware of the man who sat so very still and watched her with such keen eyes. Swiftly from the bosom of her dress she drew a letter, she pressed it to her lips and thrust it into a narrow fissure in the rugged bark of this aged tree. Then glancing round with the same fearful care, she turned and sped away lightly, swiftly as she had come; and sitting motionless, The Master watched her go, and with very troubled speculation. Suddenly he tensed and sat up, for the girl had stopped and now shrunk aside as, from behind a tall, clipped hedge stepped Mr. de Witt; he bowed and flourished his hat with an offensive exaggeration, he smiled and spoke, though what he said the watcher could not hear. The girl seemed to be pleading; Mr. de Witt smiled and shook his sleek head; she strove to pass, but Mr. de Witt set his arm about her; the girl, struggling, held him off. . . . Mr. Falconbridge rose with a very youthful nimbleness, and, once again his fists were clenched.

But at this moment from behind that same hedge shot a long arm, a clutching hand; the girl's aggressor was plucked violently backwards, and following this arm came the sturdy form of Mr. Marchdale to such effect that the pearl grey trousers described a parabola in air.

Mr. Falconbridge sat down again; the girl fled and the young secretary, having kicked Mr. de Witt to his feet, instantly knocked him down again.

"Marchdale!"

Starting guiltily at this imperious summons, Mr.

Marchdale turned to stare, re-settled his hat, pulled down his waistcoat and leaving Mr. de Witt still prostrate, came hasting to the call.

"Sir?" he enquired, stepping into the arbour.

"Thank you, Marchdale!" said The Master.

"For . . . for what, sir?"

"Trouncing a puppy. I hope you enjoyed it as much as I should have done. You are a boxer, eh, Thomas?"

"I was once, sir."

"I also fancied myself upon a time, Marchdale, many years ago. Lord, how life speeds! . . . I see our puppy has found his legs and is away, which is very well. And now, Marchdale, who is the young person he was molesting, that very handsome, dark beauty, who is she and what?"

"I believe she . . . I think she is a . . . a Miss Tutt, sir."

"Dear me! A most inapt name for such a young goddess! Well, what is she and whence?"

"Sir I . . . I fancy she is a . . . I gather she is the governess . . . next door . . . Mrs. Oliphant's children."

"Ah, young de Witt's married sister! And why must Mrs. Oliphant's governess come stealing into my garden like some beautiful, stealthy dryad?"

"Sir, I . . . I cannot say."

"And you are stuttering again, Marchdale! Was she here on your account?"

"I . . . no . . . yes."

"Meaning precisely what, Thomas?"

"Sir, I cannot say . . . you must think what you will."

Mr. Falconbridge surveyed the agitated speaker with that slow gaze of his which missed nothing,—the square, rugged face now painfully red and now as suddenly pale, the troubled eyes, the twitching hands, and heeding all this, his manner, when next he spoke, was kindly familiar:

"In the old tree yonder, just beneath the bough, is a crevice and in this crevice, a letter, will you have the goodness to . . . bring it to me?" Mr. Marchdale hesitated, glanced askance at The Master, scowled away across the sunny garden, shrugged his broad shoulders in hopeless manner and obeyed.

Taking this letter, Mr. Falconbridge stared down at it a while and then, since it bore no superscription, glanced up at the troubled face of his secretary.

"Is this your letter?" he enquired, gently. Mr. Marchdale nodded.

"Thomas, look at me, eye to eye! Now—upon your honour—is this letter meant for you?" For a long moment they stared on each other, then, as Mr. Marchdale remained silent, The Master very deliberately broke the seal of this letter, unfolded it and read this one line:

'My ever loved Anthony.'

With the same deliberation he refolded this betraying missive, saying:

"You tried to shield him, Marchdale, and to spare me the discovery, and for this at least I should be grateful, I suppose. . . . Can you tell me how long this affair has been going on?"

"No, sir, I cannot."

"Meaning, of course, that you will not. . . . I have been blind where others saw! This explains young de Witt's damned impudence. Yes, I have been very blind . . .!" Now here, remembering Bethulia Ann's gentle raillery and how she had said 'Your Anthony will never marry me,' The Master clenched fists for the third time, while there grew within him a cold anger, a slow glacial fury that congealed all the best in his nature and left only the inexorable tyrant. Yet when at last he rose, all he said was:

"You brought those plans and designs of my ships?"

"They are on your desk in the library, sir."

"Very well. You will permit no one to disturb or trouble me, no one, mind! And so soon as my . . . the instant Mr. Anthony returns you will bid him to me immediately. And, Marchdale, you will make no mention to him of this letter or the young person who brought it, not a word, I forbid it! You understand?"

"Yes, sir."

The Master nodded, and with this fateful letter in his fingers, walked slowly housewards like a man very weary, or so thought his young secretary. Reaching the library, he sat down at his wide desk and placing the letter aside, unfolded the plans of his new ships that were to be designed for speed. He studied their sweeping lines, the graceful sheer of lofty bow, the long slope of counter and stern; he measured draft and freeboard, calculating pressure and clearance, lift and stability with that assurance in his own powers and mastery of detail that was natural with him in all things. But presently his attention wandered, the pencil slipped from his lax fingers and lay forgotten, his head drooped upon his hand as, with sombre gaze upon the door, he seemed to be listening for some expected sound.

And after some long while he heard it, the quick, light tread of spurred feet; a hand rapped, the door opened and in strode his son Anthony saying:

"Sir, you sent for—" But there his voice failed and he checked suddenly as if arrested by a blow, for his father had raised his head and was looking at him.

Young Anthony's face, bold featured like his sire's, though even more sensitive, flushed darkly, though his wide, blue eyes were direct and unflinching; so for a tense moment they gazed upon each other, and now as frowned the one so frowned the other.

"Liar!" murmured the father, at last.

"Sir . . .?" gasped the son. "What . . . what in the world . . .? Pray explain—"

"For days, Anthony, for weeks, perhaps months, you have been living a lie, deceiving me with your every breath! And I have been blind, though indeed it was easy for you to dupe me because I believed my son far above such contemptible duplicity."

"Father, if you will tell me exactly what you—"

"Sitting in my garden this afternoon, I saw a young woman come creeping slyly as a thief—"

"A young—woman? Thief?" Anthony choked and his handsome face now pale as death.

"This young person crept to the old tree, took a letter from her bosom, kissed it passionately and hid it. When she had stolen away, I took this letter, opened it and read the first line, this and no more, but enough to show me—too much."

"Sir, I think this will be a letter for me—"

"As I say, I read no more of this effusion than to be made aware that you are this young person's 'ever adored Anthony.'"

"Why then, sir, it certainly is my letter. Be good enough to—"

"Poor Human Nature being what it is, I should have been prepared for something of this, for I do not expect you to be a saint, but I did cherish some fond hope that my son would at least be discreet in his amours—"

"And now, sir, I'll trouble you for my letter."

"When I am ready, Anthony," said his father taking up the letter in question and twiddling it between contemptuous fingers. "First, having regard to my wishes concerning Bethulia Ann and yourself, I desire you to inform me how soon and how best I can help you to free yourself from this entanglement with the young woman who, it is evident, has contrived—"

The Master actually gasped and opened his eyes in furious amazement for swiftly, lightly, Anthony had advanced on him, had twitched the letter from his fingers and now, as his father sat shocked and angered beyond words, he opened it, glanced at the writing and, looking into his father's eyes, pressed the letter to his lips, kissing it very fervently.

Mr. Falconbridge made to rise, but sank back in his chair again for his son, though pale and grim, was laughing.

"My dear father," said he, "how utterly you misunderstand me, which is only to be expected, I guess, since you have never stooped or troubled to be my friend—Oh, I know, I know you have always been extremely generous, you have given me most anything money can buy, you have never denied me anything except—your friendship, that close intimacy I have missed so much all these years since mother died. Not that I repine or anyways reproach you for such cold aloofness. I think perhaps when she died all your tenderness died too and followed her. Well now, father, since we are really talking to each other at last, I'll confess I am not a saint, but neither am I the heartless trifler and libertine you suppose. This, that you would dismiss so scornfully as a more or less disgraceful 'entanglement,' I esteem a holy bond, a sacred obligation, this lady whom you refer to as 'young person' is the lady who very soon, in three days to be exact, will honour me by . . . by becoming my wife."

"And pray who is this spouse elect, this wife you have chosen so stealthily, what is her name and degree?"

"She is from the South, sir, a lady of Virginia and she earns a miserable pittance by acting as governess drudge to the Oliphant brats, and her name is Virginia Tutt."

Mr. Falconbridge merely raised his eyebrows, but this was enough to fire his son with swift and passionate indignation.

"No, father," he cried, "no, sir, to disparage her unheard, unseen, merely for her poverty, knowing nothing of her, this is unworthy of you and I will not suffer it, for—"

"You . . . will not . . . suffer it, boy?"

"No, sir, not for a moment! Poverty is no slur, it only adorns and makes her the more lovely. I tell you she is as much a lady, and to me far more adorable, than Bethulia Ann with all her vast wealth. So what I beg, no sir, demand of you in justice is that you meet her and—"

"You . . . demand?"

"I do, sir, in fairness to Virginia and myself."

Leaning back in his chair, Mr. Falconbridge surveyed his tall son, from handsome flushed face to spurred riding boots, as if beholding him for the first time.

"Since you mention Bethulia Ann, shall you tell her of this very regrettable affair, or must I?"

"My dear father, she knows all about it, I told her weeks ago. Tom Marchdale knows, so does Aunt Adela. As for Ann, bless her, she insisted on meeting Virginia and being both such dears they loved each other on the spot, sir, and have been great friends ever since. And, for that matter, so is Tommy Marchdale and Aunt Adela. You see, my Virginia is so perfectly sweetly captivating that nobody—"

"So it is merely myself you have kept in ignorance? Are you proud, sir, of deceiving your father all these months?"

"No, sir. Fact is it has weighed on me like a damned incubus. It was wrong, I confess, but I feared to . . . well, to disappoint you, and—"

"A Falconbridge, especially my son, should fear no one, least of all his own father."

"Well, sir, I am a Falconbridge who fears only his father because that father, instead of stooping to be his friend, has always seemed The Master, very high and remote and perfectly unapproachable. But now I—"

"And now, Anthony, having so deceived me, you proceed to reproach me!"

"No, father, no—God forbid!"

"We will leave the Deity's name out of this."

"Certainly, sir, though I only meant—"

"You mean to persist with this rash marriage, Anthony?"

"Three days hence, father."

"Although it will be in positive defiance to my expressed wish?"

"Sir, it grieves me to think so. I can only hope that so soon as you meet her you'll know better, learn to love her as a daughter, by George, sir, I don't see how you can help it—"

"Then nothing I can say, nothing I can do will dissuade you, Anthony."

"Lord, no father! But, good heavens, sir, why should you try so devilish hard to dissuade me—why? Virginia has beauty and breeding and we, I mean you, have more money than we can ever spend. And then it isn't as though I'd tricked or jilted Bethulia Ann, God bless her! She never loved me and never would; I don't love her and never should. By Jingo, I'm growing lyrical, I suppose because I'm so happy. So come, sir, why sit perched there like a dear old, scowling iceberg, why not let all be revelry and joy?"

"Anthony," said his father, rising, "you treat the matter with a very odious levity."

"Say rather, sir, with a sense of humour. Better a joke than a tragedy."

"Yours is an irresponsible, very graceless and wholly irreverent generation, boy! Also this matter is no joke or ever can be. . . . For instance: I suppose you are quite prepared to shoulder all the responsibilities of married life?"

"Why y-yes, father," faltered Anthony becoming very solemn indeed. "Of course, sir."

"To be sure you have the income from the property your mother left you. There was also the monthly allowance I made you."

"Yes, sir—oh yes! Though I have usually spent all that and more on my club dues and other oddments. But these are just fool expenses that I shall do without, of course. But, sir, you speak of my allowance in the past tense, do I understand I must do without this also?"

"Would your wife respect you as a pensioner on my bounty?"

"No, sir, certainly not."

"Very well, Anthony. I shall leave you entirely on your own resources, and venture to suggest that you quit your present aimless existence, your life of slothful ease and prove your manhood by working to make the best of your . . . very altered circumstances."

"Never doubt it, sir. But, father, I . . . must warn you that I am . . . rather heavily in debt, this month."

"As usual, Anthony. Well, leave all particulars with Marchdale of your liabilities to date and they shall be discharged."

"I'm grateful, father. . . . We shall be pretty hard up, I guess, but, with Virginia to help me, we shall manage. Virginia is so tremendously capable and—"

"Have you any plans for the immediate future?"

"Well no, sir. You see, father, you've cut up rather, taken it even worse than I expected, and consequently things haven't gone as I expected . . . not at all smoothly, so consequently I'm somewhat at sea. But then I shall have Virginia, of course, and, as I was telling you, she is so marvellously capable, brain as well as beauty. So, even though you've rather let me down, grim Roman parent and so forth, with Virginia to advise and what not, I fancy we—"

"If, Anthony, if I can use my influence anywhere or at any time on your behalf—"

"Thanks, father, bully of you, of course. But I'm trying to tell you of my Virginia—"

"Indeed you have, Anthony, you have. You protest with no little vehemence that she is beautiful, wonderful, capable and altogether marvellous."

"Exactly! So she is! Tall you know, dark, sir, shaped like Venus—and with a brain, no end of intellect and what not. By George, sir, I can hardly wait for you to meet her—"

"Yet I fear you must."

"Oh? Wait? Pray why, sir?"

"Because under the circumstances . . . this stealthy, very random business exploding on me like a bombshell I find extremely . . . disconcerting. So if marry this Virginia you will, in such absolute defiance of my wishes, I will meet her only when she is your wife. You may bring her to me three months hence."

"Three . . . months!" gasped Anthony.

"I shall then be able to judge if she proves all your perfervid fancy paints her." So saying The Master crossed to the nearest window and stood there looking out upon the sunny afternoon with troubled eyes, while Anthony, watching him with eyes even more troubled, picked up his riding gloves, pulled them on, plucked them off, dropped them, picked them up and fidgeted generally, until at last his father broke silence, though without turning.

"This afternoon your friend young de Witt informed me—"

"Good lord, sir, the fellow's no friend of mine—"

"Acquaintance, then."

"Nor even that, sir. Fellow's an outsider. I can't imagine what brought him here."

"However, he informed me that upon the day he married—a perfectly eligible young lady of course, his father had promised to bestow on him a million dollars."

"Well, his governor's as rich as Croesus, sir."

"Well, Anthony," said his father, still without turning, "let us suppose that I made you a like offer, a million dollars to your account,—no, being myself, let us say two million dollars to forego this marriage, to think better of this rash—"

"Good God!"

Round swung The Master to stand rigid and dumb at what he saw; blue eyes that glared in face pale and bitterly contemptuous, lips back-drawn from gnashing, white teeth, powerful fists that seemed to menace him. So they fronted each other; then curbing the fury that would have strangled him, Anthony found voice:

"'Think better of it'? Sir, I think so much better of it that I . . . I scorn such detestable offer. Sir, it is vile! You? You would actually . . . offer me money to . . . to jilt my Virginia! You would dare bribe me to break my plighted word. By God, now were you not my father, I . . . I would—no! I won't say it! But near this, sir,—such offer shames you and disgusts and affronts me! You? You shall never be privileged to meet Virginia now! I say damn your money, and your power, and your cursed high mightiness! I'm done with them at last, thank God, and with you!" So saying, he turned and was gone in a blind haste, slamming the door behind him like a thunderclap, a sound so unexpectedly awful in this austere and dignified establishment, that footmen came running to halt and stare while peeping servants shrank at mere sight of this thunderous door and the youthful fury incarnate that went so blindly past them all,—out and away.

CHAPTER III

AFFORDS A BRIEF GLIMPSE OF THE SOUTHERN POINT OF VIEW

THE old mansion of Wrybourne, The Great House, looked very old indeed drowsing silent in the pitiless sun glare that showed the cruel marks of age and weather in crumbling wall and roof and chimney; for its glory was long departed, its wide lawns and terraces lay neglected all, its once noble park a desolation, the broad lands beyond, the rich plantations where so many hundreds of slaves once laboured, had reverted back to the wilderness.

Even the once teeming village was gone save for a few poor huts above which the old house rose, grand in decay. And the silent figure in the elbow chair seated drowsing in the shade, was himself like the great mansion behind him, for he, too, was old, forlorn and seemed weary with years, though, in spite of silvery hair and lined features, his head was proudly borne and the thin, veinous hand that jerked and plucked gold watch from fob, was surprisingly vigorous.

Having glanced at the dial with eyes that gleamed beneath hoary pent of shaggy brows, this aged gentleman tugged from his breast a small gold whistle attached to him by a delicate chain, and blew a shrill blast.

The morning was very hot and very still, with no sound to trouble the drowsy hush except a distant contralto voice, rich and tuneful, that sang a plaintive air, pausing now and then, only to break forth again in sweetly mournful repetition.

Presently, in the hollow vastness of the great, shadowy house, was a heavy, shuffling step drawing nearer with a tinkle and clink so very pleasantly suggestive that the aged gentleman sighed, sat up and turned as a gigantic negro appeared bearing upon a battered silver tray, divers long glasses surrounding a tall, crystal jug filled with an amber liquid wherein green leaves floated amid small lumps of ice.

A truly patriarchal negro this, older even than his aged master, whose broad, smiling visage showed the blacker by contrast with gleaming teeth and the white wool that crowned his pate. He was bedight in a livery coat that had once been a thing of splendour but which now showed sadly faded, its gold braid and gorgeous shoulder-knots tarnished with long and hard service; yet its threadbare cloth was wonderfully patched and darned, its plated buttons so carefully polished that they flashed and glittered, and he wore it with an air that matched its long-vanished magnificence.

"Dover, y' dog!" cried his master, shaking crutch-stick at him in highly ferocious manner, "Gabriel, y' black hound, you're three minutes behind time!"

Gabriel Dover set down the tray with a flourish, bowed, smiled and shook hoary head all in the same moment.

"No, suh, no, suh!" he answered, "Humbly beg to info'hm yo' lordship as yo' lordship's watch am pre-zackly t'ree minutes fast, yassuh!"

"Don't dare contradict me, y' rascal or I'll flay the black hide off ya!"

"Yassuh! An' heah am yo' lordship's speshullest medicine,—mint julep, suh, made lak nobuddy else in all Virginny can make it—no, nor nowheres else in dis yer world, an' dat's yo' old Gabriel, suh. Taste it, my lord and—smile!" So saying, the old butler filled a tall glass with this truly seductive beverage, watching round eyed as his master set it to his lips and, having tasted, nodded approvingly, drank deep, set down the depleted glass, scowled up at his anxious old servitor beneath shaggy white brows and smiled suddenly; whereupon the old negro laughed and clapped his great hands, saying:

"Say no mo', Marse' Charles, yo' smile, my lord, speaks a vollum."

"Has the newspaper arrived?"

"No, suh, not yet."

"You know the war has really begun at last, Gabriel?"

"Yassuh! Hadn't I seen young Marse' David in him grey uniform, so berry smart an' all afore him rode away?"

"Ha, and we are fighting, ye old black son of Beelzebub, mainly because there are misbegotten sons of asses in the Yankee North that say all niggers should be free! And what d'ya say to that, Gabriel?"

"Why, yo' lordship, I says fo' you to ask dem fool Yankees if dey frees all de niggers, what's to become ob all de poor slaves, suh?"

"And, by the Lord, you've hit it, Gabriel! That's the question! And there isn't a dam Yankee of 'em all could answer it,—no! They don't want free niggers themselves, there in the North, lest it cheapen labour and cause all manner of friction and competition with their working classes. We don't want free niggers, here in the South, because we're not a manufacturing country and are too poor to pay and support 'em, and because it goes flat against all our traditions. And—there you are, Gabriel!"

"No, suh,—there we hain't, my lord! Dere would be only one thing for de po' nigger to do an' that 'ud be to jest curl up an' die, suh! An' de Cunnle an' Marse' Tutt am late dis mornin', my lord."

"They are, confound 'em! Fill up my glass. And, concern your smoky hide, how often have I forbidden ya to 'lord' me?"

"Millions an' thousands ob times, suh."

"Then why, ya black numbskull, why the divil d'ya persist—hey?"

"Well, Marse' Charles suh, I presists jes' because you'se what yo' is, suh, an' dat's de lord an' Earl ob Wrybourne lak yo' pappy an' gran'pappy was afo' yo'. Dey was bofe noble lords, suh—"

"Noble fools that gambled away lands and money and left ruin behind 'em!"

"Ah but, Marse' Charles, I 'members as how dey always done lose lak de grand gen'lemen dey was, suh—"

"And made me the beggar I am! Settle my cushion and hold ya tongue, ye confounded, old, black chatter-box!"

"Yassuh! But I'se gwine hold ma tongue long time when I'se daid, suh, so why not lemme talk li'l bit while we'se alive, Marse' Charles? Le's me an' yo' talk 'bout dem grand, old days when de Great House was all alive an' eberyt'ing so—"

"No no, curse it, no! If ya must chatter, tell me of your great grandchild, little Dophy. Is she over her sickness yet, out of bed—hey?"

"Dat she am, suh, bress de good Lord! Yassuh, she am out an' 'bout again. Cried she did, Marse' Charles, wep' and sobbed suh, fo' me to bring her 'long to see yuh, suh—"

"Well, why the devil didn't ya?"

"I done think as how she might trouble yo' lordship, suh."

"Trouble me, ya fool! Concern your old black hide ya know the child amuses me! Sat on my knee the other day and told me some fool story of Jonah and the whale, facts entirely wrong, but I liked it, dam' ya, Gabriel, I say I liked it, d'ya hear?"

"Yassuh! Her mammy done tel' me as how dis chile jes' doats on yo' lordship and prays fo' yo' lordship ebery night. Which shore am bery strange an' she a babby."

"Strange, hey? And why strange? Why shouldn't she? Now devil seize your withered old black carcass, why shouldn't she pray for me, ya villain? Damme, but I wonder I don't sell ya for the few dollars ya'd bring."

"No, suh! Yo' couldn't nebber sell ol' Gabriel, suh, jes' because I'se a part ob de ol' house, part ob de ol' fambly and yo' couldn't nohow do widout me, Marse' Charles, no suh, you'd jes' nacherally curl up an' die lak a sick dog, m' lord, yo' shore would, suh!"

"Ha, curse your old white poll, I believe I should! Now go and fetch me my little playmate—no, stop! This reminds me! What's the date, Gabriel?"

"To-day, suh, am de Twenty-third day ob July in de yeah ob our Lord's Grace, eighteen hunder an' sixty-one—"

"July by God! And still no other letter from Virginia! A whole month and never a line, Gabriel!"

"Now, Marse' Charles, don't go fo' to grieve nohow, I guess Miss Virgie am shore all right, suh. Ain't she a Charteris an' de Lady ob Wrybourne an'—"

"Now curse ya nigger's wool! Why remind me o' this? A Charteris of Wrybourne . . . a governess damme! A poor drudge to No'thern brats, Yankee cubs! At the beck and call of some vulgar, moneyed harridan—my grand-daughter! The mere thought is torment! Ha, and you, ya black, treacherous hound, y' thrice accursed Job's comforter,—you must remind me of this! Come here, come within reach and be thrashed, y' dog!"

The old negro stepped forward and stood, a mighty figure, his hands clasped submissively, his white head bowed, humbly awaiting the furious strokes that never came; for the crutch-stick, raised to smite, fell clattering on the worn flagstones, the hand that had grasped it, now covered the grievous, proud old face.

Then the aged slave was kneeling, his white wool very near those patrician, silvery locks, his long arm close about his master's drooping figure.

"Dere now, Marse' Charles, fo' de good Lord's sake never take on so! Oh, curse dis ol' fool Gabriel—curse him, suh, beat him, only nebber gib way, suh. I know dese am de bad times, de ol' fambly quite ruinated lak de ol' house . . . no money . . . no servants . . . no slaves 'cept poor ol' me an' two t'ree mo'! An' Miss Virgie away, Marse' George not home, an' Marse'

David at de war. . . . I know! But mebbe dere's better days a comin' for us an' de ol' house again, an'—Laws, Marse' Charles, I hears Cunnle Phipps' ol' buggy! Dey hain't no waggin' in all ol' Virginny as creaks so almighty loud as de cunnle's ol' buggy! Lemme slick yo' hair, my lord—so! Now yo' shirt collah, suh . . . my darter Soph shore ironed dese frills good . . . !"

So the old man smoothed and patted and fussed over his old aristocrat who cursed him but submitted to these dexterous ministrations while he watched the stately approach of the time worn, weather-beaten vehicle wherein were perched his two life-long friends, to wit, Colonel Lucius Phipps and Mr. Noah Tutt, the former of whom was wont to come driving thus every morning, and always quite by accident, about julep time.

Drawn by his aged blood-horse, throned in his ancient carriage with Mr. Tutt's large, lank person squeezed precariously beside him, the Colonel, a portly gentleman of revered aspect, drove slowly, filling the air with a ceaseless clamour; for notwithstanding their slow and stately progress, his antiquated vehicle creaked and rattled, squeaked, groaned and complained as if threatening instant disruption. However, reaching the wide and lofty portice he reined up in its welcome shade and, in the ensuing blessed silence, performed the wonted, daily ritual: He socketed the long whip he was never known to use, he twisted the reins about it; he took off his wide-eaved hat with full-armed flourish and bowed, saying:

"Mistah Charteris, suh, I trust we find you well. We, suh, Mistah Noah Tutt and self, finding ourselves by chance in this vicinity, deemed it but right and courteous to honour ourselves with a brief visit."

"Gentlemen," answered Mr. Charteris, returning their grave salutes, "be very welcome and be seated, you are a little later than usual but refreshment awaits you, Gabriel, charge the glasses."

"Suh," quoth the Colonel, seating himself with a

ponderous dignity, "my dear Charles, we are beyond our customary time because the times, suh, are out of joint."

"Thasso!" nodded Mr. Tutt.

"Our whole cosmogany, Charles, is upside down, suh!"

"Our what?" enquired Mr. Tutt.

"Our Constitution, Noah, is about to split asunder, suh! These United States, gentlemen, that never were truly united and never can be, since we of the South, sired by such prouder, nobler stock and loftier ancestry, are a fundamentally different people to these Yankees, these snivelling money-grubbing New Englanders and hide-bound Puritans of the No'th."

"True, Lucius, exactly true!" nodded old Charles. "For though we all, No'th and South, descend from English ancestors, those same ancestors were bitter foes,—ours fighting loyally for King Charles the Martyr, God bless him,—and theirs for the Parliament and Usurper Cromwell, dam' em! And now it seems the old enmity still persists and we are to fight each other yet again."

"Ah, but what o' the great West?" demanded Noah, tugging at his grizzled goatee. "We're different again, —pioneer stock, English, Scots, Irish, Dutch and I dunno what all. Charles and Looshus, I'm tellin' the both o' ya, we hain't wanting ary war, no siree! Injuns is our trouble, hoss-thieves, rustlers an' bad men,— as your son George knows and can tell ye, Charles. He knows the lawless West, does George, and the Law o' the Gun, none better,—shot it out and downed a plenty badmen, has George, notches on both guns,— white men, red an' yeller bellies too! Never was a durned fightinger marshall west o' the old Mississippi than yore son George, as well I know."

"Yes, yes!" nodded old Charles. "But let us talk of this war? You were North this season with your horses and cattle as usual, Noah—?"

"I wur so, Charles, three thousand on the hoof."

"Well, you heard much talk of war, beyond doubt?"

"Charles, I shore did! And little else except the same old rant agin Slavery. But Looshus was along o' me and saw and heard a hull lot more than me, I reckon. Tell him, Looshus, all as I cain't."

"Well, neighbour," quoth the Colonel, sitting up, "I travelled in the No'th and to some purpose, Charles. I used my eyes and ears—"

"And yore tongue, Looshus, I'll bet a stack."

"I did, Noah, I cer-tainly did. I talked with Yankee folk of every degree, sort and kind, suh. I visited their mills and factories and their city offices. And, sirs, by God, I heard one wealthy mill owner declare that so long as he could find men—ay and women—to work at the lowest possible wage, he'd get every particle of work out of them and when they were worn out he'd discard 'em like broken-down machines! I also learned that they work their hands in mill and factory twelve and fourteen hours a day, right in New England, claiming such wholesome discipline keeps their labourers' morals purer!—And these are the damned Puritan hypocrites that dare to denounce us as human monsters and cruel tyrants because we own slaves!"

"Horn-toads an' side-winders!" nodded Noah.

"Charles, I also know that these Yankee Shipmasters and merchants with their hell-ships, low wages and stinking food are driving all self respecting American sailors out of the Merchant Marine and are manning their vessels with all the sweepings and scum of humanity,—ha yes, and have lately petitioned Government for the right to flog sailors at their own sweet will. These are the folk, Charles, these the ranting Abolitionists that now have the audacious hypocrisy to inflame themselves and the world in general against us because of—our abominable cruelty to these slaves of ours that are not only expensive articles to buy in the first place, but must be fed, clothed and cared for in sickness and health, as I made bold to declare publicly whenso I might, suh, but to no purpose."

"Yes!" cried old Charles, flourishing his crutch-stick. "Damn them, they've made a saint of that mad villain John Brown, who would have raised our own niggers against us to rape and massacre our women and children! They've even written a song to him, I'm told!"

"They shore have, Charles! We've heard 'em sing it, eh Looshus?"

"Frequently!" quoth the Colonel. "A doggerel rant, Charles, something like this:

"'John Brown's body lies a rotting in the sod' (or some such-earth or ground or grave). 'But his soul goes marching on.' I've heard this sung in the clear, sweet voices of delicate ladies, Charles, howled by the unlettered mob, suh, and roared forth by their tyrannous, tramping soldiery."

"An' so it goes!" sighed Noah, clutching himself by his goatee and shaking his grizzled head. "These yer Yankee moralists that never nohow had any pity for the Redskin, but tricked him, corrupted him, stole his lands and massacred him, are now arming and marching to invade us, to steal our lands an' massacre us—and all for sake o' these dam' niggers that they call 'their black brothers'!"

"Tyrannous, hypocritical humbugs!" snorted the Colonel. "Sirs, in my fair youth I fought against the Indians, I shed my blood in the Mexican War and am now prepared to pour out what remains of it (here he emptied his glass) for our noble Confederacy and our Stars and Bars—"

"And by God," cried old Charles, lifting crutch-stick as if it had been a sabre, "were I a little younger and not the halting cripple I am, thanks to my damned No'thern cousin's accursed bullet, I'd be marching with our army at this moment. But my grandson, David, is there, Charteris is riding for the South, thank God! Young David is my proxy, in every blow he strikes will be some of my strength. Should he be wounded, then in the blood he sheds will be some drops of mine. And should he die, which God forbid, so shall death be the sweeter to me for my grandson's sake! For by heaven, despite Fortune's buffets and the hardships of these lean years, the Charteris blood is still hot with life and virile as ever. The old stock is vigorous yet in my son, George, and his son, David, and through David shall so continue, I pray."

"Ah, an' by Jing, they're shore men to be proud o' raising, Charles, I swan!" nodded Mr. Tutt. "And 'specially George. I've rode with George out West, he was my pardner once, afore they made him Marshal. I've fit alongside George in more nor one gun ruckus agin bad men, white, red an' yeller. A square shooter is George—ah, an' a mighty slick an' straight too! A Southern gentleman is George wherever and however, though not like you, Charles,—no, where you're hot, George is cold, an' quiet, an' mighty deadly, when George pulls a gun there's doings. He means what he says an' says what he means,—I'll say so! Charles, old friend, I'll allow you shore should be all-fired proud o' son George. I'm tellin' ye, by heck!"

"Well, damme—so I am, Noah! Don't I say so?"

"Ay, to us, Charles. But why not to him? Seems like to me as you've allus treated George more like he was yore hired man than yore honoured son—"

"Now, confound you, Noah Tutt, what the devil d'ya mean?"

"An' there you go, Charles, blowin' off—all fire an' fury—"

"George is my son and—well, he knows his father's heart, sir, without any damned sentimental, feminine gush, sir—"

"Ah, but does he, Charles? An' do you know George? F'instance, d'ye know his reputation out West? Not you! D'ye know as he's cleaned up more nor one hell-town with his two guns an'—all alone? No, you don't,—how can ye, living seclooded hyah with yore few old slaves, year in an' year out—nohow! So by heck, Charles, I'm tellin' ye that in the badlands west o' the old Mississippi where there was no law, your son George was a power, ah, carried the law on the muzzles of his two guns, he did, and made every hell-roarin' badman respect that law or ante-up in Kingdom come. Yes, sir, I'm tellin' ye that son George was the cleanest, slickest, deadliest law man that ever belted on a marshal's guns, being ekally accurate with both. Also I'm askin' where he is, Charles? I guessed mebbe he might be around yer to-day."

"He started at dawn this morning for Richmond, with Jupiter and a string of horses."

"Ay, George knows horses, hide an' hair, inside an' out, though he ain't much of a cowman. I reckon as how he'll be j'ining the army soon, eh, Charles?"

"He will not, Noah, no sir! How the devil can he? His place is here at Wrybourne with his horses and —myself."

"Ho!" quoth Noah, tugging at his goatee. "Ha!"

"Yes, sir!" snarled old Charles. "And I now take the liberty to demand what you propose to do? You are a rich man, Noah, with your ranches and thousands of cattle and horses, what shall you do for the Confederacy, for though you live in the West, you were born in South Carolina."

"Howsomever, Charles, I claim to be a Westerner and as such I mean to take mighty good care to keep out o' this yer war—personal. But—they's a good few thousand steers and right good hosses for Jeff Davis an' at his own price, when he needs 'em. . . . And there's Looshus snoozin', the Cunnle's asleep, by Jink!"

"And our jug is empty and I never noticed! Pray forgive me, Noah. What, Gabriel! Gabriel, ya black villain—"

"No, no, thankee, Charles! No more for me, and Looshus has had aplenty." So saying, Mr. Tutt upheaved his long, lank frame and crossing to the slumbering Colonel, lifted the wideawake hat from the Colonel's nose, settled it on his reverent white locks very gently and shook him tenderly into wakefulness; whereupon the Colonel instantly declaimed and with the utmost dignity:

"These dam Yankees, gentlemen, merely exist, as I was saying, to hustle for base money, their God, sirs, is Mammon, while we Southerners live as gentlemen should,—'*otium cum dignitate*' suh,—serenely unhurried and for the mere pure joy of it—"

"And, by Jing, there's George!" exclaimed Mr. Tutt, joyfully, pointing long arm towards an oncoming horseman who galloped in a rolling dust-cloud; on he came at the same furious pace nor drew rein until, wheeling his spirited, foam-spattered animal in the shadow of the ancient house, he slid to earth with the lithe, careless grace of the born horseman and leaving the reins to dangle Western fashion, he came striding, spurs jingling and hat in hand, showing curling hair patched at the temples with silver. Tall was George, dark and clean-shaven, his face brooding, saturnine, yet handsome; a man whose movements were leisured and graceful, whose voice was low and soft, whose every word and gesture proclaimed his gentlehood.

He saluted his father and the Colonel, he grasped Mr. Tutt's ready hand very heartily; standing thus they smiled upon each other, they clapped each other's shoulders and were for a long moment quite speechless; then:

"Howdy, George?" quoth Mr. Tutt.

"Old timer," said George, "it's good to see you."

"George," cried his father, impatiently. "George, was there any news of the war, did you hear anything new in Richmond?"

"I did, sir, great news! Yes, right wonderful news, but the sight of old Noah put it out of mah head for a moment—"

"Well, well—what is it, son? Ha, damme, let us hear!"

"Well, sir, Beauregard at Manassas and General Johnson with our army of the Shenandoah met the

Federals at Bull Run, and thanks to Jackson's Brigade, defeated them, suh, utterly routed 'em—"

"Ha—victory!" cried the Colonel, rising in ponderous jubilation. "But is this glorious news true, George, are yuh sure . . . quite sure?"

"Certainly, Colonel. I happened to be there."

"You would, by Jink!" chuckled Noah.

"Meaning that . . . that yuh were actually . . . positively present at the battle, George?"

"Yes, Colonel."

"And David . . . is he safe?" cried his father. "Did you get sight of David . . . chance for speech?"

"Be sure I did, sir. He's very well, not even scratched."

"Thank God!" cried old Charles, fervently.

"Then what the 'tarnal's troublin' ye, pardner?" enquired Noah, eyeing the speaker's gloomy brow with quick concern.

"Well . . . for one thing," answered George, passing a sunburned hand across his eyes with weary gesture, "though this is sholy a great victory, the Yankees broken and on the run fo' Washington, our troops act as if the war was over and done. But such war as this can never be settled by one battle, not even such a smashing defeat as this."

"Why not, George, why not?" demanded the Colonel. "Our gallant armies are animated by the high, gay, dauntless resolution of our Cavalier ancestry—"

"Yes, Colonel, but History tells the Roundhead beat them—"

"Tell us what you saw of it, George," said Mr. Tutt, somewhat hastily.

"Much blood and many dead, for both sides lost heavily, especially at the Bull Run. Our men were driven back, their ranks shattered, but Jackson came in the nick of time and the scattered companies rallied, charged and captured a battery, only to lose it again. Twice those guns were lost and retaken before the Yankees broke, turned tail in a panic and ran for Washington and I guess they're mebbe running yet. And that was all I saw of the Battle of Bull Run."

"And have you told," cried the Colonel, "ha, George, did yuh tell any of the neighbours as yuh came?"

"No, suh."

"Then we must, Noah, we must! It is an obligation, suh, a sacred duty as patriots to spread this glorious news! Come!"

"Why, see yere, Looshus, I hain't no orator same as you, no sir!" answered Mr. Tutt. "So I guess I'll mill around a spell and rub horns with this yere old moss-head." Here he glanced with the same veiled apprehension on George, at his darkly handsome face, the glowing eye, the flare of sensitive nostril, the grim set of mouth and chin.

"Well then adieu, gentlemen!" cried the Colonel, gaily. "I speed hence on the wings of Joy Triumphant, to proclaim this gladsome intelligence, a harbinger of Victory!"

So saying, Colonel Phipps hastened where his ancient steed cropped languidly at the grass and weeds that choked this once noble courtyard, clambered heavily into his creaking vehicle, gathered up reins, flourished hat, cracked whip and rattled slowly out of sight. And when the sounds of his stately departure were muted in distance, Mr. Tutt, still viewing his old-time partner a little anxiously, questioned him in a soft-spoken aside:

"What's riz yore dander, George? What human rattler's fouled yore trail and . . . holy God!" Mr. Tutt gasped and was dumb, for George had turned and in this dreadful moment showed the haggard, twitching face of a stricken man who seemed on the point of bursting into tears; then these quivering features stiffened, the sensitive lips compressed themselves, the wistful, pain-filled eyes narrowed to shining slits, and Mr. Tutt was looking into the cold, set face of the terrible, fighting marshal.

"Last night," began George, and there was something very dreadful in his soft, slow accents, "last night I received a letter . . . and there are only two men should ever hear me tell what it says, and yuh are one, Noah—"

"Ha, did I hear you say a letter?" cried old Charles, eagerly. "Is there a letter from Virginia at last? Read it, George, read it!"

"No, father, not . . . not from . . . Virginia. . . . But it seems there's a snake needs killing, a son of a dog I must go shoot me." The old gentleman sat up, both hands clenched upon his crutch-stick, and leaned to gaze up into his son's grim face.

"George," said he, speaking also in the soft drawl and idiom of the South as he ever did when deeply moved, "yo' will done tell yo' father who and what villain yo' would call to bloody account, and why?"

"Sir," answered George, glancing from his father's aged, high-bred face to Noah Tutt's leathery visage, "the name is written here. . . . So listen, father, and you, Noah, listen and judge." And drawing a letter from the breast of his worn riding coat, George unfolded it and read these words in voice so dreadfully hushed as to be almost a whisper:

"'Dear Mr. Charteris, it is with very mingled feelings that I pen these lines because the dire news they convey must painfully grieve your noble heart and strike deep at the very roots of your honour and Southern Pride. But, sir, for sake of those happy, carefree days, three years ago, when you played host to my father and self, honouring us with the generous hospitality of your ancient, stately home, I feel it my unhappy duty to send you these tidings of your grand-daughter, Miss Virginia. How beautiful she was, how gay and high-spirited, how . . . sweetly innocent! To-day, she is still beautiful, but . . . alas to what depths of misery, despair and black shame is she plunged, solely because, being of such purely generous, fearless nature . . . she gave her all, loving too well and trusting too blindly the depraved, absconding

. . . father of her child. And the name of this abandoned villain who pursued her so relentlessly, wooed her so artfully, won upon her innocence and then so basely deserted her, is Anthony Falconbridge, only son of the Anthony Falconbridge whose enormous wealth and immense power, here in the North, are a bye-word and have won him the notorious title of 'The Master.'

"'Deserted thus by the heartless son, Virginia, being the proud, sweet lady she is, endured a while in patient silence. But her woman's dark hour approaching she, for sake of her unborn child, appealed to her betrayer's father for aid, humbly pleading assistance of the elder Falconbridge, this flinty-hearted Master, and all, alas, all in vain! Therefore, sir, in these most pitiful circumstances, I myself sought the privilege of aiding her how I might, for old times' sake, but only to learn that the poor, abandoned, creature had flown to hide her shame and broken heart,—Heaven alone knows where. Thus, sir, having sought and found her not, I write at last to inform you of her truly pitiful situation, leaving the matter in your capable hands and those of your son and her father, Mr. George Charteris, to take such further action as your pity, your ancestral pride and just indignation shall inspire. Assuring you of my deepest sympathy and desire to aid you as best I can, believe me yours faithfully to serve, Lawrence, Opdam, de Witt. Post Scriptum. He, young Anthony has, by power of money or influence, already been gazetted as Lieutenant on the staff of our General McClellan and will, doubtless, soon be riding eager to flesh his maiden sword and spill Southern blood in this truly cruel war.'"

The soft voice ended; George's slender, sunburnt fingers refolded this fateful letter, hid the dreadful thing in his breast, and still neither of these three men spoke or so much as glanced towards each other.

At last old Charles bowed white head upon the thin hands that writhed and clenched themselves upon his crutch-stick and groaned in voice of agony:

"My li'l Virginia! . . . The sweet innocent!"

"Anthony Falconbridge! Father . . . and son!" quoth George in the same dreadfully repressed tones. "Our damned cousins! It was a Falconbridge made you a cripple, father, and now—"

"Now," groaned the old man, covering his face, "Now . . . our Virginia! Shamed . . . disgraced—"

"No, father, impossible! Not Virginia, suh! The shame is on this black-souled, deceiving villain—!" And, speaking, George swept back the skirts of his riding-coat and dropped both hands upon the worn butts of the two long-barrelled revolvers holstered low upon his lean flanks. And now, with lank arms reached forth in sympathy towards grieving father and vengeful son, Noah Tutt spoke, glancing from one to the other:

"Charles old friend, an' you, George, don't let this yere dumswizzled letter stampede ye none, hold yore hosses! You all know as I've shore loved Virgie, like she was my very own flesh an' blood, ever since she was foaled. And having watched her grow up, I know—now mind, I'm tellin' ye,—I know as our Virgie's all good, through an' through! And, what's more, she hain't ary simple fool to be took in by ary black-souled, double-crossin' maverick,—nossir, by Jing! An' what's more again, I fer one ain't a-goin' to let ary cuss with a name like Lawrence Opdam, an' the rest on it, make me think different, never none, an' that's whatever! Doggone it, George, it hain't wrote right, and it don't sound right, and it don't read nat'ral, none at-all! Who the hell is this Lawrence what's-a-name feller anyway?"

"I hardly know," answered George. "I saw little of him while he stayed here. A dandified youngster as I remember, son of a wealthy father, old Hendrik de Witt, buys all the cotton hereabout—or used tuh."

"Well, what's this yere tenderfoot know of our Virgie?"

"She went as governess tuh his sister's children in N'York. And . . . Noah, she . . . she took yuhr name—"

"Did she, then? Did she so?" cried Noah, his sun-tanned visage suddenly radiant. "Well, now God bless her purty, sweet eyes! Doggone it ef I hain't tickled to death, George!"

"But . . . but Noah, old partner, she only did so . . . because . . . it was a great liberty, Noah . . . she hid our name and took yuhr's merely because . . . ha, dammit, don't yuh see—?"

"Shore I see, George! I've allus kind a reckoned as Tutt's a cussed ornery sort o' name an' fit only for a reg'lar old shorthorn like me. But now, by Jing, to know as our sweet Virgie's so honoured it makes me right proud on it, shore do, an' I'll be throwed and hog-tied ef it don't—"

"And," quoth George, his sombre eyes suddenly bright, "I say that Tutt is the name of a real white man and a true blue gentleman! Yuh're a mighty good friend, Noah, and a . . . comfort—"

"Comfort?" cried his fierce, old father, smiting the pavement furiously with his stick. "Are you my son and dare to speak or think of comfort and these foul-hearted villains walking, in their damned pride, to sin as they please and all unchallenged? Ha, damn these white hairs . . . this old, crippled body . . . damnation!" And snatching off his hat he dashed it violently to the flagstones in fury at his own helplessness, and scowled down at it through agonized tears.

"Oh God!" he sobbed, "Oh God! Were I but younger . . . maimed though I am, they should be brought to account!"

Now, stooping to this shaken, grief-stricken old man, George set long arm about him and drawing forth a snowy handkerchief wiped these old eyes very tenderly, while Mr. Tutt picked up the hat and straightened it, dusting it carefully.

"Father," said George, in his slow, gentle voice,

"indeed yuh should know me better. If this vile thing has happened, if . . . this letter tells truth, they shall answer for it. I'll bring them to account, son and father."

"You will call them out, George?"

"Certainly, suh."

"But I . . . I believe, son, that duelling, being a gentleman's method, is much out of fashion among the Yankees."

"Yet it shall contrive—someway, suh."

"And when d'yuh go, son?"

"To-night, suh."

"And how long . . . when d'yuh expect . . .?"

"A few days, father, weeks or months, what matter so that they be made to pay to the full, some time, as they surely must and shall. And now, father, if yuh'll excuse me, I'll go look to the horses. I bad Jupiter round up the likely three-year-olds. Shall I send Gabriel to you?"

"Yes, George. Go, my son," said the old man with a new, strange meekness, "But come yuh and tell me Good-bye to-night before yuh leave."

"I will, suh, of course." Then, with Mr. Tutt beside him, George strode into the desolate, old house.

"Well now," demanded Noah, so soon as they were out of earshot, "jest what d'you-all aim to do, George?"

"Need you ask, Noah? Can't you guess?"

"Shore I can guess. Yore a goin' to fork a cayuse an' ride hell bent for to shoot up these yere Falconbridge folk, pap and son, an', George, I'm sayin' yore durn wrong!"

"Wrong?" enquired George, staring in surprise, "How so?"

"All an' every way wrong, pardner, yessir! Our first duty is to find Virginia—"

"Our?"

"Shore,—our! That's whatever! I'm taggin' along with ye, George, and—I'm comin' heeled! Why, doggone it, you didn't reckon I was agoin' to let you take on this ruckus all alone, did ye? Not much I ain't! Not me—nossir! So I'm tellin' ye that our first duty is to find our Virgie, God love her, an' then, George, having comforted her good, ef so be comfort's needed, it's for us to heark an' hear her side o' this dumfoozled yarn, yessir! An' what she says 'll be true, now mind I'm tellin' ye! An' then, George, ef any dodgasted cuss needs killin', you can roll your guns an' salivate 'em with yore old side-kick to see all square,—an' that's me!"

"Damme, Noah, if I don't believe yuh're right."

"Shore I'm right! It's jest commonsense. Anyways when you ride, I ride and, come Hell or Highwater, I don't quit till our Virginia's found an' we're through with this dingbusted business one way or other."

And thus it befell that towards evening, Mr. Tutt sat with his long, horseman's legs bestriding a mettlesome animal, his sinewy hand grasping the bridle of another, while George went to take leave of his father.

He found the old gentleman reading in his great bed-chamber with its faded tapestries and antiquated furniture, a lonely figure showing very old and frail in the soft light of the candles.

"You are going, George?" he enquired, reaching out a tremulous hand.

"Yes, father, the horses are at the door," answered George, taking this pale, white hand in his strong, vital clasp and holding it rather awkwardly, for this proud old hand was rarely given to any, more especially to this silent, saturnine son, George, who now wondered in his dark, brooding fashion, to find it so thin and feeble.

"Son, you ride on a sacred mission, to right a foul wrong, to vindicate Innocence or avenge heartless treachery and wipe away dishonour. So I pray God's mighty hand shall be over yuh, my son, and bring yuh safe back. But I am old, George, older than I thought, a weary, old cripple, a mere cumberer of the ground—"

"No, no suh, indeed—"

"Yes, George, and well I know it. I have always been ashamed of my helplessness, my awkward, hobbling gait, but I hid it, ay, I hid it,—even from yuh, my son. So, George, I'd have yuh know . . . if I should not be here in the body to welcome yuhr return, I wish yuh to know at last beyond all and any doubting, that I love yuh, dear son, more than I have ever suffered anyone to know or even guess. . . . This too, George, I am proud to be yuhr father because yuh are a true Charteris and therefore I rest assured that in the hands of my son, our honour is secure. So if I have seemed cold in the past, and harsh . . . forgive it me now. . . . And so again I pray God bless yuh. . . . Kiss me, son."

Thus George took leave of his father; and presently descending the wide staircase, beheld old Gabriel hovering in the shadows like a great, black genie.

"Youse gwine away, Mars' George so I jest wait aroun' to say de good Lord bress you, afore I goes up to put yo' ol' pappy tuh bed, suh—"

"Take care of him, Gabriel! Take mighty good care of him!"

"Yassuh, yassuh! I sho' jes' will lib fo' his lo'dship ca'se him my ol' Mars' Charles, an' when he done go fo' to die, den ol' Gabriel him done die too, jes' so him shan't be lonesome in de Valley ob Shadder, an' I'se take care ob him crossin' ober dat yere black ol' Jordan Ribber, yassuh! Ol' Gabriel take care o' yo' pappy and now he kiss him ol' rabbit's foot fo' yo' own good luck, Marse George."

Then George went out where Mr. Tutt waited with the horses so patiently, and mounting, away they rode nor did either exchange a word until George reined up suddenly to glance back at the old house looming vast against a deepening twilight; then Mr. Tutt enquired:

"Pardner, what is it?"

"Why, Noah, I . . . a sort of feeling I . . . shall never see the old man again."

"Why he's plenty old, George."

"Yes. And I'm forty-two! And I'm wondering . . . which it is to be."

"Doggone it, George, let's ride! . . . In Richmond I'll mebbe buy me some boots 'n spurs, and . . . a forty-five."

So these two grey-haired men who had proved each other many a time and oft, rode forth upon their quest, bound together in a comradeship that smiles on Death.

CHAPTER IV

TELLS OF TWO GRIEVING FATHERS

GRAVES newly dug. All about him hideous, miry graves; they stretched away row on row, rank after rank, far as he could see, and each marked with roughly made cross or poor splinter of wood that bore number and name in hastily scribbled lettering.

And all these many thousands of young dead had been most vigorously alive only a few hours ago.

Colonels and majors lay here some few, with many captains and a host of lieutenants. But it was a private soldier's grave he sought, this weary, bedraggled man—yet nowhere on this ghastly field of slaughter, through these fearful plodding hours, had his expectant, haggard eyes beheld the name he sought.

4859 Anthony Falconbridge. N.Y.I.

So he trudged on, splashing through dreadfully dark puddles, slipping and stumbling in slimy ooze, stooping to peer at name after name, on and ever on until he paused at last beside a grim mound that bore no superscription.

Now as he stood thus, despairing, to wonder if this ghastly heap of mud covered the once straight and comely body of young Anthony, he became aware of one nearby, solitary like himself, a very tall man whose bowed head was crowned with elf-like locks of coarse, black windblown hair; and not troubling to glance at this bareheaded mourner or turn from this nameless grave, the stricken father, in the agony of his remorse and breaking heart, spoke:

"I seek the grave of my son . . . my one and only

child. . . . We parted as no father and son ever should, with anger and bitterness in our hearts. . . . I waited, hoping and . . . yes, even praying that he might return . . . or for some merest sight of him . . . some message . . . and all in vain. . . . He joined the army, so I hired agents to watch over him and keep me informed of his welfare. Two . . . or three days ago I learned he was dead . . . lying killed somewhere on this great battlefield. All day long I have tried to find his grave . . . names, sir,—names and numbers, thousand upon thousand, but nowhere the name of my son. . . . Yet they tell me he is surely dead. . . ."

"My dear friend," answered a husky voice, "I have no words for such grief, being only a poor, sorrowful man like yourself. I dare but offer this one consolation . . . that he died—young, and in noble cause, to preserve our Union . . . as I, too, would die and . . . as indeed I think I shall. As for this great battlefield, the precious blood that hallows it shall, under God, sanctify us who live and can feel and think, that we too, like these sacred, valiant dead, may 'quit ourselves like men,' to an ever higher and increasing purpose. . . ."

The words ended in a deep sigh; now, lifting his woeful gaze, The Master looked into wonderful eyes in an ugly, sad face, eyes indeed so gentle with the wisdom of sorrow and foreknowledge that they glorified this rugged visage and ennobled the whole man; despite gaunt, ungainly frame and ill-fitting clothes, there was in this man's every gesture a simple grandeur lending him such a natural dignity that, almost unconsciously, The Master bared his head, saying:

"Sir, I think you must be His Excellency the President . . . you are Mr. Abraham Lincoln?"

"I am that very troubled, lonely man, sir," sighed the President. "But I am also your brother in affliction, for I . . . like you . . . mourn a son. It is a wound that even kindly Time shall never heal for me, I think. . . . So here stand we, two fathers that grieve their lost sons. But all about us on this wide field of death are the grieving thoughts of many other fathers, North and South, united and at one in their sorrow. . . . So, when our warring is done, I hope and pray there shall arise from each one of these hero graves, from these dead that, dying as foes, are now united in the enduring Brotherhood of Death, a living bond of sympathy and understanding that shall knit the living, North and South, in such close fellowship that these United States of America shall be truly united at last . . . a great people sanctified and made one by this, the sacred blood of our children."

Once again the words ended in a sigh, and over this ghastly desolation a cold wind swept, ruffling the speaker's coarse, untidy hair and chilling The Master till he shivered.

"Sir," he answered gloomily, "God send this be so. But for me it shall not matter, now. Somewhere about us, among these thousands is a grave where lies all that made life worth while. So, my life is done. Of what avail now power and money? These, sir, I therefore offer to you, Mr. President, towards the preservation of this Union,—ships, railroads, mills,—all that I have. For, sir, my name, my line . . . ends with me. I am the last Anthony Falconbridge."

"I have, of course, heard of you, Mr. Falconbridge, and as a very wealthy man, and esteem your offer accordingly. . . . But I venture to think you take your grief too bitterly. You are in the full prime and vigour of life and the future should hold some ray of hope. Sir, I earnestly beg you to make the memory of your dear son an uplifting memory, inspiring you to live and work for the cause he died to save. For his sake and your own, I shall accept the generous offer you made me in some sort. Let me urge you to get back into your world for there, sir, you shall hear from me how best you can help this poor, troublous creature that is called Abraham Lincoln—"

A trampling splash of hoofs and three muddy officers of senior rank came galloping on miry, foam-spattered horses; and foremost a smallish, bearded, keen-eyed man who champed fiercely on a frayed cigar-butt.

"Hell, your Excellency!" he exclaimed, reining up, "By God, Mr. President, I've been in a sweat of anxiety! Looking for you this half-hour and more. The enemy's pickets lie none too far off and if they've any sharp-shooters out, that stove-pipe hat of yours would be a certain mark for a bullet."

"My hat?" repeated the President, turning this object in large, knotted fist to view it with a comical expression, "To be shot in the hat would be no great matter, and this one deserves it. This glossy discomfort, gentlemen, is a compulsory official tag that I do not favour and which, I am assured, in no way favours me. And this reminds me of the tale of the Cross-eyed Parson's Wideawake—but first, Mr. Falconbridge, I present Major-General Grant and Colonels Boyd and Schenk. Gentlemen, Mr. Anthony Falconbridge, of New York, of whose large interests you've probably heard. Should he visit your lines, General, let him be welcome at any time. Now lead us back to your headquarters, Grant, and keep close, gentlemen, for my story. . . . 'Years ago, into the wilds of Illinois came a parson who had the misfortune to be extremely cross-eyed . . .'"

CHAPTER V

CHIEFLY CONCERNS ITSELF WITH A VERY FATEFUL LETTER

So Anthony Three, The Master, came back to his world, a man embittered and more grimly masterful than ever; a haunted man who had but to close his eyes to evoke sudden visions of his son all glad and joyous with young life, his Anthony who, but for his own pride, might have been alive to carry on the name and family of Falconbridge that was now destined to end with himself.

Thus, bitterly lonely and driven by Remorse, The Master, wasting no time on self-pity, became more fiercely active and more sternly dominating, a vital, merciless force to speed up production, and especially munitions of war. A remote, silent man, sleeping little and eating only when and because he must; a man who, unsparing of himself, exacted the uttermost from all men.

By day and by night, he journeyed in his own express railroad car, or by dusty pikes and highways in speeding conveyances or again, astride fleet horse; from great city offices to bustling factory, from factory to thunderous mill and thence to teeming docks and echoing shipyards.

He planned and built four armoured gunboats of a new design as a present to that Brother in Affliction, Abraham Lincoln. He organized and equipped several batteries of field artillery, arming them with a new pattern of screw guns. . . . He lived but to work and scheme for the preservation of the Union, with never a stay or respite.

And yet, though busied with these multifarious concerns, despite ceaseless activity of mind and body and constant change of scene, there came upon him, sooner or later, the Black Hour when Giant Despair arose to smite him and the demon Remorse tormented him. . . . At which times he would shut himself away from all human companionship, alone with his demons, that no eye might behold his agony; as upon this stormy, windy, September afternoon in this year of blood, 186–.

All the morning his fast, two-horsed travelling carriage had waited The Master who never came. All the morning his sister, Miss Adela, this comely, gentle-souled spinster, had been in 'a dreadful taking' and 'all of a twitter' because of that locked door and silent room past which trim servant maids, stalwart footmen and even portly butler went on tiptoe because of that silent man, The Master, who sat therein and all alone. Doing what? . . . Staring down through blinding tears that would not be staunched, at a pair of worn riding-gloves, these same that he had seen young Anthony pluck off and pull on so nervously and finally drop during their last interview.

Bright and polished in its niche upon the panelled wall hung the First Anthony's old rifle, on wide desk lay the well-used gauntlets of Anthony the Fourth and, bowed between, this grief-racked man, Anthony Three, alone in his agony.

"Oh gracious me!" sighed Miss Adela to her small dove-eyed paid companion, Miss Rosine Broke (pronounced Brooke, my dear, if you please). "All the morning, Rosine, and not a word from him! I've crept to the door, oh so often but—not a sound! I even ventured to knock—once, but—no answer. And no breakfast, my dear, never a bite or sup all the morning and now—oh dear, it's past three o'clock. He'll be ill! He'll be sick, I know he will!"

"He is ill, Adela!" answered Miss Rosine in sweet, small yet very positive tones, nodding her small, pretty head, in manner rather bird-like, at the tatting she was engaged upon. "The Master is soulsick, languishing, dying—of a broken heart!"

"Oh, Merciful Goodness! Don't say it, Rosine, don't! He has always seemed so strong . . . ironlike. Yes, like his new battleboat things, invincible and quite unassailable."

"Alas, Adela, it is such iron men that are deepest sufferers when their armour is once pierced and their hearts smitten and bleeding—"

"Oh, Rosine! Oh, my dear, sometimes I have almost believed . . . thought . . . that he had . . . no heart!"

"So think most people!" nodded Miss Rosine, looking more bird-like than ever. "But I never imagined so for one moment—and Bethulia Ann knows better—"

"Bethulia—oh, her letter!" wailed Miss Adela. "I was forgetting it! Her letter to him from the fighting fields! Oh dear me!" And opening her old-fashioned reticule with its gold clasp and chains, Miss Adela drew thence a much-soiled and somewhat crumpled letter transcribed in Bethulia Ann's fine, Italianate script and smudged with such stamped and written orders as: Pass the lines. Express. Transport direct.

"And pray, Adela, why not take it to him, my dear?"

"But I did. Oh, I did!" protested Miss Adela, shaking her handsome yet woeful head at this travel-stained missive.

"But did you knock, Adela, very loudly, and shout and say in clear ringing tones 'a letter from Bethulia Ann, from the battlefield?'"

"Knock, my dear, of course I knocked. But shout—no indeed! How could one? So unladylike!"

"Then I will!" said Miss Rosine, laying aside her tatting and rising nimbly. "We both will. Come along, my dear!"

Forthwith the ladies took each other's hands and thus linked, made their way, through spacious chambers and across wide hall, to that forbidding door. Here they paused, still hand in hand; then Miss Rosine lifted one small fist to her shoulder and gave a series of smart double knocks, much like a very determined sparrow tapping with a wing.

"Now, Adela—shout!" she commanded.

"Oh, I daren't! I could not—"

"You can! Now, both together—shout, I say! Master, Master, oh Mr. Anthony, Mr. Falconbridge! We have a letter for you . . . special delivery from the battlefield . . . a letter from (now very loud, Adela) from . . . Bethulia Ann!"

Movements beyond the door, slow, heavy footsteps; then key turned, door opened a little way and forth came a hand, lean and brown, beneath delicate white wristband.

"Thank you!" said the unseen Master, taking the letter. "Adela, my dear, be good enough to send away my carriage. Tell Martin to return for me promptly at midnight. And you, Miss Broke, pray telegraph my offices, bid them have my special car hitched and the tracks cleared express for half after twelve to-night, they will understand."

"Will they know what tracks and where, Master?"

"Oh yes. Send this message at once, please."

Closing the door gently, he stood for some time gazing down at this very smudged and travel-stained letter, turning it this way and that; then, quite forgetting to relock the door, he went back to his chair and sinking wearily into it, opened the letter and read this:

"From the battlefield of Antietam.

"Oh, Anthony Three, dear man of grief, how valiant you are! To front life with breaking heart yet showing still resolute and undismayed is worthy of your dear, brave Anthony One. What an inspiration you are become! What wonders you have performed! What miracles you have caused to be wrought—your new ships, your bridges, your miles of new transport. Something of all this I know because I am become a very small part of it. I have bought and equipped a fleet of hospital waggons with a surgeon, staff and all accessories, including myself for I am by turns a driver (and a bold one for I always loved horses), a nurse (and a poor one, for I shiver at blood but am rapidly becoming used to it, alas! Also I can already set a bandage, tourniquet, etc.) I have been in five great battles and many smaller engagements. And oh, Anthony Three, the ghastly folly of it all! How brave and patient these poor wounded soldiers, South as well as North, and both believing they are right! When will it end? I do pray God soon, very soon. I have seen such horror of dying and bloodshed since last we met, you and I, that it is difficult to believe this the same world or ever can be again, or that those calm, sweet days ever really were. Yet they are for me now a treasured memory,—the old rifle, Blodwen's ring and you so very like your Anthony One.

"I have just met the President, Mr. Lincoln, a great man in every sense, I think, but very sad and almost too gentle for such cruel times as these. And yet he can be strangely whimsical too, but even then he seems to me a terribly solitary man. We talked of you, Anthony Three, it was from him I learned of your many activities. He esteems you very highly. He told me how he had offered you a position of high trust very near himself and how you had refused it. And I think you were right to keep yourself free and wholly untrammelled like The Master you are.

"You see I have written no word of your bitter loss, so far, because you being you and I being me, no words are needed, we just understand. I am now detailed with the army of General Sherman and we are moving (as I hear) to intercept General Jackson (Stonewall) who is so desperately brave and clever. So I fear there will be more dreadful work for us all, and I pray God's mercy on us all, North—yes and even this poor South, these brave Confederates fighting so desperately for what they believe to be right, also, I cannot forget that they are our own folk and so gallant. So God's mercy on them all, I pray. And God's blessing on you and me that He will suffer us to live and meet again, somewhere, somehow in His own good time. And with this prayer, Anthony Three, I end my first, and perhaps last, letter to you.

"BETHULIA ANN."

For a long time he sat bowed above this letter, reading it again and again; at first with a youthful eagerness that surprised him, then with a deliberation that dwelt on every twist and twirl, every comma and stop; and lastly with the mind's eye that strove to envisage the writer.

In some uniform she would be and writing upon some make-shift desk or perhaps on her knee in jolting waggon train,—for here, towards the end, her pen had slipped, and here again was a blot—

The sudden opening of the door startled him and glancing up angrily, he met the dark, steadfast eyes of a stranger who stood holding the doorknob in one hand, his wide eaved hat in the other; a tall, slender, shapely man clad for riding, whose brooding, saturnine face was darkly handsome and whose shabby, travel-worn garments served only to enhance the serenely assured dignity of this intruder who remained so utterly still and in whose dark scrutiny was something so vaguely menacing and sinister that for once The Master showed at a loss, sitting crouched in his chair motionless and dumb as if beneath some spell.

"I think," said a gentle Southern voice, at last, "I think, suh, yuh are Mr. Anthony Falconbridge."

"Yes, that is my name," answered The Master, rising, "May I enquire—?"

"My name, sir, is Charteris, George Charteris, of Wrybourne, in Virginia."

"Charteris? Virginia? Why then you . . . are my cousin—"

"I am, suh. It is a kinship that dishonours me."

"Dis—honours you? May I ask how . . . and why? Nay, sir, I demand to know—"

But as he spoke the door was pushed open and there entered yet another unexpected visitor, a tall, lank person whose head was grizzled like the goatee beard that adorned his leathery visage, who jangled large spurs, chewed a plug of tobacco slowly and with relish, fumbled a large hat and now meeting The Master's arrogant and somewhat disdainful stare, nodded jerkily and said:

"Howdy!" And instantly his jaws went to work again.

"Misto' Falconbridge, suh," said George, closing the door gently and locking it, "I take honour to introduce my friend, Mr. Noah Tutt."

"Indeed?" enquired The Master, his expression changing swiftly, "You are very welcome, Mr. Tutt, your name is . . . kindly familiar . . . there was a . . . very beautiful young lady . . . her name was Tutt . . . Virginia Tutt and I—"

"Not Tutt, suh," said George softly, but with a sinister curl on his clean-shaven mouth, "No, not Tutt! Noah was her godfather, but she is my daughter, suh. She is . . . or was . . . Virginia Charteris."

"Charteris?" The word was a groan, and as it passed his pale lips, The Master sank down into his chair, gazing blankly before him with such stricken look that Mr. Tutt suspended mastication to view him with quick, shrewd eyes.

"A year, suh, and more we have travelled, Noah and I, searching for her and all in vain. Then, suh, to know the truth of it and vindicate her honour, I endeavoured to find her perjured betrayer. A weary search, suh, but I have learned at last that yuhr son is dead and beyond my reach. So I have come to yuh, his father, Misto' Anthony Falconbridge, to fo'ce you to answer to me in his stead, suh."

"Her . . . her betrayer?" stammered The Master. "My son? My Anthony a betrayer of innocence? Never—never! Who dare so affirm is a vile scoundrel and liar!"

"However, suh," continued George, in his soft, deadly voice, "when yuhr indignant protests are all done, I demand that yuh meet me, here or where yuh will, in yo' son's place. . . ."

"Meet you, Mr. Charteris? Can you possibly mean . . . pray tell me precisely what you do mean?"

Light of foot, smooth and panther-like, George was at the desk and there, with motion incredibly quick, had drawn, spun and laid two long-barrelled revolvers within The Master's reach, saying:

"Here is my meaning, suh. Choose either one, I take the other and here, or across the room, we start shooting when Misto' Tutt gives the word."

Anthony Three glanced at these deadly things, their long hexagon barrels and smooth, well-worn butts, and from these, to the no less deadly face of their owner.

"Death?" he enquired, and laughed. "Mr. Charteris, you offer sleep to a very weary man, freedom to a jaded prisoner. Here indeed for me is an easy way out that I shall embrace joyfully, gratefully. But first I demand to know who has dared traduce so foully the honour of your daughter and my dear son. Speak, sir!"

For answer, George drew a certain very fateful letter from the breast of his coat and unfolding it, placed it upon the desk.

"And now," said The Master, leaning back in his chair to survey the dark, brooding face above him, "before I so much as glance at this letter, you shall hear me tell the absolute truth of this painful matter so far as I know it. Be seated."

"I prefer to stand, suh. And pray be brief."

"Listen then!" And forthwith, he told of it, a plain story simply yet graphically expressed, while George, sombre eyes keenly intent, listened mutely and Mr. Tutt, quid in cheek, glanced from placid speaker to grim hearer and sidled unobtrusively nearer.

"And so," The Master ended, "my son Anthony refused this two million dollar bribe I proffered, refused it with a fierce scorn and indignation that I . . . am very proud to remember . . . now. And thus, Mr. Charteris, to the very best of my belief . . . yes, as certainly as you now hear my words, I am confident that our children were honourably married. . . ."

"And now, suppose you read the letter, suh."

The Master took it up, glanced at writing and signature, and scowled.

"I know Lawrence de Witt for an evil-minded, ill-living young reprobate, and a proved liar."

"That you would vilify yuhr son's accuser, I expected, suh," quoth George, wearily. "However, pray read his words, at least."

The Master transferred his scowling gaze to the speaker and seemed about to make some furious retort, then raised scornful brows instead and began to read the letter, handling it much as if its mere contact might foul him. . . . But all at once he uttered an inarticulate cry and started up so very suddenly that Mr. Tutt nearly swallowed his quid and even George recoiled. For now indeed The Master was so changed he seemed another man, his pale cheeks showed flushed, his wide, bright eyes seemed staring through George,—out and away at some unexpected glory.

"A child!" said he in a strange, awed tone. "She bore a child! A son, pray God! So, the old stock shall not pass utterly away! Falconbridge and Charteris,—what better? They shall be found and the search begin this very hour—"

"Wait!" said George, sinewy hand uplifted. "What do yuh say to the letter, this accusation—?"

"Lies, lies,—all damnable lies, written by a sordid, cowardly rascal to his own base purposes. Come, waste no more time on the fabrications of this poor knave, this miserable villain. There's work to do, come then, let us get at it!"

"Yes, suh, right now!" said George, gesturing towards the revolvers. "Say no more, suh, I esteem yuhr word no better than his—"

"Hold right thar, George!" quoth Mr. Tutt with unwonted vehemence, interposing with equally vigorous gesture. "Hold yore hoss, Pardner! This yere sayso ain't agoin' accordin' to Hoyle nor yet Cocker, not like as I expected, not none, no by Jink it hain't. For, George, now mind I'm tellin' ye, if ever I see a white man, and therefore truthful, a man as antes up right smart and square, he's a-settin' in the skin o' yore cousin, Ant Falconbridge, yessir! So what I says is, ef yore said cousin Ant is so doggone willin' to help find Virgie, let him make his play and set in this yere game with us. Howandever, I'm believing him."

The Master smiled faintly.

"Thank you, Mr. Tutt," said he, then taking up the letter again, he pointed scornfully to a certain line. "Listen!" he commanded. "Here in this foul screed is a statement I know certainly for a base, audacious lie and one I will swear to,—this: 'for sake of her . . . unborn child, she appealed to her betrayer's father for aid'. . . . Well, sirs, here and now I protest upon my honour that she never did, no not once, neither by letter or message did she ever make any appeal to me. So there it is, Mr. Charteris, you must accept my word as an honourable man or be cozened by this lying indictment penned by a worthless young reprobate I have always known and always heartily despised. I can say no more. It is for you to choose, sir, and either way I shall be very gladly at your service."

Grim of aspect yet saying no word, George refolded the letter and thrust it away, sheathed his revolvers in their well worn holsters and took up his hat.

"Mr. Falconbridge," said he, gazing deep into the eyes that returned his searching regard as keenly, "knowing mah friend Misto' Tutt as I do by long experience, I'm banking on his judgement of yuh being correct, and am therefo' reserving mah judgement—on condition that yuh ride along with us and that yuh keep yo' promise and ride—now!"

"At once!" answered The Master, in his quick, decisive manner. "This moment, of course!"

CHAPTER VI

DESCRIBES AN INCIDENT OF THE WILDERNESS

UNLIMITED money, wide influence and the driving force of Anthony the Third's indomitable personality had wrought such wonders that scarcely a month later three men were riding north-westerly. They were heavily armed and splendidly mounted with a stout pack-horse to convey their supplies and gear. And they followed a trail deep ploughed by hoofs, and waggon wheels that had led them from the civilized East, through green vales and cultivated valleys to a country ever wilder and more formidable, now across barren deserts and vast alkali plains, now through dense forests, across foaming rapid, deep-flowing river, and the lurking peril of treacherous swamp and quicksand. A grim trail beset by roving bands of hostile Indians and gangs of outlaws as dangerous and more merciless; a trail of suffering, of hardship and heroic endurance littered by the gnawed and sun-bleached bones of animals that had perished on the cruel journey, the fire-charred wreck of some waggon telling of Indian battle and foray, with now and then a solitary pile of stones that marked some lonely grave; a trail of stark tragedy that led on and ever on to the lure of the Golden West.

Yet of all the many hardy adventurers who had dared this merciless trail, none more resolute and determined than these three horsemen who rode side by side, bronzed, grim of aspect and silent, their splendid animals going at that long, easy loping stride that can seem almost tireless.

Mr. Tutt, riding between his two silent companions, glanced right and left, from George's lithe figure and brooding visage to the lean shape and stern, impassive features of Anthony Three, and, taking himself by grizzled chin-tuft, he shook his head, shifted his quid and spoke:

"Lookee yere the both o' you! I reckon it's about time you buried the hatchet and got sociable, 'stead of acting like two dumswizzled, soreheaded galoots,—yessir! Pride's all right, George, an' so's dignity, Ant, anywhere except the wilderness—pride and suchlike, George, ain't of any more account in the wilderness than all yore millions and influence, Ant—nossir!"

"True enough!" nodded Anthony. "I'm the tenderfoot in this outfit, Noah, but eager to learn and prove worthy. Also I can line the sights of a rifle with fair accuracy, otherwise I'm the greenhorn and place myself equally at the orders of you and Charteris, as I told you before. As for burying the hatchet, I've none to bury, and, as Charteris knows, he can be 'George' to me or 'Mr. Charteris' as he pleases."

"Spoke like a man!" quoth Mr. Tutt emphatically. "And doggone it, nobody could say fairer! How think you, George?"

"Same as ever!" answered George, without even troubling to turn his head. "There can be no friendship while this matter lies 'twixt him and me. If we find Virginia and learn the truth from her, I shall know how to act. If we don't find her, say in the next six months, or learn she's dead, then I shoot it out with the father of her killer."

"Very well, Mr. Charteris, be it so!" Anthony answered. "And pray remember, sir, that as you are a father, so am I, and one very willing, very proud to die, if need be, in vindication of that son whose blood . . . cries out to me ceaselessly from his unmarked grave. His memory is very dear to me, sir, and will ever be,—remember this, Mr. Charteris, and if in the future you must allude to him, be good enough to temper the harshness of your tongue."

George's dark brow lowered darker, Anthony's tawny eyes seemed to glare, perceiving which ominous signs, Mr. Tutt, champing his quid, hastily interposed:

"Ant," quoth he, easing his horse to slower pace, whereat his companions did the same, "back yonder in N'York an' Chicago you were so goshdarned busy with yore traffic an' railroad agents an' specials an' clerks o' this, that an' t'other, that I kinda lost track of the why an' wherefore of it all."

"What would you know?"

"Well, first off, why are we following this yere old waggon trail, 'stead of taking short cuts and Indian paths?"

"So that we may keep in touch with the telegraph and pony express as long as possible, because at any of the bigger camps or townships or cities we may receive more certain news of the fugitives through my agents and—"

"Agents? By Jing, it seems like you 'listed a hull army of 'em! What was it they found out in N'York? Let's hear it again. And open yore ears, George, ya doggone old sorehead."

"I'm listening," growled George.

"Very well," answered Anthony, settling his heavy rifle more comfortably. "Before leaving Chicago news was brought me that my son, Anthony, being hard pressed for money, took his young wife—"

"Wife?" exclaimed George, turning to scowl. "There's no jot of evidence to prove it—"

"His wife!" repeated Anthony, turning to frown on his interrupter. "And I say so because not only was he my son, Mr. Charteris, but she is your daughter. And now, if you desire to hear me, be silent till I'm done. . . . These children then, in their poverty, found refuge with my son's one time head groom, a man named John Hoyt and his wife Martha, and in their poor house the child was born. Then came Lincoln's call for soldiers and my son, I suppose for the miserable bounty, enlisted and . . . was killed. The news very nearly killed Virginia also, but owing to the devoted care of Martha and John Hoyt, she recovered though with complete loss of memory. I learned also that the Hoyts, to escape the war and make a new start, joined a waggon train bound

West for the new gold strike at Elk City and Oro Fino, in Idaho. So our search must be far and wide and may take much longer than six months, Mr. Charteris."

George merely frowned at the hazy distance ahead and eased his heavy, low-slung guns. In which moment, Mr. Tutt spoke softly, his keen eyes narrowing suddenly upon that same wide prospect:

"George, d'you see what I see?"

"A dead mustang, Noah."

"Where?" demanded Anthony, unslinging his rifle.

"Over yonder, Ant, in the shade o' they cotton woods. And in this yere country a hoss means a man, and a man frequent means quick triggering. So foller George an' watch out!"

Reaching this dead horse they saw, beyond trampled grass, hideous splashes and stains easy to follow, leading to a huddled shape of misery that stirred feebly at their cautious approach and gasped:

"Drink . . . gimme . . . water—"

Anthony reached for his canteen, but Mr. Tutt was down first and ministering to the stricken traveller while George, after one brief glance, lounged in his saddle, but his dark eyes were very keenly alert.

"Stranger, how come?" enquired Noah, bending above the grey head upon his knee.

"Slim Travis . . . got me, Sonora Slim . . . two gun killer. Joe Peden too . . . for our dust . . . Joe's in . . . the river . . . shot an' drowned, and now . . . I—" The feeble voice ended abruptly and, laying the touzled grey head down very gently, Mr. Tutt rose.

"Dead?" enquired George.

"Ay, he's cashed in, poor feller. Did ye see his forehead, George?"

"Very bloody."

"Shore is, and no wonder! He's been branded, George, an S ripped wi' the foresight of a sixgun. I'm guessing this same Sonora is sure enough pizen. Slim Travis of Sonora . . . ever heard of him, George?"

"No."

"Nor me. I guess he's a disease infests these yere parts since our time."

"Maybe so we'll cross his trail, Noah."

"George, if that's a promise it'll shore be like the halcyon days of our youth."

"Has the poor fellow any letters?" enquired Anthony. "Any papers to identify him?"

"Nary a one, Ant," answered Mr. Tutt bending again to search, "No money either, he's been cleaned out . . . wait though! Ay, here's an empty, crumpled envelope and says . . . 'Josiah Morris, Lewiston, Idaho.' A lucky prospector, I reckon, homeward bound, a miner from the new placers at Florence or Bannack or Oro Fino, going home with his dust an' murdered for it!"

"Well, we know the name of his killer!" murmured George, his sombre eyes questing the distances before them, "Let's ride!"

"Wait!" said Anthony, glancing askance at this piteous, marred shape. "We can't leave him so, he should at least be decently buried—"

"Suttenly suh!" sneered George, wheeling his horse, "scratch him a hole with yo' knife; but Misto' Falconbridge, suh, I'm riding."

"Then do so, Mr. Charteris," said Anthony scornfully. "Your cynical callousness is matched by your sullen and unreasoning—"

"Ant," quoth Mr. Tutt, again interposing, "friend Anthony, we shares and respects yore feelings, but seeing as we've neither pick nor shovel and this yere trail 'pears some infested by human snakes an' polecats, I guess pore Josh M'll take the will for the deed, and however, he's shore beyond caring any more about his wore-out old carkiss,—yessir! So up with ye, Ant, an' let's go. Come, friend, pore Josh has got home at last, leastways the best part of him has, I reckon, so leave him with the Almighty."

Now looking into the grim speaker's leathery visage,

Anthony surprised such look there that his own frowning brows relaxed and laying his hand on Mr. Tutt's dusty shoulder, he nodded, saying:

"Yes, friend Noah, I guess you're right." Then Mr. Tutt swung to saddle and they went on again, but now with George riding solitary before them.

On they went through the noon-tide sunglare and a country ever wilder and more desolate until the rocky trail, trending upwards towards barren foothills, narrowed to a gloomy canyon where flowed a small, dark, unlovely river and no living green thing grew.

It was as they eased their horses to the ascent that a bullet whined viciously between them and from the riven crags beside the way rose a puff of smoke and the echoing report of a rifle.

George was the first to rein up and lift his hands, whereat his two companions did the same; and sitting thus defenceless all three, they heard fierce cries, jeering laughter and beheld armed men leaping and clambering over the rocks towards them. Six they counted, human castaways unshaven and unkempt, as wild and ferocious as the country about them, and foremost of these a tall, red-headed fellow in the tattered blue uniform of the Union and a slim, dark man dressed like a Mexican. Being come within easy speaking distance the big red-headed man halted his fellows and, with finger on the trigger of the musket he carried, leered upon the silent, watchful three; and now Anthony saw one of this motley company was a mere boy.

"Well, pilgrims," said the big man, jovially, "it looks like we got the drop on ye—"

"Ker-rect, stranger," answered Mr. Tutt, spurting tobacco juice, "it shore does! An' now what?"

"Well, I guess it's howdy and good-bye—"

"If it's money you want," cried Anthony, urging his horse forward, "take mine and let us go—"

"Keep your hands up!" snarled the big man, with threatening gesture, "An' as for going," said he, baring yellow fangs in evil grin, "to bring the vigilantes down on us, I reckon not, Mister. But we'll take your money, you c'n bet, an' yore guns an' clo'es, hosses an' hull dam outfit, seein' as ye won't be needin' 'em never no more—"

"Si, si, Beel!" cried the Mexican joyfully, spinning his revolver and levelling it with lightning dexterity. "Shall-a I shoot now these-a men pronto, Beel?"

"Not yet, greaser, be a shame I reckon to muss up an' spile their dandy clo'es. First we'll make 'em strip an' then you can show us some fancy triggerin'—"

But now George spoke in his smooth, soft drawl:

"Ah'm wondering," said he, viewing these six merciless faces, one after the other, with his darkly brooding gaze, "does either one of yuh happen tuh be Travis of Sonora . . . Sonora Slim?"

"Nary one of us, feller," answered the big man.

"No,—ah—no!" cried the Mexican. "Ha-a, my friend. He ride-a South, he go, eef not you all-a keeled. Sonora he shoot so queek-a, he keel then-a talk,—not lak thees beeg Beel that onlee talk—"

"Shut yore trap, greaser!" growled the big man, scowling. "I guess I know my business. You an' Charlie go take their weapons an' then—"

George's horse reared suddenly; his hands swept down and from each hip gushed flame and smoke through and beyond which Anthony glimpsed stricken men in the act of falling as, like an echo to his guns came George's fierce command:

"Lift yo' hands!"

And now Anthony, dazed by the speed of it all, beheld four men who cowered, hands aloft, gazing down at two of their fellows who sprawled upon the trail very silent and very still.

"Oh . . . oh my God!" whimpered the boy. "He's shot 'em both . . . Bill an' the dago . . . they're, they're . . . dead!"

"KER-rect!" nodded Mr. Tutt. "An' that's whatever!" Then dismounting leisurely, he proceeded to unarm the living and the dead, tossing their weapons into the stream that hereabouts ran deep and still. And now ensued an ominous and dreadful silence while George, lounging in his saddle again, held their dismayed assailants helpless and blenching before the threatening muzzles of his guns, until the boy, unable to endure, uttered a piping, inarticulate cry, and sinking to his knees, covered his sweat-streaked face in shaking hands.

Shocked by this sudden killing, Anthony gazed at these pallid, shrinking men, at the sobbing boy, the sprawling dead and lastly at their executioner; and George's eye was bright, his brow serene, his shapely mouth contorted in dreadful smile that showed a gleam of teeth, a revolting smile, or so thought Anthony, and therefore spoke on hot impulse:

"Is it your pleasure to kill them all, Mr. Charteris, even the weeping boy?" George never so much as glanced at his questioner, but, as if in answer, his right-hand gun roared again and one of the men, uttering a shrill cry, clapped a hand to his head.

"A notch," said George, softly, "A notch in yo' ear. Listen now and answer me or I'll notch all yo' ears. Now are yuh listening?"

"Yes, sir! Yes! Yes!" cried the four, instantly.

"Well, then, being wishful tuh meet up with this Slim Travis of Sonora, I'm asking yuh-all to inform me where I'm likely to cross his trail. And—I want the truth!"

"He's rid for the noo mines at Bannack," cried one man eagerly.

"Or else for Beaver Head!" cried a second.

"How long since?"

"Not an hour ago, sir."

George looked up at the sun, glanced at the quaking four, sheathed his deadly guns and spoke:

"Listen again all of yuh. I've a good eye fo' faces, especially such gibbet heads as yuhrs. If ever we meet again Ah shall shoot yuh on sight with a deal mo' pleasure than I can say."

"Hold on a minute, George!" quoth Mr. Tutt, whipping out his own revolver with the speed of an expert, "ef you're done with these dingbusted skunks an' coyotes, I ain't—nossir! They're foul inside an' out, by Jing! An' so," said he, turning on the four and gesturing to the stream with his pistol, "into the crick with ye,—jump, dang ye, jump!" The four, turning as one man, incontinent jumped. Then Mr. Tutt re-mounted; and thus, while their late aggressors floundered, gasping in the icy waters, the three rode on again, though more than once Anthony must turn to look back at those ghastly sprawling shapes ere distance and heat haze blotted them from his vision.

Now after some while Mr. Tutt, riding beside him and perceiving his look of frowning disgust, leaned nearer and spoke:

"Well, Ant, I'll opine as no man ever see purtier shootin', though I told ye George was mighty accurate right and left—"

"But," said Anthony bitterly, "you did not tell me, you never warned me the man was a killer and—enjoyed it!"

"Now stop right there, Ant! George has never killed ary man, and he's downed a plenty, except he was compelled so to do, nossir! There's men in this yere world—an' especially hereabouts, as jest naturally needs killing, they shore do! Ah, like this yere Slim Travis an' them hellbenders back there. It was them or us, an' I'm free to own as I'm mighty glad that George made it them—at least two o' them—"

"But, Noah, there was no need to kill, he might simply have disarmed them."

"Shore he might, an' left 'em for some other pore cuss to kill . . . or be killed! No, sir-ee! That ain't George's way to leave unto others what he can do better hisself, and it hain't my way—and, if you're the Ant I take you for, it won't be yore way either. . . . And there's George signallin' to stop . . . dinner time, I guess, and yore turn to rustle grub an' cook."

CHAPTER VII

TELLS HOW THEY GOT NEWS

LONG weeks of hard travel through a savage country of tremendous mountains, frightful chasms, scowling canyons and ravines; hours of dreamless sleep beneath the palpitant splendour of stars; constant alertness against natural dangers and the stealthy perils of human foes red and white,—all this had transformed the stately Master, this dignified potentate of towns and cities, into a lean, bronzed and hardy adventurer. Vigorous youth was in his light tread, a quick vitality in his every movement and the flashing glance of his tawny eyes.

And, day by day, his feeling for Noah Tutt had deepened to a warm friendship and respect for his shrewd wit and simple-hearted sincerity; even George's gloomy moroseness and persevering hostility irked him less, these days.

It was morning and the sun's early beams, shooting athwart a cloudless heaven, touched even the harshly forbidding landscape to strange and unexpected beauty, —the naked desolation of rocky barrens, frowning gorges and rugged mountains rising peak on peak flamed with vivid ever-changing colours, blues and purples, scarlet, amethyst, yellow and glittering gold,— a beauty almost unearthly; or so thought Anthony as he stood viewing it all and lathering his chin while George, bearded now, was tending the horses, and Mr. Tutt, whose original goatee was lost in whiskery undergrowth, busied himself preparing breakfast.

"Coffee smells good!"

"An'll taste better!" answered Mr. Tutt, instantly, and it was to be noted that the further West they travelled, the broader grew his speech. "My coffee hain't only coffee, Ant, it's dreams come true, it's an inspiration, yessir!"

"Like my flapjacks, eh, Noah?"

Mr. Tutt snorted.

"Ant," quoth he, "you've got yore gifts, you're good as George with a rifle, ay an' me too—purty nigh! Yes, you've got yore p'ints—but—yore flapjacks ain't one,—nossir! An' jest now, pardner, I'm wondering why, here in this yere goshdarned wilderness, you must scrape all the hair off'n yore features so reg'lar. Sorta labour in vain, hain't it?"

"Why you see," said Anthony, busy with razor, "shaving is a habit I guess, a sort of rite, part of the daily ritual, just as regular as breakfast,—which reminds me I'm mighty hungry this morning."

"Which don't sapprise me none! Yore appetite's growed like my dam whiskers! You tackles yore grub these days like ary youngster."

"And I feel absurdly young, Noah!"

"An' look it, Ant. This yere doggone, allfired country shore agrees with you."

"My father was born in the wilderness, Noah, so I guess it's in my blood. Anyway, it's been a grand trip, Noah, so far."

"Yes, we been mighty lucky—so fur!"

"And the farther we travel the more certain I feel that we shall find the child . . . my grandchild, Noah!"

"An' George's likewise, Ant!"

"Of course!" said Anthony, glancing askance where George sat remote on the craggy steep above them, solitary as usual.

"I wish," sighed Mr. Tutt, shaking his head at the battered frying pan he chanced to be holding, "ay, I shore do wish the two o' ye could grow a piece more friendly like."

"So did I at one time," answered Anthony, packing away his shaving kit, "but now,—well, he's about as pleasant and sociable as the toothache."

"Ant, if you'd only try to savvy him better—"

"I have, man, I have, and he has so constantly repelled me that now I can do no other than ignore him."

"Hah!" growled Mr. Tutt. "You hardly spoke him a word all yesterday,—which shore was some powerful ignorin', Ant. So, I'm kinda wondering what would happen without me taggin' along between ye?"

"Without you?" repeated Anthony, seating himself beside the fire and laying hand on Mr. Tutt's bony shoulder, "I fear we should quarrel, perhaps even fight and then I think Charteris would kill me—almost certainly. . . . Which would be very well, considering I've nothing to live for, or . . . very little, I guess."

"Little? Why yes," nodded Mr. Tutt, "this yere grandchild o' yore's 'll be very little, I reckon."

"And there is also . . . one other," said Anthony pensively, "one who, if I should die, would cherish this child for its own sake and . . . mine, I hope."

"Eh, a woman, Ant?"

"Yes, Noah."

"Would you trust me with her name, Ant?"

"Ann . . . Bethulia Ann. At the last ranch house we stopped at I wrote her my wishes regarding the child. This letter is in my pocket here, so if anything should happen to me, I ask you to see and make very certain she gets it."

"Friend Ant, I shore will! Ah, an' so will George, yessir, or die for it same as me, because Ant—now mind, I'm tellin' you—you've got George all wrong! There hain't a whiter, truer, cleaner man in all God's earth than George Charteris."

"And you're a great friend, Noah, your middle name should be Loyalty. As for Charteris, I can only judge a man by his acts, and he seems determined to think only the worst, and his persistent hostility to myself is beyond all reason. Then also, his first thought now seems to be—not for his lost daughter or even the child, no—wherever we've halted lately his first enquiry has been for this vile murderer Travis, Slim of Sonora."

"Well, and ain't we hearin' tales o' the skunk, robbery, murder an' mutilation? Well, I guess George has a hunch and means to discourage said Travis's heinous propensities. Ye see, Ant, the most determined killer is apt to lose all interest in murder when he's dooly fitted with a wooden overcoat, yessir! Howandever," said Mr. Tutt, whisking frying pan from fire, "let's eat, breakfast bein' ready. Hey, George!" he roared, clattering spoon in cup, "Come an' get yore grub else I'll throw it away!"

So down came George, and seated together about the fire they ate and drank with that keen relish that only hard work and the open air may bestow.

Anthony was in the act of refilling his coffee mug when faint yet unmistakable upon the clear, windless air, rose the crackle of far away rifle fire. Instantly the three were afoot; and peering down over the natural parapet that defended their camp, they beheld a distant horseman coming at wild gallop.

"He's seen our smoke!" said George, for this speeding rider was heading towards them.

"An' he's shore riding!" quoth Mr. Tutt, coffee mug at lips.

"And no wonder! Look beyond those bluffs." Mr. Tutt glanced whither George directed and choked.

"Good grief!" he spluttered, "Injuns!"

"How many d'ye make 'em, Noah?"

"Nine!" answered Mr. Tutt, peering.

"Thirteen!" said Anthony.

"Fifteen as I count 'em!" said George.

"Fifteen it is!" nodded Mr. Tutt. "An' enough too!"

"How can we help?" demanded Anthony, turning to snatch his rifle. "What can we do?"

"Eat our breakfast," said George, and sat down again.

"An' that's whatever!" sighed Mr. Tutt, shaking his head.

"But, great God!" cried Anthony, fiercely indignant, "the poor fellow may be captured . . . killed!"

"Suttenly, suh!" answered George, eating with very evident relish

"Do you mean you can sit there and see murder done without stirring a hand? Even you, Noah?"

"There hain't anything we-uns can do for said pore feller. I reckon he's doo to cross the Great Divide, Ant."

"That be damned for an excuse!" said Anthony bitterly, "I at least can make the attempt—" But, even as he spoke, Mr. Tutt had risen and clamped his wrist in iron-like clutch.

"Mist' Anthony," said he, angrily, "d'ye think George an' me wouldn't risk our skins for a feller traveller any time, any place, if there was a chance? If ye do so think, then dang ye for blind fool. I'm tellin' ye again it'll be all over with yonder pore cuss afore we could cinch up,—he's booked to cross Old Jordan, sure. . . . See now, there he goes! What did I tell ye!"

Following Mr. Tutt's finger with quick glance, Anthony saw the pursuers blotted out by puffs of smoke, heard the rattle of their guns . . . the fugitive's horse seemed to falter, step awry, then, striving to recover, went down headlong, throwing his rider heavily; whereat, faint with distance yet terrible, rose his pursuers' triumphant war-hoots; then they were up with the fallen man . . . some of them dismounted and bent over him. . . .

"Snatching his ha'r!" sighed Mr. Tutt. "Mebbe they'll be taking ours soon, eh, George? I'm allowin' fifteen ag'n three is fairish long odds, pardner."

George took off his wide-brimmed hat to smooth his own thick hair, covered it again and nodding, smiled almost happily.

"We'll suttenly do our best tuh keep it where it is," said he; then draining his coffee mug, he rose, tightened his belts, eased the two heavy weapons in their holsters and taking up his rifle, went to peer down from this natural fortalice that his keen eye had selected as their camp against just such an emergency.

Guided by the smoke of their camp fire, the Indians advanced at an easy gallop, riding in open order, until they were so near as to be seen quite distinctly; fifteen lithe shapes splendidly equipped and hideous with war paint, long black hair streaming on the wind, each head adorned with eagle-feathers while from elbow and knee fluttered white skunk tails with narrow strips of antelope skin; and each of them flourished musket or rifle in right hand, guiding horse with his left and on every back a bow, ready strung, and quiver of arrows. On they came until just within range, then wheeling into line they began to circle this rocky bluff that sheltered their foes.

"Blackfeet, by Heck!" sighed Mr. Tutt dolefully. "Which I'll opine couldn't be worse!"

"Why so?" enquired Anthony, watching the proud bearing and superb horsemanship of these Indians with a feeling very like pleasure.

"Because of all the red varmints that infest the North-West, these yere Blackfeet are the most pizenous!"

"Meaning they are bold and valiant as they seem?"

"No, suh!" answered George but without turning his head, "Meaning they are the devils they look, murderous savages, suh, with mercy for none."

"Has the white man shown them much of mercy, Mr. Charteris? I answer—no! Having first stolen their country we have tricked, cheated and hunted them ever since. In his native state, before we corrupted him, the Indian was as courtly, as proudly honourable as any other gentleman."

"Noah, d'yuh hear him?" sneered George, his watchful gaze on the menace below, those circling warriors who were riding ever nearer. "Misto' Falconbridge it seems has lived so long among his red brothers he can tell us all about them!"

"However," Anthony retorted, "it revolts me to think of slaughtering any—"

"Then sit down, suh, and wait for them to slaughter yuh! Noah, how many of 'em are riding now?"

"'Leven—only eleven, George. There's four on 'em up to some deviltry . . . watch out now, they're coming, take cover!"

A scattered volley from below, buzzing and whine of bullets in the air above them; but Anthony crouched on knees, turned from those circling horsemen below to glance up and around behind him, and thus glimpsed eagle-feathers behind a rock unexpectedly near, a naked shoulder, a hand and arm that steadied a musket at George's back, and levelling his own weapon, fired; saw a stricken warrior leap from concealment and fired again. . . . And now for Anthony was an unforgettable memory of desperate effort, of rapid point-blank firing through drifting smoke, and once a fierce grappling body to body, an elemental struggle for life . . . until sudden as it had come, this fury of attack melted away. . . .

There was blood on George's face, Mr. Tutt's left hand dripped red, Anthony felt weak and bruised and saw his right shirt sleeve was ripped away. But among the rocks nearby three of their foes lay dead and five more upon the rocky levels below with nine of their horses, while the survivors, having galloped out of range, now seemed disputing together.

"Which I guess that powwow," quoth Mr. Tutt, biting off a chew of tobacco, "means as we've give 'em 'bout enough."

"I wonder we are alive!" said Anthony.

"Which George wouldn't be except for you, Ant. Wherefore, considerin' yore sentiments ag'in slaughter, I allow as you've done purty fair."

"Are you much hurt, Noah? Your arm—"

"Hain't looked yet, but feels like hell."

"Then let me—"

"No,—wait! See there!" Glancing down and away where their discouraged foes were congregated, Anthony saw one wheel his horse suddenly and come galloping, a slim young-seeming warrior; scornful of danger this Indian youth checked his steed in full career, leapt to earth and began lifting one of the dead who, it seemed, from the splendour of his adornment, had been a chief.

Instantly George's ready weapon was levelled against this young warrior, but almost as instantly Anthony's quick hand thrust it aside.

"To shoot now would be sheer murder!" said he imperiously whereat Noah gaped and George scowled through his mask of blood. "He's such a youngster," Anthony explained, "and that dead chief may be his father. Besides, the fight's over, they've had enough and—anyway, let that boy go with his dead—"

Scowling but dumb George once more took deliberate aim, and once again Anthony interposed; then, dropping his rifle, George turned and struck, but Anthony, avoiding the expected blow with a boxer's practised ease, clinched, and for a moment they stood locked in powerful grip. A hissing bullet whipped through George's hat; Mr. Tutt's rifle cracked and like an echo came his hoarse cry:

"Quit . . . quit yore foolin'! Fight . . . doggone ye . . . fight. . . ."

Crouched again, side by side behind their rocky parapet, they plied rifle and revolver for their lives until the spent survivors of these valiant Blackfoot Indians, smitten at last beyond endurance, broke and fled.

And when George had reloaded his weapons, he wiped the blood from his eyes, took off his hat, looked at the hole in it, glanced at Anthony and turning on his heel, went to unhobble the horses. Then Anthony made shift to wash and bind up the painful bullet-graze in Mr. Tutt's left arm, which done he went to help George collect and pack their gear, each avoiding the other's eye and both of them speechless.

Thus presently the three mounted together and rode down from this well-chosen camping place which, thanks to George's experience and foresight, had proved their salvation.

Silently they rode, even Mr. Tutt's ready tongue was

dumb until they reached that ghastly, scalpless thing that had striven so desperately to live, but a short while ago.

"Pore cuss!" sighed Mr. Tutt. "They've took his weapons along with his ha'r!"

"And his horse needs killing!" said George, and promptly shot the gasping, stricken animal.

"I reckon we-all had better go through his pockets, eh, George?"

"Suttenly, Noah, his friends will want tuh know."

Then while Anthony sat nearby with head averted, the two partners dismounted and together began their search.

"A sack o' dust!" announced Mr. Tutt weighing it in his hand, "Valley, let's opine, about three hundred dollars, also fifteen more in eagles."

"A pipe and plug of tobacco!" said George.

"Which last I'll doolly appropriate with gratitood seein' as late owner has riz up and beyond such earthly consolations."

"A pocket-book!" said George, "with fifty-five dollars in green backs, and a letter in envelope . . . addressed tuh Mr. Jos. Stevens, Yankee Flat, Lewiston. Take and read it, Noah."

"That will be this new capital of Idaho," said Anthony.

"That's whatever!" nodded Mr. Tutt; then standing above the dead man, he unfolded the letter and cleared his throat: "Begins: 'Bannack Mining Camp. Dear Joe,' and ends . . . why . . . by the 'Tarnal it's signed . . . John Hoyt!"

"Then read it, man, read it!" cried Anthony impatiently, which Mr. Tutt did, in these words:

"'Dear Joe, I hope this finds you as well as it leaves me, for I've struck it rich here in Bannack and am writing this to give you the word. I don't forget as how you saved my life that time when the dam Indians surprised our waggon train and killed so many of us. So I'm sending you this so you can stake a claim at Bannack. My Martha is well also the child when last seen, she don't know my luck yet, poor soul how glad she'll be to be rich. So come immediate to Bannack. Yours, John Hoyt.'

"Well," exclaimed Mr. Tutt, glancing down at the silent thing at his feet, "doggone me if this hain't the dumswizzled luck! This yere pore feller might have told us all we want to know."

"Mentions his wife, Martha," muttered George. "Mentions the child, but never a word of my Virginia!"

"Mebbe he just kinda forgot," suggested Mr. Tutt, consolingly.

"And most likely she's . . . dead!" murmured George in his soft drawl, but glancing askance at Anthony with very ominous expression. "Well . . . if she is dead indeed, I shall know how to act."

"Meaning," enquired Anthony, meeting the speaker's dark look with level gaze, "meaning you will exact summary vengeance on me, Mr. Charteris?"

"Yuh've guessed it, suh!" nodded George, turning to his horse, "come, let's ride!"

CHAPTER VIII

TELLS HOW GEORGE DELIVERED BANNACK OF ITS TERROR

NIGHT was falling when before them showed twinkling lights that grew and multiplied as they approached, while the solemn hush, the deep primeval stillness was troubled by a vague, uneasy sound, a confused noise, a blatant, swelling dissonance that, growing hoarser and more plain, became a mingled hubbub, an unholy rant of many lawless voices that shouted, laughed, hooted and sang to the wailing squeak of fiddles, tinkling thump of wiry pianos, thudding of heavy boot-heels; an all-pervading din, a raucous, never-ending clamour that was the voice of this young mining town of Bannack.

"Shore sounds like old times, George!" quoth Mr. Tutt peering through the rapidly falling dusk.

"Like Hell's delight, rather!" said Anthony.

"Yes, tuh both!" answered George, easing his guns.

"Hell's delight?" repeated Mr. Tutt, thoughtfully. "Well, I guesso, Ant. Ye see they's thousands o' folks yonder, men an' women, good, bad an' indifferent—"

"Though mostly bad!" growled George.

"Ah, 'specially the fe-males, pore souls!" sighed Mr. Tutt, expectorating mournfully, "Yessir, I'm mighty glad I warn't born a woman, I shore am! 'Specially in a minin' camp! Howandever, all o' them men an' women, good an' bad, has only jest one idee, —to get rich quick. The best of 'em work hard for it all day wi' pick, pan, shovel an' sluice, an' the worst of 'em works for it all night with cyards, dice or painted faces,—it's hard come an' easy go, but that's human an' nat'ral, I guess."

"The question is," said Anthony, glancing toward George's slouching figure, "do we enquire here for mother and child or—this damned criminal Slim of Sonora?"

"Why I reckon both, Ant."

"Very well then, you and Charteris may do as you please, but I shall not leave Bannack until I have exhausted every possible source of information."

And now they were entering this riotous town, a wide street with raised wooden sidewalks, a very busy thoroughfare athrong with pedestrians, horsemen and vehicles and bright with gleam of lamps and candles, from the open windows and doorways of clapboard houses, rough shacks hastily thrown together with here and there fairy-like structures of canvas or calico tacked to scantling poles, these set between larger and more durable buildings formed of split logs and dignified by rough-painted signs and such inscriptions as: Fairlight Hotel, Happy Chance Saloon; but everywhere was light and noise and ceaseless movement.

It was before one of the larger saloons calling itself 'The Miners' Joy,' that George dismounted, hitching his splendid animal to the rack set there to such purpose, whereat his two companions did likewise.

"Now, Ant," said Mr. Tutt, taking up a notch in his gunbelt, "foller me an' watch, for I'm allowin' you may see something. C'mon!" With which gleeful, cryptic utterance he led the way from noisy street into the blatant glare and joyous uproar of the Miners' Joy Saloon, owned, as Anthony noticed from its sign, by one Harry Plumer.

An unexpectedly spacious building was the Miners' Joy, with flights of stairs leading to broad galleries above a long bar, displaying racks of many shaped bottles, whereat rough-clad men drank or jostled each other in loud good-natured horseplay, this at one end; at the other, stood many card-tables where sat other men playing poker, euchre or faro, and between these a wide, open floor where close-embracing couples danced boisterously to the thumping accompaniment of tinny pianos, shrill flute and squeaking fiddle; men these, of all descriptions, though mostly in the rough garments and heavy boots of miners, and women old and young, some of whom filled Anthony with a cold disgust and some with deep and fatherly pity.

"Well, there they are!" murmured Mr. Tutt. "Right plenty o' fools with hard-earned dust, an' plenty o' slick gamblers an' daughters o' joy, Lord pity 'em! to take it away from said fools—ah now, watch George! Keep yore eyes on—" As he spoke George's slim right hand flicked gun from holster and fired into the floor, stunning the tumultuous merriment to sudden quiet; then on this silence rose George's soft, smoothly pleasant voice:

"Beg yo' pardon, folks, but Ah'm here tuh ask a question. Yuh, Mr. Bartender, can yo' please tell me where a friend can find a Misto' John Hoyt?"

"Sure can, Mister," answered the plump, keen eyed man of bottles, "he's in our noo cimetery. We planted him in Boot Hill three days ago. . . . It were three days ago, eh Cherokee?"

"It were, Bob!" answered a bony, woeful, dark-avised man, "Ye see, Stranger, he got hisself shot up some by this here Sonora as comes pirooting into town frequent and forever hellbent."

"Ah?" murmured George. "Hoyt is dead, is he?"

"Stranger," answered Cherokee, shaking his lank head, "I've never see nobody deader. This here Sonora shot him fuller o' holes 'n a sieve, an' the pore cuss hardly knowin' one end of a gun from t'other."

"Meaning Hoyt had no chance, Misto' Cherokee?"

"About as much as a snowball in hell, Stranger."

"Then may one enquire if this Misto' Sonora Slim is still in Bannack, suh?"

"Why, I guesso, Mister," answered the plump barman, "you'll likely find him down street at the Happy Miner, but you being a stranger, I'm shore advising you not to nowise monkey with Sonora, it ain't healthy none!"

"Unless," said Cherokee, edging nearer, his voice low and more mournful than ever, "he's went an' took his departure which this commoonity shore wishes he has, for he's . . . a killer, a cold-blooded slayer, Stranger. Also he's a two-gun pilgrim and lightning fast on the draw. So if you now, bein' also two handed, was kinda thinking o' calling the turn on him, I'm warning you that—" Cherokee coughed and was discreetly dumb as loud voices were heard approaching, heavy feet trampled, spurs jingled and framed in the wide doorway appeared three men, at sight of whom, the growing buzz of conversation died away again while all eyes focused upon the man who, advancing before his two companions, now stood lounging against the wall, a lithe, hawk-faced man who glanced around about upon the awed assemblage with the narrowed eyes, the sneering, arrogant contempt of the practised terrorist. And when his leisured, roving gaze had made itself felt, he spoke in voice mockingly contemptuous as his look:

"I'm aiming to know what daring citizen has been lettin' off his li'l pop-gun behind my back."

"Ah did, suh!" answered George in his smoothest, softest voice and, speaking, re-holstered his revolver. "May one venture to ask if yo' name happens tuh be Travis, called Sonora Slim?"

"That's me!" answered Travis, and, hooking thumbs in his crossed cartridge belts, he fixed George with his cold, inflexible eyes, the compelling, hypnotic stare that had shaken the nerve and thus had been the death of many a man before now. "Yes, I'm Travis of Sonora. Who's askin'?"

"Mah name is Charteris."

"Charteris? Oh! And then—what?"

"Ah kill snakes!"

Now in this great, crowded saloon was an almost unearthly stillness while these two men fronted each other, eye to eye, the hushed concourse waiting . . .

waiting for some word, some movement that it seemed would never come, a deadly suspense that grew so nerve-racking as to become unbearable at last; women screamed suddenly and fled; then was frantic stir, men leapt for distant corners, behind or under tables—anywhere to be out of the line of fire; but still these two faced each other, George erect, Travis lolling against the wall. Suddenly one of his companions, uttering a breathless oath, whipped out his revolver but, before he could level it, came the thunderous crash of Mr. Tutt's swift-drawn weapon, and the would-be assassin, twisting on his toes, fell to lie motionless across the threshold.

"Plump centre!" quoth Mr. Tutt, his voice loud on the tense stillness. "Now you!" he snarled, gesturing with smoking pistol, to Sonora's other companion, "step up an' onbuckle yore gunbelt, then grab at the roof!"

Speechlessly the man obeyed, an ill-looking fellow with broken nose and a hare-lip, and stood, hands aloft, staring at Sonora who, like George, had never so much as moved.

And now George spoke again:

"Travis, way back on the trail yuh killed a lone traveller and . . . branded him."

"Well, I gen'rally marks my kills—"

"Yuh also shot another defenceless man lately in this town."

"Oh? Did I? Well, mebbe so, if I did, he asked for it."

"Well, now I'm asking for it."

"What's this mean? A dee—fi, hey?"

"A hole!" answered George, his lips curling in their dreadful smile. "A hole in the ground for one of us, Travis, and I'm offering any odds yo' rank carcass will fill it."

Sonora's slender body stiffened, he laughed harshly.

"Mister gunfool," said he, nodding, "I'm taking that bet blind, all you got agin all I got, an' I'll be collectin' it from yore corpse."

"Enough talk!" said George, bitterly scornful. "Get to it! Yuh wear two guns and I'm told yuh're fast, well—show me! Fill yuh're hands . . . I'm waiting."

Someone's uneasy foot scarped nervously; someone drew a long, shuddering breath. . . . Travis of Sonora moved at last and with almost incredible speed; but George's matchless hands moved even faster, his guns, just clearing holsters, were belching flame and smoke a fraction of time the sooner, and Sonora, pulling triggers as he fell, shot holes in the floor that next instant was wet with his life.

"Dead!" announced Mr. Tutt. "Dead afore he hit the boards! And that's two pizen-toads the less—" Then his voice was lost in sudden uproar, a jubilant pandemonium. Cheering men capered or tossed up their hats, others came thronging with eager hands outstretched, proffering drink and even gold-dust to this stranger who had rid them of this two-legged incubus whose murderous guns had held them thralled with sickening dread these many months.

But George, shaking his head, forced his way through this vociferous, hero-worshipping crowd; and presently the three were riding along the riotous street that already buzzed and roared with the news:

"Sonora Slim's dead! Give a cheer, boys, the Sonora Killer's dead!"

CHAPTER IX

GIVES SOME PARTICULARS OF WHAT BEFELL IN BANNACK TOWN

"AT your service, gentlemen!" He stood in the doorway of their private sitting-room and bowed; a very distinguished-seeming personage, who smiled. His smooth-shaven, nearly-handsome face looked neither young nor old, his linen was spotless, his frockcoat well-fitting, his spurred riding boots highly polished; yet George having surveyed this very seemly personage, lowered dark gaze to his plate again; Mr. Tutt, knife and fork suspended for a moment, glanced up and merely nodded, while Anthony rose instinctively to greet the speaker.

"You wish to see me, I think, gentlemen?"

"Yes, sir," Anthony answered. "If you are Mr. Plumer, the owner of this hotel."

"And I repeat entirely at yore service, sir. I am honoured to welcome you-all to Bannack and especially to this hotel. We are a little rough, I'm afraid, but we are new, sir, we are new—but clean and thriving like our town, pioneers, sir, of a far-flung civilization. Pray what may I do for you-all?" And his smile was engaging, his voice soft like the white hand adorned with flaming brilliant that he now extended in such ready welcome; and yet Anthony loosed this hand rather suddenly as he answered:

"Mr. Plumer, an unfortunate man was killed here recently—"

"Alas, sir," sighed Mr. Plumer, shaking his head, "such things happen all too frequently, our death rate is distressingly high, lead poisoning, sir, in almost every case! A man died of it this very night, I understand, a stranger . . . name of Davis or Travis—"

"Two men, suh!" murmured George, in gentle correction.

"Ah, to be sure!" nodded Mr. Plumer, affably. "And you gentlemen were present, I believe?"

"We was!" said Noah. "And two was the number."

"And Ah'm wondering, suh," continued George, "since yuh know the name of one, if yuh know the name of the other?"

"No!" answered Mr. Plumer, his smile slightly less bland. "How should I? All I know of this Davis . . . or Travis is that he was a two-gun terror, fast as lightning yet beaten to the draw by a man even faster."

"Faster is shorely the word!" quoth Mr. Tutt.

"It's no business of mine, gentlemen," said Mr. Plumer with engaging frankness, "but, I may as well confess, you three were pointed out to me as the parties concerned and I'll own I should be proud to shake hands with the gun wizard who could out-draw this . . . this Davis—"

"Or Travis!" murmured George, plying knife and fork.

"P'raps," suggested Mr. Tutt, reaching for the whisky bottle, "p'raps you might know this yere Travis better by his nomme de gore—which is Sonora Slim?"

Mr. Plumer's steel-blue eyes seemed to chill the warmth of his ever-ready smile as he answered, almost loudly:

"No, sir! Never heard it—"

"But," interposed Anthony impatiently, "all this is quite beside the question! . . . Pray sit down, Mr. Plumer,—perhaps you'll take supper with us?"

"Honoured, sir, but I've already eaten. However, I'll take a seat, with pleasure."

"Why then, a glass of whisky?"

"Thanks again, sir, I'll smoke instead, if I may. I rarely drink and never Valley Tan."

"Briefly then, sir," said Anthony, "we desire to

learn everything possible about a man lately shot and killed here in Bannack, a miner named John Hoyt."

Mr. Plumer, in the act of cutting a cigar, paused and sat turning it, this way and that, in long, white fingers, then he trimmed it with extreme care, put it in his smiling mouth and shook his head.

"I pass, sir!" said he. "The name means nothing in my life."

"Which," quoth Mr. Tutt, "shore sap-prises me! Yes, by Jing, it cert'nly do!"

"Indeed?" said Mr. Plumer, beaming. "May I enquire why the amazement?"

"You may. And I'll answer: When a miner strikes it rich the hull camp gen'rally knows all about it an' said lucky miner is a marked man. Well, this pore cuss struck it so rich an' was such a marked man, he's laying in his grave, all shot to pieces. . . . And—you ain't heard of it!"

Here Mr. Plumer paused to ignite his cigar with a very solicitous deliberation, which done, he answered lightly:

"Not a word."

"Which, I repeat, shore amazes me!"

"And I ask again, pray why?"

"Because you run a saloon and this yere ho-tel an' in such places folks meet, and when folks meet they talk! And I know as there was, and is, talk of John Hoyt's luck. And you've got a pair o' y-ears. And you hain't deaf! And—that's why!"

Mr. Plumer laughed very pleasantly, though the eyes down-bent to his cigar were more steely than ever; but before he could speak, Mr. Tutt continued:

"One other thing. Since John Hoyt, being so completely dead, has riz beyond such carnal vanities, I'm kinda curious to know what's become of his dust an' likewise who now owns his claim? Which queries no citizen o' Bannack as I've made occasion to ask, has been able to answer."

"And yet it's all perfectly simple," said Mr. Plumer, stifling a yawn, "Bannack is no longer a mere mining camp but a town where so many citizens have been successful lately that one here and there is apt to escape notice. There's plenty of gold being dug around Bannack and plenty more to find, I guess."

"Then you have no information regarding John Hoyt?" enquired Anthony, a little grimly.

"Regrets, but not a word!" answered Mr. Plumer, with airy flourish of cigar. "But there are others, sir. I guess some citizen should have heard something and be ready to impart, but—not me, sir." So saying he rose, opened the door and turned to enquire: "Are you gentlemen intending to use this hotel, any?"

"Yes, our business may keep us a day or so before going on."

"Further West, sir, Lewiston way, or back East?"

"This depends," Anthony answered, evasively.

"Then, gentlemen, you couldn't do better than stay here,—single beds in every room with washstand, soap and towels complete, and the best of service, for though young, sirs, our watchword is—comfort." So saying, Mr. Plumer smiled, bowed and departed, closing the door behind him; whereupon, and before Anthony might speak, Mr. Tutt held up an arresting finger, listened a moment and rising silently opened the door and in walked Mr. Plumer, cigar in mouth.

"Forgot something?" Noah enquired.

"I have," smiled Mr. Plumer, "I omitted to tell you-all that breakfast is usually at nine, and also to make a suggestion."

"Whereunto," said Mr. Tutt, sitting down again, "we are listenin' with doo attention, sir."

"Well, gentlemen, if you should happen to be riding further West, towards Lewiston, say, I can tell you-all a short cut through the mountains will save you a goodish few miles. Or, better still, I could show you. I'm riding with a friend or so to the capital very soon and should be honoured by yore company."

"Sir," answered Mr. Tutt, "yore suggestion meets with our gratitood but, seein' we hain't settled when we ride nor where, we leaves it at gratitood for the present."

"Suit yourselves, gentlemen," said Mr. Plumer, smiling, "I bid you *au revoir*, reminding you we carry several very excellent brands of liquor." Once again he departed, and they heard his spurred heels go jingling along the uncarpeted passage and down the stair till lost in the busy stir below.

"Which I'm bold to aver," said Mr. Tutt, producing a well-seasoned corn-cob pipe and filling it thoughtfully, "yessir, I here an' now ass-everates as how Mr. P. is a slick customer, a smooth article an'—carries a hideout!"

"Shoulder holster, left arm!" nodded George. "Eh . . . what now, suh?" he demanded, for Anthony had risen and was reaching for his hat.

"I'm off to enquire about poor John Hoyt, of course, Charteris. I've travelled these thousands of miles to find my grandchild and I'm beginning—now! You and Noah do as you will, but I'll waste no more time."

"Well, Ant, now doggone ye for a mole which is born without ary an eye!" exclaimed Mr. Tutt.

"I don't know what you mean," said Anthony, putting on his hat, "but anyway—I'm going."

"Which," quoth Mr. Tutt, rising, "I'm bold to say—you hain't."

"Noah, what on earth do you mean?"

"Such a dingbusted lot I dunno how to begin."

"Then keep it for another time, because—"

"Another time wouldn't hardly do, Ant, because I'm guessin' you'll be dead—"

"Good God!" exclaimed Anthony. "What are you suggesting?"

"Come away from that door an' lemme try to tell ye. . . . Ant, if you go walkin' down into that street to-night, I'm gamblin' a blue stack you'll never come walkin' back—nossir!"

"Oh, nonsense, man! No one here knows me, no one can have anything against me. There is only one man in Bannack who threatens my life—"

"Meaning me, suh?"

"Yourself, Charteris—"

"Ant Falconbridge," whispered Noah, drawing him yet further from the door, "now you listen to me! In the law-abidin' East I'm allowin' you air a mighty powerful citizen, you can handle money an' rule men—specially men yore money pays for,—but—constant protection by the law has made you the sort o' man that without such protection, yore helpless as a child—yessir! So I'm tellin' ye that in such place as this where only gun law rules, you'd be snuffed out afore you knowed it."

"However," said Anthony, becoming the imperious Master, "I'm going—"

"Then George an' me'll have to tag along an' most likely get shot in the back or knifed—"

"But why, man, why? Surely not because you killed those ruffians in the 'Miners' Joy,' that bloody business made you heroes all over this wild town."

"What? Can't ye see it yet, Ant?"

"No, I'll be damned if I can!"

"Then, George, you tell him, I'm through!"

"Because," said George, keen eyes on the door, "Hoyt was shot fo' his gold and because Someone wanted his claim, and we look like stirring up trouble for this Someone, on Hoyt's account, and therefo' it's up to this Someone to silence us and have us planted along with Hoyt."

"And that's whatever!" nodded Mr. Tutt. "We've horned in on Someone's game an' Someone, not knowin' how little we know, is mighty anxious therefore an' waitin' to get the drop on us."

"But this," said Anthony, impatiently, "all this is merest conjecture, empty surmise and vague suspicion, for neither of you has advanced one iota of proof. You evidently distrust the man Plumer, well, so do I heartily, but—" Something flipped up through the open window to bounce lightly from wall to table, and Anthony picked up a tightly-rolled ball of paper; unrolling this very carefully he glanced at the hastily scrawled words and then, sinking his voice, read aloud this message:

> "'To warn you three there are six out gunning for you when chance offers. If further info. wanted, I'm in room nine, eleven o'clock. Cherokee. Burn this sure.'"

Passing this paper for his companions' perusal, Anthony sat down, glancing from closed door to open window and round this small room in sudden apprehension.

"So it seems your suspicions are justified and that I owe you an apology," said he, "unless, of course, this warning is a hoax."

"Speakin' personal," said Mr. Tutt, knocking out his pipe, "I'm gamblin' this yere Cherokee is on the square."

"Me too!" nodded George.

"Why then," said Anthony, glancing at his rifle in adjacent corner, "I have generally found that the best defence is attack, instant and determined. Therefore I propose we begin our search at once, but take Mr. Plumer with us as hostage for our safety."

"A hostage—by Jing!" chuckled Mr. Tutt, slapping his knee.

"And why Plumer?" demanded George, a new light dawning in his sombre eyes as he surveyed Anthony's alert, determined face.

"Because he rings false. I read him as a bold, unscrupulous fellow sufficiently educated to dominate the more ignorant and perhaps be a power among them—"

"Shore as I'm born!" quoth Mr. Tutt, slipping off his boots and rising. "Yes I'm bettin' Mr. P. is the king-pin of this town. . . . Now what's o'clock by that gold time-piece o' yourn, Ant?"

"Just three minutes after ten!"

"Which," said Mr. Tutt, easing revolver in scabbard, "gives me time for a mite o' scoutin'."

"Then we'll come with you, eh, George?"

"Suttainly, suh!"

"Which is plumb ridiculous!" snorted Mr. Tutt, laying hand on the door knob. "One's enough to size up the gen'ral sitooation and that one's—me."

"And I insist we toss for it," said Anthony, taking out a coin.

"Toss nothin'!" snarled Mr. Tutt. "Mind that winder, George. I opine as they're liable to start somethin' any minute. So long!" And with a curt nod he stole forth, shutting the door softly behind him, and left his companions to stare at the lamp, at the window and at each other while Anthony, ever craving action, grew more restless until his mounting anxiety forced him to speech at last:

"Charteris, if our situation is really desperate as I now suspect, there's death for us in every corner of this hotel."

"And all over Bannack tuh, Falconbridge!"

"We . . . we should never have allowed him to go. . . . If anything should happen to Noah—"

"We should probably quarrel, and even fight and yuh think Charteris would suttenly kill yuh!" murmured George, faintly mocking.

"So you overheard me say that?"

"Mah y-ears are fairly sharp, suh."

"They must be."

"Yes, suh!" And so was silence again, each listening keenly alert to catch, above the ceaseless hubbub of crowded street and boisterous stir of the hotel, the uproar of sudden fight.

"If," said Anthony at last, "if any harm should come to Noah, by God I shall never forgive myself!"

"Why not, suh?"

"For permitting him to run such risk."

"Could you have stopped him?"

"I could have been more insistent! . . . It's men like Noah Tutt sweeten this world and make life worth enduring."

"Yes, suh!" Again they were mute, while Bannack

roared at them, until up started Anthony to pace restlessly.

"Falconbridge—sit down!"

"Eh? What d'you mean?"

"The window! Yo' head against the light."

"Eh? You think someone may try a shot at us so openly?"

"Well," said George, smiling. "Let's see." Taking his rifle he withdrew the cleaning-rod, balanced his hat thereon and edged it slowly round a corner of the heavy window frame as if its wearer had been peeping stealthily down into the busy street that clamoured on apparently all unheeding this proffered lure. But very patiently George sat there moving rod and hat gently, every now and then, much as though he had been fishing; and presently, sure enough, a fish seemed to nibble, for on the opposite side of the street and directly opposite, rose sudden outburst of passionate voices in fierce altercation, drowned suddenly by three or four echoing reports fired in rapid succession . . . something hummed in at them through the window to thud into the log wall, the hat swayed and fell, the furious uproar in the street subsided and was gone.

"A rifle!" said George and drawing the hat within reach, picked it up. "And that's two!" he nodded, showing Anthony where a second hole now pierced it. "So yuh see if my head had been where someone thought it was, I should have been killed . . . accidentally, and no one to blame."

"Dastardly!" exclaimed Anthony.

"But an old trick."

"The situation becomes grimmer, Charteris! Do you suppose Noah was mixed up in that shooting below there?"

"Not he."

"Do you think he's all right?"

"Yes."

"However," said Anthony rising, "I think I'll step out and look for him."

"As yuh will," said George, rising also. "And seeing this sort of thing comes more natural to me, yuh'll suffer me to go first, suh."

"I've no wish to force any needless risk upon you, Charteris."

"No, suh, but yuh are."

"Then, for God's sake, let me go alone!"

"Suttenly not, Falconbridge! Noah Tutt was mah friend long befo' yuh ever saw him. Shall we go?"

"No—wait!" said Anthony in his masterful way. "George, look at me!" In the act of adjusting his crossed gun-belts George's slim, brown hands were stilled and he fixed the speaker with a wide, dark stare.

"Well, suh," said he, "Ah'm looking."

"Talking of . . . friendship," said Anthony, coming a pace nearer, "because, under prevailing circumstances, our talking may end to-night for ever, I would first say that I beg your pardon for anything I have done or said in the past that has anyways hurt or affronted you. And secondly I . . . would ask your friendship. Our families have been predisposed to hatred and enmity for a generation and more, ever since our grandfathers met in battle, yours to die at the head of his men, mine to be killed later in a duel. But all this was long ago, and to-night, if you are willing . . . let us banish this old, bitter rancour, for good and all . . . George, let us forget!" George drew both guns, viewed and tested them heedfully, nodded, sheathed them and spoke; and now his soft voice had lost its languorous drawl:

"To forget may be easy fo' yuh, suh, but quite impossible fo' me. There is a . . . hobbling cripple, I allude tuh mah honoured father, suh . . . and he is a constant reminder that he was so crippled for life by yo' father's bullet. And then besides—"

"No need for more!" said Anthony very bitterly. "The old curse must live, it seems. Well, thank God, it will die, for I am the last Anthony—"

Instantly and together they turned to face the door, as

upon a panel came the quick, softly insistent tapping of a finger.

"Come!" said Anthony, hoarsely, whereupon the door opened, closed, and the man Cherokee stood viewing them with his mournful gaze.

"'S me, gents!" he nodded. "Called Cherokee, an' I ain't a mite hostile so you can leggo yore lead-slinger, friend."

"What yuh want?" George demanded, hand still on gun-butt.

"Jest rambled in, gents, to know if you-all got my warnin'."

"Was it you wrote this?" enquired Anthony, showing the crumpled paper.

"Shore did. And—asked you to burn it, bein' my death warrant, shore as shootin', if found."

"Watch then!" said Anthony and set it to the lamp flame.

"Gents," said Cherokee, when the paper was no more than crumpled ash, "to-night you salivated two human wolverines as killed frequent and took joy therein . . . but there's others as needs yore like attentions in particular—one, the slickest, coldest-blooded murderer in this whole dam state of Idaho, and—infestin' this here hotel at this moment, seein' it's his!"

"Yuh meaning Plumer?" enquired George.

"Keno!" nodded Cherokee. "Harry Plumer's the pest I been livin' to ex-terminate, hangin' on in this hell-fire town, waitin' for chance to e-liminate same! Ah!" sighed Cherokee, his mournful features transfigured with a terrible glee, "to line on him with a double-bar'l, sawed-off shot-gun! Ye see, gents, he shot my boy . . . my only son, or had him murdered and jumped his claim . . . name of Edward Francis . . . used to call him Frank . . . just twenty-two years old, which is mighty young to die, and . . . of a bullet in the back! So here came I to exact bloody vengeance on his killer. . . . But no luck, gents, no luck . . . for Plumer's guarded night an' day, hired gunmen an' bouncers, so a lone cuss like me has no chance, and the miners, an' such, prefers to buck the tiger 'stead o' buckin' Plumer's hellish game an' hangin' him for the murdering vermin he is."

"But what of Miners' Courts?" enquired Anthony. "And this new-raised company called Vigilantes?"

"They ain't half-organized, Stranger, and a miners' court needs real men to run it, men as ain't afraid to be a real jury and pass a true verdict. But these here Bannack miners ain't got a backbone among 'em. So this is why I'm waggin' my chin at you-all and consequently liable to be shot along with ye."

"Then why risk yourself with us?"

"Because to me it shore looks like three real men has come into Bannack at last, gents. I see the way you handled Sonora and yore friend out-drawed Butch Maloney—two of Plumer's fastest gun-toters. Now, gents, when guns is in question I'm some fast myself but I'm sayin', with my hand on my heart, that I've never seen such speed an' accuracy so harmonious wedded. An' this brings me to the crux which briefly is—I want to throw in with you-all, I want to offer self an' guns in yore service, until yore safe out o' Bannack or till I've got Harry Plumer where I been waitin' so patient to get him, an' that's—lookin' down the business end o' my guns, whereafter, gents, he'll go, very completely dead and you an' me free to go or come unmolested. Well now,—what's the word?"

"Yes, fo' me," answered George. "I guess yuh'r straight; anyways I'm willing to take a chance with yuh, if my two partners agree,—what d'yuh think, Anthony?"

Now here ensued a minute's silence while Anthony, gazing on Cherokee's sad yet mournful visage, could think only how this was the first time in all their travels that George had deigned to utter his name; but now Cherokee, misunderstanding his silence, laid a hand on his arm with look and gesture almost of entreaty.

"If you're worryin' any about my financial status—"

"I'm not," said Anthony.

"And—you needn't," quoth Cherokee; "I'm well fixed for money, also I got a horse an' outfit, so if you agree—"

"Oh, I do," answered Anthony, "it only remains for Mr. Tutt—"

"Then Keno, friends!" exclaimed Cherokee, almost joyously. "He's agreeable already, Mr. Tutt and yore's truly has talked."

"Why, then, where is he . . . is he safe?"

"Shore is. I left him bellyin' down on the floor of a loft with eye and ear alternate at a knot-hole as I've used frequent and to good purpose—"

"Listen!" said Anthony, starting from his chair, "What on earth—?" A hurry of spurred feet upon the stair, trampling feet that seemed almost to run; George's lightning hand had armed itself, Cherokee, leaping to stand beside him, had produced a short, double-barrelled derringer as the door swung wide and in upon them strode Mr. Plumer impelled by the muzzle of Mr. Tutt's revolver.

"Keno!" exclaimed Cherokee, in dreadful, hushed jubilation, and, closing the door softly, locked it.

CHAPTER X

TELLS OF A DUEL IN THE DESERT AND HOW THREE BECAME FOUR

MR. PLUMER smiled no longer, also he was pale, but his steel-blue eyes glanced round upon the hostile faces about him boldly and his bearing seemed perfectly assured.

"Well, gentlemen," he demanded, "perhaps one of you will explain the meaning of this outrage? In the private office of my own hotel, your friend here creeps upon me, rams a gun into my back and forces me here! Well, I'm demanding what it all means?"

"Which," answered Mr. Tutt, holstering his revolver and pulling forward a chair, "which, instanter I'll dooly relate. Set you down, Mr. P. an' get an earful. So . . . . now! Pardners, I am pervadin' the upper premises o' this yere ho-tel when I runs into this Cherokee feller some onexpected and demands instant explanations—"

"With yore gun in my stomach!" nodded Cherokee.

"Explanations satisfactory, we talk an' he brings me into a sorta loft with no winders but a knot-hole in the floor lookin' plumb down into this yere Plumer's private office, whereby I sees and hears enough to know our Mr. P. for a two-legged, public misfortin' as soars way beyond all our expectations."

Mr. Plumer's assurance deserted him, his eyes quested, shifting from door to window, while, beneath his crisp hair, spots of moisture crept, as Mr. Tutt's harsh inexorable voice went on:

"I sees an' hears Mr. P. describe the three of us very acc'rate to his killers, six or seven, an' how we must be shot an' planted immediate . . . 'Because, boys,' says he, 'these here pilgrims are here to raise hell on account of Hoyt an' his claim. I told Sonora,' says he, 'as it should be done private, but the fool must shoot him up in the street. Well, Sonora's dead for it,' says he, 'an' so will you-all be—shot or kickin' in so many nooses if these three is allowed to ask questions. So it's them or us!' says he."

Mr. Plumer was cowering now, the hand that dabbed snowy handkerchief to his moist brow was shaking, his eyes, rolling wildly from face to face, fixed themselves suddenly on Cherokee who, leaning against the door with folded arms, was speaking now in a voice and accents of the cultured East:

"Harry Plumer, it seems there is a God whose all-pervading justice may shorely reach into this lawless town you've ruled too long, this hell on earth called Bannack, to bring you up for judgement and a full accounting."

"And that's whatever!" nodded Mr. Tutt. "Are our horses waiting where an' as agreed, Cherokee?"

"All ready, Mr. Tutt. Let us go—

"Wait!" cried Plumer, struggling against the hands that clutched him. "What . . . where are you taking me? Are . . . God, are you going to . . . murder me?"

"No!" murmured George.

"Certainly not!" answered Anthony.

"We hain't yore doggone sort!" quoth Mr. Tutt, contemptuously.

"Then let me explain . . . let me speak . . . what are you going to do with me . . . what?"

"Which," said Mr. Tutt, pulling his whiskers pensively, "is shore the present, burning question!"

"Hang him!" suggested George, putting on his hat.

"No!" said Anthony, taking rifle from the corner, "we will escort you to Lewiston for a fair trial."

"Or, best of all, gents," said Cherokee, reverting to the vernacular, "yank him outa Bannack, take him away into the desert, give him a gun an' turn us loose, him an' me, lettin' Chance or Fate or the Etarnal decide. How of it?"

"Yes!" nodded George.

"Shore goes with me," said Mr. Tutt. "And it hain't no use shakin' yore head, Ant, so c'mon! Step careful, Mr. P. and make just one wrong move an' I crack down on ye with my Colt's! Now, get a-goin'! Show the way, Cherokee."

Along carpetless passages they hurried and, avoiding the main stair, followed their guide until they reached and descended a narrow flight of steps, past clattering kitchens and out into a still night lit by great stars and the radiant promise of a full moon; a vague twilight that showed where, beyond dim-seen, untidy piles of rotting crates, boxes and tin cans, stood their horses in charge of a dark-faced Indian youth who, at word from Cherokee, nodded and vanished silently amid the shadows. So, with scarcely a sound, they mounted and rode from roaring, flaring, hectic Bannack, out and away into the vast, deep quiet of this rolling, desert country; on and on, mile after mile until the moon was up, mounting in pale splendour to show a wide desolation all about them, a dreary prospect of sand and scrub and jagged storm-smitten rock.

Here Cherokee, lifting one hand, eased up his horse and nodded.

"This'll do, eh friends?" he enquired.

"I guesso," answered Noah, and dismounting he beckoned their prisoner to do the same.

"Wait!" said Henry Plumer, hoarsely and making no effort to obey. "Is this . . . murder or . . . a square deal? What are my chances?"

"Plumer," answered Mr. Tutt, looking the very figure of doom in the vivid moonlight, "what we should do, considerin' yore record, is swing ye in a rope. But this yere Cherokee, having first call by reason of his murdered son, gives you a chance to shoot it out, fair and square—"

"And how if I down Cherokee?"

"Then, like my pardner says, we'll ride ye into Lewiston to be tried by the law which I'm hopin' thereafter to see ye well an' dooly hung. Now—ged-down! So! George, loan him one o' yore guns, I'm keepin' him covered with my own."

Mr. Plumer took the weapon, examined it critically, balanced it in practised hand, then started to Mr. Tutt's harsh voice:

"One wrong move, Plumer, an' I kill ye my own self. Now, you an' Cherokee git back to back."

Jingle of spurs and whisper of footsteps in the sand as the two men placed themselves; and now, standing thus in the pervading silence of this vast, glimmering landscape, Cherokee spoke, his solemn voice loud upon the great stillness:

"Plumer, when we turn to shoot, you will be facing two men, myself and my dear son, the boy you murdered. So, I guess one of us will surely get you. Now, pray give the word, Mr. Tutt, we're ready."

"Then listen again, the both of you! I'm agoin' to count five, an' you're goin' to walk five paces and on the fifth, turn and fire. Now,—are ye ready? Go!"

Four leisured strides they made to Mr. Tutt's count and on the fifth, leapt about firing as they turned, and advanced against each other veiled in smoke that was split by rapid spurts of red flame; ensued a sudden deadly stillness, broken by jingle of spurs as Cherokee, his face dripping blood, stepped forward to look down on his fallen adversary who lay face down, the still-smoking pistol beneath the lax hand whose immobility seemed more manifest because of the fiery life and sparkle of the great solitaire ring that flared on limp finger,—or so thought Anthony.

"Snakes die hard!" said Cherokee, his bedabbled face ghastly in the moonlight. "So, best make sure!"

"Be content!" pleaded Anthony, grasping his pistol-hand. "To kill in a duel is one thing, to shoot in cold blood is damnable! Be content!"

"And anyways," said Cherokee, turning away, "I reckon 'twould be wastin' lead."

"He didn't git you bad then, Cherokee?" enquired Noah.

"No more than creased my visage, friend, which seein' I've no hankerin' to be mistook for Adonis, don't grieve me none."

"Well," enquired George drawing his revolver from Plumer's nerveless grasp and reloading it instinctively, "What are yuh aiming tuh do?"

"Bein' a lone cuss," answered Cherokee, holding sodden handkerchief to his lacerated cheek, "a ramblin' feller as roofs all his fam'ly an' responsibilities under his hat, I can please myself an' no ways better than taggin' along with you-all, if agreeable?"

"Speakin' for the three of us," quoth Mr. Tutt, glancing at his two companions, "we're agreein' full an' free. And we're ridin' for Lewiston."

"Then pardners," said Cherokee, nodding at each in turn, "from now on, your troubles an' enemies is mine. Let's be goin'."

CHAPTER XI

TELLS HOW CAME FRIENDSHIP AND A PARTING

It was as they broke camp of an early morning that George, being first mounted, rose in his stirrups to stare back along the way they had come (as he was for ever doing of late), this winding, mountainous trail that had been broadened and smoothed recently for the better passage of wheeled traffic and, more especially, the stage coach that bore to and from thriving Lewiston a heterogeneous cargo of parcels, passengers, special delivery letters, gold in dust, and gold in coin, and, consequently bristled with artillery yet which frequently proved all too inadequate against the bandit gangs infesting these wild and desolate regions.

"What is it, George?" enquired Mr. Tutt, peering also along this lonely road. "What's bitin' ye this time?"

"There's dust!" answered George, pointing. "Way off yonder, just crossing the divide. See it?"

"No, my eyes hain't like yourn."

"I do," said Anthony, "a small cloud and travelling fast."

"Me too!" nodded Cherokee. "Not 'nuff dust for the stage but plenty for a lone rider. P'raps they's more than one, gents from Bannack, say, with guns yearnin' for sight of us."

"No, there's only one," said George, "but riding hard."

And now, being mounted all, each man looked heedfully to his weapons and thereafter sat to watch this rapidly approaching horseman who, presently aware of their threatening posture, checked his speed and now rode watching them in his turn; perceiving which, the four lifted their arms high in the universal peace-sign of the open, unarmed hand, while the horseman approached at the same cautious gait, rifle held ready for instant use. Suddenly Cherokee took off his hat and flourished it, saying:

"Bust me if it ain't Childers, Zeke Childers o' the Pony Express. Zip-ee, Zeke!" he roared. "'S me, Zeke, Cherokee with friends. Come right on!" Thus assured, the rider shouted hoarse greeting and came on again, a lean man, coated with dust and bronzed as an Indian: to whom cried Cherokee joyously:

"Why, Zeke, consarn yore hide, ease up old timer an' swap noos."

"I'm the Mail, Cherokee an' some late now," answered Childers reining up to salute the company. "But seein' it's you, here's how!"

"Got any noos, Zeke?"

"Not any . . . except the stage was held up beyond Bannack an' they got away with twenty-fi' thousand in dust and specie, three jaspers tried to stop me at Runnin' Horse an' I got two, an' Harry Plumer's been shot up."

"Is the polecat dead?" enquired Mr. Tutt, champing his quid.

"Not when I came through. Leastways he was lively enough to tell the tale how four bandits kidnapped him an' how you shot him, Cherokee."

"Which I cert'nly did, Zeke, an' he creased my cheek, here."

"I been noticin' that same. So then you did give him a man's chance, Cherokee, like I said you did, you bein' you,—gun to gun, hey?"

"My friends here can so witness, Zeke."

"Yore own word goes wi' me, Cherokee. But Plumer tells different."

"He would!" nodded Mr. Tutt expectorating fiercely.

"But," enquired Childers, "how come you bungled it, Cherokee, how come he ain't dead all proper an' complete?"

"Snakes," sighed Cherokee, mournfully. "Snakes die hard, old timer."

"Shore do!" nodded Childers, also mournfully. "An', what's more, this snake's yearning to sting! He's offerin' fi' thousand dollars for yore scalp, Cherokee! And what's more again, he's organizin' a posse, leastways some of his picked gun-slicks, to hunt down said bandits . . . which I'm thinkin' these friends o' yourn is them same. And what's lastly an' most of all,—they know as you're ridin' for Lewiston. So, you might pass it up and take the trail to Boise City, or strike across the mountings for the Beaver Head; yore hosses shore looks the best I seen this side the Rockies, an' all in prime condition, so I guess you should make it. So good luck, freends an' Cherokee! I'm late . . . so long!" And with flourish of hat and thud of quick hoofs, away went this hardy rider with his precious Mails, off and away at stretching gallop that very soon had taken him out of sight.

"The question now bein'," quoth Mr. Tutt, masticating with added grimness, "do we ride to Lewiston or bear away across the badlands?"

"Lewiston, of course," answered George, scowling back along the trail.

"'S all one to me, freends," said Cherokee, easing his rifle in its sling.

"What says you, Ant?"

"Nothing!" answered Anthony. "Under the circumstances, I am compelled to leave the decision to you and George."

"Eh? What circumstances?"

"If I hadn't interposed so . . . disastrously, this new danger would never have arisen. It seems I saved a scoundrel's life."

"Dis-asterously is the word, Ant! Prudence an' general savvy urged Cherokee to kill a pizen-toad, which yore on-reasonin' humanity prevents, and—as you now says, an' which I agrees to,—disasterously!"

"And yet, Noah, I think, under like circumstances I should act again precisely the same. . . . To shoot a helpless man in cold blood—"

"Might save the chance, Ant, of four men bein' shot in hot or cold blood—"

"However," murmured George, still frowning on the distant prospect, "Ah can begin to appreciate Anthony's point of view, Noah." Mr. Tutt very nearly swallowed his quid.

"Hell's bells!" he exclaimed. "Can ye, by Jing! Well, I guess we all acts accordin' to our lights."

"And I," said Anthony glancing at George's averted face, "I'm grateful . . . very—"

"And so," continued George, as if neither of them had spoken, and with keen gaze still questing the country behind them, "I'm asking yuh . . . yo' advice: Do we ride on to Lewiston direct, or take Childers' advice, strike off for the Beaver Head and wait till this hunt fo' us is over?"

"To Lewiston, at once! And I thank you for permitting me a choice," said Anthony, little guessing how tremendous and far-reaching were to be the results of this decision.

"I take it yuh'r fo' Lewiston also, Noah?"

"Oh shore, George! An' if Plumer's killers should fetch up with us, I'm ass-sertin' they'll get a plenty an' then some!"

"Pards," nodded Cherokee, "there's a pretty good book, though wrote by a Frenchman, with a line in it as fits the occasion, and it goes: 'all for one and one for all,' and friends, if needful I aim to be that one. And now let's be goin'! If we do some sure-nuff ridin' we should make Lewiston sometime to-morrow."

And thus it was that in the slumbering heat of next day four dusty horsemen came riding into Lewiston; this frontier community that had grown so rapidly from lawless mining camp of tents and shacks, to the present dignity, solid comfort and ordered respectability of a city and capital of the so rich and immense State of Idaho. Its pioneer makeshifts had given place to well-built homes; its wide main street boasted numerous more or less ornate hotels, office buildings and thriving stores, with stage and telegraph office, and one or two prosperous-looking banks.

But just now, the hour being high noon, Lewiston lay drowsing in the sunglare; upon the porch-rails of house and hotel the boots of divers citizens exposed themselves upon the languorous feet of their slumberous owners asprawl in chairs. But high and clear above all other sounds of drowsy life rose the shrill and joyous clamour of children who, scornful of temperature, scampered and gambolled in the wide, dusty street.

"Doggone me!" exclaimed Mr. Tutt, reining up before the first hotel. "Doggone my whiskers if them innocent voices hain't sweet music in my y-ears!"

"Yes," answered Anthony gazing wistfully at this uproarious company of very small citizens. "Children seem scarce in this mighty West . . . perhaps one of those little folk yonder may be . . . our grandchild, eh George?"

"And somewhere hereabouts . . . my daughter . . . perhaps . . . my lost Virginia . . . perhaps!"

"Speakin' personal," said Cherokee, dismounting to secure his horse to the hitching-rail, "the first thing intimated is—a drink!"

"And a bath!" added Anthony.

"A talk wi' the town Sheriff!" quoth Noah.

"Tend the horses!" sighed George.

This being beyond all or any argument, off rode they to the city livery stables, themselves to care for the proper comfort and refreshment of their animals. Thence to the largest hotel where Anthony secured accommodation for them all; and it seemed the fame and name of 'The Master' had reached even here, thus service was instant and of the best. Insomuch that Mr. Tutt, having discarded his quid outside, was moved to speech:

"By Jing, Ant, money plus position shore talks an' is a power! Come you in reach of a telegraph an' you're a reg'lar dumswizzled po-tentate,—yessir!"

"The telegraph!" repeated Anthony. "Yes, by Jingo,

there should be news waiting for me, I hope! . . . But first—soap and water!"

Thus after some while, bathed, shaven and mightily refreshed Anthony hastened across to the telegraph office (this new marvel) and there found a message reading thus:

"Anthony Falconbridge. . . . To be called for. According to your orders have equipped three waggons with all necessaries and competent nurse for mother and child. Starting to-day and hope to reach Fort Benton by the 3rd, when shall wait further instructions how and where to meet you. Marchdale. General Lee's surrender expected any day."

With this telegram was a letter transported all these weary thousands of miles by stagecoach and pony express, a letter which he carried unopened to the seclusion of his bedroom and there, seated beside the open window, he read this, the second letter he had ever received from Bethulia Ann:

"Your long and very Anthony Three-ish letter reached me just before our guns began firing in this last battle which I think, and humbly pray God, may indeed be the last of this long and cruel war. So I read it first with the horrible thunder of artillery in my ears, this your very first letter and, reading it hurriedly, loved it—almost. But since then I have read it much more carefully (having little else to read, sir). You see I was hurt a little in the battle and was in hospital. So I read your letter again, such a long letter, and tried to picture you writing it by fits and starts, now by some camp-fire, now jotting down a part while halted on the dreadful trail which you describe so vividly. But your letter is more vivid in other parts, revealing you to my feminine perceptions, sir, with such complete masculine unconsciousness that sometimes I have felt indignant and sometimes I have laughed. For this letter is various as yourself. In parts you write me like an extremely prim and proper spinster aunt penning platitudes for behoof of a bread-and-butter niece, or as a very ancient, hoary greybeard to a tiny, though feminine, tot. . . . Oh Anthony Three! But sometimes your pen runs away with you (bless it!) and then you show to a very understanding woman so much of your great, lonely heart that she dares to know even more.

"Poor yearning heart, how unutterably lonely it is! As for B.A. (myself) she has seen and endured so much these last years that she is now far, oh far older than her years and in some ways more knowing and much more ancient than the dominating person and spoiled boy I call Anthony Three."

He had reached thus far when he was interrupted by a loud knock on the door and sighing impatiently, closed his letter and cried "Come in!" Whereat entered Mr. Tutt closely followed by Cherokee and a squat person chiefly remarkable for fiery whiskers, sharp eyes and rawhide boots with enormous Mexican spurs.

"Ant," said Mr. Tutt, seating himself on the bed, "meet Sandy McIver, sheriff o' Lewiston, which Sandy, bein' friend of Cherokee you may reckon one hundred per cent an' aces up. Sheriff, this is my other pardner, Mr. Anthony Falconbridge, o' N'York an' other places East."

"Prood tae ken ye, sir," said Mr. McIver gripping hands, "your name is familiar. I'm hoping ye'll be findin' oor toon o' Lewiston, forbye it's a city, no sae verra wild as ithers I could name."

"Indeed," answered Anthony, smiling, "it seems a very haven of peace and does you credit, Sheriff."

"Well, it's no juist pairfect, sir, but we're no sae bad, we've had nobody shot here in two, three weeks,— not properly shot, ye'll understand. But though law rides this toon high, wide an' handsome, we hae oor troubles, there's several neckin' Valley Tan at this meenit, especially a quarterbreed as calls himsel' Pancho Sims been liquorin' up and heftin' his colt-gun since 'long aboot eleven o'clock a.m. an' the cause I suspicions is a telegram from Bannack."

"Which telegram," added Cherokee, "at my suggestion, Sandy had the clerk read over to us, whereof I takes a copy, an' it says this: 'To Pancho Sims, Lewiston. Cherokee riding in with three bandits. Warn sheriff or get them, especially tall dark one called George, two-gun killer. Attend to him personal then return Bannack. By order.'"

"And where," demanded Anthony, starting up from his chair, "what of George?"

"Settin' on the porch," answered Cherokee, "looking the town in the face through the smoke of a see-gar."

"And I reckon," quoth Mr. Tutt, rising, "them steaks I ordered 'll be waiting. Comin', Ant?"

"No, I'll be down later, I've an important letter, needs my attention."

"Why then don't go rovin' the streets casual, not any, Ant, I suspicion that telegram means more trouble."

"And," sighed Mr. McIver, shaking his whiskers, "all my deppities happen to be awa'!"

"Well, let's eat!" quoth Mr. Tutt, leading the way; whereupon, so soon as the door had closed on the Sheriff's clanking spurs, back went Anthony to his letter:

"The war, really and truly, is nearly over. General Lee's army of half-starved, ragged heroes, outnumbered twenty to one, is completely surrounded at last and Lee is faced with annihilation or surrender. So I returned to my house in New York, soon as they let me out of hospital, and reading in the newspapers some account of your travels, I called on your sister, Miss Adela. She told me your faithful Marchdale was in Chicago, fitting out an expedition to meet you and your recovered Virginia and grandchild.

So to Chicago went I and, to poor Marchdale's dismay, declared myself in, and am travelling with this expedition towards you now, yes indeed, sir, even while you read these words! So Anthony Three, after such busy years, we are to see each other—soon. And I thrill with expectation to see what changes time has wrought. You, of course, will be much younger, I suppose a very hardy, tanned, young man who will find poor B.A. old—very, very old, and paler, thinner (not too much) yet more consciously alive than ever she was—oh, and with one of her 'beautiful white arms'—which you deigned once to notice in these very words,—just as white (thank Fortune!) though scarred by a minie bullet.

"And now, poor, solitary man, knowing how bitterly you are yearning for this grandchild, to succeed you someday, and to fill your empty heart to-day, I end with a prayer you will find him and his gentle mother, and that I shall hold him close in my arms because someday he may become your Anthony Five.

"Yours now and ever

"BETHULIA ANN."

For some time he sat looking down at this signature so boldly written yet with no unnecessary flourishes and in his dreamful eyes an unwonted tenderness; then starting up as on hot impulse, he took paper and pen and began to write:

"Oh woman,—my dear, in your written words you show me the actual spirit of Womanhood, comforting, tender, yet so vital and alluring that I am inspired to dream like a youth,—wildly, wonderfully, so that I tremble; till, striving to draw nearer I awake and am lost in fearful doubts because, despite my reawakened youth, my hair is grey with nearly double your years. And yet in all those years, never, no never have I felt so eagerly young, so passionate with and for life as now,—"

"Tchah!" he exclaimed and snatching up what he had written, wrenched and tore it in fierce hands. Then taking another sheet of paper he began again:

"MY DEAR AND ONLY ANN,

"To know that you are so unexpectedly near fills me with a complexity of emotions, and one of these anxiety lest the ardours of such journey should prove too much for you and so lately out of hospital, such silly, madcap whim and yet so gloriously like you. I hope it may benefit your youth only half as much as it has revitalized my age, child. We reached Lewiston at noon to-day where I hope to find certain news at least of our fugitives. Thus one half of this great journey is accomplished and has been, with the exception of one or two incidents, not so eventful as fiery Imagination painted. For, despite my age and experience of life, I am a very dreamer, the kind of self-deluder who visions for himself all that he has missed in life, those deep and breath-taking joys that, though I have been husband and father, have passed me by. And this my tragedy—that I should have found the perfection of my dreams—too late! A woman, of course, a face, form and intellect all that I dreamed and sought in my too young manhood and finding not, soothed and hid my bitter disillusion in many traffics, creating a world that I could dominate, a life that I might order how I would. And yet at forty-four years of age, and so very much older by experience, I am a dreamer still.

"And, you were wounded, and from all you leave unsaid I think death must have come very near you . . . had you died the world would have been darkened to one man's eyes. As to your arm—did I, despite the cold restraint of my seniority, dare so speak? And is it badly scarred, my dear? So shall its beauty seem more lovely and this scar a place for my most reverent—"

"Damnation!" he exclaimed, and frowning at this letter, tore it up as before, and essayed a third:

"MY DEAR BETHULIA ANN,

"Rode into Lewiston this noon after a fairly uneventful journey, all of us, like our horses, in prime condition and none more so than your humble servant. I believe my fugitives are in this town and am about to turn it upside down to their discovery. But before doing so, I write to thank you, my dear, for the comfort of your precious letters and to endeavour, vainly I fear, to express with what strangely delicious trepidation I look forward to our meeting. To see you again! To hear your voice—"

"Damme, I'm bewitched!" exclaimed Anthony, and had just scored out these last two lines with furious pen-strokes, when the door opened and George stood looking at him, and in his eyes such pain, such abysmal grief, that Anthony rose, not daring to question him. And when they had viewed each other thus for a long, tense moment, George spoke and his voice seemed smoothly soft as ever:

"She's dead, suh! I know at last . . . my Virginia is dead. . . . But I've brought yuh . . . this." And, stepping forward, he held out a slip of worn and crumpled paper; now taking this, Anthony saw it was a licence of marriage between Anthony Falconbridge, bachelor, aged twenty-one, and Virginia Sibella Charteris, aged twenty-two; and looking in these names and record of their ages so pitifully short, all he found to say was:

"I'm glad . . . very glad!" Then folding this paper, he laid it beside his unfinished letter.

George closed the door and crossing to the window, leaned there, with bowed head averted, and presently found speech again:

"Have you nothing else to say to me, Falconbridge?"

"No, Charteris."

"And it's like yuh, suh, to take it so quietly . . . not one word of reproach . . . no least show of triumph, and this . . . makes me only the mo' humble, and . . . comforts me, suh. Yuh see I know at last beyond all doubt my Virginia is dead . . . of hardship on the journey here . . . they buried her on the trail . . . one of those lonely graves we passed was . . . hers. . . ." Here the soft voice faltered woefully and was dumb; but Anthony stood mute also, and presently George went on again:

"She was my daughter but also . . . yo' son's wife! And therefo' suh, I ask yo' pardon very humbly that I ever doubted yo' honourable dead, the son yuh grieve as I my daughter—"

Then Anthony spoke at last, but in voice so harsh, so broken, that George turned and saw a face convulsed with a grief more bitter even than his own:

"God forgive me . . . it is I am humbled, Charteris, I who should plead forgiveness for I . . . hold myself responsible for their dying! It was my cursed arrogance and pride drove them to their deaths . . . your sweet daughter . . . my own brave son—" He choked, his head drooped, his hands clasped and wrung each other until they were seized by other hands that gripped and held them fast, hands of grieving man striving to comfort his fellow.

"Forget the past!" said George. "Take comfort in the thought that our children are still—together. Can yuh believe this, Anthony . . . a life eternal?"

"With all my heart, George. It is my one consolation . . . now!"

"Why then," murmured George with unwonted fervour, "I'm hoping these children of ours are together now . . . in a happier life. And because of this hope, I'm asking yuh to make their memory a bond between us . . . of friendship, Anthony."

"Yes," he answered, deeply moved. "Yes, it shall be, and forever!"

"This means beyond death!" said George, with his

rare, wistful smile. Then giving the hands he held a hearty shake, he turned back to the window again, while Anthony gazed down upon the crumpled marriage licence and with his eyes thus intent, spoke:

"Did you find our grandchild, George?"

"No, he was playing somewhere about the streets. Mrs. Hoyt is out looking fo' him now with Noah and Cherokee."

"Then let us go help them, shall we, George?"

"Why ye-e-s," he answered, moving to get a better view of something in the street below, "yes, we'll go but . . . not just yet. There's a small matter I must attend to first. So finish yo' letter, Anthony. I'll come back fo' yuh."

"My letter can wait."

"But Anthony Ah'm . . . asking yuh. And I'll be back . . . soon I guess." So saying George crossed to the door, smiled, nodded and was gone. So Anthony sat down again to finish his letter, but had not written many lines before he was startled by the terrified screaming of a child, so very sudden and near that he rose and leaning from the window saw that he was never to forget: George stood facing a man who, crouched low, menaced him with revolver levelled across the shoulder of a struggling child clutched to him in brutish hug; and George's guns were out, but for once these unerring, deadly weapons were silent and useless, and seeing the reason, Anthony leapt to the corner where stood his rifle, but even as he seized and cocked it, heard the report of a shot; then he was back at the window, had levelled his weapon and dwelling a breathless moment upon his aim, fired. George's assailant, in the act of shooting him again, started up convulsively, dropped the child and plunged head foremost into the dust; but George was upon his knees and sinking.

Anthony sped from the room and down the stair, thrusting aside all such as barred his way, and running with great strides, came where lay George coughing in weak, horrible manner and sprinkling the white road with blood so vividly bright that Anthony groaned in a fearful despair while, gently as possible, he lifted this drooping head to pillow it on his breast and hearken to a feverish, breathless muttering:

"The li'l child, Anthony . . . fetch the . . . child. I . . . couldn't—"

"No no," murmured Anthony, settling him more comfortably, "There, old fellow, are you easier?"

"Yes, but . . . the child! Let . . . someone bring the li'l child."

"George, don't . . . don't try to speak . . . yet!" said Anthony, striving desperately to check the life that bubbled between George's lips. "Hush, man . . . don't talk."

"Must, because . . . going soon, Anthony and . . . the child . . . that's why I couldn't . . . shoot. Now let some of . . . these folks get me . . . the child—"

"D'ye hear?" cried Anthony harshly, glancing swiftly up and around at the ring of staring faces that already hemmed them in. "Good God, can't some of you, one of you, bring him the child? And somebody fetch a doctor, hurry—hurry!"

Then the murmurous crowd swayed, parted and Noah came striding up like a wild man, and, behind him, Cherokee with the sobbing child in his arms.

"How come, George old pardner, how come?" cried Noah, gazing down on his stricken friend with grim visage all convulsed with passionate grief. "Did some dam buzzard git you in the back?"

"No, I had him . . . covered, Noah, but . . . the child, I couldn't. Ah, Cherokee, show . . . look, Anthony, look, this li'l man has . . . yo' golden eyes . . . look!"

Now glancing at this terrified child, Anthony saw he was indeed staring with wide, tawny eyes. Then heard George's gasping voice, fainter now, though glad:

"Our grandchild, Anthony . . . our grandchild,

surely . . . call him . . . Anthony, Noah, George . . . in memory—"

Settling himself more cosily, George pillowed his cheek on Anthony's breast, murmuring faintly:

"Ah'm going, Anthony . . . to prove our belief and . . . find our children . . . I hope. . . ." Then, sighing deeply, he closed his eyes sleepily nor stirred to Noah's harsh cry, nor heeded Anthony's tears that wetted his pale cheek; for silent, brooding George had himself passed—out and away into the Great Silence.

CHAPTER XII

TELLS HOW THEY LEFT LEWISTON

ANTHONY, fifth of that name, clung to the worn petticoats of this small, grey-haired, haggard woman who was the only mother he had to remember, and, from this secure haven, stared up fearfully at the tall, bronzed man whose yearning arms were reached out to him; and seeing this man's look was all imploring gentleness, the child therefore grew bold enough to frown, but shrank still further away.

"Ye see, sir," little Mrs. Hoyt explained in nervous apology, "the poor lamb's still scared, an' no wonder, him bein' mixed up in that double killin' yesterday."

"Yes," sighed Anthony, "yes, I suppose so. But I . . . I rather hoped he would not be afraid of . . . me."

"Why, Mr. Falconbridge sir, the poor mite's that sensitive! He'll need to learn your ways, I guess . . . an' besides he's a bit backward-like in his talk."

"Mrs. Hoyt I have tried to express something of my deep gratitude for your faithfulness and unswerving devotion to my son and his wife, but——"

"Lord, sir, me and my poor John would ha' done anything for Mr. Anthony . . . and her . . . so sweetly patient to the very hour of her death, dear, sweet lady."

"Death!" repeated Anthony, bitterly. "It seems to have been all about me! And I so well and strong! But you, Mrs. Hoyt . . . for you my gratitude is beyond any words. . . . I have arranged an annuity that should make you comfortable for life, should you need more, at any time, you have but to mention it.

. . . No, no, please don't thank me, I can never repay you adequately for your devotion to my son . . . and daughter——" A loud rapping interrupted him and round the crazy, ill-fitting door, a woeful visage peered.

"'S me!" said Cherokee, "an' I'm wantin' yore advice."

"What now?" demanded Anthony, stepping into the noon heat.

"Friend Noah! He's up yonder in the cemetery, campin' by George's grave—and I don't like his looks."

"What, is he ill?"

"Come an' take a peek. Ye see, Anthony, he's talking to George as if he was still alive." Reaching this grim, unlovely place, they beheld, seated beside a newly-raised mound, Mr. Tutt, who saluted them cheerily.

"So here's the four on us again," said he. "Old George has gone plumb silent, but then he never was a chatty sort o' cuss—nossir! These is his guns, I'm totin' them from now on . . . the guns as never missed nor failed till this yere grandchild o' yourn injects hisself into the scenery so onexpected, and George, bein' George,—takes it! An' now me, bein' me, an' kinda fond of him, is jest a-waitin' the chance to go find him across the Great Divide. . . . Don't kinda seem nat'ral-like—me here an' no George."

"You're wrong, Noah, you're quite wrong!" said Anthony gently, and yet speaking with the utmost conviction, "George has risen beyond death and is more alive than ever. Indeed he is so vital still, that I can feel his presence beside me now."

"No, Ant, no! When a man's dead he's dead . . . put inta a hole an' there's the end. Well, George was put inta a hole . . . yesterday or to-day was it . . . or a year ago? Anyways, all as I ever knowed o' George is a layin' under this yere heap o' dirt, an' it do come hard-like t' leave th' darn ol' cuss!" Here Mr. Tutt patted this heap of new-turned earth with lean, brown hand while his eyes held such stricken look that Cherokee turned away and Anthony felt the sting of painful tears.

"Noah," said he, sitting down beside this man whose grief seemed beyond all consolation, "you were George's one loved and trusted friend, but only a little while before he . . . passed, George honoured me with his friendship, too—"

"I'm glad o' that, Ant, I'm mighty glad . . . you know now that he was a . . . man!"

"He was indeed, Noah, and one who had faith to believe in a life beyond the grave."

"Which shore needs a mighty faith, Ant, such blind faith as reason and intelligence mocks at, yessir!"

"Yet, Noah, perhaps Faith sees more than ever may coldly logical Reason and so can lead us when stumbling Reason fails."

"Mebbeso, Ant. But all as I'm sure on is that George is layin' there, four feet under my hand . . . they buried him shaller—"

"And I'm just as certain that George is alive, a vital presence for good. . . . I tell you I feel him near us now, I think I always shall. And I believe he will ride on with us the rest of this hazardous journey to see us safely through."

"Ay, George never was a quitter. So mebbe yo're right Ant. . . . an' we'll shore be needin' him by all accounts. And I guess the sooner we're back-trailin' the better. Let's get goin'." But as they rose to leave this ill-tended graveyard, they beheld the Sheriff approaching, and Mr. McIver's hairy visage showed moist and anxious and his huge spurs jingled loudly with his haste.

"Hech, sirs," said he breathlessly, "I'm here tae warn ye, they're here! Plumer's gunmen is juist rode in, six of 'em frae Bannack, harrd cases all on 'em. Sirrs, this bein' a peaceful toon and myself shorrt-handed, my airnest advice tae ye is—git!"

"Certainly!" said Anthony, glancing about them anxiously. "But where? We can't take the road back through Bannack—"

"Na na! My advice is—strike out across the desert

. . . two days o' hard riding North East an' ye should reach a settlement in the foothills called Medicine Bow, three days beyond that is Helena. And sirrs I'm bidding ye hurry. These Bannack killers'll be oot gunning for ye so soon as they've liquored up sufficient."

"Noah . . . Cherokee, what's your advice?"

"Well, Ant, if George was along, I'd say shoot it out wi' these polecats seein' they're only six; as it is, I reckon it's the desert for us."

"'S all one to me!" nodded Cherokee.

"Then will you and the Sheriff see our horses saddled while I send a telegram. Come, Noah!" Mr. Tutt tightened his gunbelts, took off his hat and looked down at George's grave.

"George," said he hoarsely, "old pardner, yore sperrit may be with us like Ant says, which I'm shore hopin' powerful it is,—but yore body's a-layin' there and, old pardner,—now mind, I'm tellin' ye for the first and last time,—I reckon there never was a man like you . . . also, I got yore guns an', George, I aim to live an' die worthy of 'em. An' now it's us for the home trail an', whether you come a-ridin' a ghost along with us or lays there asleep till Kingdom Come, I'm wishin' ye all the best in life and death, an'—so long!"

Then they turned and hastened their several ways; but reaching the wide street, Mr. Tutt paused, to say:

"Which I notice, Ant, as you ain't heeled . . . well, I'm wearin' two guns as was ever the fastest and most acc'rate East or West o' the Rockies an' they gotta be kept so."

At this slumberous hour the telegraph office was deserted and here, while Mr. Tutt sat pensive in a corner, Anthony scribbled full particulars of his change of route for Marchdale's direction with a warm message of greeting for Bethulia Ann.

The sleepy telegraph clerk checked the message through, Anthony paid the charge and then, to his amazement, saw the clerk, suddenly very dreadfully awake, cower to his knees and glancing round to know the reason, came face to face with a man who stared at him through slitted eyes above the shot-gun he was slowly raising.

"I reckon you'll shore 'nuff be one o' them!" quoth this man, and said no more, for Mr. Tutt, unheeded in his corner, had gone into swift action with both guns; two thunderous reports and the man lay a crumpled heap.

"Send that message—at once!" cried Anthony to the dazed and blinking telegraph clerk and stepping across his would-be slayer, saw four other armed men running towards him up the street; but once again Mr. Tutt, saying no word, ringed himself in smoke, firing rapidly from either hip and so truly that three of these assailants went down in as many moments and the fourth limping for safety, when Cherokee appeared with the horses.

"Up!" he cried. "Up an' ride for yore lives!"

But as they swung to saddle pandemonium broke out behind them, clatter of feet, fierce outcries, the quick reports of firearms.

"Mrs. Hoyt's shack—spur!" cried Anthony, and up the echoing street they rode like a whirlwind.

CHAPTER XIII

SOME DESCRIPTION OF SUFFERING AND A GREATER DEVOTION

LEWISTON had vanished in the haze behind them and the sun was low when, easing up his horse, Anthony glanced round about and spoke:

"I thought Cherokee meant to ride with us."

"He did so, Ant. But he can't, seein' as he got hit that last crack they took at us."

"I hope not seriously."

"To which I says 'amen', Ant! An' another thing,—we're goin' to do without the best part of our outfit an' some o' them comforts you bought for . . . young Tony there."

"What d'you mean, Noah?"

"That our pack-hoss is hit too an' failin' rapid. Ease up. An'—one other thing—"

"What more, in God's name?"

"Yore own hoss has ketched it likewise—"

So perforce they halted and found the pack-horse injured indeed beyond recovery; and so when they had transferred what they might of its burden to their own animals, Noah shot it and turned to examine Anthony's horse, whose wound he pronounced likely to heal with proper care and attention, while Anthony Five, a small shape in a Navajo blanket, watched great-eyed, whimpering fitfully.

Then, having consulted their compass, they mounted and rode on again north-easterly until came evening with a rising moon to light them.

"I'm wondering," said Mr. Tutt, pensively, after

some while, "if we shall happen on any water in this hell-fired country?"

"Why worry, Noah? We have a plenty, Cherokee saw to that."

"We had, Ant. But we were shore plumb unlucky makin' our exit,—ye see the shot as ketched our pack-horse, holed our biggest canteen, so we'll be on short rations till we find us water."

At this dire news Anthony glanced down at the precious bundle on the saddle before him and clasping his small namesake and heir more tenderly, set his jaw, but uttered no word.

Silently they rode on, knee to knee, ever deeper into the desolation of these 'badlands' until the moon was high in the heavens, on and on through a ghostly, brooding solitude until in a place of rocks apt to defence, Anthony drew rein.

"How about camping here, Noah?"

"Soots me! I'll doctor yore horse while you tends yore grandson."

"He's asleep at last, thank Heaven! So I——" But here Anthony Five began to kick and struggle, filling the air with his lamentations while Anthony, rocking him in cherishing arms, strove vainly to quiet and comfort him.

"Li'l fellow don't seem to cotton none to the desert, Ant, and no wonder."

"I guess he needs feeding . . . or, God help me! Perhaps he is in pain," said Anthony, a little wildly. "Mrs. Hoyt said something about 'spasms' . . . what d'you think, Noah?"

"Try feeding him."

"Why then, hold him. Mrs. Hoyt boiled some milk and stuff, catch hold of him while I find it."

"Not me, Ant! 'Sides I gotta doctor this yere four-legged animile."

"Well, hold this two-legged one a moment."

"But I hain't used t' fosterin' children none at all—"

"Take him!" Awkwardly enough, Noah complied,

whereupon Anthony Five, instantly mute, reached up two small hands to grasp Mr. Tutt's whiskers and, evidently soothed by the feel of them, smiled up into the face that now smiled down on him.

"By Ding, Ant, yore young Tony's took to me amazin'! —with both hands!" And when Anthony, acting upon Mrs. Hoyt's reiterated directions, had prepared his grandson's meal, they contrived to feed him between them, which done, Anthony took him in cradling arms to hush him to sleep whereat this small rebel kicked and wailed and sobbed anew.

"Tony want ba-ba!" he cried. "Oh ba-ba!"

"God bless me!" exclaimed his agitated grandsire. "D'you think he's ailing, Noah?"

"I'm kinda wondering what he means by this yere ba-ba, Ant."

"Heaven only knows! Perhaps a pet name for Mrs. Hoyt. . . . Hush, Anthony little son! Hush now, cuddle down, little man . . . ! Lord, he can howl!"

"I'm kinda wonderin'," repeated Noah, turning from his completed surgery, "if he might be meanin' . . . these yere whiskers o' mine?"

"Try him, man—let's try him." Once again Noah took the child and lo! once again up went those little eager, clutching hands, and Anthony Five, smiling, was hushed and presently fell asleep on Mr. Tutt's wide breast; who now gazing down upon the small, lovely face, spoke in a tender murmur never heard from his grim lips before:

"Doggone me, Ant, but I shore think there must be a powerful lot o' George in this grandson o' yourn! Anyways, I've took to him con-siderable. . . . Though Noah's certainly one hell of a name for such a pretty li'l creetur. . . ."

"It will be his name anyway!" said Anthony, now preparing their own supper. "George, Noah, Anthony, as George himself suggested."

Supper done, they examined their horses very heedfully, took stock of what was left of their provisions, more especially their water supply and, estimating how long it must last them and their animals, agreed on a daily ration.

"And from now on, Ant, we cuts out all ablootions —yessir!"

They were up and away in the dawn, through a waste of sand where nothing grew save scant patches of soap-weed or grease-wood, a glaring desolation with here jagged rocks, great boulders or stretches of choking, gleaming alkali dust.

Sunglare and blinding dazzle, stifling heat and growing thirst all day long and, by night, a stealthy wind from far distant mountain ranges to chill them with presage of death: yet ever and always thirst that plagued them waking, that haunted their troubled slumbers and grew upon them always until it was a raging torment, that through the burning day, cracked their lips and swelled their tongues; yet needs must they deny themselves, for the horses must drink to be their salvation, and the child must have no stint lest his feeble life flicker and go out.

So these silent men suffered and endured until came that tragic moment when Anthony's horse, more deeply hurt than either had dared suggest to the other, swerved, faltered and went down beneath him.

Speechless at such catastrophe, Anthony gazed on this poor, dying creature and from this to his little grandson cradled in Noah's bridle-arm, and, licking cracked lips, he broke the long silence.

"Lord . . . Lord help us, Noah, what d'you say to this?"

"Be a savin' of water!" croaked Mr. Tutt.

"Noah . . . by God, you teach me fortitude! Come now, let us all drink and heartily for once." So when with merciful shot, Anthony had ended his horse's misery, they sank down in the shade of a great, overhanging rock and there drank of their precious water more abundantly than they had dared and with a sublime joy no words might ever tell. Then, with

Anthony Five very lively between them, they took their midday meal, nor stirred until the day's heat was somewhat abated.

Up at last and on again but very slowly now since while one rode, the other must trudge afoot, ploughing wearily through yielding sand or stumbling painfully over unseen, rocky tracts and ledges.

Thus, with every toilsome hour their peril increased and Death crept nearer as they struggled on through this cruel desolation, this monotonous never-ending waste that seemed to bring them nowhere. Until upon an evening they sat leaning against a great boulder, almost too spent to eat, moistening their parched lips with the few swallows of water that seemed only to make their consuming thirst the more tormenting.

Now as they sat thus, seldom speaking, slow moving, like the dying men they were, often their smarting eyes were turned towards vast misty shapes vague and dreamlike with distance yet tipped just now with glory by the sun's last rays; and with his yearning gaze turned thither, Noah spoke:

"Them mountings don't seem to come no nearer, Ant . . . watched 'em all day, I have. I'm beginning to think, if some miracle don't happen purty soon, this'll be the end of the trail for we-uns, pardner."

"Yes, Noah. The Wilderness is beating us at last . . . killing us by inches, and I . . . I am to blame!"

"No no, doggone it—"

"Yes!" said Anthony, all his bitter self-scorn and fierce condemnation finding utterance at last. "Looking back on the past I can see how my own pride of will has cursed me. . . . A blind fool, Noah, that drove my son to death . . . killed George, and now . . . my little grandson, this innocent! In my stubborn pride I sowed the wind and in my present torment of body and anguish of mind, I am reaping the whirlwind . . . My son Anthony, his gentle wife, George, you, the child! Was ever remorse more bitter than mine?"

Here Anthony struggled to his feet and went limping to and fro until his passion of grief had spent itself; then Noah beckoned to enquire how much water they had left.

"Just about enough for one more day, I guess."

"And them mountings is purty far," sighed Noah. "Two days, I reckon—"

"Say three," groaned Anthony.

"Say two days an' a bit! An there's water aplenty there, Ant, cool streams a-flowin' . . . waters o' life. . . ."

"And beyond our reach!" said Anthony bitterly, stooping to peer down at the sleeping child.

"Well, mebbe some miracle will happen, Ant, yes . . . mebbe I guesso! Waters . . . o' life! It's powerful comfortin', this yere belief in a life . . . beyond death, Ant."

"For you and me, Noah, yes," sighed Anthony laying his hand very tenderly on the small sleeper, "but this little soul has . . . scarcely lived."

"Ah!" nodded Noah, "so I'm thinkin' the little feller should be given a chance. You an' me, we've had our share o' life, Ant, you bein' forty-three—"

"Forty-four, Noah."

"An' I'm sixty-two, or three, never could be shore which. Anyways, I've certainly lived, though a lonesome cuss ever an' always, except for George . . . that's why I'm kinda missin' the ol' son of a gun so constant. But it's a great idee, Ant, to believe as he's riz into eternal life an' is waitin' somewhere to greet his ol' pardner—"

"And me too, Noah, I hope and pray."

"Why shore you too, Ant! An' what a meetin' it's agoin' to be . . . the three of us! What a shakin' of hands! What a slappin' o' backs . . . by Jing, Ant, doggone me if I ain't growin' all worked up and impatient. . . . And I reckon you should reach them mountings in two days easy."

"With one day's water, Noah!"

"Ay but, I'm tellin' ye, p'raps along'll come this yere miracle. So cheer up, pardner, I gotta kinda feelin' as we'll win out yet!" So saying, Noah set one long arm about Anthony's drooping, disconsolate figure, then grasping his hand, sat thus silent a while. At last, laughing a little oddly he rose, saying:

"Sleep's the word, Ant. Get us some shuteye, let's hit the hay. I reckon it's kinda good to sleep . . . specially at such a doggone, dingbusted time as this yere. . . . So good night, pardner, an' dream as happy as you can."

Wrapped in their blankets down they lay, the moon very bright above them, Noah to sink at once into profound slumber, or so it seemed, Anthony to listen enviously to his deep breathing, to plague himself anew with bitter self-reproaches and fevered rush of anxieties and fears, now thinking curses on himself, now sighing prayers for his little grandson until at last his wearied body relaxed and upon his woeful mind crept the sweet oblivion of sleep.

He awoke suddenly in a grey dawn, his ears yet ringing with some fugitive sound, and sat up to blink drowsily; then started to his feet, broad awake and ran where lay Noah, arms wide-tossed, one of George's guns clutched in right hand, a crumpled paper in the other.

Sinking on his knees beside this motionless form, Anthony lifted his eyes to the dawn and striving to pray, choked in his grief.

"Noah!" he gasped. "Oh . . . friend. . . ."

Now as he crouched thus, the sun rose, making a glory all about them. And after some while, he drew the paper from these dead fingers and half-blinded by scalding tears read these hastily scrawled words:

"Dear Ant, with my horse and what's left of the water you will make out all right, with George an' me to help, for if there is life, we're with you right through to the end. Anyways, good luck to you and the precious child. So long and Good-bye. N. Tutt.

"P.S. If you can manage me some sort of a grave, I'd like George's guns buried with me."

And when Anthony had walked some time, being desperate in his loneliness, he collected a pile of loose rock and boulders, and then set himself to dig a grave as well as he might; then gathering this good friend in his arms, held him close in long farewell, and thereafter laid him reverently in his last resting-place with hands upon the worn butts of George's two guns. So Anthony buried him and built a cairn above him; piling it high as possible and with every rock and boulder, praying for the strong, faithful, valiant soul of him; and so remained, heedless of time, until the child began to cry. Hurrying to his little grandson, Anthony took him up and found him very flushed and feverish.

And thus to grief was added fear lest this last Falconbridge should not endure, this precious little life be snatched from him and Noah's great sacrifice be all in vain. Therefore he spared some of the water to bathe this little hot face and fevered body,—with wordless supplications to that God Who, in this cruel waste and wide desolation shut in by dazzling sand and sky of brass, seemed so infinitely remote.

And when he had coaxed the child to eat, and all in vain, and suffered his gaunt horse to drink a few gasping swallows of this water that was their very life, he lifted his little, wailing grandson to the comfort of his arms, got to saddle and, with no backward glance at the solitary grave they were leaving, rode on toward those distant mountains that never seemed any nearer, glimmering dreamlike, taunting his eager sight . . . for life was there. And now he recalled Noah's words:

"There's water there, Ant! Cool streams a-flowin'! Waters o' life. . . ." It seemed almost that Noah was back, beside him again, speaking him brave words of comfort; so that, more than once as the long hours dragged by, he turned expectantly, but seeing only empty solitude and shimmering haze, began to mutter curses on these for tormenting hallucinations. Yet they persisted; he was haunted by visions of dim-seen faces, the echoes of remembered voices. . . . Haunted thus he rode on and ever on, losing all count of time. . . .

Sun and sand, heat and thirst, failing horse and failing strength and on his breast a child who moaned in fitful slumber or whimpered in fevered wakefulness. And thirst, ever and always thirst, the plaguing lust to drink; a ceaseless strife between dying body and resolute mind. . . . Travail, suffering and, lastly, the growing fear of approaching madness . . . these echoes, these glimmering faces seemed all about him, pressing nearer, filling this cruel waste, the very universe; until he made hoarse outcry at last in answer:

"George! Oh, George, if you are there . . . come near! Did you find our children? . . . Noah's followed you, so . . . if you are together now, by God you have the best of it! Come near, for I'm alone . . . and dying, George, dying . . . and our little grandson with me, unless you can do . . . something for us . . . you and Noah—"

Mountains whose jagged summits stabbed the hot void . . . sand, pitiless sun . . . and a moaning child who would not be hushed . . . And the water nearly exhausted.

Times of agonised suffering and wild despair; spells of sudden strange respite when, thirst and horror forgotten, he laughed and talked with George in a great and glad new friendship and listened to Noah's chuckling laugh . . . on and on until he was lying beside his dead horse and the water all gone. But the mountains were near, he could see the blessed green of shady trees . . . and Noah's cheery voice was in his ear:

"Cool streams a-flowin', Ant! Waters o' life! Up, pardner, up and live!"

So Anthony struggled to his feet and, clasping his small grandson and heir, hushed to sleep at last, went on again through pain and gathering darkness towards those mountains, stumbling through death towards life.

And it was just about now that Mr. Thomas Marchdale, descending the lower slopes of these mountains ahead of creaking waggons, began to stammer very nervously:

"I . . . Miss Ann . . . I always suspected . . . feared—" Here he turned from the bright eyes that watched him so kindly to glance back at the lumbering waggon-train. "Yes, I . . . I always had the . . . the dread that there might be . . . someone else, yet I dared hope . . . because this love of mine for . . . for you can never quite die . . . until I'm buried, and perhaps not even then."

"Dear Tom Marchdale," murmured Bethulia Ann, looking at his troubled face with eyes of tenderest compassion, "this is because you are such a man that I dare open my heart to you and tell you how I have loved him always . . . from the very first."

"Love's a . . . a mighty queer thing!" sighed poor Marchdale, his reverent, adoring eyes surveying this bewitching creature who rode beside him, all vital womanhood from windblown hair to the slim, dusty riding boot beneath her clinging, dusty habit.

"Heavens, Tom!" she exclaimed, a laugh in her eyes, "have you only just discovered this?"

"Why no," he answered, gravely, "I was thinking of . . . of The Master—"

"So am I!" she murmured.

"I was thinking, Miss Ann,—forgive me, but . . . The Master never seemed, to me at least, a man women could . . . love."

"Perhaps," said she, in the same tender voice, "this is why . . . a woman . . . does!"

"And will you tell me, Miss Ann . . . dare I ask . . . if he returns your love?"

"Why, of course!" she murmured, in voice tender as the look that made her eyes even more beautiful. "Yes, and has done so through these last weary years, very deeply, very intensely, though . . . being Anthony Three, he is quite unaware of it . . . yet."

"Un-aware of it?" stammered Mr. Marchdale.

"Or, if he has just discovered it, he will be profoundly shocked, of course."

"Shocked?" repeated Mr. Marchdale, faintly, and merely stared at the lovely smiling speaker whose dreamful gaze was on the distance, that vast barren waste below them that stretched away and away into a hazy infinitude.

"Look, yonder!" said she, suddenly alert, "surely there is something moving . . . there across the desert?"

"Why yes," answered Mr. Marchdale, reaching for his glasses, "Too small for a horse—"

"Let me look," said she, reining up. So she took the binoculars and sat very still to peer at that distant object.

"It's a man," said she at last, "a man with . . . something in his arms, but . . . he walks so . . . so strangely! There . . . he is down! Now he's struggling up again, but . . . Ah merciful God!" she cried and in that moment set her horse galloping so wildly that Mr. Marchdale cried out to her in panic, then spurred in desperate pursuit. . . . Headlong down the steep they rode, over the green levels and out across the trackless desert until, at last they saw:

A madman who shouted and raved and sang, whose bloodshot eyes glared left and right upon the empty air while dry tongue and cracked lips made dreadful, cheery, half articulate clamour:

"George . . . George, old fellow . . . Noah man, by God . . . we'll do it . . . yet—"

A terrible, half-naked wretch who clasped and cherished a dead child in his arms.

CHAPTER XIV

WHICH ENDS VOLUME TWO

GROANING with return of consciousness, Anthony opened his eyes to see himself in bed and Tom Marchdale's anxious face bent over him.

"So then," said he faintly, and surprised at his sense of deathly weakness, "we . . . . did it . . . . thank God!"

"You did, sir, thank God!" answered Marchdale, watching the speaker's haggard face and roving, eager glance apprehensively, "Though since we found you it's been touch and go, thought you'd have died in the waggon, sir, and I guess you would have but for . . . for Miss Ann. She's sleeping now . . . up with you all last night, sir . . . shall I call her?"

"No no. Fetch him, if . . . how is he?"

"He, sir? D'you mean—?"

"Him! My heir! The child two splendid men gave their lives to save. . . . I mean George, Noah, Anthony Falconbridge, God bless him . . . the last and latest of the name! How is he, Marchdale? Where is he? Is he asleep . . . is he well?"

"Why . . . yes sir, I . . . yes."

"Then let me see . . . the little man. Bid his nurse bring him to me, at once . . . d'ye hear?"

"Yes, Master. But . . . indeed . . . you see, sir, she's out . . . the nurse, I mean, and—"

"Out? With the child . . . my little George? Well, have them found instantly! I . . . must and will see my grandson. Go now! Damnation, man—go! Or must I—"

"No no, sir! You see, Master, I . . . what I'm

trying to . . . to tell you is . . . I think Miss Ann should see you first . . . she'll be so . . . so glad and . . . and besides she can tell you better than I . . . I mean, sir, being a woman and . . . considering you are still so . . . so very weak and . . . so forth. I . . . if you'll excuse me, I—"

But Anthony propped himself on feeble elbow and stared up into the speaker's averted face with eyes widening to horror and a blasting dread.

"Marchdale," he gasped, "Marchdale . . . look at me! Now, cease your stammering and tell me . . . my little grandson, is he . . . dead, too?"

'Sir, I . . . I cannot . . . Miss Ann should be here, for—"

"Answer me, Tom Marchdale! Has this precious life . . . been taken from me . . . also? Is he dead?"

"Yes, sir. God help you and—"

From Anthony's twitching lips came a sound between laugh and groan, terrible to hear; but with this heart-broken cry was another:

"Anthony! Oh my dear, my dear—!"

But with eyes fast shut, heedless of these cherishing arms and the yearning passion of these gentle eyes, he turned away, muttering between clenched teeth:

"Dead! And after . . . so much! Then God has deceived . . . mocked me! George and Noah suffered and died . . . in vain!"

So cried Anthony in a bitterness of soul far beyond the reach of any comfort or solace of tears, and hid his face and was dumb and heedless of all save fury of despair. For in his grandson's little grave was buried, it seemed, all his hope of the future, and he grieved to be alive. Also he yearned desperately for the strong, warm clasp of silent George's hand, the valiant, cheering voice of faithful Noah, and, knowing these lost to him, longed to share with them the eternal comradeship of death. . . .

But the Dark Angel will not always be bidden; and

thus, waking upon a day to a radiant sun, Anthony saw Bethulia Ann seated near, her shining head bent above some dainty garment she was making; but her needle was still and as he gazed upon her warm loveliness, a tear fell, sparkling; and when she had wept thus silently awhile, quite unaware of the eyes that watched her so eagerly, Anthony spoke:

"Ann . . . child, why are you crying?"

For a moment she neither moved nor spoke, then lifted her stately head with its shining coronet of bright hair to look at him through her tears.

"Need I answer this, Anthony?" she questioned, gently.

"Yes," he answered, leaning a little nearer, "yes, because I think you know I'm . . . fated to live. Death will have none of me, it seems."

"And this is the reason I am crying," she said, bowing her head again. "Because though I love you so, Anthony, yet all my love is not strong enough to make you even wish to live. I think indeed you are too old, much older than I thought, too old to ever know all the passion and pain and joy of a great love. . . . But, that I so deluded myself all these years, Anthony, this hurts me very much. Well, it is only natural, my dear, you are forty-six or seven and—"

"Forty-four," he corrected.

"Yet older than I deemed," she sighed, "and now your illness has aged you even more."

"Yes!" he muttered, "yes . . . at least I fear my hair is even greyer. But—"

"And so, dear Anthony Three, though I love you, as you know, it is such love shall ask no more than . . . merest friendship—"

"No!" said he, with something of his old masterfulness. "There can never be mere friendship for us, it must be all or nothing."

"So now," sighed she, busied with her needle again, "now that you are growing stronger, will you drive me from you, my poor, dear man?"

"I . . . couldn't!" he answered, in strange, choked voice. "I'm starving for you—"

The needle paused suddenly, then went on again, flashing to and fro, but very much at random.

"Starving for me?" she repeated softly. "You never let me suspect it, Anthony. . . . Oh why?"

"I was ashamed!" he answered with a humility she thought very pitiful. "Ashamed! I have proved myself such a failure, such . . . arrogant, blind fool! And yet I . . . dare to love you, Ann, and shall love you always. To look at you is my joy, to . . . touch you would be such happiness that I cannot—"

Away went her sewing and uttering a soft, broken cry, she was beside him upon her knees, looking at him above clasped hands with radiant eyes.

"Oh, Anthony Three," she murmured, "my Anthony, if you love me, need me so, I am here . . . for your arms! So take me, my own dear." So he drew her near, to hold her close, to smooth her bright hair and kiss it.

"That you should stoop to me!" he murmured. "You in your splendid youth and beauty . . . and I no more than . . . what I am—"

"Dear, silly man," she answered, nestling closer yet, "were you the poorest, crippled wretch I should love you. . . . Soon Love shall make you your own strong self again and then—"

"But now," he sighed, "now I am almost afraid! I have brought death on all those I most loved. . . . Death has seemed all about me—"

"But here is Life!" she answered, kissing him. "And if . . . if God is kind He may give us other lives . . . little lives to cherish, my Anthony. . . ."

BOOK THREE

BOOK THREE

On and upward, mounting from strength to strength, this new Republic has become a dominant race.

The message, penned so many years ago to be their own inspiration, the stated belief that Freedom and Happiness are the birthright of all, has become a trumpet call ringing across this troubled world, a glad rallying-cry for the poor distressed of mankind:

'Come all ye that are broken, destitute or grovelling beneath the heel of Tyranny, come ye now and learn, at last, the joy of living.'

And through the years they have come, an innumerable host of every creed, race and colour, fleeing to this Land of Promise to find their salvation; to live for it, die for it, and leave their children part of this great American Nation.

Freedom and Equality for all! And all such as prove fit and able have risen and achieved; for in this new land with its vast areas and incalculable natural riches and resources, room has been found for all men, and all such as are men indeed, have prospered.

But alien blood, ever-growing power and immense wealth have brought their attendant curses; for with national prosperity the hectoring giant Mammon has arisen to hustle into the background that old, reverent spirit of High Principle and Rectitude which inspired those devoted men who, long ago, framed the constitution of this Republic. But these men are long dead, their ideas old-fashioned, and therefore contemptible, their stern morality and the ideals for which they strive, are deemed utterly impracticable in this modern, hurry-scurry age,—more especially in the World of Business where material gain is the one and only aim, where money, instead of a means to an end is become The End to be obtained by any or every means.

So, instead of Integrity is Astuteness; instead of a Brotherhood of Commerce, business is waged like war wherein, according to the cowardly, cynical, old adage, 'all is fair.'

Thus, huge financial combines have come into being that, waging business without mercy or respite, have thriven exceedingly,—soulless, machine-like organizations that have builded them towering structures, veritable shrines of Mammon where men labour, slave-like, in offices lifted heavenward but with their every thought bent, very pertinaciously earthward, becoming themselves, in time, no more than so many working parts of these huge, money-churning machines.

And of these vast concerns no two more powerful or more bitterly antagonistic than those bearing the names of Falconbridge and de Witt, both engaged in a war, with drug and every commercial weapon, that in this ominous year of 1913 was to end in the triumphant aggrandisement of one and the utter destruction of the other. And who more remote from and apparently heedless of it all than the solitary, old creature, little regarded by any, these days; an old man long and long past his allotted span,—the bony, huddled shape of seeming decrepitude peering into the fire,—all that a century of years had left of Anthony Falconbridge the Third.

Of whom (if you will) you shall read—over the page; beginning there:

CHAPTER I

Of this Third and last Book

CHAPTER I

TELLS HOW A VERY AGED DREAMER WAKED

CROUCHED in his deep elbow-chair, gazing pensively into the fire that scarcely warmed his aged bones, sat old Anthony Falconbridge, third of the name. A frail and withered shape of time-worn humanity so long past the allotted span of life that he had become, for such as knew him, an ever-growing, awesome wonder, and, to the world in general, a curiosity.

Thus to-day, seated in his library, alone as usual, Old Anthony was gazing wistfully into the fire that burned winter and summer; so quiet was he and so very still that he might have been dead but for the gleam of his tawny eyes beneath their thick, white brows. Except for this one room the great house about him, like the world outside, had known many changes while the mighty River of Life, this ever-flowing, ever-broadening stream, bore him on and on through light and shadow, by foaming rapid and gloomy deep, a long, long journey with the heartbreak of many cruel partings,—loved faces that smiled and vanished:—on and ever on amid new scenes and other faces until to-day he sat an old, old man desolate and forlorn in this new world of speed and stress, alone with his deathless memories.

For here, in this unchanged room, surrounded by objects so long familiar, great desk, old-fashioned furniture and the ancient rifle in its niche above him, his aged eyes glimpsed visions of other days. . . .

A comely youth, bold and eager for life, and yet who stands, flushed and stammering while he fidgets nervously with a pair of well-used riding-gloves,—who drops them to lie unheeded and with last half-pleading, half-defiant look, turns and strides away . . . to death, to a nameless grave on a great battlefield. . . . Comes another vision, a shape of gay loveliness in dainty, full-skirted gown and furbelows, who laughs at and names him 'Dear Anthony Three.' So young, so lovely, this the mother of his two sons. . . . And all dead these many weary years. . . . Oh, sweet visions of the vanished long-ago, bright angels of a happier day, fading too soon, where are ye now—and one here so old, so weary and very lonely, one who cannot die,—where are ye now?

His old eyes grew misted, and closed to the smart of slow, painful tears.

'And yet while she lived, what joy in life! Truly the long years had not been all vain, or wholly barren.'

So now yearned Old Anthony the Third, this relic of the forgotten past, this creature of another age and world, whom Death had passed by and refused to gather in; a tall, lean, silent ancient who sat thus for ever staring on the fire, apparently quite lost in his memories, seldom speaking and so contemptuously heedless of the new world about him that he had ceased to count in the busy hurry-scurry of everyday life and was become just a solitary old man content with his dreams, whom nobody heeded very much these days; a figure of death-in-life, impotent and therefore—negligible. Yet the eyes of him beneath their thick, hoary pent of brows, were still bright and strangely vital; and never more so than upon this particular morning of early summer when the dreamer was to wake, the moribund to arise in new life, these nerveless old hands find strength to grasp the reins of Circumstance, yet once more, and thus guide the destinies and alter the lives of so many. . . .

Came a sudden rapping on the door, but Old Anthony never heeded; came one in horn-rimmed glasses, an earnest-faced youngish man from whose bosom a stethoscope protruded and whose long fingers grasped a small phial; the old man never moved:

"You, Penley?" he demanded, without glancing up.

"Yes, sir. I've brought your pills."

"Eh? Bills? Take 'em away, burn 'em, I don't want 'em!"

"Pills, sir!" repeated the young doctor more loudly, "your pills."

"Well, I don't want them either. Throw 'em on the fire!"

"But, sir, they are most necessary to your health, vital in fact, a heart stimulant! At your great age, your heart, sir, is—"

"My what?"

"Heart, sir—your heart—"

"My heart is strong and young as your own, Penley—younger! And will remain so in spite of physic and nostrums. I need no medicines, never did, and I'll not swallow 'em."

"Mr. Falconbridge, as your new resident physician and in constant attendance upon you of late, I can assure you that your heart . . . your stupendous age—"

"Resident fiddlestick, sir! I've no sooner rid myself of Stern than you descend upon me, and by whose order?"

"Your grand-daughter, sir, the Countess of Riderwood engaged me, at the earnest solicitude of an old friend of yours, a Mr. Keith, I believe."

"They should know better, especially Keith! He knows how I detest being fussed over."

"But, sir, it seems you are his first and chiefest consideration and of course quite rightly—"

"No, wrongly! Wrongly! I have set Keith in sole charge of great affairs . . . my representative . . . my mouth-piece, and Falconbridge Amalgamated must and shall come first with him. As for my grand-daughter, she should mother her own wilful children instead of pestering me with resident physicians, doctors and nurses, pills and potions,—as if I were a miserable invalid. . . . Rubbish!"

"If, sir . . . if," stammered the young doctor, fidgeting nervously with his horn-rims, "if you desire to be rid of me also—"

"I haven't said so—yet. Wait until I do. Good God, young man, don't look so distressed! Here, give me a pill or dose of physic . . . can't do me much harm! Eh, a pill? Very well. . . . Never mind the water. There! Well, what are you staring at?"

"Sir, I . . . I find you . . . rather amazing. At you great age such . . . such enormous vitality is almost . . . unearthly . . . superhuman!"

"Nonsense, boy! I come of clean ancestry and lived in a much saner world, long before your brain-shattering, bowel-blasting, modern cocktails."

"Excuse me, sir," ventured the young medico, settling his glasses again with nervous fingers, "but, may I suggest, cocktails are not a modern invention."

"I know it, sir, I know it. We had our ginslings, sherry cobblers, juleps and saratoga-coolers with many others, and I drank 'em all. But these were milk for babes compared with your modern explosive poisons. 'Kick' is the word, I believe? Everything to-day must have a kick in it, irrespective of morals, manners or health. Yes, mine was a saner world, we drank less and with more knowledge, we worked harder and with little or none of this present-day fuss and flurry and senseless speed."

"But, sir, this is the age of speed, we think faster and act quicker—"

"And to very devastating, ruinous purpose, young man, judging by the present universal mess! I see about me a world of general incompetence. . . . Rush and hurry and—havoc! Deliberation of thought and considered action received its deathblow from the telephone as the radio is now killing the art of conversation. Yes, mine was a saner, happier epoch . . . simpler, cleaner, more reverent. And pray what do you propose doing with that stethoscope?"

"Why, as a matter of fact, sir, the Countess suggested it might be as well if you allowed me—"

"No! I tell you it will be much better if I am left completely undisturbed." And sinking back among his cushions Old Anthony closed his eyes and became so particularly deaf, so serenely unconscious of the world in general, and Dr. Penley in particular, that this young medico, after making one or two tentative gestures with his stethoscope in the region of his indomitable old patient's waistcoat, sighed, shook his head and departed.

It was a sunny morning and so warm that the long windows of the aged man's room had been thrown wide to the broad, old-fashioned verandah beyond which lay the garden whence breathed a fragrant air with, ever and anon, a vague murmur of voices that slowly drew nearer, and thus presently resolved themselves into Number One, a man's flutey tenor and Number Two, a woman's rich, full-throated contralto now declaiming rather passionately, thus:

"And that'll be all from you, Arthur de Witt! I don't want to hear another word, and that's final!"

TENOR: (*Mockingly.*) Is . . . that . . . so?

CONTRALTO: (*Fiercely.*) It certainly is, so let's drop it right now!

TENOR: (*Drawling.*) Ah . . . no, loveliness, not on your sweet . . . precious life! (*Sinking to harsh baritone.*) Say, listen now, Barbara, you can't quit on me cold like this,—you just can't, I'm telling you.

CONTRALTO: (*Becoming almost soprano with wrath.*) Oh, can't I? Well now just wake yourself up enough to watch and see!

TENOR: I don't have to, Sweetness, not me! I'm wide awake all right, I sure am! Sit down, Babs, here in the shade and I'll tell you just how much awake I am. Come, let's sit.

CONTRALTO: No, I'm going indoors.

TENOR: Oh, really? Then, after you, Babby. I'll go find the Coun-tess and ask her ladyship, with proper dejection and sigh effects of course, just why her one and only lovely daughter is crossing her wishes and turning down this very devoted and mother-chosen suitor—my woeful self. 'Dear Coun-tess,' I'll say hopelessly, 'can it be there is another—er—pebble on our lovely Barbara's beach? If so, who—ah, who can it be? A jewel of price? Some Prince of Romance perhaps, say a . . . Falconbridge truck-driver, overalls, cap and brass-badge complete!' . . . Well, Sweetness, now . . . don't you think you'd better sit down and do a spot of explaining, come to a commonsense understanding? Do let's, eh, Darlingest?

Petulant creak of rustic settee on the verandah just beside the open window; then the Contralto voice in hushed and broken question: How . . . what . . . how much do you know?

TENOR: Quite enough! For instance: Tall fellow drives a motor truck, peak cap, etc., labelled 'Falconbridge Amalgamated' like every other chattel around the place. Still, said fellow isn't a bad looker,—you've an eye for male beauty, eh, Babs? . . . And your humble Adonis answers to the name of Bill Romney. . . . Well now I guess this'll be about enough to let you know I'm just awake and able to take an intelligent interest in things, eh, Babs? So, my dear, own wife-to-be,—what d'you say now?

A silence, but one very eloquent of fierce, gloating triumph and quick-breathing, speechless dismay; while the old, old man lay back amid his cushions, motionless as usual, only his eyes, those strangely vital, bright eyes glanced askance towards the open window, much as if his seemingly deaf ears had distinguished every word. Then the Contralto voice spoke again and bitterly contemptuous:

So you . . . you've been spying on me, Arthur!

TENOR: (*Cheerily.*) Admitted, Sweetness, admitted. I've watched you good and plenty! I know you've been meeting your Truck-driver on the sly and pretty often. I know you've hung about waiting for him, lucky guy! Question is,—does he know all his good fortune? Is he aware his so ardent sweetie is lady Barbara Riderwood?

CONTRALTO: (*In hissing whisper eloquent of fury and despair.*) S-s-stop!

TENOR: (*Placatingly.*) Righty-right, old thing, don't get yourself all worked up, there's really no need. I'm not kicking about your truck-driver, not me! The sky's the limit so far as I'm concerned. So play around and enjoy your lovely self all you know how. I'm merely showing you just why you can't throw me down, Sweetheart, and exactly why you're going to obey your mother and please my governor by marrying me in due course as per arrangement between our families.

CONTRALTO: (*Dispassionately.*) Arthur, what a perfectly foul thing you are!

TENOR: Babs darling, sometimes I really do believe you love me.

CONTRALTO: If I go and tell George of your vile spying and beastly insinuations . . . !

TENOR: Ah, big brother George! What a hope! Poor old George is too busy splashing ink or cocktails to give a hoot for anything else. . . . Listen, Barbara, you know our folks agreed we should marry, fixed it up between them long before I left Harvard. Well, my old man's so dead set on it that, to be quite frank about it, unless I do marry you he'll boot me off without a bean. So you see—

CONTRALTO: It's just a matter of business, of course.

TENOR: Why, sure it is,—but there's a whole lot more to it, there's yourself, Barbara, and you're a very lovely thing, fill the eye well and a husband's arms better, and, believe it or not, old thing, I'm just crazy about you really, though not such a sap as to be jealous, either now or when we're married. I guess I'll make a sensible husband . . . go our own ways . . . and if you must see your truckman now and then, it's O K by me, only—be discreet and —what, must you go, Sweetness? Then I'll tag along . . . what, pay our respects to your aged Methusaleh? Right-o, I'm game. Marvellous old boy, of course, though, rather like a mummy, better dead I'd say, though I guess if—

The speaker was suddenly dumb, for Old Anthony was looking at him with a slow, unwinking gaze that roved down his slim, elegant person from shining hair and pale, nearly handsome face to glossy shoes and as slowly up again.

But Arthur de Witt merely smiled and, with his usual effrontery, the careless insolence that is sometimes the outcome of limitless wealth,—waved his white, carefully manicured hand in airy salutation.

"Morning, sir!" he piped. "Don't suppose you can hear me but anyway—greetings and Good-bye. Come on, Babs, let's ske daddle, your Aged Person eyes me as if I were a—"

"Slug," said Old Anthony, frowning; "they sometimes crawl in from the garden, but you are a de Witt also. Once upon a time there was a Lawrence de Witt."

"My worthy grandfather, sir."

"Many years ago your grandfather proved so extremely un-worthy I had occasion to order him from my house. It seems the evil of him persists in you . . . such blood as yours shall never mingle with ours. I therefore, here and now, positively forbid my grand-daughter to you. I also forbid your presence here in the future. You may go."

"Eh, go, sir—go? Oh but look here . . . I say you know, look here—"

"I am!" nodded Old Anthony, grimly. "And the sight affronts me, it is an offence shall be removed," and speaking, he touched one of the electric bell pushes on the small table at his elbow, while Barbara viewed him in dumb amaze.

"Wrong, old sir, you've got it all wrong!" said Arthur de Witt rather stridently. "You don't want to quarrel with me. I'm part of the scenery around here. Barbara and I are engaged, we're to be married in a month . . . it's all fixed—absolutely, so if you don't like me it's just too bad—"

"And your sound is offensive as your look!" said Old Anthony placidly.

"Well, that's a shame too, sir, seeing I shall be your something-or-other-in-law so soon. I'd like you to appreciate and like me, of course, but if you won't, well I guess you're too old to matter anyway. Oh, I know you were a power once, everyone used to call you The Master, but that must have been donkey's years ago, and values have all changed since then. To-day my father stands where you did, or pretty near, he means quite a lot in finance and on The Street, and it doesn't do to cross him. Now his idea is to unite Falconbridge and de Witt in both business and social sense, merger and marriage, multi-millions to wed millions, and that's where Barbara and I come in . . . it's the dream of my father's life,—and mine, of course."

"But only a dream!" said Old Anthony gently. "And one that shall never materialize." Now, mild though his tone, the tawny eyes of him glowed with such fire, his lean, age-worn features showed so keenly resolute that Barbara's amazement grew and Arthur de Witt lost his temper, he laughed angrily:

"Mr. . . . Falconbridge . . . sir," he drawled, "why stir up trouble and at your age! Should you stop this marriage, supposing you could, my father won't take it lying down, ah no . . . he certainly will not!

He'll put a crimp in Falconbridge Amalgamated that'll pretty well bust the whole concern big as it is, yes sir! We de Witts have always been a power to reckon with, and to-day more so than ever. And we want to be friends, so—why not?"

It was now that a knock sounded on the door and a man entered, a trim, upright figure in neat chauffeur's uniform; a middle-aged man for his hair was grey, a grim man small of nose, large of jaw and wide of shoulder, a very powerful, extremely formidable-seeming person though, as he stood cap in hand, looking down on the aged figure in its deep-cushioned chair, his small, bright eyes held such look of doglike devotion as quite gentled and transfigured him.

"Tom Pegg," said his Master, "conduct Mr. de Witt off my premises. Take him out through the garden and see he does not return, then report to me." Tom Pegg's saturnine visage was lightened by the grim ghost of a smile, his bullet head gestured towards the open window. "Mr. de Witt, sir," he murmured respectfully, "if you please."

Arthur de Witt frowned on the speaker, seemed about to retort, but laughed instead.

"Oh, righty-ho!" he nodded. "*Au revoir*, Mr. Falconbridge. I only hope you're not starting something you'll regret bitterly, sir, bitterly! Toodle-oo, Babs darling, bye-bye Sweetness, I'll be seeing you mighty soon, so don't worry or grieve any, old thing." Then with airy gesture he went out into the sunshine with Tom Pegg close behind.

"Well . . .!" exclaimed Barbara, Lady Riderwood, drawing a deep breath, "That's—that! . . . But you, great-grandfather so very much alive! And not a bit deaf! Really you're terrible unexpected, quite shattering—absolutely! Of course Arthur's a poisonous microbe, quite septic in fact, but mother can't see it, she's all for him, and when she knows you've given him the air, well—something's going to pop! You know what mother is when she goes in off the deep end—"

"Come you here, Miss! Here where I can look at you."

Obediently she came and stood before him: a tall, vivid creature all subtle provocation: from short, lustrous hair to slim, silken ankles she was as curvingly feminine as the prevailing fashion allowed: her grey eyes, large and broad-set beneath slim brows, shone down on him between long lashes heavily beaded, her full-lipped, rather wide mouth, though impossibly red and shaped, nevertheless showed firm and resolute.

For a long moment they surveyed each other in silence and very steadfastly; but the old man's keen glance, wise with long experience, was so shrewdly critical and coldly disparaging that the girl's cheek flushed hotly, and when she spoke it was in tone of sullen defiance:

"So . . . that's what you think of me, is it?"

"What else?" he questioned, sadly. "The innocent child I loved, the little school-girl I played with has grown into a slangy, painted creature utterly strange to me."

"And yet," she retorted, frowning down on him, "in spite of time and lipstick, I'm the same Barbara and in the best sense, may be innocent still. Believe this . . . if you can."

"I will!" he answered, in tone almost humble.

"And if I seem strange to you, if we've grown away from each other, as we have,—it's your fault, shutting yourself away here, allowing no one to see you except Mr. Keith and Tom Pegg, letting everyone think you're half-dead, half-blind and deaf as a post! In the old days I used to adore you frightfully . . . called you 'Gramps'—do you remember? And I'd have gone on adoring you if you'd only let me,—but not you, oh no! When I came back from college you were quite changed. When I came home from Paris last year, you were a recluse and seemed almost a corpse. And now . . . now when I've found you again, now we've discovered each other—it's too late!"

"Never say so, child!"

"Oh, but I do,—I do!"

"Suppose you tell me why?"

"Just . . . because!"

"Can't you trust me, Barbara?"

Once again she looked deep into the eyes that were now viewing her so wistfully.

"Yes," she answered. "Yes, I can. I will." She glanced from closed door to open window, then, with swift and supple grace, sank to her knees beside him and leaning close, spoke in a whisper:

"Swear you'll keep it dark, not a word to any living soul, on the honour of a Falconbridge."

"You have my word, Barbara."

"Well then, I'm skipping. . . . I'm going to cut off, clear out for good!"

"All of which means precisely what, pray?"

"My truck-driver! Five days from now I shall be . . . his wife! There! Now I suppose you're perfectly outraged, scandalized, shocked and shaken to the very marrow?"

"Not at my age," he answered in tone so unexpectedly gentle that for a moment she could only stare.

"Well, but," she gasped, "what about our dashed family pride? Think! Just imagine the beastly blurbs in all the foul tabloids:—'Titled heiress elopes with humble Adonis in overalls!' And such vile rot. Ponder this, my poor dear, and then thunder your Jovian wrath upon the devoted head of your wilful great granddaughter. . . . Not that she'll mind . . . very much, because she'll soon belong only to Bill, and he's a man, her man . . . yes, the one . . . the only man in all the world. Now—now what have you to say?"

"Only this," he answered gently, "if you are sure you have found the one man at last, if you are perfectly convinced, I can only wish you all and every happiness, dear child."

"Happiness?" she repeated, breathlessly. "You? You of all people are big enough . . . wise enough to wish me happiness. . . . And not one word of reproach—" Gone now was all her flippant cynicism; her deep eyes brimmed with tears, her voice, tenderly murmurous, broke to a sob and covering her face she bowed her bright head upon the old man's knees:

"Oh, Gramps . . . oh, my darling," she whispered brokenly, "if you only knew how desperately . . . lonely I've been! How I wanted . . . yearned for someone to confide in . . . a friend to tell me I was doing right . . . choosing well. . . . And now, now to find you are my friend . . . you! Oh, dash it, there go my eyelashes! Yes, I'm crying like a fool just because I'm so happy, so . . . relieved. . . . And you're such a comfort because you seem young again . . . yourself . . . masterful as ever, and yet so kind . . . so gentle. Why, why are you so sweet to me?"

"Because," he answered, laying his frail-seeming hand upon her lustrous hair very tenderly, "because a woman who dare make such choice as yours, is either the poor, frivolous victim of a wanton fancy or a true-hearted woman whose valiant devotion honours her. . . . Now, tell me more about your man. Does he know exactly who you are?"

Barbara sat back on her heels to dab quite recklessly at her eyes and shake her handsome head.

"Well—no!" she admitted. "Frankly, he hasn't the foggiest, he'd have been too utterly fed, if you see what I mean?"

"I do not! You frequently become wholly unintelligible."

"Well then, Bill, being Bill, has such quaint, old-fashioned ideas that I daren't let him know. You see he thinks a wife should be entirely dependent on her husband, especially for money, odd, of course, and yet I rather like him for it—though he put off our wedding till his wages were raised."

"How much does he earn?"

"Twenty-five dollars a week! Think of it, Gramps!

Why I've paid as much for a hat! And he works so hard and such long hours!"

"And you are quite, quite prepared for the mortifications and hardships you must endure as a poor man's wife?"

"Yes, I've thought it all out from every conceivable angle and it just comes down to this: I'd rather eat dry crusts with a man like Bill than bloat on dainties with a worm like Arthur de Witt! And besides, it won't always be crusts. Bill's got ideas, big ambitions and he's a hustler. . . . And . . . oh my dear, we've got the dinkiest little flat, two rooms and a kitchenette, rather larger than a loose-box! And can you see me cooking things—me!"

"Perhaps I shall!"

"Oh . . . you mean . . . do you mean you'd visit us?"

"If I'm invited, certainly!"

"Darling . . .!" she exclaimed, with a break in her rich, husky voice, "you're making me so . . . happy I shall cry again. . . . Oh, aren't you the dearest, the . . . the most perfect lamb—"

"Certainly not, Miss! Remember my years!"

"Oh," sighed she, cuddling down against his knees, "I'm so proud . . . so happy I don't know what to say . . . how to express it."

"Suppose you start at the beginning and tell me all about it, just how you first met and where."

"Oh, my Precious, I'm simply dying to—"

"And in your narration, my dear, endeavour to speak plain, sound English."

"Why, of course, dear. But first let me shake up your pillows. There, is that comfy?"

"Very!"

Then, folding her shapely arms across his knees and looking up glad-eyed into the wise old face above her, she began:

"It all started really at Patricia Van Dorne's cocktail party because she thought it would be rather a rag for the whole gang, about fourteen of us, to barge into a cheap, down-town dance hall—"

"Do you mean break in?"

"Something of the sort. Anyway, we went, togged for the part of course. It was a pretty tough crowd and I got separated from our bunch and was being so pestered by two or three near-hoodleums to dance and drink that I got rather scared, so I blew—"

"But what precisely did you blow, child, and why?"

"I mean I ran out into the street, but two of them followed and caught me and things were beginning to look rather ugly when—along came Bill, from work, peak cap and all complete with its brass badge labelled 'Falconbridge Amalgamated' like a great big Saint Michael in overalls. So I screamed for help and he certainly helped . . . and so quickly it was all over and he was walking me safely away almost before I knew it. And then, Gramps, what must he do but start lecturing me like a Dutch uncle about going near such places . . . and I the meekest, humblest thing! And, ah my dear, Bill was different! Bill was different to any man I'd ever met, for though he looked all smudged and oily outside, he was clean inside, all clean and white and . . . nice! He asked me to meet him again, and I did. And the oftener we met, the more I liked him, he was so sweetly naïve and simple. He told me he had worked his way through college and was driving a truck while he looked around for a proper engineer's job . . . driving one of your trucks, my pet! So I told him I was Babs Mason and worked in an uptown store—"

"And did he believe it, Barbara, with all this paint and stuff on your lips and eyelashes?"

"Oh, my dear! I dressed the part,—simplest little frocks and no make-up! And that's the joke of it because one evening the dear, silly goof presented me with a silver compactum and lip-stick complete . . . and so shy about it I could have kissed him and didn't. And that was the night he popped—"

"I presume you mean 'proposed'?"

"Yes, of course. Mother thought I'd gone to a swell do at the Harrison's, so I had, just long enough to get out of my party rags—Betty Harrison is the only one in the know,—and then I stole away to Bill. We went for a trolley ride and the car was packed, frightful horde, but we saw only each other, so what did we care. . . . Now all this time, Gramps darling, believe it or not, Bill had never been sloppy, not a word of love-stuff and never even offered to kiss me though of course I knew he was just dying to, but that's Bill's funny way and I respected and loved him so much for it that I determined he should—and of course he did, for, all at once, we were strap-hanging at the time, he leaned near and said: 'How about it, girl?' Well, I was waiting for it, as I say, but I just naturally said: 'What, Bill?' Then he looked down at me, ah the gentlest, dearest look, and said: 'Are you on?' So I said 'Yes.' And well—that's all."

"God . . . bless . . . my soul!" murmured Old Anthony. "And in my day we so revered our women that we actually knelt to them at such times."

"Ah, my Aged Blessedness," she murmured, "and yet I'm sure that, way deep down, love is just the same to-day, just as true and sacred, only we hate to show it or be theatrical—"

"But why be ashamed of it, Child? True love is such a very holy thing it should be revered as such, and real emotion is always so unconscious that it cannot be vulgarly theatric. And nothing in life is more sacred than marriage, and nothing more sublime than the wonder of Motherhood,—no, nothing!"

"I know, my Blessed, I know!" she murmured, touching his silvery hair very reverently. "The very thought of it all, as you say it, makes me want to weep again. . . . And yet . . . if Bill had gone down on his knees to me I . . . should simply have . . . hooted with laughter. But you are very wise, dear one, and very kind, I think because you must love very greatly."

"I did," he answered softly. "I did indeed . . . and knew in return such sweet devotion as reaches beyond the grave, my dear, such love as I pray you may know."

"And there go . . . the last of my eyelashes and all your darling fault!"

"Eyelashes!" he snorted, blinking his own, "yours are positively grotesque!"

"Yes, my Precious," she answered, meekly. "But you see we're all so grotesque we should be more grotesque to be anything else. . . . Oh, my darling, now your dear, golden eyes look like Blodwen's in the old picture, so kind and sad as if they might weep too. I'd simply love to kiss and kiss you only I know I should smear red butterflies all over you!"

"Lipstick—bah!" he exclaimed, "your mouth is prettier as God made it. Why will you use the vile stuff?"

"I should be so crudely conspicuous without it, Sweetness," she sighed.

"However, I possess a handkerchief, Miss!"

"Oh!" cried she. "That means—!" Then leaning forward the better to clasp his frailness in the warm, soft vigour of her young arms, she alternately kissed and wiped him until she was arrested by sound of approaching footsteps and voices,—or rather, one—a clear, rich contralto much like her own though far more imperious.

"Oh, ten curses,—the Mater!" she exclaimed, in sudden dismay, "And my eyes all dashed bleary! I must fly to repair damages, but I'll come back to you, darlingest, I'll be back." And with a final caress she rose and sped away out into the sunny garden.

Then sinking back amid his cushions, Old Anthony closed his eyes and instantly became the very personification of doting senility, as, with no ceremony of knocking, the door swung wide and his patrician granddaughter, accompanied by the young doctor, paused on the threshold to survey him.

Rowena, Countess of Riderwood, tall, superbly gowned and coiffeured, was middle-aged but did not look it; she was darkly handsome and of commanding presence, also, like most of the Falconbridges, she possessed—a chin.

"Doctor, how is he to-day?" she demanded, advancing graciously towards the motionless figure. "He looks very, very old and seems deafer than ever, he never so much as moved when we entered. How is he?" Dr. Penley adjusted his glasses the better to peer at his apparently heedless patient.

"Well, your ladyship," he answered, shaking his head, "he's alive, and this in itself is a miracle, considering his stupendous age."

"Oh yes, yes of course," she answered, coming a little nearer, "And yet—so deaf! So blind! So little real interest or joy in living, poor old man! Ninety-five is a cruel, a preposterous age. You tested his heart thoroughly, I hope?"

"Why, yes, after a good deal of persuasion. . . . Oh yes, yes, I ran over him as well as I was able, yesterday—"

"Yesterday? But I distinctly asked you to examine him very thoroughly this morning."

"And, madam, I . . . I endeavoured to do so, but he . . . we . . . I . . . I found it quite impossible."

"Ah, he was troublesome?"

"Extremely impatient, my lady. I deemed it wiser not to . . . to anger him . . ."

"Quite rightly! He can be dreadfully stubborn, and you mustn't rouse him. He discharged poor Doctor Stern at a moment's notice. . . . And I must have a resident physician always ready—in case anything should happen. You examined him yesterday, you say?"

"I did, madam, and found him remarkably,—I must say amazingly sound! He is a—quite a phenomenon!"

"That's very well, Doctor. I'm greatly relieved, because I desire to move him out of this dreadfully shabby old room, at once. I thought . . . to-day. It must be completely altered and redecorated. I shall require the whole of this floor, of course, for my daughter's wedding and— Do you suppose he can possibly hear us? . . . I fancied his eyebrows twitched at me."

"Well," answered Dr. Penley, stooping above his aged patient, "I have sometimes doubted—"

"Then don't! I can!" answered Old Anthony, so suddenly that Doctor Penley jumped, and even the stately Countess started violently.

"Grandfather, you . . . you startled me!" she stammered.

"Good!" he nodded, opening his bright eyes. "Glad of it! And, Rowena, I'll not be moved! D'ye hear? And no one shall touch this room! Let 'em dare!"

"There, there my dear!" said she, becoming her stateliest self. "We do only what is best for you—"

"Then don't! Instead, you may be seated. And bid your doctor leave us."

"But . . . Grandfather—"

"Sit down, Rowena! I'm going to talk to you."

The Countess frowned from the doctor's hurriedly-retreating person to this indomitable old face that frowned back on her, then threw up her imperious head, exclaiming:

"Well, upon my word!"

"No, upon a chair,—this one!"

My lady sank obediently upon the chair with something less than her customary studied grace, her white, bejewelled hands began to pull and twist at the laced handkerchief they were grasping, her delicate nostrils were dilated, her fine, large eyes were glowing with that battle-light before which all lesser humans had been wont to quail, especially her son and daughter.

"Really, Grandfather!" said she, speaking loudly that he should miss nothing of her indignation, "I'm quite unused to being ordered around—and so harshly! Indeed you are very strange to-day! Are you sure you are quite well, quite yourself?"

"Quite!" he answered, a little grimly. "I am! And pray cease fidgeting with that handkerchief. And you needn't shout at me, I'm not deaf,—at least, not at present. For instance, I heard you speak of your daughter's marriage. Well, to whom do you propose marrying her?"

"Why of course to Arthur de Witt—"

"And pray why 'of course'?"

"Because it is a matter perfectly agreed and understood,—as you should know, Grandfather."

"I've been too long a-dream!" he sighed. "But I'm broad awake at last and, despite my years, so very far from dying that I mean to live every hour, every minute until Death calls me. . . . I've work yet to do, it seems."

"Work, Grandfather?" she repeated, shaking her head at him reprovingly. "At your age? Impossible, quite unthinkable! You must relax, my dear I insist, you must rest and take your ease because now, as some poet or other, I forget who, writes: 'now is the evening of your days—'"

"So I'll be up and doing before the night falls, Rowena."

"But how?" she demanded. "And you so terribly old! Remember your heart . . . old hearts are always tired! Too much exertion would certainly kill you and—"

"Good!" he exclaimed. "Better die on my feet than smothered in bed. However, Rowena, I tell you this marriage shall not be."

"Dear Grandfather, how very wildly you talk! And don't, please, oh please do not distress yourself to no purpose. I regard this union, dear Grandfather, as most desirable, an excellent marriage and consequently it is all quite settled, all arranged—"

"By yourself, Rowena."

"Well naturally, I—"

"Always you and yourself, Rowena!" he nodded. "But what of your child?"

"She will, of course, be ruled . . . guided by me—"

"Yourself, Rowena, fills for you the very universe, it seems, now as ever! I remember you as a spoilt and pampered child, a headstrong miss and self-willed woman. You could have married David Charteris or Malachi Tutt, yes, or Donald Keith, good Americans, but you hankered for a title, and your ever-indulgent father bought you one. But by the grace of Heaven you wed a man, for Riderwood was a fine fellow, had he lived, you and your children might have been happier and more united,—instead of which—"

"Stop! Stop!" she cried, between fury of anger and passion of tears. "How can you—how dare you so reproach me?"

"Instead of which," the thin old voice pursued relentlessly, "your son George is an idler, a do-nothing clubman who rarely comes near you, and now you would drive your daughter from you by forcing upon her this hateful, loveless marriage—"

"Grandfather!" she exclaimed, rising majestically, "you are cruel . . . you are unjust! I'll not stay here to be affronted, I—"

"Tantrums! Tantrums!" he retorted. "Before you run away, answer me this—if you dare! Do you believe that Barbara loves young de Witt?"

"Why of course—"

"No!" cried a third voice, rather breathlessly. "No—absolutely not!" and in from the sunny verandah stepped Barbara herself, re-eyelashed and complexioned, who, now entrenching herself behind her great-grandfather, fronted her redoubtable mother with a desperate levity: "If, Mummy, if you're talking of Arthur, you may as well know I think he is definitely the limit in warts and altogether poisonous—"

"Barbara!" quoth her mother, in terrible voice, "do you know what you are saying?"

"Oh perfectly, darling. I've been telling Gramps, and he quite agrees,—don't you, my lamb?" And having thus shamelessly dragged her aged champion to her defence, Barbara took out begemmed compactum and began to touch up her lips with extreme care, though quite needlessly.

"Grandfather!" the Countess challenged. "Can this be true?" The old man merely blinked at the fire. "To undermine my influence with my daughter! To interpose between the sacred relationship of mother and child,—you! You that I have tended and watched over as one quite done with earthly concerns and fading gently out of life,—do you rise against me now to abet my wilful child—?"

"Oh, Mums—darling!" sighed Barbara, wearily, "why be so frightfully high-hat?"

"Silence, Barbara!"

"But, Materest, 'wilful child,' you know, and the word 'abet,'—too terribly archaic and what not—"

"Barbara, hold your tongue! Grandfather, am I to regard you as the gentle old man you have seemed, or beware of you as a . . . a monster of duplicity, the menace to a mother's authority, a subtle inspirer of rebellion? Answer me!"

Now here, seeing Old Anthony only blinked more owlishly than ever, Barbara knelt suddenly to set a protecting arm about him, as her stately mother continued implacably.

"I am quite aware how very sedulously you have nursed and fostered your bitter animosity against the de Witt family all these years, despite their efforts at conciliation . . . and although they have made themselves so charming to me and mine, old Mr. Lawrence particularly so, he has been extremely gracious to me in many ways—"

"Not to mention," added Barbara, "the block of shares and things he gave you for a birthday present, Mummy!"

Old Anthony seemed to tense and stiffen, he raised his white head suddenly and spoke with his old time voice of authority:

"Barbara, go and put on your bonnet, you shall take me out."

"'Bonnet,' my blessed Aged One?" she laughed, "there hasn't been such a thing in the world for ages,—

but I'll do it anyway. Don't let my little Mummy trample you too hard, my Precious!"

"Rowena," said he, so soon as they were alone, "how much exactly was this bribe?"

Her ladyship recoiled.

"Bribe—?" she ejaculated.

"Yes. At how much, precisely, does Lawrence de Witt rate your daughter's marketable value? Her cash value in shares—"

The Countess gasped; she rose superbly to her stately height; she struck an attitude of magnificent indignation; but now (alas) before she could find utterance, a hoarse English voice said cheerily:

"Mr. A. de W. has went, sir, like a lamb. All's clear!" And Tom Pegg appeared on the verandah, saluting smartly, like the old soldier he was.

"Then come you and help me on with an overcoat, Tom."

"Overcoat, sir? My oath—asking pardon, sir, but does this mean—?"

"Overcoat!" snapped Old Anthony rising from his many cushions with scarcely an effort.

"Grandfather!" exclaimed the Countess in very real amazement, "you are never going out—?"

"Why not, pray?"

"Your heart! Doctor Penley says—"

"Fiddlesticks!" snarled the old man, struggling into the somewhat shabby garment Tom Pegg held out for him, so eagerly, saying:

"Lord, sir, I hain't drove you nowhere since I dunno when, sir."

"At least, Grandfather, you'll take Doctor Penley with you."

"Not I, Rowena, no!"

"And which, sir," enquired Tom Pegg, buttoning up the frail old body with strangely tender solicitude, "which car'll you have,—the Rolls, the Packard, the—"

"Any one of 'em, Tom, so long as it's open and not a box on wheels—"

"But this," exclaimed the Countess, tragically, "this is madness!"

"No, sanity, madam, stark sanity! Now, where's my hat? Oh, here it is . . . rather worn, rather decrepit —like myself. Reminds me of Lincoln's hats—generally looked shabby. Old Abe! . . . Off with you, Tom, don't keep me waiting."

"Not me, sir, not me! This here is a occasion, this is, ah and one as I've been a-hoping for with all me 'eart, sir!" And away strode Tom Pegg, jubilant.

"Grandfather," said her ladyship, viewing him in growing apprehension, this gentle, old dreamer who, casting off his dotage, had awakened to such grimly-vigorous and resolute purpose, "Grandfather, I demand, I . . . no, I beg to know where you are going . . . what you intend to do . . .?"

"My child," he answered gently, but with something Puckish and mocking in his smile, "since your demand becomes a plea, it shall be answered: I am going to meet the husband-elect of your daughter."

"And . . . oh my Precious Dear," cried Barbara, running to clasp arm about him, "here she is, and so frightfully grateful . . . take her away before she snivels—!"

CHAPTER II

DESCRIBES HOW AGE SET TO WORK

FALCONBRIDGE AMALGAMATED, this huge machine, was grinding away at full speed; and like so many wheels and cogs of this great money-making engine, its every member, from grey-haired Donald Keith, chief of executive, to red-headed Timmy McGee, youngest of its many office boys, was busied according to routine.

And Old Anthony, leaning back in his open car and peering beneath the brim of his shabby hat, looked up at this great structure that, dwarfing most of its tall neighbours, soared dizzily aloft rising, floor on floor, from the gloom of busy street up and up high against the afternoon sunglare; this solid evidence of his wealth and far-reaching power whose ramifications stretched away across continents and seas.

"It's perfectly mammoth, Gramps!" exclaimed Barbara. "I've hardly ever seen it so near. But I never glimpse it in the distance without a thrill."

"And its shadow," he murmured, glancing round about, "its shadow falls where, in this ever-changing city, once stood the pleasant, tree-shaded tavern in which my grandfather, Anthony One, was killed . . . and upon just such sunny afternoon as this; the building itself is rooted on the garden and house-plot where they brought him to die . . . Blodwen's garden. Not so very long ago, but the world and life so greatly altered."

"But so much for the better, my Aged Precious One," answered Barbara, giving his arm a little hug.

"Oh, surely, surely all for the better, confess!"

"I were fool to doubt it, child,—and yet," he sighed, and beckoning to his ever-watchful Tom Pegg, prepared to descend, "I must ask you to wait for me, Barbara, drive around . . . come back and enquire for me at about half past three. . . . No no, Tom, don't embrace me! Give me your arm and I shall manage. Now, easy does it! All my age seems to have got into my confounded, old legs!"

The sidewalk achieved, he paused a moment to get his breath and glance about him at the ceaseless bustle and stir of unending traffic; then baring his silvery head to Barbara, he turned in at the imposing, pillared doorway and entered the great, busy place; here he paused again, standing aside from the bustling throng, an aged, lonely figure propped upon crutch-stick, looking up and around from marble pavement and fluted columns to lofty ceiling, so very wistfully that a tall superman resplendent in gold braid and buttons, extremely stiff as to back and square as to shoulder, but whose Irish heart was touched by this vision of forlorn age and seeming decrepitude, strode up and enquired solicitously:

"Is ut meself now can annywoise serve ye, Granddad?"

"Thank you. I am here to see Mr. Keith. Mr. Donald Keith."

"Have ye iver an app'intment, now?"

"Well no, but—"

"Ah, thin 'tis sorry I am for yez, Pop, for the Governor niver sees annyone widout."

"He will," answered Old Anthony, taking out his card. "Show him this." The superman took this pasteboard, glanced at the name inscribed thereon, stared, goggled and becoming squarer and stiffer than ever, saluted with quivering smartness, saying:

"This way, sorr—av ye plaze!"

Forthwith Old Anthony was whirled up to a certain floor and there met by a man who gazed on him in wide-eyed disbelief; a middle-aged man this, tall and of commanding presence though just now his lean, comely features showed careworn and in his eyes, as they met the old man's shrewd gaze, dawned a look very like consternation that flickered and was gone and Donald Keith, masking his secret apprehensions like the able and much experienced man of affairs he had so often proved, was greeting his unexpected visitor with joyous eagerness.

Yet the old man had seen; the thin, nervous fingers, withdrawing themselves from Keith's clasp, gestured towards a chair, the ageworn voice, unexpectedly full and resonant, spoke with the old, well-remembered note of command.

"Sit down, Keith, and tell me your trouble. Is it merely circumstance? Or the sight of me—or both? Out with it, man." And Donald Keith, present ruling head of this great organization, who yet as a boy and young man had been wont to obey this imperious voice, now and instinctively obeyed it again; he sank into the chair and leaning haggard brow on clenched fist, answered brokenly and with sudden and almost terrible humility, using the epithet of long ago:

"Master . . . I'm thanking God you're back again! Had I dreamed ye were strong and able as ye seem, I should have sought your advice. . . . For the world's run mad! The power o' money is destroying itself as Fear is destroying all faith and credit. . . ."

"Then," said Old Anthony, throwing back his silvery head, "it is time I awoke. Now pray be more particular, Donald, what of us? Our interests are so various and widely scattered—"

"Ay, true enough!" groaned Keith. "But why . . . why should we stand forever immune when other concerns as great and powerful are tottering or have gone? How can you expect Falconbridge Amalgamated to weather such tempest?"

"Still I do, Keith, I do. Show me why I should not? Tell me the worst . . . tell me all, Donald."

"Then listen!" And Keith told a story of rates cut to impossible minimum; of slow yet ever-growing disaster. ". . . And then . . . to cap all is the Orellana Dam, that immense irrigation scheme you mapped out years ago."

"To tame the wilderness,—yes!" nodded the old man. "It was my dream to make the desert rich and fruitful . . . transform it from blasting curse to blessing . . . a worthy home for valiant people. This should have been done long since."

"We've been at work on it three years, Master, and it's still far from completion . . . matters have gone from bad to worse . . . heat and cold and cloud-bursts, a wicked climate . . . and the workpeople striking for higher wages . . . and money tight! Things looked pretty desperate, we simply had to have ready money, liquid cash and plenty of it or the work would stop . . . that meant a loss of millions in plant and machinery alone,—we had to have money, we had to carry on or—fail utterly."

"Ah-h-h!" sighed the old man, thin hands tight-clenched upon his stick. "And then de Witt seized the opportunity! How?" Donald Keith started, rose to his feet, apprehension changing to stark dismay.

"How . . . who . . .?" he stammered, "the transaction is known only to—"

"Tush, man! I know Lawrence de Witt too well,—vicious, unscrupulous, merciless—! Sit down and explain precisely how far we are in the slimy clutches of this bloodsucking octopus, and who is his agent, his go-between. Sit down and answer me!" Once again, Donald Keith, now the pale wraith of his usual calmly impressive self, sank down miserably, dabbing at brow and cheek with snowy handkerchief.

"As I say, we . . . we were in desperate straits, Master . . . of course money was there and could have been found with due time, but time was the factor denied us. Then word came to me—"

"How and by whom?"

"Well, by Julius Fischer, it seems he is acquainted socially with the de Witt family and—"

"Fischer being, as I recall, one of our chief consulting engineers?"

"He is the sole head of the field department now, sir, and a very able—"

"You mean he is in charge of the Orellana Dam operations. . . . Well, for what amount is this loan?"

"The amount, sir," repeated Keith, busy with his handkerchief again, "the amount is about . . . nine million dollars."

"Call it ten!" nodded Old Anthony. "And what collateral did Lawrence de Witt demand? What security? When does repayment fall due?"

Bowing his head and with looks averted, Keith made such answer that his aged hearer sank back in his chair as from a blow, his hands fumbled aimlessly, his eyes closed as though in sharp pain, from quivering lips issued a broken murmur:

"De Witt then . . . then de Witt holds the controlling interest . . . Donald Keith, you have sold me out! Except I find ten million dollars Falconbridge Amalgamated will be ruled by de Witt! This man who brought ruin and death and bitter anguish on those I loved! Who has built his fortune on the ruthless destruction of others,—he will be master here."

"Sir," said Keith, after a tense and painful silence, glancing furtively at the sightless, stricken old face opposite that showed now so very worn and seemed to mirror something of the many sorrows of his long life, "sir, I can only say that I . . . I'm sorry, but acted for the best, and now . . . beg you to accept my . . . resignation."

The old man made no answer, but slowly the fluttering hands grew still, slowly they clenched themselves, the golden eyes opened and he spoke with the look and tone of The Master.

"No, Donald, I refuse your resignation. I shall need you beside me now more than ever. In the old times all things were secure, to-day we face jeopardy undreamed . . . we have much to do. . . . And first I will see the executive, your staff, the managers of every department—No, first send out a general call for truck-driver Number Two Hundred and Forty-Seven, William Romney—"

"A truck-driver? Here, sir?"

"Yes. Let him wait until I can see him. And now summon to me all the chiefest members of your staff."

Thus presently Anthony sat surrounded by men old, young and middle-aged all of whom surveyed this silent, hoary figure with emotions ranging from awe and pity to merest curiosity.

Suddenly the silvery head was lifted, the vivid eyes glanced from face to face and instinctively each man, suddenly intent, leaned nearer as the old man began to speak:

"I am, sirs, a very aged, a ridiculously old man and all the years seem to have got into my legs, so you will forgive my not rising to greet you." Here a polite though confused murmur stilled by Old Anthony's uplifted hand as he continued:

"Gentlemen, for some years now I have been a ghost heedless of time and the changing life around me, living only in my cherished dreams and awaiting my final exit. To-day I am awake and find myself in a strangely troubled world . . . for it seems that this great concern, this once powerful house of ours is shaken. But, worse than this, I learn we are in danger of falling into the clutches of . . . an organization whose business principles and methods I have always heartily detested because they and it have ever been a power of ruthless destruction, trampling down all weaker rivals remorselessly, whereas we have been constructive and must and shall so remain while I live. But, sirs, as you see, I am a very old man. I was born long and long before the fathers of any of you and I lived in a much simpler, more reverent age, when God seemed nearer and men were not ashamed to call on Him. . . . I, sirs, have prayed with and beside Abram Lincoln, two grief-stricken fathers on a blood-soaked battlefield. So here and now, gentlemen, I humbly invoke God's blessing on us, our coming efforts, and that He will endue my old body with all needful strength to make one last fight . . . that we, you and I, may keep this great business house clean and honourable and a power for good now while I live and long after I have won to the Great Beyond.

"Many of you I know, of course, by long association, but others I see for the first time, yet you are all parts of this ancient and honourable business house that was once, instead of a soulless machine, a living entity, and I ask you, one and all, again to make and keep it so,—help me to carry on to yet greater power and prosperity."

"Ay, by God!" cried Donald Keith, blowing his nose like a trumpet and turning to his nearest neighbour, "we will that! What d'ye say, Dana man, and you, Jefferson—?"

"Never doubt it, sir!"

"Trust us!"

"We're with you, sir!" cried they all in hearty chorus.

"I'm . . . grateful!" sighed the old man, sinking back in his chair, "your young strength shall prop my feebleness, your faith inspire me. . . . Long ago, in the full pride of my vigour, I was called The Master. To-day I am heavy with years, chastened by grief, humbled by experience and therefore, I hope, a little wiser. So to-day instead of Master I am comrade to you all, your brother in arms to share with you this fight which I think shall be my last—"

"No! No!" cried Donald Keith, rather hoarsely. "You are The Master as you always were and will be! And to-day more than ever, I guess! Eh, Trowbridge? Dana, Erickson . . . McClure,—what of it?"

"Yes! Sure! The Master! God bless you, Master!"

"Then," said Old Anthony, rising at last with an effort and Keith's ready assistance, "then so be it. Once again I thank you from my heart. . . . And now in regard to the Orellana Dam. The work must be completed, and soon as possible, yes—before the end of this year or we are faced with disaster. So I ask you, each one, to bend all your energies to this one purpose. Submit to me any schemes for speeding up the work, any time-saving devices no matter what. The loyal spirit of you all comforts me greatly. . . . Go now and inspire your various departments; let the word be 'Speed.' Lastly,—this business that has become a mere machine, must live again and find its soul, and it is upon your strength I am going to rely for this."

And so, presently, with a new-born enthusiasm that found expression in flushed cheek, glowing eye, or fervent hand-clasp, these that had been mere working parts of a great machine, went forth men eager for action, to spread the news that The Master was back again and great achievements in the air; news that spread from lip to lip until the whole great building hummed and buzzed:

"The Master is alive! The Master is back again!"

And sunk in his chair an old, old man gazed on vacancy with such troubled eyes, a silent, tragic form so deeply stricken yet so dumb and uncomplaining that Donald Keith, unable to endure the sight of such mute suffering, broke this too eloquent silence at last, and being himself so deeply moved, reverted to his native Scots:

"Oh, man—speak! Ye look sae sair waefu', and fine I ken the wherefore 'ot,—speak! Ye'll be thinking better we'd gaed smash than tak' up wi' this loan?—Speak!"

"Far better, Donald!"

"Aweel,—oot wi't,—reproach me, blame me, I'll be feeling the better for't, mebbe."

"Hardly a year, Donald, to complete the Dam and we are safe! But the time is so short! If we double the labour, you tell me it will be scarcely possible."

"Ay, it will that!"

"So here at last is the opportunity for which Lawrence de Witt has waited all these years! Eleven months hence he takes possession—except a miracle happen!"

"And," groaned Keith, "the age o' miracles is long bye with!"

"I wonder?" murmured Old Anthony. "I wonder? However, with belief in a just and merciful God and faith in myself I shall do my utmost to contrive such miracle. . . . Ten million dollars! Give me the reports! By stripping myself I can raise . . . perhaps half this sum immediately—"

"And I can offer ye another million."

"You would practically ruin yourself, Donald."

"Ay, I would that, Master—though I'll confess this wad no juist ruin me precisely—if it should come to't. But I'm hoping for your miracle, ay! And I've unco' faith in you, Master, though in little else, these days and so—" Here the buzz of a telephone interrupted him.

"It's yon driver man you sent for, sir. Will you be for troubling with him at such a time?"

"Certainly. This moment. And, Donald, I'll see him alone."

CHAPTER III

TELLS HOW A NUMBER WAS MADE A MAN

COMELY of face, tall and powerfully built, young Bill Romney stood very conscious of his work-stained overalls, the luxurious splendour of his surroundings and, most especially, of this silvery headed, keen-featured ancient throned behind the great desk; this lean, stately old gentleman whose strange golden eyes were surveying him with such calm, dispassionate appraisement, eyes which in their long experience had thus reckoned up the strengths and weaknesses, plus and minus, of so very many other faces ere now.

So Bill stood silent, fumbling his weather-beaten cap in hands which, though grimed and roughened by hard toil, were well shaped; his wide-set grey eyes were steady and thoughtful, his mouth, though sensitive, was firm-lipped and resolute, while every movement of his lithe, young body told of speed and strength. Having duly noted all of which, The Master spoke:

"You are a boxer?"

"I was, sir, and had good hopes—at first. But the game's crooked, at least I found it so and turned it up."

"And to-day you are driver Number Two Hundred and Forty-Seven, William Romney?"

"Yes, sir," answered Bill, twisting his cap more nervously. "And you, I think, must be . . . The Master, Mr. Falconbridge?"

"And what d'ye think of me, boy?"

"I . . . I shall know better, sir, at the end of this interview . . . perhaps . . . I hope."

"You are an Englishman?"

"Why . . . no, sir . . . though my father was. He came over here to paint portraits, but died before he could make good . . . mother died in England . . . I was a boy then."

"How old now?"

"Twenty-six, sir."

"You have worked your way through college,—which?"

"Yale, sir. Though I hardly worked . . . not honest to goodness work, I mean. You see, sir, I was pretty good on the diamond and grid-iron,—that's how."

"You have passed your examinations as an engineer?"

"Why . . . yes, sir. But how . . . who—?"

"Then why do you drive a truck?"

"To live, sir. Engineering jobs are mighty hard to find, especially—"

"And you earn twenty-five dollars a week."

"No, thirty, sir. I got a rise lately."

"To be sure, I was forgetting. Well, it seems that on thirty dollars a week you are about to wed Lady Barbara Riderwood, my great-grand-daughter."

Bill dropped his cap; he opened his grey eyes much wider than usual; he parted his shapely, clean-shaven lips and striving for speech, was dumb; at last, falling back a pace, he contrived to stammer breathlessly:

"I, sir? I . . . marry your. . . . No, sir—no! You've got me all wrong! It's not . . . not me, sir, good Lord —no!"

"Yet she herself assures me of the fact. She tells me you proposed marriage to her, and very inadequately in my opinion, strap-hanging on a crowded street car,—that she accepted you and that five days hence you set up housekeeping as man and wife in a,—I believe the word was 'dinky'—little flat. Well?"

Bill shook his head, much as if he had just taken a short-arm jolt to the chin.

"Sir," he answered in a dazed sort of way. "Sir, I . . . I . . . what beats me is . . . you have some of the facts right, because I . . . in five days' time I am getting married, sir, but her name is 'Mason' and she works in a—" A telephone buzzed again and taking the receiver The Master answered:

"Yes, at once. Yes, I'm waiting."

A moment or so of expectant silence, then the door opened and:

"Bill!" cried a voice; he started and swung round:

"Babs!" he exclaimed. Then, quite heedless of his grimy overalls and her own dainty finery, she was clinging to him, his arms fast about her.

"Oh, Bill," she sighed, "I'm glad you know all about me at last!"

"But I . . . I don't!" he stammered in troubled voice: and now as he became aware of all the subtle elegance of her that was so eloquent of boundless expense, his arms fell and he stepped back in a dismay so painfully sincere as to be almost tragic. Once again he shook his head as if shrewdly smitten by some invisible fist, and chancing to espy his tumbled cap he took it up, dusted it carefully and began to polish its worn, brass number plate so industriously that she laughed, then frowning snatched the shabby thing from him, dropped it to the carpet and set her daintily shod foot upon it.

"Now!" said she; and both so lost in each other as to be perfectly oblivious of the golden eyes that regarded them so wistfully. "Well?" she demanded, "what is it, Bill? What's got you now?"

"Then you're not," he retorted in gloomy accusation, "you're not just a . . . a poor work girl?"

"Well,—no, Bill old thing, but—"

"And you are really . . . a lady of title?"

"Yes, but you can't blame me, it's no fault of mine, definitely not. I'm just the same 'Babs' or . . . or anything you will, so . . . well, what about it, Bill-boy?"

"Oh, not much," he answered, between quivering lips, "only it's mighty certain you're no wife for . . . a cuss like me. So,—here's where we say 'Good-bye!'" and, saying it, he turned and strode towards the door, but ere he could reach it Barbara was there barring his way.

"Bill, don't . . . be such a . . . perfectly ghastly . . . goof!" she panted. "You shan't walk out and leave me . . . just because I'm not poor and happen to have a tag to my name . . . you can't!"

"I can!" he answered very grimly. "And I shall because I am and haven't! So your ladyship will please stand aside and save me the trouble of lifting you. I'm going back where I belong—"

"Bill, don't be such a frightful worm! Your foul humility or loathsome pride doesn't cut any ice with me or Gramps."

"For the last time, will you stand out of my way?"

"No!" she answered defiantly, "I certainly won't . . . and dare lay your great, oily paws on me, Mr. Bill Romney, and see what happens!" Bill put on his cap, sighed heavily, picked her up lightly, set her down gently and reached for the door-knob; but now, in her extremity of helplessness she cried on her champion for aid:

"Gramps! Oh, my angel, stop him for me . . . don't let him go—!"

"Come here!" said The Master, "both of you!" So back came they, side by side, to stand mute, Barbara frowning at Bill and he scowling at the thick rug beneath his feet.

"I guess, sir," said he, "I've been a pretty considerable fool."

"Definitely!" nodded Barbara, "you're every kind and size of fool to pull all that prideful humility stuff."

"We are all of us fools, boy, at some time or other," said Old Anthony, with the ghost of a smile. "Do you love this double-faced, deceitful creature . . . my great-grand-daughter?"

"Yes, sir," answered Bill, yet scowling at the carpet. "So I'm getting out, sir. I'm quitting my job . . . going to give in my notice, right now."

"And I accept it," nodded The Master. "Driver Two Hundred and Forty-Seven is dismissed and William Romney is engaged at a salary of sixty dollars per week, to begin with."

"Sir—?" muttered Bill, then, meeting the speaker's look, choked and was dumb; so the old voice, and more kindly now, went on:

"Trusting to Barbara's judgement of you—and my own observation—I will essay your capabilities as an engineer. Report here to-morrow and ask for Mr. Keith—"

"Oh, my precious dear!" cried Barbara and kissed him till he gasped:

"Don't . . . don't butterfly me, Miss! Wipe . . . wipe 'em off—!"

"There, my adored angel, there!" she murmured brokenly. "But you're so . . . so big! So tender, so —godlike . . . you're making me shed my dashed eye-lashes all over you."

"Then stop it, instantly! Here, William, take her away . . . take her home. But send Tom Pegg back with the automobile. There now, off with you."

"Sir . . . Master," answered Bill, rather hoarsely, "I'm no sort of good at saying things, but you've given me the chance I've hoped for, the chance to . . . to live and be worthy . . . Barbara and you, and I can only say 'thanks' and promise to make good or . . . or—"

"There's no 'or' about it, my dear silly lummox," cried Barbara tearfully. "I know you'll make good, so does Gramps or he'd never have bothered about you. Now let's be going or I shall be making more butter-flies on him. . . . Good-bye, my silvery angel, you've touched the world and made it beautiful for me, so wonderful, I . . . I feel like saying my prayers again! . . . Oh, Bill, isn't he the most absolutely utterest—it?"

"Surely!" answered Bill, fervently, pausing in the doorway to glance back radiant-eyed at the solitary old figure. "Anyway he's The Master for me, from now on."

CHAPTER IV

WHICH IS MORE OR LESS A MERE BUSINESS CHAPTER

"TEN million dollars!"

Mr. Malachi Tutt ruffled his thick white hair with clutching fingers; his blue-eyed glance shifted from the speaker's placid old face to the floor, to the ceiling, to the window and finally to his young partner's dark, inscrutable features; and then all he said was:

"Gee-whizz!"

"Yes," nodded Old Anthony, "it is a tolerably large sum, but I am offering as security a controlling share in the Orellana Dam and Irrigation System which will fertilize an enormous tract of desert waste and certainly transform this vast desolation into habitable and extremely valuable virgin land. Well, gentlemen?"

Malachi Tutt, sighing deeply, touzled his hair more furiously and, once again, glanced at the brooding, saturnine face of his youthful partner who, meeting this appealing look, now spoke in his pleasantly soft Southern accent:

"And pray, Mr. Falconbridge, why come to us?"

"For two reasons, Mr. Charteris. First because this Western Development Company of yours stands high, is extremely rich and powerful. And secondly because your company has always been prepared to spend largely to such good purpose and upon precisely such projects."

"Perfectly true, sir," murmured young David Charteris, viewing this serene, old face with dark, impassive eyes, "but, as you know, we are not, like you, a one man organization, we have our board and thousands of shareholders, and to advance such a loan, even to you, on a project which we know is far from completion and may never be so,—to risk so much of our shareholders' money would be sheer gambling. Also having regard, sir, to the vague rumours that are abroad to the effect that Falconbridge Amalgamated is pressed for money, I regret to say that as co-director with Mr. Tutt of the Company, I, for one, feel that this loan must be refused. What do you say, Malachi?"

"Me?" quoth Mr. Tutt, heaving his tall, bony person erect with surprising nimbleness, "I'm saying a whole goldarned earful yessir—and then some! Mind now, Davy, I'm not saying yore wrong, none whatever, I'm only putting it up to yore intellects—whether there can be any friendship in business, and if gratitood or gain counts most? Wherefore and therefore, Davy boy, heark to me good and listen yore damdest. We—all, you and me, and I guess the whole business world, know that the name of Falconbridge stands for all that's best, cleanest and most honourable in business, by Jing! I'll say so!

"Now, first off the bat, Davy, I'm telling you, but for Anthony here, this Western Development Company would never have been. Years ago, long before you were born or thought of, Anthony seeks out yore father and me, we were youngsters at a loose end with mighty little money and no prospects,—he brings us together, sets us in charge of one of his smaller companies and we make a success of it. . . . You've heard something of this, maybe?"

"Why, yes, Mal, a very little. But—"

"Then listen you some more! The business we'd made a success, Anthony insists on selling to us,—and way below our own valuation! And later when we hit a snag and were up against it good an' hard, he finances us,—he carries us till we're strong enough to go alone, as we have been ever since, and from strength to strength, glory be! So here's another reason why he's come to us now, I guess."

"There is yet one other," said Old Anthony, smiling

up into Malachi's grimly-serious visage, "a better and more natural reason, because I feel that we are akin . . . of the old stock, Americans all, as were our forefathers. You, Malachi, speak to me in the voice and idiom of your uncle, my loved and honoured friend Noah, God bless him! . . . And you, David, Nature and the years have honoured by making you so very like my one other dear friend George, your noble grandfather."

"Ah!" exclaimed young David, moved at last and eager, "my grandfather . . . you saw him killed, I've heard you shot his murderer—"

"And he died with my arm about him, David," sighed Old Anthony, bowing his head. "A man's death! . . . And after him . . . Noah . . . in the desert. . . . Yes, these were men! Their memory is always with me. They come to me sometimes in my waking dreams, vigorous and hearty . . . and I so worn and feeble! God send the world such men as these! . . . When we were perishing in the desert,—Noah, the child and I, minds and bodies failing us, Noah pointed me to the distant mountains:

"'There's water there,' said he, 'cool rills and streams, —waters of life. You should be there to-morrow!' That night he died that the child and I should live . . . died of the desert where I buried him with George's guns belted about him. It is in his memory that I schemed this great enterprise and am now building the Orellana Dam. Before I die, if God is kind, I'll break the curse of the desert, bring the blessing of water to this thirsty waste, change its cruelty to kindness,—if only for the honoured sake of my loved friend, Noah, whose lonely grave makes every desolation a hallowed place for me. . . ."

The murmurous voice died away and for a long moment not a word was uttered; then, uprearing from his chair, Malachi spoke:

"Davy boy, here's a scheme we-all should shore be in on, by heck, I'm saying so! To break the curse of the desert! Man's work, Davy, man's work I'm telling you!"

"Sure enough, Mal!" answered his young partner. "And if we had ten million dollars of our own, Mr. Falconbridge should have it right now."

"And that's some talking, Davy. But not having the money—then what? We might raise a million or so between us—"

"About three million, to be exact," murmured David. "Would this be of any use, sir?"

Old Anthony looked from one to the other glad-eyed, and when he spoke, his voice too sounded glad:

"Friendship is a potent blessing. In hour such as this it brings comfort and great solace and repays us for past griefs—almost. Now, if I may, since you have blessed me with your sympathy, I will give you my confidence. Briefly then: Years ago I retired from business altogether, investing Donald Keith with full power and authority."

"And," quoth Mr. Tutt, heartily, "knowing Donald, I'm saying you couldn't have made a wiser choice."

"True, Malachi. But there was constant trouble on the Orellana Dam, strikes and so forth. . . . There was, and is, also a certain Julius Fischer! Money was needed instantly or the work would stop, money at once and plenty of it. Then to Keith at his wits' end, in this exact psychological moment, comes Fischer with proffer of this ten million loan, and from—Lawrence de Witt."

"Him?" exclaimed Malachi Tutt. "Well, I'll be everlasting doggoned—"

"And so," continued the placid old voice, "Keith, desperate as I say, accepted this loan, pledging the whole of our interests as security. Hardly had he done so than comes the shattering news that the company who was to take over the Orellana Irrigation when completed, had broken its contract, being on the verge of bankruptcy—"

"Ha!" cried Malachi. "And I'm betting a blue stack de Witt was onto this beforehand!"

"So I believe. I am convinced it was all of his contriving."

"And oh doggone it,—twice in the past, Ant, twice you had him on the brink of ruin, squealing for mercy and you let up on him, and I'm asking you—why?"

"That his final ruin might be the more bitter and complete. I held my hand that he should endure to suffer. . . . So to-day I am at his mercy."

"But why, sir?" enquired David. "May I ask your reason for such inveterate hatred?"

"Because," answered Old Anthony gently, "it was Lawrence de Witt who wrote the vile lies that brought death upon those I loved most on earth,—to your Grandfather, my friend George, to my trusty comrade, Noah Tutt, to my son and his young wife themselves almost children, and to their child, my little grandson. . . . Physically a coward, de Witt kept beyond my reach. So I made myself his Nemesis in business. I became his constant menace, over-bidding and underselling him, thwarting all his endeavours, arrogating thus to myself the powers of that God Whose ways are ever beyond our finite understanding . . . and now, it seems, to my own destruction. . . . My friends, my children, and now. . . ."

The old man rose and leaning heavily on his stick came slowly to the window and stood looking up at the serene, cloudless heaven almost as seeking there some enlightenment; while behind his back, eyes questioned eyes, dark head nodded to white, and Malachi spoke:

"Anthony . . . old friend, you and I belong to a generation that's dead, I guess, or dying mighty fast, a generation when we used fewer lawyers and seldom needed the signed contract to ratify and make us keep faith with each other,—no, sir! Now this Irrigation Scheme of yours is just our mark and mighty near our hearts, yessir! So here's our proposition. . . .

Make yore play, Anthony, finish the Dam, let's see it completed and perfect, as it shore will be seeing it's a Falconbridge job, and the Western Development will take it over for ten million dollars cash down and shares to be agreed later. This, old friend, without any written agreement we guarantee to do, relying on yore repute and our weight to swing our board, knowing such transaction will greatly benefit our stockholders. But, Anthony, and here's the snag for you if any,—we're so fixed that you must undertake to complete—nine months hence."

"And one week!" added David. "This is our extremest limit."

The old man turned and, looking from old face to young, smiled:

"So speaks Friendship!" said he. "And so am I made strong. Life has its compensations, even a life so long, so weary and troublous as mine. You have made me resolute for one last achievement. Nine months and one week hence the Orellana Dam and Irrigation works shall be handed over to you complete and perfect, I pray God, or I shall have risen above all caring. . . . To wear instead of rust out! To die in harness! What man could ask better? And David, my son, I thank you for that extra week."

Then shaking hands with these strangely-assorted partners, he went between them to the door; but there he paused.

"Tell me, Malachi," he enquired suddenly, "do you ever see your godson, young George, these days, my great grandson?"

Mr. Tutt ruffled up his thick, white hair again and shook his head rather guiltily.

"Well—no!" he answered. "What with young George being an earl and his ma a coun-tess and dowager of this, that and t'other, I kinda feel that old Mal Tutt wouldn't ante up high enough to their polite game not none, they're too . . . too—oh well I guess you get what I mean, Anthony?"

"I do indeed! Yet despite all their affectations, I hope, I believe, the jewels of truth and sincerity are there for the trouble of finding."

"Why shore, Ant. The Coun-tess . . . Rowena is straight-bred Falconbridge, hide and hair, and I guess that's good enough. But it'll be all of ten years since I spoke to her . . . Rowena. . . . She was a mighty fine girl, I'll say so, yessir!"

"I'm asking you to visit us again, Malachi, and you also, David."

"Thanks a heap, Anthony, but—not me! Jiminy Christmas, no. I'd not fit in . . . but Davy would."

"And will!" nodded David. "And so shall you, Mal. Thanks, sir, we'll surely come."

"In the meantime," said the old man, "have you an hour to spare now, Malachi, for me?"

"Shorest thing you know!" answered Mr. Tutt, heartily. "What's the play, old friend?"

"I want you to help me know this great grandson of mine a little better, Malachi. I'll tell you how, as we go. . . . But first I'll tell you what I think about these repeated strikes and constant labour troubles on my Dam. . . ."

So they went away together, arm in arm, leaving young David Charteris to look after them with the dark brooding gaze of George, his grandfather.

CHAPTER V

WHICH CHIEFLY CONCERNS ITSELF WITH ONE, GEORGE, EARL OF RIDERWOOD

THUS it befell that another George, to wit young George, Earl of Riderwood, rather more languid than usual by reason of 'the night before,' long-limbed, well-featured and recumbent on cushioned settee, turned his dark, somewhat ruffled head on its downy pillow at the sudden opening of the door behind him and spoke feebly plaintive:

"Bring me s'more cracked ice . . . eh, that you, Milvey?"

"Yes, m'lud!" answered a distinctly agitated voice, and a large somewhat flaccid face presented itself at the door, "yes, indeed, my lord, but there is a . . . a person, my lord, demanding—" The face was withdrawn rather suddenly and a disdainful, rather nasal voice was heard instead:

"Suppose," said Mr. Tutt, advancing one pace and leaving the door ajar, "let's suppose yore lordship, my lord, troubles to take a peek and see."

The dark head was raised and turned; blue eyes opened, shapely lips smiled and shaking off his lassitude quite surprisingly, George rose, both hands outstretched.

"Why dash me if it isn't the Tutt-Tutt!" said he, almost joyfully. "Old Malachi, friend o' my tender years and innocent childhood. Greetings and so forth! Be welcome, old horse!"

"Which I reckon is no way to welcome yore god-dad, son!"

"However, it's heartily sincere, my dear old chappie."

George Riderwood of Riderwood and ninth earl, was tall and more so for the silken dressing-gown that enfolded him; his features, clean cut like most of his family, were pleasing; he was young, he also occasionally and quite needlessly, but for a purpose, wore an eyeglass, for which he now fumbled vainly since it was in his bedroom.

"I'll be darned," quoth Mr. Tutt, glancing from George round about the luxurious apartment, "I'll be tee-totally goldarned if you don't listen and look more English than the Union Jack, yessir! I'm saying so."

"And you, Mal, you sound too American to be real."

"Well, son, I'll tell you. Your furnishings are all so English, yore dood butler-feller's so all-fired English and you're so near-English that all the Yank in me, South and West, shore rises up and snorts!"

"Godfather, old bean, you're forgetting, as per usual, that I'm half English."

"Shucks, son, I certainly am! Question is,—how much of you's just plain, hustling American and how much donothing English aristocrat?"

"A problem, Mal, a vexed question I have never been able to resolve—yet. Meanwhile, sit down, old timer, perch with me and let us together gargle," said George, reaching for the large, silver cocktail shaker that stood in reach. "A snifter, eh?"

"Nary snift, boy—nossir. You kinda look as if you'd been on a ripsnorting toot recent."

"Last night—yes! B'gad 'ripsnorting's' right!" sighed George, hand to brow. "Some fool or other was getting married, to-day or to-morrow, and other fools, self included, poured forth many and divers libations to the poor fish's departing bachelorhood, with the result that you behold me a somewhat shattered wreck, distinctly mouldy and what not, hence the aspirin and dry martini . . . dog's-tail and so forth."

"Well, son, I'm here to talk, if you're not too drunk."

"Never that, old horse! Speak, shoot, unbosom—no, wait! First unbonnet and park the person,—lo, a pew!"

So saying, George relieved Mr. Tutt of his hat and inducted him into a deeply cushioned arm chair.

"Now," quoth he, "grim friend of my vanished youth, to what do I owe the pleasure and cetera? Come you upon me like 'gentle dew from heaven' or a dam downpour?"

Instead of answering, Mr. Tutt sat frowning on the graceful, lounging figure opposite, but with such troubled look that George, reaching languidly for the cocktail shaker, laid hand upon his visitor's bony knee, instead.

"Old Timer, what's biting you?" he enquired. "Why the beetling brow, stony eye and dumb reproach?"

"George, boy, you've shore got me guessing, though I've known you since you were little lad and such dog-gone tough handful—"

"Quite!" nodded George. "I was a foul brat, as I remember, a peculiarly scaly urchin. But you were always my friend and champion, Malachi."

"Yes, we always got along," nodded Mr. Tutt, "even when you went to college,—and an all-fired wild proposition you were, George."

"A perfectly foetid youth, Mal! A revolting memory to shudder at, so why dig it up?"

"Wild or no," sighed Mr. Tutt, "you were all straight American, son, before yore ma sends you to that Oxford College way over in England. To-day yore so changed that—well, as I say, you've shore got me guessing! What are you? Which are you? How much of you is real genu-ine man, English or American?"

"Dammit, Mal, I've had myself guessing over this for donkey's years! Myself is to myself neither and both,—a damfool conundrum without an answer. . . . 'Why is a mouse when it spins?'—that sort of tosh."

"But, George boy, you come of a great old family that has achieved greatly—"

"Why yes," said George, masking a smile, "I believe my ancestors did some pretty hefty stuff—in armour and what not,—Crusades, Creçy, Agincourt and so forth, their motto—'Riderwood rides let stay who will' —or some such rot and—"

"Hell—no!" snarled Mr. Tutt. "The grand old family I mean is 'Falconbridge'! It's done great things, boy, and always succeeded."

"*Ad nauseam!*" murmured George into his glass.

"And, son, first and foremost, being the son of yore mother, you're a Falconbridge and therefore American!"

"But being the son of my father I am lord of Riderwood, old horse, and therefore English."

"And I'm telling you, George, that to be a Falconbridge is better than any doggone title in the whole round earth!"

"Says you!" murmured George.

"Yessir, I do and, by heck I mean it!" nodded Mr. Tutt, fiercely. "Being a lord and an earl's all right, I guess, so long as it pays,—which in yore case, son, I happen to know it shorely don't."

"True enough!" nodded George. "When my father got himself killed playing polo, he hadn't a bean, not a single sausage to his name. . . . But for the mater's money and the Ancient Respected's princely allowance I should have been in the cart, absolutely and long ago, of course. . . . You knew my governor rather well, didn't you, Mal?"

"Shore did, son. And, though an earl, he was a regular feller, yessir—I'll say so! And he shore knew horses! But I'm talking about yourself, and what I'm saying is this: To call yourself Riderwood and English but yet to live on Falconbridge money, don't seem so good,—no, sir,—unless you live for and act up to the Falconbridge side of yourself, which I'm saying is the best side, being American. And what's more, I reckon it yore dooty!"

"Ah—Duty!" groaned George, "in thy ghastly shadow how many dashed unpleasant absurdities are spawned! If you know what I mean, old timer."

"I don't, son, not me!"

"Then get this instead, old scout, to wit: Though

born a dashed Falconbridge and confounded Riderwood, I prefer to live my own existence, go my own way, and be merely my own humble self."

"The hell you do?" snorted Mr. Tutt, fiercely. "Why then I'll tell you precisely what yoreself is, young George—"

"Right-ho, Mal, but have no foolish diffidence, endeavour to be quite frank,—now, let it come!"

"Well then, young George, you're just something makes a shadow in the sun,—a spineless gink, a poor lummox spending money better men have earned! You're not even a has-been, you're a never-was, and I'm beginning to think, a never-will-be!"

"Dear, old, candid friend, topping—absolutely!" sighed George, through the smoke of his cigarette. "A distinctly sound, red-blooded effort, hot stuff, pep, vim and what not,—and all so dashed true—up to a point. But and however—"

"Son, you ought to have had to scratch dam hard for a living 'stead of having too much of everything handed you on gold plates, yessir! Too much is worse than too little! I guess this is what's wrong with us here in the U.S.A.—too much belief in the power of the Almighty Dollar and too little faith in anything else. So consequently we look like heading for a tee-total almighty smash—some of us! And that's why I'm here, son, for what with all this and our own dam rackets, strikes and panics—even the Falconbridge vast credits have taken a fierce jolt. Things look mighty ugly. . . . And what d'you say to that, young George?"

"Well," answered George, flicking the ash from his cigarette, "being for the nonce English, Mal, I remark: 'No, really?' 'Just Fancy!' or, more bluntly: 'Blimy!' Becoming American, I exclaim: 'Shucks!' 'Do tell!' or 'Holy Mackerel!' But, as myself, I say that if Falconbridge Amalgamated was swept clean out of existence it would leave me cold—absolutely."

Mr. Tutt arose, surveying the languid young speaker with eyes of horror.

"Well, dog—doggone everything!" he stammered. "Falconbridge's can't go, it's rooted too deep, like a part o' the constitution,—it stands for all that's best in American commerce,—it couldn't go, it mustn't and shan't, nossir! Yet you, George, goldarn ye, you have the gosh-blamed disrespect and gall to say—"

"That freed of its shadow, Mal, I should walk in the sunlight of possibility and attainment. . . . Dear old bean I'm not quite the idle waster, the damfool playboy and nitwit you think me and that I may probably seem; for I've achieved, somewhat, and not as Falconbridge or Riderwood, but in my own way, under the name of Roger Falcon,—I've succeeded quite to my own astonishment, Malachi, old son!"

"Eh? Succeeded? You? And just how?"

"Pen and ink, Mal. In the drawer of my desk there, is the manuscript of my fourth novel,—already sold, and for a dashed surprisingly good figure! What with book, serial, screen and dramatic rights I'm well,—pretty hot. So at last, old horse, if and whenever needful, I can arise as the stately head and benefactor of my stricken family . . . roof and what not . . . with an occasional meal, kindly comfort not blatant luxury, and throw a protecting wing over the sparse silvery locks of my amazingly aged progenitor, poor helpless old bird—"

"Eh? Bird?" demanded Mr. Tutt. "Helpless? D'ye mean your great-granddad, The Master?"

"The Master—yes!" said George in altered tone. "Once a giant to be obeyed, a colossus bestriding his world,—to-day, feeble with years, shrunk to a pigmy no one bothers for! Somewhat grim and rather ghastly, Mal, eh what? Oh dammit! Let's hope we don't live too long, let's die in good time and escape such bitter tragedy!"

Mr. Tutt sat down again, rather suddenly.

"You haven't seen yore great-granddad recently, eh, George?"

"Not I, he hates to be disturbed,—cushioned chair, chimney corner, daydreams and so forth,—slightly ga-ga I believe."

"How d'ye know all this, George?"

"The Mater. She tells me he's breaking up fast . . . quite doddering."

"Dying, you mean?"

"Absolutely! Wobbling on brink of grave, teetering on verge of the Beyond, poor old boy. . . . Yet no wonder, he's certainly had a dashed long innings,—amazing! Poor old chap's become a sort of anthropological curiosity, a national asset and so forth."

"Son," quoth Mr. Tutt grimly and glancing towards the slightly open door, "I'm saying you've got one hell of a surprise coming to you. . . . Suppose now I tell you I'm here to bid you report for dooty at the Falconbridge Building to-morrow at eleven a.m. sharp?"

George very nearly dropped the cocktail shaker and, setting it by, sat back to regard his godfather in wistful reproach: sighed he:

"Were you to ask such fool thing, Mal, then I, as an Englishman, should instantly rejoin that you were 'balmy on the old crumpet'; as an American freeborn, I should say you were 'all wet and had gone haywire'—"

"However," quoth Mr. Tutt, "by reason of one dam thing or another, you, as the one male descendant and heir of Anthony Falconbridge, are expected there to-morrow at said hour."

"Whereto, Malachi, speaking as myself I instantly observe: 'Tutt-Tutt! No, no! and Nothing doing!' My dear, old, faithful bird of ill omen why, oh why, if the business is toppling, why come to me, the Original Broken Reed? You know I've no head for business, that I detest business, that I—"

"Hold right there, son! Now try and forget yourself a second, if you can, and think of others! Yessir, all the many thousands dependent on F.A. for their living. Think of this and go to it, boy! Get down to it and do yore little best to keep things agoing. Get you into the battle, George, for battle it shorely is. Doggone it, son, if ever this old world needed men and heroes, it needs 'em right now, yessir, it shore does!"

"Unlucky world!" sighed George, sinking back upon his pillows. "I've never felt the least inclination to be a hero."

"And I'm believing you!" nodded Mr. Tutt, scornfully.

"Quite!" murmured George. "Tales and legends of heroes and supermen, classic and modern, peerless valour, noble of self-sacrifice and all such sentimentally romantic dashed nonsensical swash make me sleepy!" And he yawned forthwith.

"Ye poor, doggone, dingbusted young fish!" snorted Mr. Tutt, ferociously. "Yet I guess you're not too young to remember there were some pretty fine things done in this old country one time or another and not all for glory."

"My dear, old bean, that's all ancient history, the world's moved on since then—"

"Shore has, George, and I'm wondering just where it's a-moving to?"

"Oh up, old horse, up—skyhigh probably,— . . . or . . . along the Circle, I mean to say the Wheel of Life . . . down and up and back again to the Godhead . . . if you know what I mean."

"It's going down and out, I reckon, son, and just what the end'll be, God only knows."

"But does He, Mal? Is there a God?"

"Better and wiser men have believed so, boy, yessir! Your own grandfather, ah and great grandfather weren't ashamed to pray to their God . . . and on their knees, yessir!"

"And in nightgowns, I'll swear!" chuckled George. "They used to wear 'em in those days, made of flannel and what not. Must have looked whimsical, extremely dam comic,—man in flannel night rail kneeling so dashed solemnly and perhaps in a pointed nightcap and so forth—"

"Not a nightcap," said a gentle voice at the door, "I don't remember that I ever wore a nightcap even in my far distant youth, though I've seen them. But I do wear flannel, George, being such a very old person."

George sat up to look; George stood up to stare, he opened his lips quite speechlessly, for on the threshold, leaning upon crutch stick, golden eyes vivid with life and a faint smile on his clean-shaven lips, stood The Master.

"Won't you offer your ancestor, your aged progenitor a seat, child?"

George complied, awkward with haste and still dumb; and sighing, the old man sat down.

"George, my boy," said he, leaning back the better to survey this tall descendant of his, "I have been eavesdropping very carefully and was struck forcibly by one or two of your remarks. . . . You may seat yourself, my child. . . . The object of this visit was to form, as an unseen spectator, some estimation of your general character. But you are so extremely modern, of a world so remote and, in some few things, so far ahead of mine that I confess myself still somewhat at a loss. You will therefore be good enough to answer my questions, frankly of course and fully as you may. And please believe I ask with respect because you are one of this new generation in whose charge lies the future destinies of humanity. First then: Is there anything in this Creation that you humbly reverence and truly revere?"

"Oh yes, sir, I should say—Intellect."

"But, my son, this surely is a gift rather for wonder and admiration?"

"Sir, I venture to think it the power whereby Man has raised himself from the slime."

"Yet Intellect is a gift so rare, George, so coldly remote that I dare affirm it never was and never can be an inspiration to others. . . . Personally I think we should most revere the Power of Loving,—a love that is fearless and far-reaching, from which naturally flow the blessings of sympathy, a deep, instinctive kindliness and faith in our common humanity, a faith that, casting out craven fear and distrust, breeds Friendship and Brotherhood and is itself a direct manifestation of that great Spirit of Infinite Good,—indeed that God to whom I still pray—and in flannel, George, though these modern garments are pyjamas. . . . If you desire to smoke, George, or fortify yourself with stimulants, pray do so, for I haven't done. Age is garrulous and remembering my length of years, be prepared. My Second Question is:—Have you yet been in love?"

George reached a cigarette, looked at it and put it down again.

"Frequently, sir," he answered. "That is to say . . . now and then, off and on—"

"You mistake me, George. I said Love, not callow infatuation, or animal passion. I mean that mighty uplifting transport of the soul that is so nobly pure it fires with a yearning not so much for the beloved object as to be worthy of her surrender, nay her least caress? Boy, have you ever known what it is to tremble at the pure light in a woman's eyes, or even her mere approach? To hold her so sweetly sacred that you scarce dare touch her?"

"Well, no, sir, no . . . not exactly. What I mean is . . . absolutely not."

"Then, my poor boy, you have certainly never known love in its truest, most sacred and enduring reality. I can only hope you may. For such love, and I speak from experience, thank God! such love is man's inspiration, his sweetest solace and a deep, joyous content, a flower that the years cannot wither or even death destroy. So Heaven send you such love, my child. . . . Now my Third Question, as to your future. That you are ambitious, I know. You wish to succeed as a writer. Well, I pray God prosper you. But to write enduringly you must feel greatly and therefore—suffer. Suffering, either bodily or mental, is the fire, the acid test,—the weaklings cry out feeble complaints, the strong are made stronger and, enduring, grow wise. You will write, I guess, to please yourself, but don't forget your readers altogether! And remember, George, there is so much bad in the world that if there were not greatly more of good, Civilization could not last a day. Long experience has taught me there is good in the very worst if we will but trouble to find it. So in your books let there be some message of hope, some word of encouragement for our poor Humanity that, struggling up from the original dark, is beginning to glimpse the light and climbing on and up to ever greater achievements. Therefore in your writing be as comfortable, as pleasantly hopeful as you may, George."

"But, sir," said George, sitting up, "what about Realism? I mean painting Nature naturally, stark and unashamed?"

"By all means, my son. Be truthful. But how? For instance, one man describes a rat on a dunghill, another shows us two happy lovers kissing in the sunset; both pictures are true—but with this great difference: Someday, soon or late, rat and dunghill shall be cleaned away, but so long as man exists, lovers will kiss and Old Sol go down in glory. All foulness is ephemeral, thank God, beauty and goodness everlasting. . . . And here, poor boy, my verbose lecture ends and, alas, on a difficult . . . perhaps dangerous . . ." The old man broke off suddenly and, sighing, bowed his silvery head.

Now, viewing this intent, old face, the latent power behind luminous eyes and lofty brow, with a new vision, George beheld something of the valiant, deathless soul and indomitable will that shone through, that, revitalizing this frail, old body, seemed to crown the silvery head with the serene and assured dominance of leadership.

Greatly awed and somewhat shaken, George instinctively rose to his feet and, not knowing exactly what to say, spoke at random:

"Absolutely!" he murmured. "I apprehend, sir, spot of trouble and what not threatening F. Amalgamated. All hands to the jolly old pumps and so forth. And so, sir, blood being thicker than H 2 O, what I mean to say is absolutely right-ho! Eh, Malachi, old be—godfather?"

"Son," quoth Mr. Tutt, crossing his long legs with a sort of triumphant flourish, "you have shore said it, yessir! Now's the time to be all good American and stand by another dam good American yore great grand-dad and help keep his old flag a-flying, the business flag that's been kept clean and lifted mighty high."

"I get you, Mal. Now being the time for all good men to come to the aid of the party and so on. Therefore, great-grandfather, here am I, sir, to rally around you forthwith and right heartily if you'll tell me precisely how, when and where—" Old Anthony looked up at him so wistfully and with such smile that George stood dumb again, and taking the pale, thin hand that now came groping for his, held it in both his own, clasping it tight ere he let it go.

"The right stuff, Malachi, the right stuff!" sighed the old man. "The breed runs true."

"Shore does, Ant! Yessir, and in spite of being half English and a whole earl—"

"No, because of it, man, because of it! England and America, great Sire and mighty Son,—these, Malachi, but for the Boston Tea-party, might have ruled and kept order in this troubled world,—as they may yet, who knows?"

"Which," quoth George, "would be a perfectly sound egg! And now, great grandfather I am, metaphorically, all ears. Speak, sir shoot me the woeful tale."

Briefly and with no redundancy of word or gesture the story was told, the situation described so vividly that George's eyes shone, his shoulders squared themselves, his languor was forgotten.

"So it's war," Old Anthony ended. "I'm beating up recruits, ordering my forces. But when the battle joins I want you beside me to help me win my last fight."

"And, by God, sir, I'll be there!" said George, fervently.

"But first, my son, I am sending you on a secret . . . and I fear, dangerous mission to the Orellana Dam. You have risked life and limb frequently on polo-ground and foot-ball field, to-day I'm asking you to take such risk again but in better cause and to worthier purpose. Well, George?"

"Quite, sir, music to my ears and so forth, absolutely. When do I go?"

"Come to me in the Falconbridge Building to-morrow at eleven o'clock and we will hold council of war."

"And, sir," answered George as he helped the old man to rise, "I shall be very truly honoured."

"And, George," said The Master, thin hand for a moment on George's broad shoulder, "because I believe you are sincere and mean this, I am made so much the stronger to meet—what is to be."

CHAPTER VI

TELLS OF A VISION AND A REALITY

REACHING home, Old Anthony, supported on Tom Pegg's ever-ready arm, went forth into his old-world garden, for the Westering sun was genial and the air, balmy.

"Let them bring my tea into the arbour, Tom. Bread-and-butter, not too thin, and plenty of butter."

"Yessir! Cakes? You've had a pretty hard day,—what about a sandwich or so—ham, sir? Or a bit o' cold chicken like?"

"No. Just lettuce. Extreme age is seldom very hungry."

"Well but just a sliver o' ham, sir, or a—"

"No no."

"Very good, sir."

"Look at it, Tom!" said the old man, halting suddenly.

"What, Master?"

"The tree, Thomas, the old tree. There it stands, older than myself by perhaps a thousand years! Only a tree and yet so enduring, so strong and vigorous, while I . . . ! How frail a thing is this mortality, so quick to fade, to wither and pass away!"

"Well, yes, Master, ordinary folks,—but you, sir, you're so—you're such—"

"Oh, I'm an anomaly! I'm an example of the confounding perversity of things, Thomas. Having frequently wished to die and be free, Death pertinaciously shakes his grisly head at me and passes on,—but not very far, he's waiting close at hand to summon me—when least expected, of course. So it behoves me to do what I must while I may. Go fetch me paper and pencil, you'll find them on my desk."

They had reached the bowery old arbour in which fragrant shade stood a deep armchair beside a table whereon was a telephone, with electric bell switches. Here seated, Old Anthony gazed dreamily across the sunny garden, breathing deep of its flowery fragrance and lost in wistful reflection.

"Paper, sir, and pencils," said Tom Pegg, setting them upon the table very precisely.

"Right, Thomas. I'll have tea when I ring. Till then, let no one disturb me—nobody!"

"Nobody shan't, Master, never a soul!"

Left alone, The Master took pencil and paper to scheme out details of the vast undertaking before him, like the wary and much experienced tactician he was; but after some while the busy pencil slowed, grew still, was laid aside and, leaning back wearily, the old man gazed away where, beyond clipped hedge, trim walks and shaded lily-pool, rose that mighty and age-hoary tree. And, once again, his old eyes beheld vision of the long-vanished yet ever-living past:

A lovely, timid creature in plain, small bonnet and simple gown, who steals upon his sight, often pausing to glance so fearfully around, then, flitting silently to the old tree, she takes a sealed letter from her bosom, kisses it, hides it in the rugged bole and flits as silently away—back into the shadowy past.

The old man closed his eyes to the smart of sudden, painful tears and so remained, lost thus in grievous thought, until, roused by an extremely unexpected sound, he glanced up and thus beheld an even more unexpected object that bounced, that rolled and came to rest within a foot of his chair. Now peering down at this, he saw it for a disreputable looking old tennis ball so worn and grimy by long service that he judged it the joy of some childish heart and so, reaching out the crutch-handle of his stick, he drew it beneath his chair. . . .

A vague murmur of voices; a scrambling sound; a rustling upon the ivied boundary wall; silence.

Footsteps, very light and furtive, stealing nearer, pausing, coming on again. . . .

Old Anthony caught his breath, gazing now with wide, though disbelieving eyes.

A young and lovely creature, plainly dressed, who stole upon his sight, often pausing to glance fearfully around. . . .

Old Anthony sighed deeply and once more closed his eyes: heard these light feet steal near, looked again and spoke, gently:

"Under my chair."

The young trespasser, starting violently, turned to front him, head back thrown, one hand to her round bosom, one slim foot poised for instant flight, an attitude the more graceful because so utterly unconscious.

A handsome girl whose worn dress served only to enhance her young body's slim yet generous shapeliness; an oval face, somewhat too pale, framed in short, glossy curls of night-black hair; a mouth, full-lipped, and almost too wide for perfection, above a round chin firmly moulded; a vivid arresting face lit by that almost indefinable quality of innately mental loveliness which is far beyond and more enduring than mere beauty of feature. All this he was quick to note, but it was the eyes of her that drew and held his wide gaze, for, between their well-opened, thick lashes, they were golden as his own.

"I . . . I beg pardon!" said she, breathlessly, "I know I'm trespassing. But a little girl, such a poor, little mite, lost her ball . . . in your garden here some place. I guess it means a whole lot to her, so I just . . . came after it."

"And, as I say, you will find it under my chair," he nodded. "Pray forgive my not rising, but I am less agile than I was."

"Oh, thank you!" she answered, pale cheek flushing as she returned his searching regard. "Please don't move. I can reach it." Lightly she came to kneel and grope beneath his chair; and now his quick glance was instant to notice the trim gown so very skilfully mended here and there, the little out-worn hat and shoes that spoke of dire poverty; he saw also certain livid marks that shamed the rounded beauty of her white throat.

"Child," said he, in voice so tenderly compassionate that she started and glanced up at him, "ah, my dear, what brute has savaged you?"

"Oh, the usual sort," she answered bitterly, "goes on two legs and calls itself a man. I've had to fight with the beasts before now. . . . But this one was the worst yet. . . . I answered his ad.—went to his office that wasn't an office. . . . I've got pretty hard, so I don't scare so easily as I used,—but this time . . . ! You see he locked the door and grabbed me, but I fought him off and got out of the window, down the fire-escape. Then I wandered around till somehow I found myself in the yard at the back here . . . and a little mite in tears because she'd lost her ball. So, being pretty miserable myself and not caring much just what happened, I . . . well, here I am! And now—what?" Uttering the question she rose with a swift, supple grace, for Old Anthony had pressed one of the electric switches on the table. "Are you going to have me thrown out?" she demanded; and now the sensitive beauty of her face was disfigured by a hard recklessness that is so often the defence of a nature too easily hurt. "Don't bother to ring for help, I can still walk, and I'm doing it—right now."

"On the contrary," he said gently, "I beg you will favour an old man with your company to tea."

"Tea—?" she repeated, glancing about rather wildly.

"If you will honour me."

"But . . . where . . . ?"

"Yonder!" he answered, as a resplendent footman approached bearing in fashion stately a well-laden tray; a plumpish young footman whose round eyes became rather more so as they encountered The Master's unexpected visitor.

"Another cup and saucer, Rogers, and bring some jam and ham sandwiches and cakes and stuff, cold chicken and so forth. I find myself extremely hungry. And, Rogers, hurry!"

"Yessir. Hat once, sir!"

"First set a chair for the young lady, here by mine. And now, child," said Old Anthony as Rogers sped away quivering with haste, "when you've returned the ball, be good enough to sit and pour tea."

For a long moment she stood looking at him with eyes so bitterly experienced and so very like his own, then without a word, did as he bade. The grubby old ball was tossed back over the wall to be welcomed by an elfin shriek of rapture.

And presently seated beside him at the little table, looking down at her nervously clasped hands, she spoke very softly:

"So you knew I was . . . hungry?"

"There, at least, we are alike," he answered, lightly, "so get busy with that teapot, pray. And do not trouble to make polite conversation. Let us eat!"

Now while this was doing, she intent upon the dainty fare before her with a youthful appetite and an eagerness she took pains to conceal, Old Anthony watched her with a musing intentness: The sweetly prideful carriage of her head, her delicate hands and wrists, the gracious ease of bearing that spoke of breeding and refinement. At last becoming conscious of this keen regard, she smiled faintly and shook her head at him.

"For one so hungry you don't eat very much, while I . . . if I make rather a pig of myself, please forgive me because . . . well, things haven't been . . . I mean . . . oh I mean you guessed right, I was so hungry, so famished I could have devoured your nice plump footman—almost!" Now, though her lips smiled on him, her eyes were suddenly abrim with tears.

"A little more milk this time," said he, passing his empty cup. "You are of the South, I think?" he enquired, watching her deft, pretty hands.

"Yes. We lived in Virginia . . . Richmond, just mother and father and me . . . such quiet, home folks. But when mother died I . . . oh I came on to New York, hoping to make my way. But the only ways that seemed to offer led nowhere, or else—" Here, once again, her face showed bitterly hard. "But I've tried pretty nearly everything beside, indeed I have. I've been a cloak model, I've worked in an office, I've sung and danced in a musical show, I've even been a scrub-woman and cleaned out office buildings, yet here I am, still hunting a job."

"Have you no friends?"

"None—that count any."

"You are not married?"

"Oh no—no!" she answered fervently.

"Nor engaged?"

"And never shall be. I—hate men!" said she fiercely; then meeting his look, "young ones," she added.

"The distinction comforts me," he answered and with such smile that she, relaxing, smiled also.

"You don't use that abominable lip-stick or powder stuff, I notice," he pursued.

"I can't afford to!" she sighed.

"Meaning you would if you could—hum! Do you know shorthand?"

"Why, yes,—" she answered with hushed and rather dreadful eagerness, then shaking her head, sighed wearily, "No, I'm lying! My shorthand's rotten and I'm not much better with a typewriter, otherwise I might have got some secretarial job, but—"

"You have," he answered. "I have engaged you."

"En . . . engaged . . . me?" she stammered.

"As my personal secretary. Your salary will be fifty dollars a week and your duties commence now,—and your first is to refill my cup. Why on earth are they made so ridiculously small?"

"Fifty . . . ? Dollars . . . ?" she echoed in faint, gasping manner. "But you . . . you don't . . . I can't give you any character or—"

"But you have!" he answered, with his serene air of finality. "It is in your eyes, your voice, your every gesture. The matter is settled."

"But you don't so much as even know my name . . . or I, yours."

"I am Anthony Falconbridge—"

"You . . . ? Mr. Falconbridge? The . . . Mr. Falconbridge?"

"I am indeed that so aged person, and with a cup waiting to be refilled!" The teapot was lifted, but her hands so unsteady that she put it down again.

"Please," said she in voice tremulous as her hands, "you're not doing this . . . just out of pity? And yet I guess . . . I know you are! Of course you are! And yet even if . . . if you are—"

"Well?" he enquired.

"I shall accept just the same, because this means . . . life to me . . . or more than life . . . self-respect . . . hope. Ah, you don't know and I can't tell you just how much it does mean . . . if . . . ah, if only your offer is real! But is it . . . oh, is it?"

"Of course!" he answered, fumbling in his breast pocket. "Don't I look real? Do these bills feel real? Your first two weeks' salary in advance. Take it, come take it, this moment! And it would be as well to tell me your name."

"Jennifer," she answered, stuffing the money blindly into her little handbag, "Jennifer—Claire, Trent."

"Well, Miss Trent, don't think this is going to be any sinecure! Far from it. I am an extremely busy man and shall be increasingly more so, and this will entail a great deal of hard work, close application for you."

"And I," she murmured, "I'm not making you a lot of promises, Mr. Falconbridge, only . . . this: I'd come so low, no money and so desperately alone and afraid of what hunger might force me to, that I was going to end it all to-night and go back to mother so she could kiss and welcome me—unashamed. Well now, the life you've saved I would give up for you . . . gladly. Oh, believe!"

"I do believe you," he answered, gently. "And the life you offer me I will take and use to good purpose, for myself and your own future happiness. . . . Come here, my child, kneel here beside me."

Swiftly, and mutely wondering, she obeyed and thus upon her knees, gazed up at him with an expression very like awe.

"I am," said he, "such a very old man that God, being ever merciful,—to offset the weakness of this poor, old, weary body,—has blessed me with vision and sight, eyes that see with strange clarity and an unfailing intuition; thus I see so far beneath the surface of things . . . the false and the real. You, child, have known suffering and bitter disillusionment,—but by suffering our characters are formed, for good or evil. But your eyes, though sad with knowledge of evil, are still bright with truth and sweet with purity. So to-day instead of dreaming girl you are a woman of such character shall make her beauty a power for good, whose intellect and faith in herself shall help me in what is to do. Just what this is you shall know to-morrow. Come to me in the Falconbridge Building to-morrow at eleven o'clock. Now off with you, child, you'll be wanting to shop, I guess. Tom Pegg shall take you in the automobile, it will save time." So saying, he turned to reach a certain one of the electric switches and in so doing, let fall his stick; now as he groped for it Jennifer caught it up, pressed its worn, gold handle to her lips, thrust it into his grasp, rose to her feet and bending to smooth her shabby skirt, murmured brokenly:

"Shopping . . . oh joy . . . !"

"You rang, Master?" enquired Tom Pegg, cap in hand; "you want the auto again, sir?"

"Yes, Thomas, for this young lady, my new secretary, Miss Trent. My dear this is my chauffeur, Tom, he is also my old friend, eh Tom,—is friendship old at fifteen years?—such little time! Until to-morrow then, Jennifer, at eleven o'clock."

She clasped the frail hand he offered; she spoke no word, but in her eyes was a glory; and when she turned and followed Tom Pegg through the sunny garden she went with lovely head proudly borne, walking like a young goddess.

CHAPTER VII

WHICH IS A CHAPTER OF MERE TALK

GEORGE'S eye (despite monocle) lit on her first as she entered the crowded elevator, and becoming instantly aware that she was of a distinct type and entirely new even in his varied experience, he viewed her, faintly curious; he looked away and back again with quickening interest: Her face, air, costume, and the form it contrived to reveal, pleased his aesthetic and almost too fastidious judgement, waking vague memories of dreams unrealized, callow imaginings, desires unfulfilled.

So George looked; he gazed, he stared until she, as if sensing this persistent scrutiny, turned her head (so beautifully poised, thought George) and meeting his eyes, frowned (and very properly, thought George) and, thus frowning, contrived despite the throng, to turn her back on him (such adorable and shapely back, thought George) as he followed her out of the elevator in time to hear her say to the gold-braided attendant:

"Miss Trent to see Mr. Anthony Falconbridge, by appointment."

"Most excellent egg!" quoth George within himself; and was still following this so alluring, feminine back when a powerful grasp checked him, a tall, immaculately garbed person gripped his hand, smote him in joyous welcome and hailed him by the familiar nickname of his not so far off college days.

"Porges, old man! Can this be you?"

"Bill!" exclaimed George, smiting as heartily in return. "Why, Bill, old son," said he, becoming all American, "you old son of a gun, this is great! Where've you been keeping yourself all this time?"

"On a truck mostly," answered Bill, slipping a hand within his friend's ready arm and beginning to walk him up and down the wide corridor, "yes, a truck, old lad! And that's one of the amazing things about it all, because, d'ye see, it was a Falconbridge truck!"

"Oh?" enquired George and being at a loss, fumbled for his monocle, screwed it in his eye and was instantly English.

"A truck, eh? Quite! Oh absolutely! Not that I know what the dickens you're talking about, but if you say a truck,—right ho! But, let me tell you—"

"And, George, what's more,—you don't know it, of course, and I didn't until yesterday, but the further astonishing fact is—I'm shortly becoming your brother-in-law!"

"Amazing!" said George, shaking hands again. "Astounding, but all to the good! I rather thought the Mater had selected the de Witt bloke whom from adolescence I have ever regarded as a poisonous amœba, a pestiferous egg and extremely scaly bird! Wherefore, Bill, old skate, in congratulating you, I felicitate myself—"

"But the really wonderful thing is," continued Bill, as they paraded to and fro again, "I thought I was marrying another girl altogether—"

"Mum's the word, my William, mum! Spot of wild oats and what not,—all understood. Hush-hush and so forth, tell it not in Gath and dumb as an oyster—"

"No, no, George—no! Not a bit like it. I'm trying to tell you this girl—"

"Quite!" said George. "One came in here just ahead of me, a vision of all the wistful, disembodied yearnings of my vanished youth, if you get me. The Absolute She, in capitals, Bill! The Concept Feminine I've hunted and sought vainly in so many other shes. And here to-day, Bill, here in these mundane mercantile surroundings she dawns upon me like—"

"The Master," said a voice behind them, "will see you gentlemen now." Incontinent and silently they followed a uniformed attendant to a door whereon he knocked and thereafter ushered them into the presence.

Old Anthony glanced up from the papers before him, looked from one intent young face to the other and nodded.

"It would appear that you already know each other?" he enquired.

"Yes, sir," answered Bill, looking at George.

"Absolutely!" said George, glancing from Bill to this aged relative. "Yale, sir, same year. Bucked the line together frequently, Bill was centre, I was inside right tackle. Bill was also our star 'man in the box'—pitched us to victory two seasons running, which was some performance."

"I'm glad you are friends," said The Master, "because you will be associated, and together in the particular work I am asking of you. And I am asking, not ordering, because you may encounter personal danger, even to life itself. So, before going further, I must know if you are willing to take such risk?"

"Sir," answered George, screwing in his monocle, "I'd no idea business could be so interesting, not to say dashed alluring. The job was made for me, absolutely!"

"And me, sir!" said Bill.

The old man glanced at these young faces, each so very different yet both so virile and resolute; then bowing his silvery head almost humbly, said gently:

"It seems I have somewhat underestimated this generation,—well, I'm still young enough to learn. Now, William," he went on briskly, "under these circumstances I suggest it might be as well to defer your proposed marriage. I have set the facts before Barbara and she, having quenched anger in tears, has agreed to abide by your decision. Well?"

Bill rose, said "But, sir—" choked and sat down again, whereat George, dropping monocle the better to see his friend's stricken face, leapt instantly to his defence:

"Oh, I say, Gramps," said he, using the childish pet-name in stress of the moment. "What I mean to say is, poor old Bill, you know, not to mention Barbara,—seems too dashed footling to let a spot of danger hold two loving hearts, and so on, apart and yearning—if you get the idea. Besides there's the Mater! I gather she's no end peeved because you booted Arthur de Witt, hoofed him out of the picture and what not,—which, allow me to add, puts you ace-high with me, sir, and proves you the absolute and original—It!"

"George, your flow of eloquence is, I fear—"

"Turgid, I'll own, sir, yet sincere. One further spate and I'll dry up. Briefly then, in re, the Mater and de Witt, knowing what she is when on the warpath, and Arthur being such a pernicious germ, I suggest we take Bill, Barbara and Time by the jolly old forelock, marry 'em forthwith, honeymoon 'em, then let them come West with me to the Orellana Dam. Barbara can cook and keep house for us, teach her domesticity and so forth,—which I humbly submit is a perfectly sound egg, eh Bill?"

"Perfectly! Yes!" answered Bill with fervour, "If The Master will only agree. Will you, sir?"

"So be it!" said Old Anthony. "Once, years ago, I strove to part two lovers such as you . . . in my prideful folly, God forgive me! Death and bitter remorse have made me wiser . . . Now hear what it is I ask of you. . . . For some time there have been labour troubles on the Orellana workings which I am convinced are being wilfully fomented by some secret agency, troubles which I expect will grow and become worse and, unless checked, must end in disaster. Your duty will be to discover by what means these irregularities are inspired and—by whom. William, you, being an accredited engineer, I am sending as another assistant to Julius Fischer who is at present in sole charge. You, George, will go as gang supervisor, but chiefly as yourself, I mean as one who, forced by harsh circumstances to an odious task, does little and complains much."

"Quite!" nodded George. "Fits me to a hair, sir. And I suggest dropping the handle, for the nonce I'll be George Riderwood or, better still, Rider."

"So then," continued The Master, "you will be my eyes and ears on the Dam. You will live together in a suitable cabin I am having built and fitted up for you, somewhat removed from the camp and in direct telephonic communication with this office. Should this private line be discovered and interfered with, you must contrive to telegraph in code, daily. Now is all understood?"

"Yes, sir," answered Bill.

"Not quite," George demurred, "concerning this dashed pussyfoot business, this dark and dirty work at the cross-roads, I rather gather you suspect someone, sir?"

"I do!" nodded The Master, grimly. "But towards whom my suspicions point I won't say lest you be unduly prejudiced and because I may be mistaken, though I fear not. This is all I have to tell you at present except that, knowing youth's reckless spirit, I do beg you will take care to run no unnecessary risks, for if this peril comes it will strike swiftly."

"When must we go, Master?" enquired Bill.

"Remembering," added George, "this forthcoming marriage and what not, sir!"

"Well," said Old Anthony, musingly, "the sooner the better, of course, but under these circumstances let us say a week hence."

"Thank you, sir, indeed!" said Bill rising, "I'm . . . oh I'm tremendously grateful to you. And now with your permission . . . Mr. Jefferson is waiting to give me all necessary data for—"

"Certainly, my boy, off with you. . . . See me again at four o'clock before I go."

"A ripe specimen, sir!" quoth George as the door closed on his friend's stalwart form. "Extremely sound bloke! Zeal, initiative and so on, no end. Which naturally reminds me of myself, George Rider, sir, at your service—ever ready, up and at 'em, what's my present job, how shall I achieve, pray?"

"By studying the map, my son, and scale plan of the Orellana workings, getting them and the vicinity by heart. I have them here for you . . . somewhere. . . ." The old eyes began to peer, the thin, frail hands to turn over the many papers and documents on the great desk before him. "They were somewhere here," he repeated. "If I live much longer I shall be requiring spectacles! I know they were here. Ah, perhaps—" speaking, he touched a bell; George resumed his monocle; a door opened and—the monocle tumbled to dangle unheeded. . . .

She had laid by hat and coat, she also appeared entirely serene and self-possessed and thus (thought George) showed more than ever the dream incarnate.

"Miss Trent," said Old Anthony, "there was a—ah, I see you have it, thank you!" His quick eyes had, of course, noted George's froglike stare and now, unfolding the map, he spoke:

"By the way, Miss Trent, this is a relation of mine, Mr. George Rider. George, Miss Trent, my secretary."

"How do you do!" said she, coolly.

"Quite!" answered George, his usual calm assurance tottering, "Absolutely! What I mean is,—seeing you in the jolly old elevator, I, as it were, looked at you, you looked at me, deep called to echoing deep and so forth, the answer being: Here we are again!"

The beautiful face became almost hard, the long-lashed, golden eyes swept him with a very evident dispraisement and passed on, but when she spoke, her smooth, soft voice was kindly gentle:

"Were you in the elevator?"

From behind the widely unfolded map that Old Anthony seemed studying, issued a small sound that was neither cough, sneeze, nor laugh, a vague sound yet sufficiently remarkable to draw the momentary attention of both hearers; then George drew a deep breath, smiled and became his serenely complacent and quite competent self:

"Miss Trent," said he, "I fear you misapprehend me entirely. I stared at you, as I am doing now, with an expression of admiration, amazement and profound awe because, though we have never met before, I felt and do feel that long ago I knew you very well. Perhaps this is because of your golden eyes so extremely like my respected—er—relation's, perhaps because you are a type I've seldom seen. However, I beg you'll notice my speech is respectful as my look,—and as your humble servant henceforth, I'm honoured to make your acquaintance which I hope may lead on and up to ever better things . . . the realization of a long-forgotten dream."

"Mr. Rider," she answered, with expression less hard, "if you are joking I don't think it funny. If you are serious I don't understand you in the least. Mr. Falconbridge, will you go over those manifests now?"

"No, later, my dear. Bring them along home with us and we'll go through them together after tea, in the garden."

George resumed his monocle and gazed mutely from hoary, reverend age to vividly blooming, adorable youth and remained thus dumb until the door had closed behind her, then:

"Tea!" he murmured in tone of deep reflection.

"Miss Trent seems well able to take care of herself, George."

"Most girls can, sir. The simpering *ingenue*, bleating baa-lamb innocence . . . absolute back numbers. . . . But—tea! In a sunny garden!"

"George, do you mean that Innocence is out of date with our top-hats and Prince Albert coats?"

"No, sir, only that Ignorance is. Our modern lasses, bless 'em! . . . know their way around these days, which I submit is all to the good. . . . Though the burning question that consumes us is—tea! Sir, there are sundry great-grandfathers, even in this harsh world, would certainly ask their humble relation to pop along and chink a convivial cup and what not."

"Probably, George, but this great-grandfather is an exception."

"Sir, may I venture to ask why?"

"Your erotic predilections are too manifest."

"In this case—admitted, sir! The rosy archer got me first crack, dead centre. Absolutely clean bowled,—and for the first time in our experience. Wherefore this case is, well—different."

"It always is, George."

"Quite! But this is a case that most truly is,—'pon my honour. There was I, at eleven this a.m., full of *joi de vivre*, keen as mustard and burning with zeal to rally around and so on, when—there she is! And there am I wondering what hit me,—until I remembered the picture and your stories."

"My stories? George, what on earth—?"

"And the picture, sir! The portrait of my how many times 'great'? grandmother, Blodwen. Well, you often told us about our beautiful ancestress when we were kids, Barbara and I, with her on one knee and me on the other. You inspired me with tales of Blodwen's loveliness, her courage, her marvellous rifle-shooting, how she saved her Anthony's life and he hers, and how she and her baby were saved at last by Mahtocheega, the Tuscarora. Do you wonder she became my boyish heroine and that I worshipped her beauty as a youth . . . used to stand gaping up at her portrait? Sir, it was on that picture, that type of feminine beauty, I based my callow dreams of the She I should someday fall for . . . I mean love and so forth. Well now, isn't Miss Trent her breathing image—no, Blodwen back again in the flesh under another name?"

"You seem to have noticed the likeness, my son."

"And you to have grasped the fact, great-grandfather."

George's comely face was so unwontedly grave, there was such deep sincerity in his every word and gesture that the old man's austere features softened wonderfully, beneath their thick, white brows his eyes twinkled, but his tone was quite uncompromising as he answered:

"However, Miss Trent being Miss Jennifer Trent and my private secretary, I suggest you direct your amatory exuberance elsewhere."

"Not so, revered sir, oh no! I'm through with all that, long since. Dalliance and what not is dust and ashes, ab-so-lutely! Henceforth, Respected Ancestor, I am out to woo, to, if possible, win and wed this long-sought Blodwen of mine who calls herself Jennifer Trent,—which is a prettier name and extremely apt. Meanwhile, sir, the sun being over the fore-yard, I suggest we beetle forth together and snatch a hasty one and thereafter gnaw a bone or toy with a chop. What, no? Then I'll totter alone, or with Bill, returning to yon slave-bench at two-thirty sharp. But . . . this afternoon at four o'clock, or say—four-fifteen . . . who knows?"

Reaching the door George turned to glance back rather wistfully at that solitary old figure.

"Quite sure you aren't taking on too much, Gramps?" he enquired. "This mammoth business is hardly a one man job. Why not trip along with me for half an hour,—spot of rest and what not?"

"Thank you for such thought, my son," answered the old man, gently, "but in two minutes I am conferring with the staffs of all departments. I mean to knit these men together in a vital fellowship, yet make each one know himself a responsible entity,—one power, one soul made up of the many. . . . Come back to me, George, at two-thirty. I shall have more data for you concerning the Dam, with a name-list of the men we can trust there, men I know personally."

George went from this quiet office out into an atmosphere of purposeful stir; hurrying feet and intent faces seemed all about him, an atmosphere so infectious that George himself forgot to lounge. Meeting Bill, as alert and purposeful as any, George hailed cheerily with proffer of refreshment.

"Good lord—no, old man!" answered Bill, shuffling the papers he held. "The Master's called a conference, and, George, the more I see and hear of him, the more I marvel at him—"

"Quite!" nodded George. "And we all thought—yes, I thought he'd gone all loopy, ga-ga, just a poor, futile old—"

"He's a wonder! A superman!" quoth Bill fervently. "Now I'll push or he'll be waiting . . . mustn't and can't be. So long, old lad."

So George ambled his solitary way through the orderly bustle around him and, knowing the inspiration of it all, his respect and wonder grew.

For truly the soul of this great business was awake again; instead of mechanical routine and parts of a vast machine, were human beings, each with an individual duty to perform, and each one of them conscious that with them and of them was a leading force, a power that inspired confidence by its calm acceptation of all final responsibilities; all knew The Master was back with them, fronting this uncertain and troublous future undismayed.

So sped this busy day until came four o'clock when The Master's roomy car, with Tom Pegg at the wheel, rolled smoothly homewards; and at approximately three minutes past four, a long-bonneted speedster, with George at the wheel, rolled smoothly after.

Thus it befell that, as Jennifer sat in the arbour with papers and documents before her, she became aware of a scrabbling sound nearby, and stepping forth into the garden glanced up in a certain direction, frowning and expectant; nor had she long to wait,—for:

George's monocle, with George's eye behind it, rose above the wall and peered down at her; and George smiled, swung himself to a sitting posture with remarkable ease, removed his extremely natty hat and bowed; murmuring:

"And here we are again!"

For a long moment she stood looking up at him with a level gaze wherein was no hint of coquetry, anger or embarrassment, surveying him from expensively shod feet to crown of sleek head, noting the quiet elegance of his perfectly tailored garments, his length of limb, width of shoulder and, lastly, his face with its arrogance of nose and chin, his changeable eyes that could be alert, dreamy, impish and wistful in as many moments; and as she thus gazed up at him in dispassionate appraisal, so he gazed down at her. Finally she spoke:

"That's a very easy wall to climb."

"Quite!" he answered, eyes still intent.

"You see, I climbed it once."

"Oh, really?"

"Yes—really! I came after a lost ball. What are you after, please?"

George shifted his gaze, fumbled for his monocle, put it into his pocket and answered plaintively:

"Well, I did hear something about—tea."

"Does Mr. Falconbridge expect you?"

"Why, yes, in a way he certainly does, — oh quite!"

So saying, George vaulted gracefully to earth, tripped, lost his hat, picked it up and beamed. "Not at all according to plan. However—"

Silently she turned and went back to the arbour and silently George followed; here she pointed him to a table laid daintily for tea.

"Two cups!" she murmured.

"Strange oversight!" said George. "Doubtless another is to be had—"

"So you are not expected to tea, Mr. Rider. And I know you are not here to see Mr. Falconbridge. So I ask again, please why are you here?" And her voice was so softly, smoothly gentle, her dark lashes so demurely adroop that George, thus lured, took heart of grace and answered:

"To be perfectly honest the answer is—you."

"Me?" she repeated. "Oh? But why me?"

"Because," said George, his voice deepening, "though our acquaintance seems so short, I'm resolved to marry you at the earliest possible moment. You've but to say the word—no, you've merely to look your consent and—"

"Marry me!" she murmured, and still without looking at him, "it was . . . 'marry' you said?"

"Absolutely! And just as soon—"

"Then you are either madly rash or . . . merely insulting."

"Hardly rash, but never insulting," he answered gravely, "but ever and always your humble, respectful servant, oh quite! It may sound ridiculous, at such short notice, a bit odd at first, but the more you think over it the less—"

Then she laughed,—so harshly, so bitterly that George, fumbling for his monocle, stood motionless; for, crossing to the doorway she leaned there to look back at him over slouching shoulder, her face disfigured again by that same hard recklessness; she lounged, hand on rounded hip, long-lashed eyes half-closed, shapely lips thinned to a mirthless smile.

"Say," she drawled, "get this, Lothario! I'm no snugglesome, google-eyed baby pet. I've been around places and know all you can tell me—and then some! Just because I'm pulling this 'real lady' stuff to keep my job, don't fool yourself it's all honest-to-goodness, dyed-in-the-wool. I'm sure wise to your sort, I'm onto your play and it doesn't go with me none whatever, so you can cut it right out."

Perching himself on an arm of the easy chair, George swung a leg, shook his head at her, answering forthwith:

"Well now, Sweetie, that's just too bad, it certainly is! Because I'm aiming to play Ro-meo to your Juli-ette, and sooner or later you're going to act up to me good and strong and plenty,—and you're going to like it, baby—see? And now, Miss Jennifer, having thus broken the ice, as it were, I beg to inform you that my name is George, and if you'll can the tough stuff, babe, and become again your own true and sweetly gentle self, I'll endeavour to explain how and why this apparently ridiculous offer is very real, very sincere, —so, Miss Jennifer, please listen. . . .

". . . There was once in my family a very lovely, a very noble and valiant lady, she lived in the Independence War days, we have an old portrait of her and she is so beautiful that I loved her as a boy, but to-day I adore her! And Miss Jennifer, you are her breathing image! Her brave, sweet, gentle soul looks at me from your golden eyes—now, yes now! So it's my hope that some day I may see them even more beautiful with the love I shall wait for. . . . Well, Miss Jennifer, my dear, there's my explanation and I can only humbly ask that you'll try to believe me."

Here, once again they viewed each other steadfastly; then her ruddy lips, now softly sweet and tenderly curved, parted for quick speech and yet were dumb; she shook her head.

"But at least you do understand?" he pleaded, and quite humbly.

"Why yes,—oh yes," she answered, "it makes things more . . . thinkable. But, Mr. Rider, you're not in love with me, you love a disembodied spirit. I may look like her picture, but I'm quite different . . . not a bit . . . noble—Besides, I . . . loathe the whole idea. I hate men and the thought of marriage is just . . . horror! I may not be so hard as I acted just now, but I've seen enough to make me. . . ." She shivered violently and into her eyes came such look that, for once George found no word adequate; then, upon this painful and rather dreadful silence, rose the tap-tapping of a stick and glancing round, George beheld his great-grandfather approaching and from a totally unexpected direction, but off came George's hat with an airy flourish and he hurried towards the old man, saying, cheerily as ever:

"Greetings, sir. Pray take my arm. It seems we are short of a cup and saucer. You see I'm doing myself the honour of inflicting myself upon you for tea."

"Indeed?" said Old Anthony, taking the proffered arm. "At least we can talk business. Miss Jennifer, oblige me by fetching the Code Book, you will find it in the rack upon my desk. . . . Now!" he continued, so soon as they were alone, fronting George rather grimly, "be good enough to tell me if your proposal was as sincere as you contrived to make it sound?"

"Eh . . . what, sir . . . proposal? You mean to say you were . . . listening?"

"Why, of course!" answered The Master, rather testily. "You are my heir, the last man of our line and I am naturally interested in whom you choose to be the possible mother of—my descendants, your children."

"Chil—! My word!" exclaimed George, feebly. "Looking a trifle ahead, aren't you, sir? I mean to say somewhat previous and so forth. However, here we are! Will you sit down, sir?"

"No, not in the arbour, let us walk, come this way. . . . So then, though entirely ignorant as to her nature, antecedents or past you are urgent to marry this young woman, eh George?"

"Quite!" answered George, lightly, but his face showed grimly resolute as his great-grandfather's.

"You are then determined on this and sure of yourself at last, are you?"

"Abso-lutely!" answered George. "What I mean to say is, well absolutely, definitely, if you know what I mean?"

"I think I do, and am therefore glad to assure you Jennifer Trent comes of sound stock, a family long resident in Richmond, Virginia. Her mother was a Stukely, her father, purebred American, was a doctor,

Miss Jennifer acted as his dispenser until he killed himself with overwork, last year."

"But how, how the dickens—?"

"You forget I have agents in all our larger cities. Also there are telephones, airplanes, wireless and suchlike double-edged tools."

They had reached a rustic bench set in secluded corner beyond sight of the arbour and here the old man sank down.

"And now," said he, motioning George to sit beside him, "as to Miss Jennifer's character, her past—"

"I say, sir, you—you've never been digging into that, for heaven's sake?"

"Well, no George, no—"

"Then don't! No, not on your life! You see," said George fumbling his eyeglass, "a woman's past . . . well, it's her own, I guess, or should be—"

"Until she marries, George?"

"Yet, even then . . . it all depends and . . . oh, to hell with it anyway! It's what she is that matters, not what she was,—it's not the past, but the present and future that counts . . . eh, sir?"

"Right, my son, may you always believe so. . . . Lastly, as regards her fierce antipathy to men and marriage."

"Why that's it!" nodded George. "If only you'd seen the perfectly ghastly look she gave me!"

"Well, how do you propose to combat this?"

"The Lord knows!"

"Of course. But I'm asking you."

"Oh well, there are ways . . . a gentle persistence, masterful humility, say it with flowers and what not."

"Your usual methods, George?"

"Yes and no, sir. You see I've never been like this before, she's so new in my experience yet so marvellously like Blodwen that I seem to know her, and yet of course I don't and . . . by the way, sir, why the cross-examination, this interest, why trouble your wise old head at such busy time? Does it mean,—by the Lord, Gramps! are you with me in this—are you?"

"Heartily, my son!" George rose to grasp the frail-looking old hand that clasped his own with such unexpected vitality. "To know you happily and worthily married, George, with the assured and blessed hope of children! Ah, to know this before old Friend Death takes me by the hand, would make up to me for past griefs and failures! To leave behind a clean and worthy heritage . . . the new America! For ours is a good breed, my son, a clean strain. It is on such that the very foundations of this America rest, this country, that, great now, shall be greater. It is the old, vigorous strain of the first colonists and early pioneers that is still the chiefest basic alloy of the American character, thank God! That undying Spirit bequeathed to us through the ages by a great ancestry . . . British, Roman, Saxon, Norman and English, fighters for and lovers of freedom all,—the unconquerable spirit ever most merciful in counsel, fiercest in battle, readiest to die for its ideals, the Spirit that still inspires this English-speaking race and shall be yet, I think, the ultimate salvation of all men."

The old man's pale cheek had flushed, his golden eyes had kindled, so also had George's, but all he said was:

"Absolutely!" yet the trite word was uttered with such reverence and Old Anthony nodded so comprehendingly that George continued:

"Such great tradition, sir, is hard to live up to, and must bring an enormous burden of responsibility."

"Of course, George, of course! But only the coward and weakling shirks responsibility,—this is the hall-mark of Manhood and of a nation's vigour."

"But, sir, how about the old slogan and ballyhoo of 'minding our own business and only our own,'—'America for the Americans' and so on—?"

"No! Someday it must be America, with England,

for the world, that way true greatness lies, my son. . . . I shall not be here then, and yet I may be helping, working hard to bring this about,—yes, still hard at work, George, though on grander scale. Meanwhile, my boy, tea is waiting,—tea and—"

"Blodwen!" said George, rising.

CHAPTER VIII

TELLS HOW GEORGE WENT FORTH TO ACTION

THE busy days have sped; Barbara has wed her man and followed him into the great South-West; but George is still kicking his neatly shod heels in New York, as indeed he is doing literally at this precise moment, perched on a corner of the desk, looking down at Jennifer's lovely down-bent head as she sits opening and sorting the great pile of correspondence for The Master's attention an hour hence; for it is ten o'clock and the morning sun is lighting small fires in her chestnut hair.

And Jennifer is frowning at her work and George at her, though very wistfully.

"It's got my goat!" sighed he, at last. "It beats me why you can't appreciate me, not at my true worth, of course, but approximately. Just permit me to mention one or two of my more obtrusive perfections: I'm steady in my paces, seldom off my feed, sound in wind and limb, go easily in single but better in double harness—"

"You make yourself sound like a horse, Mr. Rider."

"And the horse, remember, child, is a noble animal."

"That's why I prefer horses to men."

"And—I asked for it!" murmured George.

"Mr. Rider, I do wish you would go and let me get on."

"Name being, Ever-devoted George, Jennifer darling," he sighed. "And Ever-devoted George sits confounded, George cannot imagine what you find to kick at in George with such dam persistence."

"It may dawn on him eventually," said Jennifer, slitting an envelope quite viciously.

"Oh, absolutely, of course, but what, pray?"

"That he—"

"Meaning George?"

"Yes."

"Then say it."

"That George Rider simply doesn't enter into her scheme of things."

"Poor soul!" murmured George. "How dark, how desolate must be her scheme of things, whatever they are, poor lass! A scheme and—no George! A weary, dreary waste and no blink of George to transform it into a golden Eden of Joy, of bliss and marital raptures surrounded by choiring throngs of rosy amoretti—"

"Oh, for heaven's sake!" she sighed, frowning yet laughing also, "if you've nothing better to do, take this and read something worth while," and catching up a volume that lay nearby she thrust it into his unwilling grasp. George took it, glanced at its title and down fell his monocle.

"Eh,—Roger Falcon . . . *The Increasing Flame*?" he exclaimed, "So—you read his stuff?"

"Yes, and why not? It's new, and happens, for a wonder, to be clean."

"Too, too much so!" he answered, shaking his head at it. "Old-fashioned hero and heroine, a he-him and feminine she, virtue triumphant and so on—"

"Well, virtue is triumphant sometimes," she retorted almost bitterly; "it must be or we should act like savages and brutes still. And anyway this book and others like it are better than the sordid beastliness so often called 'Realism,' of the frightful stuff written by perverts for degenerates, showing just one vile little out of the way corner of life at its very worst. . . . It's only those who've never really seen, never really felt and known such rottenness and the awful waste . . . the tragic horror and . . . terror of it who love to write and read about it." Her wide eyes stared on vacancy, her shapely hands, no longer busy, were tight-clenched. Then, looking up at him, she laughed, mocking herself and his gravity.

"Oh fudge!" she exclaimed. "Will you listen to me! As if it mattered anyway. It doesn't help to take anything too seriously, especially ourselves."

"Only now and then!" said he, more solemnly than ever. "And, Jennifer dear, whatever rottenness you've had to face hasn't hurt you, it couldn't. So just think of it as only a bad dream never to return."

"I do," she answered. "And a book like that of Roger Falcon's is a help."

"Oh? Is it? How and why?"

"Because, though Life's so mixed, it tells mostly of the best."

"Well," said George, fluttering the pages of the book in question, "after all it's only the best that endures. However Rog Falcon should feel pretty bucked."

"That sounds almost as if you knew him. Do you?"

"Eh? Know him? Why,—as a matter of fact, yes I—what I mean to say is, somewhat—"

"Oh!" she exclaimed. "What's he like,—to look at, to speak to,—tell me!"

George dropped the book, picked it up, screwed in his monocle and answered:

"Stick upon the torso of the young Augustus the head of the young Antinous; fire the eyes with genius, tip the tongue with eloquence and, well—there you are!"

"No, there he is! And he doesn't sound a bit convincing."

"No?" enquired George.

"No! And frightfully uninteresting!"

"In fact, a washout," sighed George.

"As you describe him, yes. Anyway he's clean and must have a nice mind."

"Which," said George, "naturally brings us back to Ever-devoted George! Because George is nice, George is also clean inside and out, so . . . Jennifer, my dear, what about him?"

"He'd better go, because The Master will be here in about—five minutes," said she, glancing at the clock with a tenderness surely wasted on its unresponsive dial.

"Ambling forthwith!" answered George, rising obediently. "Though first, the oft-denied appeal: Luncheon—will you honour me? Is it the harsh 'No thanks' as per usual. If so, so be it. Or—why, Jennifer, is it yes?" For she was looking at him, and a glitter of tears on her lashes.

"You are so . . . different!" said she, with a break in her smooth, soft voice.

"And that's pinning on the blue ribbon, absolutely!" said he, flushing. "And to keep 'different' I . . . I'll refrain from kissing you though I'm all yearn from head to heels and the only way is to buzz off. So, my dear, lovely, tempting angel, I'm buzzing—watch a hero!"

Thus at precisely eleven o'clock The Master found him extremely busy with gauge-rule and dividers upon a scale plan of the Orellana workings, yet instant to help him off with hat and overcoat and full of chatty greeting:

"Morning, Governor! All well and hearty, we hope?"

"Amazingly so, George, considering. Hard work seems to suit me even now, as it always did. What are you doing there?"

"Oh, stewing over the dam Dam, sir. Quite a town you've got here it seems,—club-rooms, theatre, baths, recreation ground. A somewhat hefty job by the looks of it and involving a dollar or so, eh sir?"

"About fifty million, George. The Dam will hold ten billion gallons of water and will take two years to fill. It is two thousand, one hundred and fifty feet long at the crest and will absorb some five million cubic feet of concrete. Its seven million dollar electrical scheme should produce power which, over a fifty year period, will repay the cost of plant and structure, plus interest."

"Oh? Quite!" murmured George, feebly. "I mean to say . . . my hat . . . no idea . . . sir, it's stupendous! But the time limit seems dashed short!"

"Yes!" said the old man, frowning. "Yes, and yet it will suffice,—but there must be no more strikes, no more mysterious accidents."

"Well, everything seems quite serene and what not, sir."

"Seems, yes, George. But were I young enough I should be worrying. Age, however, has taught me that worry is mere waste and futility."

"And anyhow, sir, Bill's report on the phone yesterday was all to the good, so far."

"Yes,—so far! None the less I'm taking every precaution."

"You mean against any more dashed dirty work. Of course the de Witts are at the bottom of it all, eh, Gramps?"

"*Cui bono*, my son! Had I but the least tittle of evidence . . . !" Old Anthony drew a deep breath, his hands clenched themselves and so passionately that he viewed them with a faint surprise. "Dear me!" he sighed, shaking his head at them, "it seems the mere name still has power to rouse the Old Adam in me. . . . I am convinced Lawrence de Witt will stop at nothing to achieve my ruin, and now at last is his opportunity. I believe trouble is brewing . . . danger threatening. . . . I can sense it in the air. Well, I'm prepared. Also, this week I am despatching another thousand men who have worked for me all their lives, like many of their fathers before them, loyal and trustworthy every one."

"When do I go, sir?"

"George, I don't know. For once I'm unable to make up my mind. How soon could you be ready?"

"Whenever you say,—to-morrow, the day after,—" answered George, glancing very wistfully towards a certain door.

"And pray," enquired The Master, instant to heed

this eloquent look, "how speed matters in that direction?"

"Eh? Direction? Oh, I get you sir,—fairly bobbish, thanks."

"And are you still as certain, George?"

"More, sir, more! With every breath certainty becomes more assured, oh quite!"

"By the way, I bought a novel by Roger Falcon called *The Spadesman.*"

"Oh? Really?" muttered George, fumbling with his monocle. "Fairly putrid in places, but you see it's the first."

"I haven't read it—yet, George, but my eye was caught by a poem—"

"Sorry, sir, but my hero bloke, though a man of his hands and what not, has a curse of rhyme and breaks out, ever and anon."

"It struck me as a worthy effort, George. . . . Now as regards your going to the Orellana Dam. . . . Step over to Keith's office and talk it over with him."

Left alone the old man sat a while lost in troubled thought; at last espying a bunch of roses that graced his desk, he drew them near, inhaling their fragrance gratefully, then setting them by, touched one of the many electric bells at his elbow.

"So," said he as Jennifer entered with the letters, "so you don't forget me, it seems." And he motioned towards the roses.

"How could I?" she answered. "Oh, how could I ever? I only wish I could tell you all my gratitude . . . how I feel, but . . . I can't?"

"But you do!" he nodded. "It is in your eyes, my dear." And then, because these eyes began to fill, he busied himself with the letters she had set before him, glancing at, scanning or perusing them according to their importance; finally he leaned back in his chair, saying:

"Nothing here of any particular moment."

"Why then," said Jennifer, rather nervously, "I've made you an egg-nog, will you please drink it if I bring it now?"

"Very gratefully," he answered.

So the pick-me-up was brought, tasted and pronounced excellent.

"Thank you, my dear!" said he. "Sit down, pray, and watch me drink it. In one so young such gracious-thoughtfulness can touch hoary old age. . . . Youth!" said he wistfully, "youth is a glorious season, my child!"

"Age is more wonderful," she answered, "though I think rather terrible. Yes, I mean you, Master! For with so many around to do your bidding and . . . love you, there are times you seem so remote . . . so tragically alone."

"Age is always solitary, my dear. And yet though my world is dead long since and life so changed, my memories are green and fragrant as your roses here. . . . But lately I've renewed my youth, the last flicker of the flame, perhaps, but it shows me wonders undreamed, I am even beginning to understand this present, your, generation a little! This very perverse, so extremely self-conscious generation that hides its best and flaunts its worst, seems ashamed of its many virtues and overstresses its fewer vices. For instance,—this book!" Here, he took a volume whence it lay and opened it at a certain page, saying:

"This is a modern novel entitled *The Spadesman* and written by an extremely modern young man, one Roger Falcon, yet in this book I find these verses, pray listen." Then The Master read aloud, this:

"'God made a man of goodly earth
Then sent him forth to try his worth
By hardship, pain and toil.
Man suffered much, but wrought amain,
Grew rich and, strong with pride of gain,
Made Wealth his god and his disdain
The good and cleanly soil.

'So Mammon made of Man his slave;
And to this golden god, man gave
His best in painful toil.
He laboured fiercely day and night . . .
Then Right was wrong and Wrong was right.
For, thralled by Mammon's golden might
Man scorned the cleanly soil.

'But, on a day, the Great God spake:
Oh Man! Oh Son of mine—awake!
Look up, thou slave of toil.
'Tis I that with my strength have stayed thee
Since first to be a man I bade thee
And in my living image made thee
Out of the good, clean soil.

'So, learn of me now, sons of mine,
In work shall be a joy divine
And glory in your toil
If, in a kindly brotherhood,
Ye labour for each other's good

And dwell together as ye should—and there,' said Jeremy, reaching for his tankard, 'the old bean conks out!' whatever that may mean!" said Old Anthony, frowning at the words in puzzlement. "You see, my dear, our author, being young and so extremely modern, becomes self-conscious all at once and jibes at his own earnestness. . . . As poetry these verses have little merit, perhaps, but they embody a thought, which at least is something. . . . But the surprising thing is that this Roger Falcon turns out to be that apparently average, rather brainless young man, my kinsman, George Rider. . . . You, too, are surprised, I see!" For indeed Jennifer had risen and was gazing down wide-eyed upon the open book, and her ruddy lips, parting to a rosy O being yet dumb, the old man continued:

"Indeed, like his generation, George is so much more than he cares to appear or has allowed me to suspect, that I hesitate to send him into danger . . . perhaps risking his life on the Orellana Dam."

"His . . . life?"

"There has been trouble and will be more,—an ugly stealthy business and George is eager to risk himself to uncover it—"

"But you . . . you are The Master!"

"And suggested he should go, my child. . . . But now—? However, let us hear what he says."

So George was summoned and came forthwith; beholding their solemn faces he closed the door with exaggerated caution, glanced from hoary age to glowing youth and back again and folded his arms.

"Hullo—hullo!" he exclaimed, "am I called to judgement? Is it crown of bays or dungeon for mine?"

"George," said the old man, "I am greatly minded to keep you here in New York as my unofficial lieutenant, or rather as a kind of *aide-de-camp*."

"Now pon my soul, Gra—sir, I'm no end bucked to know you want to have me on tap, dodging around and so on. I'm touched, sir, flattered, absolutely. We do seem to rub along surprisingly well, don't we? But for office or staff work I'm the world's positive worst, oh quite! It's the open spaces for me, sir, out there with old Bill. So, with your permission, I'll push off fairly soon, say the day after to-morrow. But before I go, if you—"

A desk telephone buzzed suddenly; a muffled voice said:

"Long distance, sir. Special from the Dam. Through right now, sir." A series of clicks, a moment's silence, then:

"Falconbridge speaking. Is that you, William?"

A small, thin voice answered, the ghostly whisper of speech uttered three thousand odd miles away; and hearkening to this faint voice, Old Anthony tensed, his white brows slowly knit themselves, his mouth closed grimly; and when, sudden as it had begun, the ghostly voice ceased, he sank back in his chair, showing so stricken and so very, very old that Jennifer instinctively clasped a protecting arm about his drooping shoulders and there met George's arm, and thus for a moment their three heads were very close together. But glancing up left and right from one anxious face to the other, Old Anthony smiled:

"Dear me!" he murmured, "I thought I was going to be kissed."

"You looked pretty wonky!" said George.

"Please," said Jennifer, producing a small, silver flask, "please sip this!" And, with murmur of thanks, Old Anthony meekly obeyed.

"Suffering snakes,—a hip-flask!" moaned George. "Booze positively upon the person! . . . Well, sir, what about it,—bad news from the Dam?"

"Death!" answered The Master, squaring his shoulders. "A premature explosion. Nine men killed and injured. Of course this may be an accident—"

"Or the beginning of more devil's work," said George. "However, I feel myself summoned hence in no uncertain manner. Miss Jennifer, our luncheon, alas, is postponed because I'm hencing immediately."

"What, George, immediately?"

"Yes, sir, I shall go by air."

"Air? You mean a flying machine! To be sure, I had forgotten such dreadful things existed. . . . Desire Keith to summon a conference here at once. And, George, don't fail to see me before you go, I've a list for you, names of men we can trust."

Thus, while The Master sat surrounded by men who, beneath his direction, ruled the destinies of so many, George, perched once more on corner of a certain desk, was taking leave of Jennifer in characteristic fashion:

"I've tottered in just to say cheerio for the nonce and hope you'll not instantly forget your Ever-devoted George, but will rather steel yourself for the inevitable against his return."

Jennifer had taken up a pencil and was drawing twirls and flourishes upon the pad before her, and, thus intent, she questioned him:

"'The inevitable' being what, please?"

"Taking him for better, worse, richer, poorer and what not."

"Are you proposing again?"

"Quite!" said George, fervently.

"Why?"

"Eh?" he exclaimed, somewhat startled. "Oh, well, just because you are you and I am I. I mean to say—made for each other, love at first sight and so on."

"Love?" she enquired, turning a squiggle into a bird with an extremely curly beak. "Did you actually venture to mention the word?"

"Certainly! Why not? Yes,—love. Absolutely! And the genuine article. Not to be fulsome I love you and I love you just for breathing, and with my every breath, and with each breath I love you more. So, Jennifer,—how about it? . . . What's that you're sketching there, an eagle or a parrot? Dashed good!"

"No, not a parrot, and not an eagle exactly," she answered, touching up her sketch with firm, deft strokes, "it's meant to be a . . . falcon."

"Eh? Oh, a falcon,—quite!"

"When we discussed him this morning, I think you rather over coloured your description of him, Mr. Falcon."

"Ah! I get it!" nodded George. "You're on, it seems."

"Your great-grandfather informed me a while ago. He also read me some verses out of your book, *The Spadesman.*"

"Too bad!" murmured George.

"I'm also aware that Mr. Rider is really the Earl of Riderwood."

"Did the old boy tell you that, too?"

"Oh no, my ears and eyes and such intelligence as I happen to possess."

"Which," sighed George, "judging by your dashed aloof air, has probably torn it somewhat. However! Take a chance, my dear, let's beetle off and get wed, then fly with me to Orellana as Mrs. Rider or my countess. What d'you say, girl?"

"No!" she answered, firmly though very gently.

"Any reasons?"

"Not worth mentioning."

"Then better luck next time. . . . I rather like your falcon drawing, may I have it to wear against the old throbber, with appropriate posy: 'To beloved G. from his everest, ownest J', or some such,—may I?"

Obediently she added the date and, giving it to him, looked up into his eyes: so George took the sketch and her as well, folding her close, drawing her near, and she all unresisting, only she murmured brokenly in small, pleading voice:

"Be . . . different . . . still!"

"As possible . . . beloved!" he answered, murmuring also; then, brushing her lustrous hair with his lips, he loosed her, turned, and strode away.

CHAPTER IX

RELATES, SUCCINCTLY, DIVERS ACTIONS OF MR. RIDER

HERE on the fringe of the desert all things were on prodigious scale: rugged foot-hills, jagged mountains, range after range whence soared rocky giants, peak on peak, flaunting their everlasting snows in the sun's very eye; the desert itself,—this vast desolation of weary distances lost in a shimmering haze of blistering heat, a place of torment by day, an awful mystery by night whence breathed an air chill as death; the mighty dam that rose sheer between craggy walls of a yawning canyon,—this man-made cliff that was to collect and contain the precious water, streams of very life in this barren wild, that had been seeping to waste through countless ages.

And here wrought men, frail-seeming, puny creatures against this tremendous background, men who laboured day and night; an army of pygmies and yet so potent, dowered with an intelligence so godlike, that mountains crumbled before them, the wilderness shrank sullen upon itself, even the grim desert, this place of desperate travail, suffering and death, was to be tamed, its stark terrors done away, itself transformed from cruel desolation to smiling homeland. And all by these laborious men, these godlike pygmies who, having tamed and harnessed Giant Steam, have set Titans to aid them in this stupendous battle with Nature.

Engines blare shrill warning as they clatter to and fro over miles of rails, dragging long trains of trolleys, cars and trucks; huge steam shovels scoop and delve; steam drills clamour and rave as they drive deep into stubborn rock for the charges that are to rive the mountains asunder; powerful cranes move as if dowered with human intelligence, they haul and sway their mighty, iron arms like the obedient and hardworking Titans they are.

Heat and noise, dust and ceaseless effort; and amid it all, chiefest of all,—Mr. Julius Fischer. He is a tall man, blondly handsome, whose powerful frame is set off to advantage by the dusty, though well-cut, riding garments he wears; he is also a masterful man who knows his business, for his eye is quick to heed as his voice and hand are to direct.

"Well, what is it, Jake?" he demanded of a heavy-shouldered, hard-bitten fellow who now approached. "Still more men arrived?"

"Yeah!"

"Be damned to 'em!" exclaimed Fischer, scowling. "Here's nineteen hundred new men on the job since The Master took hold again! How many this time?"

"One."

"Eh? Only one? What sort of one? Where is he?"

"Over there. Guy in dood ridin'-pants an' eyeglass, says his name is Rider."

"Well, let's hear from him. Fetch him along,—wait! If I don't get another chance alone, remember to warn the boys for to-night."

"Sure, boss. O.K. Same time and place?"

"Dammit—no! At Number Two sluice, the old shack, eleven o'clock." Jake nodded and lumbered away to return presently, followed by a nattily attired, very languid person who peered round about through his monocle with an air of dejection tempered with disgust.

"Ah," exclaimed Fischer, viewing this immaculate tenderfoot with scarcely veiled contempt, "you're a Britisher, I guess?"

"Thereabout!" moaned George. "Somewhat!"

"Oh! Well?"

"Is it?" queried George, shaking his head at this

hot and dusty prospect. "Looks like hell to me. Feels like it, too!"

"Don't like it, eh?" demanded Fischer, fixing the forlorn speaker with his large, blue eyes.

"Yes, like hell!" sighed George.

"So? And what d'you want?"

"To get away again speedily and forthwith. However! At present I'm on the prowl for a dodger named Fischer."

"That's me—"

"Oh?" enquired George, peering.

"My name's Fischer—"

"Is it?" murmured George. "Why then the odds are you're the bloke I'm after—"

"What 'n hell d'you mean?" demanded Fischer, large blue eyes suddenly bleak with menace, while Jake slouched a heavy pace nearer.

"I mean," answered George, with fatuous smiling nod, as he fumbled in the breast-pocket of his well-fitting coat, "exactly what I say, or somewhat, I'm on your track and what not, old bean, hunting you and so forth, chivvying you with a chit, missive or epistle, if I haven't lost it, dammit! No, here it is—"

Uttering no word, Fischer snatched and opened the letter; but as he read, his scowl vanished and he glanced at George with a contempt more evident than ever.

"Mr. Rider," said he, "Donald Keith writes here to say you are sent to me as a 'roving' gang-boss,—whatever that may mean, for it's a new one on me. Just what does it mean?"

"Ask me another!" sighed George. "I pass this one,—unless it happens to mean precisely what it says,—that I'm destined to rove and so on, flitting from gang to gang and what not, like a dashed bee or butterfly. It's all one to me and perfectly accursed anyway."

"Keith also writes," continued Fischer, consulting the letter again, "that you're to bunk with Romney and his wife—"

"Bunk?" repeated George, wincing.

"I'm telling you,—with Romney, another of the Old Man's new appointments,—"

"Yes, but old Scout,—bunk! I mean to say, you know,—sounds so dashed indelicate! However! Where shall I find this Romney bird?"

Laughing scornfully, Julius Fischer turned his back: "Show him the way, Jake!" he called over broad shoulder, and strode off towards that range of dusty buildings where was situate his office.

"C'm on!" growled Jake.

"Right ho, Puck!" answered George. "Lead on, thou jovial sprite, I follow eftsoons,—excelsior!"

"If you gotta talk, talk American and I'll answer—maybe."

"Then, say bo, are we having any strikes lately? Do tell?"

"Whajermean?" demanded Jake, halting suddenly to view his cheery questioner askance with small, fiercely suspicious eyes.

"Echo," quoth George, surveying this unlovely fellow with sleepy though keenly speculative glance, "silvery echo, my frolic lad, answers merely—'what?' Do we go much further, sweet wag?"

"Na,—up the gulch there a little ways."

"Then let us stagger on, whistling merrily as we go."

Jake stared, shook his head and trudged on again without another word.

They climbed an ascending path that led between rocks and boulders, that dipped and wound and turned sudden corners, leading them up and away from the great bustling camp and remote from the dust, the roar and racket of those labouring Titans; and thus George heard, suddenly and to his surprise, the notes of a guitar softly strummed and a richly melodious voice in murmurous song. Turning a sharp corner they came full upon the singer, a slim youth perched upon a rock.

"Dam greaser—!" snarled Jake and, stepping forward, he kicked this unfortunate musician so brutally that his singing broke to a shrill, anguished cry and he fell heavily; next instant Jake himself was staggered and amazed by a sharp pain in his own person and, turning, espied George in the act of kicking him again.

"What the hell?" growled Jake.

"Quite!" nodded George. "Old-fashioned tit for tat, and I hope it hurt. If not, we'll try again."

"Says you!" hissed Jake, and leapt; but his passionate blow was deftly avoided, a powerful fist smote his craggy jaw with such force and nice precision that he spun round and went down violently to sprawl half-stunned upon the rocky path.

"Silly ass!" said George. "To offer me your jaw like that! Get up and let's have another smack at it—"

Hasty feet on the path above them and round a corner strode Bill, a stalwart figure in knee-boots, khaki breeches and shirt.

"Hullo—hullo!" quoth George, winking. "Who may you be, pray? I'm Rider, a poor, dam tenderfoot reporting for duty."

"Yes, but what the hell's all this?" demanded Bill, taking his cue.

"Spot of bother with Jake here. Jake booted yon songster and I booted Jake. Jake tried a haymaker and I snapped Jake on the button. Q.E.D., and so forth."

"What d'you say, Jake?"

"I says as this dam Mex oughta be on the job. And if Mr. Smarty in the pants wants any more I'll be waitin' for him this time. Nobody ain't agoin' to down me an' git away with it."

"That'll be all from you!" said Bill, angrily. "Guilio's on night shift. And next time you speak to me say 'sir'! Now get t'hell out of this and pronto!"

Jake got heavily to his legs, scowled, and went his way, muttering evilly.

"Not so good!" sighed George, looking after his departing form. "Not so good, Bill! This may cramp my style as a sleuth, somewhat. In me you greet a blend of Sherlock Holmes, Mr. Fortune, Dr. Thorndyke and the whole shooting-match of unfailing 'tecs, and now this dashed gorilla, Jake, will be onto me forthwith. I shall probably be watched, which is all distinctly to the bad. However, I'm delightfully anhungeed, what's Barbara fixing for supper and how is she?"

"Porges, she's wonderful. Ah, George, old man, she's the most—"

"Quite!" nodded George, "I've known her ever since she became my sister,—but what does our songster want?"

"*Signori,*" said the young musician, taking off his hat with one hand but cherishing his guitar with the other, "I am not dam Mex,—no—Italiano—I! That-a Jake he no good—ah no! He ver' bad-a-man! He creep-a, creep,—he spy and peep—"

"All right, Guilio boy," answered Bill, "go ahead to the cabin and tell Mrs. Romney we'll be right along. . . . And talking of Barbara, old man . . ." Bill talked and George listened, pensive and patient, until his brother-in-law paused for breath, then:

"Abso-lutely!" he nodded. "But what's all this about premature explosions and what not?" Hereupon, Bill entered upon a very particular and highly technical description of the accident with reasons and causes thereof, probable, possible but all extremely hypothetical.

"In fact," said George, this laborious explanation ended, "nobody knows a dam thing about it, I mean to say, the direct cause, whether a genuine accident or—and there she is! And looking the complete home-comfort, housewife, helpmeet, and better half, absolutely! Greetings, Kid!" he called; for Barbara coming to meet them, had appeared on the path above, a radiant vision in the brief sunset glow. A bare armed Barbara, fresh from her home duties, her shapely form showing the more so by reason of the large flowery apron that swathed her; a Barbara whose eyes were bright and joyous and whose welcoming kisses left no scarlet butterflies or stigmata.

"My child," quoth George, surveying her with pleased, though fraternal eye, "old thing, you look all to the candied violets! The roseate bloom on that damask cheek comes from Nature's box, wedlock and old Bill seem to be suiting you—By George, you're actually blushing! Thought you'd forgotten how ages ago, but—"

"George," she laughed, "don't be such an absolute assinine goof!"

"Rather nice arms, too! Eh Bill?"

"I'll say so!" murmured Bill, fervently.

"Idiot!" said Barbara, "you've seen my arms heaps of times and never noticed them."

"True, Mrs. Romney, but never thus adorned with smudges of flour. . . . Which reminds me I'm dashed hungry! Eh . . . goulash? Lead me to it!"

"And why," demanded Barbara as, arm in arm all three, they began to ascend the path, "why are you a fortnight behind your time, George?"

"The answer is Woman, my child, the ultimate, the capital SHE."

"George, you're never—honest-to-goodness in love, at last! Not really?"

"Ah, but I am. And with reason."

"But—you, George, you! Who is she? What's she like? Do I know her? Is she dark, fair, tall, short? For heaven's sake speak! Say something! Tell me!"

"Blodwen's picture!" he answered. "Multiply it by two and you've got her, absolutely. Name's Jennifer Trent and she's great-grandfather's private secretary. . . . And is that the shack?" he enquired, as they came in sight of a log-house throned upon a green plateau where trees grew, for her a rill bubbled down the steep in a small cascade. "Looks more like a young county club-house. The old boy's certainly done us extremely well."

"Yes, it's cosy and roomy—and with every home comfort!"

"For which last, benedictions on his old, white head."

"Well, come in and help me dish up,—both of you."

So in they went, filling the place with cheery bustle, merry voices, laughter, the pleasant clatter of dishes. . . . Seated about the cosy supper-table they ate, they laughed and talked, especially Barbara. Under her remorseless cross-examination George hazarded the belief that Jennifer's hair was neither bobbed nor shingled, black or golden but precisely the absolute It; that she might take four in shoes or possibly fives; that she was not too tall and certainly not too short; that though not plump she appeared to be very far from thin—"

"In fact," cried Barbara, at last, "you hardly know what she's really like!"

"Oh yes,—Blodwen!" he answered patiently: then glancing across at silent Bill:

"What do you think of this Fischer cove?" he enquired.

"Knows his job," answered Bill, heartily, "yes, he certainly does. There isn't a better engineer, and that's sure."

"Yes,—but as a man, Bill?"

"Well . . ." Bill hesitated.

"Exactly!" said George. "Same here. And now I suggest a modicum of shut-eye is indicated, the hour being eleven and—" In the act of rising he sat suddenly arrested, glancing towards the window, for on the pane a ghostly finger was tapping. George rose, Barbara snatched from the high mantel-shelf a heavy automatic pistol; Bill smiled and threw wide the lattice:

"That you, Guilio?" he called, softly.

"*Si si*, Signor Beel!" a voice whispered and in through the open window came the young Italian's sleek head. "I come tell-a you thees bad Jake, he creep-a . . . he crawl. He down by Number Two sluice . . . and other *hombres* . . . five, six."

"Methinks," said George, rising, "the spot of shut-eye is deferred for the nonce. I'll away and take a furtive slant at these creepy crawlers."

"Good!" said Bill. "I'll tag along with you."

"Not so, my bold Benedict, not on your life!" answered George, with all the superb finality of his great-grandfather. "No, my lad, you are merely an engineer and only a married man, so stay with your engines and wife and what not, leaving the sleuthing business to George, Sherlock, Fortune and Co.—"

"Not much!" quoth Bill, looking round for his hat.

"You're certainly not going alone, George!" said Barbara.

"Now why all this dashed fuss?" he demanded, "I'm merely following a hunch . . . spot of blindman's buff, puss in the corner and so forth. And I'm going alone. If you came lumbering along, Bill, you'd simply put me off my stroke . . . anyway, if you go, I don't! So be a regular fellow and keep your old bean out of it. This is definitely my pigeon, so sit back like a sportsman and leave it to George."

"Oh, all right!" growled Bill.

"Well then, you just take this!" said Barbara and into her brother's unwilling grasp she thrust the pistol; George looked at it, tiptoed delicately to the hearth and set it back on the mantel-shelf with exaggerated caution.

"Not for me,—no, no!" said he. "Should I run into anything worth while, I prefer—this!" And from his pocket he drew an extremely useful looking knuckle-duster. "So for the nonce, my children, chin-chin!" And, with an airy flourish, he slipped out of doors,—out into a velvet darkness topped by a splendour of stars.

"You take-a my hand," whispered Guilio, "the path he tweest."

"Right-ho!" whispered George. "*Avanti!*"

Borne to their ears upon this windless dark came a throb and murmurous hum where the distant Titans clamoured over their ceaseless labours; between dark earth and star-spangled heaven they beheld an up-shooting, palpitant radiance and, turning sudden corner, they glimpsed the great dam lit by hundreds of powerful flares and twinkling lights by the thousand, then a turn in the path hid all from sight except that up-streaming radiance where Man was battling so relentlessly against stark Nature; and ever the sound of this unending strife waxed louder until George checked, suddenly arrested by his companion's hand and voice:

"There, *Signor!* Look, my sir!"

George made out the loom of a small building, glimpsed a spark of light, and loosed his companion's hand.

"Wait here!" he whispered and turning from the path, began to creep towards this twinkling light, but stumbled in the darkness and a loose stone went rolling. Somebody whistled softly, the light was instantly extinguished and George sensed stealthy movement below, shapes unseen that skulked away in different directions, and, immediately changing his tactics, he cried out in his most English voice:

"Hallo there! Oh, I say! Is anyone about? Half a mo! I've lost the dashed path. Hi there, somebody, anybody . . . hold on! You there, be a good bloke and help a chappie!" George slithered down a yard or so of rocky slope towards something his keen eyes had glimpsed.

"Ah, what the hell!" snarled a familiar voice.

"Eh—what?" cried George, cheerily, but freeing his armed hand for instant action, "is it my old pal Puck? Oh, good egg—"

"I ain't no pal o' yours and me name ain't Puck—see? So you jest can the bull-con and don't gimme no more o' your old buck,—djear?"

"Right-ho, laddie, but—"

"Didjer see anything?"

"No, dash it I can't,—that's why I lost the jolly old path."

"Huh!" growled Jake. "Then whatya doin' around here? C'mon, nosey Parker, let's have it—what?"

"Well, old playmate, I believe I'm on what they call a night shift, and I don't mean any sort of garment and what not, and I'm looking for the Superintendent's office, to know whether or no. Do you show me whither to go, yes or no, with a rumbelow and a heave ye mariners haul-oh, and so forth. How about it, Santa Claus?"

"A blamed nice time to be reporting. And why the Sup'rintendent?"

"The better belate the better the deed, if you know what I mean, sweetheart—"

"And don't give me no more o' your dam fancy funniment neither!"

"Or what?" enquired George, softly.

"I'll push your nancy face in, for a starter,—see. I'll alter your map—"

"Listen—you!" said George, in fierce contempt, "I'm saying you're just a four-flushing plugugly as yellow as you're mean and straight as a cork-screw! Get that? Now get on, before I bust you on the jaw. Go on,—show me the way. And keep ahead of me. Don't try anything or I'll sock you for a home run. Get!"

Jake hesitated; George, crouching purposefully, advanced a slow pace; Jake, breathing thickly but uttering no word, turned obediently and led the way down and out from the dark and silent canyon into the light and ceaseless activity of the great camp.

"There y'are!" he growled, pointing to a long range of lighted buildings.

"And I said the Superintendent's office. Lead me to it!"

"If only," said Jake, with a kind of wild animal whimper, and glancing at the pocket that hid George's right hand, "if only you didn't tote a gun!"

"Then what?"

"You'd see!"

"Listen, Jake: I don't want trouble with anyone, I'd rather be friends. But if you want it the other way and give me the least cause, I'll make you a hospital job and be mighty glad to do it. Now,—which is it to be?"

Jake hesitated, then essayed a smile, a somewhat repulsive facial contortion, and held out his hand.

"Why, friends for sure, Mr. Rider," he answered; but his eyes, meeting George's keen, searching gaze, flinched and glanced away; so George's hand remained in his pocket.

"Think it over and tell me to-morrow," said he. "Now show me Mr. M'Cloud's office."

Thus George was ushered presently into an inner sanctum hung with maps, scale-plans and blue prints where a broad-shouldered grey-headed man was busied.

"Mr. Hector M'Cloud?"

"Ay! That's mysel', sir."

"My name's Rider, sir, and The Master told me to look you up and show you this list—"

"Bide a wee, sir." Opening a desk drawer Mr. M'Cloud took thence a letter and conned it over.

"Here the Master writes, sir, touching yourself . . . I'll run ower a line or so: 'Hector, my dear old friend' (ye'll be pleased to note the familiareety, sir), 'I am shortly sending on special service my great-grandson George, Earl of Riderwood, who for obvious reasons shall be known as "Mr. Rider." He comes to take counsel with you, my dear Hector' (I've kenned auld Anthony since I was a bairn, my father was one o' his chief engineers) 'and he' (that's yoursel', sir) 'has my full authority for the taking of all or any measure to ensure the work shall progress with no further interruptions, and also to discover the secret cause of past disturbances. To this end you will, of course, do all you may to assist and advise him' (which I am verra willing to do, sir). 'I have made him no least mention as to the direction our suspicions point and suggest you be as reticent lest we prejudice his judgement and set him upon a false trail. . . .' Weel, Mr. Rider, I'm happy to be acquaint. Pray how can I help or sairve ye?"

"First, Mr. M'Cloud," answered George as they shook hands, "what about this recent premature explosion?"

Hector M'Cloud frowned in troubled manner, shook his grizzled head and, leaning near, spoke below his breath, and to such effect that George's face grew troubled also.

"Then you are convinced it was deliberate," said he, "murder in fact?"

"Mr. Rider, I am that."

"And no means of so proving it?"

"Not the least in the worrald, sir. Whoever contrived it was a skilled engineer."

"Quite!" murmured George, frowning on space. "I suppose the camp is policed,—watchmen and so on, sir?"

"Day and night, Mr. Rider." George took out his wallet and drawing thence a folded paper, gave it to M'Cloud, saying:

"This, sir, is a list made out by my great-grandfather, names of men, of all grades and ratings, known to him personally, fellows he can trust implicitly. From these I want you to select ten of the heftiest for my own secret service corps, men who can handle themselves, quick of hand, but quicker witted. Tick off their names, tell me why and leave the rest to me."

So Hector M'Cloud, with Scottish caution and due deliberation, made choice of ten names, giving his reasons therefor. This done, they sat knee to knee talking in lowered voices, rapid question and deliberate answer, until a knock roused them and a clerk entered to say Mr. Romney was outside.

"Right ho!" answered George, rising. "Say I'll be right with him. Thanks, Mr. M'Cloud, for your information, it will be priceless to me, and besides I feel I know these ten chappies already. Good night, sir. I'll pop around now and then, if I may."

"Ay, come often, I'll be glad o' ye, Mr. Rider."

So away strode George to meet six feet or so of indignation.

"Hell!" growled Bill, in angry relief. "We began to think someone had beaned you; Barbara couldn't stick it, so here we are and past midnight, dammit—"

"Sorry, darlings, bless your pretty hearts!" quoth George, kissing Barbara's anxious face and slipping a hand in the arm of husband and wife, "Let's to bed right speedily! Take George home to bye-bye!"

CHAPTER X

DESCRIBES, BRIEFLY, OTHER ACTIONS OF MR. RIDER

So, day and night, the Titans wrought amain, the brief months shortened to weeks, the army of pygmies laboured and the work went on apace beneath fierce sunglare and the cold light of stars.

But at all seasons George took his seemingly inconsequent, aimless way, yet with eyes and ears constantly alert and, ever and always, in touch with one of his chosen ten.

He forgathered amiably with all and sundry, though more especially with such of the men, high and low, whose names appeared on The Master's long list. He also dallied with pick, spade or shovel of the humblest labourers, talking as he worked. He sauntered frequently into Mr. Julius Fischer's field-office, and always in haphazard fashion, to pass the time of day and rail fatuously against the fate that doomed him to such slavery. And every day, at four in the afternoon he made report to The Master in far away New York.

And yet, despite his vigilance, there were furtive eyes that watched him unseen and dangers that menaced. . . . As upon a certain evening when, turning into the deeper gloom of the canyon, he heard a rustling on the steep above, glanced upward and leapt for the providential shelter of a rocky outcrop as a heavy boulder came hurtling down to crash splintering on the path perilously near. . . . Now as he crouched thus, peering, his hand lighted by chance upon a stone, a smooth, round stone somewhat smaller than a baseball but much heavier; clutching this, he groaned dismally and saw a shape vague against the shadowy rock-wall, a creeping figure that very stealthily drew nearer, nearer yet. George balanced the stone in practised hand, for he had not been a star First Baseman without acquiring that accuracy of eye and hand that is one of the marvels of this ever-wonderful game. George arose; his would-be slayer, turning to flee, was for a moment outlined against the sky; George hurled his missile and the running form went down as if poleaxed.

A smallish, dark-avised, Italianate man whose face showed quite unfamiliar. Removing the man's broad belt George pinioned him therewith securely and, grasping him by the collar, dragged his inert captive to the little rill that bubbled nearby and there seated, bathed the unconscious man very patiently until he gasped and struggled to sit up.

"Feeling better, Machiavelli?"

The man merely groaned.

"Quite!" said George. "Now let's hear why you tried to kill me. Come on, talk!"

Ensued a spate of breathless speech, passionate denials in fluent Italian and broken English.

"Absolutely, my lamb!" sighed George, wearily. "But cutting out the fairy-tale, let's know who set you on to heaving rocks on my unwary bean. Speak Mac., and the truth, mind, the truth, d'ye hear?"

The writhing man was seized by a powerful hand, plucked to a sitting posture and shaken savagely to and fro,—a groaning, spiritless shape of misery that could but gasp, over and over again:

"Me no heave-a da rock . . . !"

"Of course," mused George, eyeing his wretched captive askance. "I might kick the truth out of you . . . and yet. . . . Oh hell!" He sighed mournfully, then, setting fingers to lip, emitted a clear, far-reaching whistle that was answered, like an echo, from somewhere beneath them; and presently two burly forms came clambering.

"That Ole Jansen and O'Brien?"

"Ay, it bane us, boss."

"Is anything doing, sorr?"

"Only this!" answered George, pointing to his terrified prisoner. "Either of you know the bird?"

"Not me, sorr!" answered the small, fierce Irishman.

"Wan guinney ban so same lak another guinney, boss! What he bane doing of?"

"Tried to spoil my appetite for supper. I don't know who or what he is except that he's a pretty evident wart and general bad actor. Take him along and stick him in jail, lock him in the pen and see who asks for him, if any. If we can find any of the crowd he's been running around with it'll be all to the good. Get going, boys. I'll be around to visit the posts before turning in."

"Right, sorr. Come on—you!" And away they went through the gathering darkness, the moaning prisoner hustled along between them.

But, after some while, as George pursued his solitary pensive way, the moon began to rise, filling the rugged canyon with pale radiance, and touching all things to strange, new beauty, this devious path became a glory perilous whose vivid brightness by contrast made shadows the blacker to hide lurking evils. So George watched these patches of shadow and halted suddenly, fiercely alert, for amid this darkness something darker had moved.

"Come out!" he commanded, right hand in coat-pocket. "Out with you, d'ye hear? Come out or—" His harsh voice was suddenly dumb and he fell back a step gazing with disbelieving eyes at this oft-dreamed, so beloved and unexpected vision.

"Jennifer . . .?" he murmured, incredulously.

"Yes," she answered. "Yes, George, I came to meet you. But why so fierce?" He caught her hands; he drew her into the moonlight, but content awhile to gaze upon her loveliness, made no attempt to kiss her . . . and thus read in her eyes a gratitude that touched him beyond words; so for a long moment they stood hand in hand, viewing each other in this magic light.

"Well, well!" said he, at last, drawing her arm within his own. "I mean to say—Here we are again and so forth, if you get what I mean?"

"I do, oh I do!" she answered fervently, giving his arm a little squeeze. "I know you so much better than I thought that I . . . I'm happier to be here than I ever expected."

"Sounds a trifle involved," said he, laughing a little shakily, "but I . . . oh well, I'm so dashed glad . . . the old throbber bounds responsive . . . if you only mean what I hope you mean. And you look so much more dashed lovely even than I dreamed, that . . . oh, let's walk,—though not too fast, the night's so absolutely you-and-me-ish!"

"You don't ask me why I'm here, George."

"No," he answered, "no, I'm so perfectly content to know you are here that nothing else matters. And I simply love the way you say 'George.' But of course I perfectly adore your dear voice whatever you say,—so talk, dear heart, talk!" At this, naturally, she became dumb, so, too, was he; but they went on together in a very eloquent silence, a closer, sweeter intimacy than they had ever known.

"I'm rather hoping," said George, at last, "that you won't always want me to be so . . . so dashed . . . different, my dear."

"But you will always be different," she answered, keeping her head averted, "yes, always, because you can't help it . . . thank God!"

"Jennifer?" he questioned. "Oh, my dear, does that mean you'll be content with me as I am . . .? I mean to say . . . someday you'll let me be just as ordinary as I feel?"

"Yes," she answered, very tenderly, "yes, George."

Now, uttering his name, she looked at him; and George read in this look so much, that he lifted her hand to his lips.

"Lord!" he murmured, kissing her slim fingers, "it's a grand old world,—absolutely, now you are here!

And why did you come? The Master sent you, of course."

"Of course, George."

"Blessings on his old, white head! I wonder he could part with you and your egg-nogs. Well, what's your job here?"

"I'm private secretary to Mr. Fischer."

"Not so dashed good!" exclaimed George, frowning. "No, this is definitely all to the dam bad!"

"But, George, please—why?"

"Oh . . . well . . . let's hope I'm wrong! However, I shall never be very far from our Mr. Fischer henceforth."

Nor was he; for every day and at all hours, his apparently haphazard ramblings would take him in the vicinity of the Chief Engineer's office.

And thus it befell upon a certain afternoon that Mr. Fischer summoning Jennifer into his small, private office, was so unwise as to commend her shape and to remark somewhat fulsomely on her beauty and general loveliness:

"You are," said he in the voice and with the assured air of one well used to easy conquest, "a very peculiarly luscious thing, Jennifer, all S.A. darling, from pretty toes to bewitching head. So what do you say, Sweetness?" Jennifer would have said much, but her eyes had read a name upon a certain paper among the many that littered the untidy desk, and she stood dumb; but when his powerful arms enfolded her she struggled wildly, fired with the old, sick fear and rageful disgust; and when, forcing her near, he would have kissed her, she screamed. The answer was instant, for someone, seemingly all arms and legs, came scrambling in through the open window.

"Hullo! hullo!" cried a voice. "Loose the lady and put 'em up, Fischer. Turn round, Mr. Satyr, and take what's coming to you." And Julius Fischer obeyed: that is to say, he clenched his fists, he faced the speaker and quivering for action, checked to stare;

for George's smile, no longer fatuous, was such as signalled a warning, more especially to such as Fischer who had 'roughed it' more than once, ere now; therefore, reading this smile aright, he wasted no breath in vain words but leapt to instant, vicious conflict.

Both men were young, powerful and skilled at the game, thus as this merciless strife progressed, Jennifer, crouching in a corner, was spattered with the blood of each; she watched in horror as the office went to ruin about these grappling, smiting, reeling fighters; she heard vague shouts and cries, was aware of peering faces at broken doorway and shattered window, but saw only these two fierce battling men. . . . Glass shivered, chairs splintered to ruin, over crashed the littered desk and Jennifer leaping thither, caught up a small, stout book and crumpled a certain paper between her clenching hands. She saw George lurch backward to the wall, steady himself and leap; she heard the dreadful impact of two hard-driven blows, a groan, and silence except for gasping breath and muttering voices.

"Pretty . . . business!" panted George. "Will that . . . be all . . . Fischer? If not . . . up with . . . you—"

But Julius Fischer lay a battered, bruised and crumpled heap. "What . . . no?" gasped George. "However you're . . . better than I . . . thought! Look after him . . . some of you. . . ." Then he followed Jennifer out from the wrecked office, watched her don hat and coat and so away through the gathering crowd, and without a word between them. Nor did they pause or speak until they were in the canyon, George because speech, just then, was decidedly painful, and Jennifer because words were beyond her.

Then said George, behind stained handkerchief:

"Sorry, girl! Though a jolly little fracas. Fischer's no end of a microbe, of course, but a fairly tough one. I was lucky to get off so dashed lightly."

"Lightly?" she repeated, shivering.

"Well, I mean to say! He nearly had me twice,—

that upper-cut was a rattler! And the jolt to the point . . . shook me, absolutely! Bulldog breed and what not! What I mean is—Oh, my dear love," he broke off in tones of horrified contrition, "there's blood on your sweet, white throat——"

"Yes," she sighed, shivering again, "it's yours, or —his. . . ."

"Ghastly! Let me wipe it off."

"No!" she answered. "If it's his you can't wipe it clean enough and if it's yours it was shed for me and is—precious."

"Darling—"

"No, please, George! Come indoors and let me bathe your poor face and do what I can before the others see you."

"Am I very awful, dearest?"

"Rather frightful. And yet I never . . . liked you so much."

"Glory!" he exclaimed. "By Venus, I'd kiss you—if only my mouth felt less like a dashed tomato."

"No, George . . . ah, my dear, please don't ever try until—"

"Yes, yes,—until?"

"Until I kiss you, George. Now come in and be doctored."

So she bathed his cuts and bruises and every touch of her cool, soft hands a delight. Then seating him in the easiest chair, she brought another beside him and from her bosom took a crumpled screw of paper, smoothing this out carefully on the chair-arm, she drew him near, and watched him as he read.

"Holy . . . jumping . . . Moses!" he exclaimed and almost in a whisper, for what he saw was a telegraph form with these words in Fischer's handwriting:

"Wittax: Prosper, recondite, artichoke, music, contraption, waywardness, benevolence, exult, pertinacity."

"And this ends Fischer!" said George, grimly.

“But it’s in code, you can’t read it—”

“Enough to prove Fischer’s treachery. That first word Wittax is the de Witt telegraphic address. I wonder what new deviltry. . . . If only I could read the dam thing. However, it behoves us to act, girl, and that right presently.”

“What must I do, George?”

“Kiss me, someday. But for the nonce, go you and seek out Fischer’s code-book, meanwhile, I’ll set divers eyes to watch the blighter.”

“Some day I . . . surely will, George.”

“Will . . . what, loveliness, what pray?”

“Kiss you . . . someday! But now, the code book,—here it is!”

“Well,” quoth George, taking the book and hand that held it, “I mean to say, of all the lovely, adorable—”

“Quite!” said Jennifer in tender mockery. “Ab-so-lutely! I love you to tell me so, but wait. First, let’s decode this message—now, George, this moment!”

“Quite!” said George.

CHAPTER XI

TELLS WHY MR. RIDER WAS KISSED

Day by day, the Master sat, watching, warding, guiding and directing. And yet, though his mind proved alert and judgment swiftly decisive as ever, it was now that his frail, old hands began to drop things, especially the gold-handled crutch stick also his step seemed slower, his lean frame more bowed, his silver head less boldly carried, would droop often, as if feeling at last the weary burden of his many years.

But in these moments of growing bodily weakness, his lips would form words and, with the assured faith of his own generation, he would utter such prayer as this:

'Lord of Mercy, Master of Life, let me endure this little while . . . until the end; let me endure in Thy strength until my work is done?'

This morning he sat at his great desk intent upon the writing of a letter, no matter of dictation this but one inscribed by his own hand, though he paused often as though he found it a labour almost beyond his powers, and often closed his eyes as if he felt them failing him; and these the words he had written so laboriously:

"My dear Jennifer

"I miss my morning egg-nog more than I deemed possible, which means, as I suppose, that I miss its maker even more. Age must be creeping on me with a vengeance at last, for to-day I feel more lonely than—"

He had written thus far when his desk telephone buzzed and a voice announced: "Long distance, sir."

"Well, put it through!" said he, sharply; and then to his distant caller: "Falconbridge speaking."

"That you, Gramps, good egg, sir!" answered a thin, far off voice there was no mistaking. "I've gotten a line on things at last . . . pretty big and dashed surprising—absolutely! Now . . . are you there, sir?"

"Yes, my son, yes."

"Well, sir, there have been doings, yes. Hell was going to pop, down here, was—but isn't because we've rather crabbed their game! I've got the absolute king-pin, the Big Shot. To-day we shall bag the whole dam outfit. . . . Are you there, sir?"

"Yes, George, yes. And beg you to be plainer."

"Right-ho, Gramps! Now listen and hearken! This whole black business has been run—"

The far away voice was lost in a sudden sharp and painful crackling . . . a muffled explosion.

The receiver dropped from Old Anthony's nerveless grasp and deafened, half-stunned, he sank back in his chair, gazing at the telephone with aweful eyes that widened to anguished fear and growing horror; then from his lips issued a broken cry:

"George . . . oh, my boy . . . not you too! Oh God, show mercy . . . not George—" His white head sank and for a moment he cowered . . . an old, old creature, dumb-struck and helpless. Then he straightened; his steady fingers sought and pressed certain of the switches on the desk and in to him came hurrying the chief members of his staff and, foremost of all, Donald Keith.

"Gentlemen," said he, looking round on them, calm-eyed, "there is more and sudden trouble at the Orellana Dam and I must be there. I am leaving Keith in charge here, and my faith with you all. And I go at once! Order me a special train—no, an air machine. I'll fly. See to it yourself, Donald, and immediately—"

Speaking, he arose, stumbled, clutched at the air and would have fallen but for the ready arms that caught him.

"You are ill, Master!" cried Keith anxiously.

"I am old, Donald, no more."

"Lie down, sir."

"You surely can't travel at present."

"He ought to be in bed!"

"At least, sir, try to sleep a little."

"Not yet!" said Old Anthony, rising unaided and smiling upon the anxious company. "Soon I shall sleep very deeply awhile, to wake young again, I hope and pray, glad with eternal youth. But now, I must be away. Call a taxi . . . order the fastest of these flying machines,—see to it, Donald Keith! . . ."

And while The Master was thus issuing his orders at one end of the wire, at the other end lay George, bleeding and helpless with none to aid . . . until one came running fleet as a deer, one who, heedless of creeping flame and drifting smoke, caught him in cherishing arms, who pillowed his stricken head on her bosom, wetting him with her tears and whispering in breathless, passionate supplications:

"George! Oh, my own dear, look at me,—speak! . . . Dear God, don't, don't let him die . . . don't take him from me! George . . . oh my beloved, speak to me!"

And presently, sure enough, George looked, gazed at her with swooning eyes and, despite pain and weakness, contrived to gasp:

"Jennifer . . . dear, I think . . . now . . . at last . . . a . . . kiss is indi-cated, abso—"

And kiss him indeed she did, though George felt nothing of it, for now he had sunk to deeps beyond even her reach.

CHAPTER XII

IN WHICH THIS NARRATION BEGINS TO DRAW TO AN END

IT was on a morning that George opened his eyes and turned bandaged head on his pillow; then his welcoming smile vanished and he blinked to see, instead of Jennifer's loved and lovely face, the silvery locks and lion eyes of his great-grandfather.

"Eh? Why . . . oh, greetings, sir! Cheerio, Gramps!" he mumbled and contrived to stretch forth a hand that was taken and held firmly between the old man's bony fingers.

"Well, my son," said The Master, with such smile as warmed George's heart, "so they didn't quite kill you!"

"Lord no, Gramps! Lots of kick in me yet! Up and about in a day or so, absolutely! But you? Pray how—?"

"By air, George. I flew. A quite astonishing experience."

"Dash me, but you're a marvel!" exclaimed George so vehemently that Old Anthony smiled and pressed the hand he held:

"Such praise tickles my pride, George, but is hardly merited," he answered. "For I was very fearful, my nervousness indeed quite astonished me, and when we arrived I had to be lifted from the machine and put to bed like the poor, old wreck I was."

"Ah but," said George, "by God, sir, it's just such wrecks that become traditions to live up to . . inspiration,—do or die . . . bulldog breed and what not. Sir, I'm dashed proud to be your great-grandson . . . I mean to say—quite! If you get what I mean."

"Thank you, my son," answered Old Anthony. "When Death, that good angel, lifts me up into the fuller living, I shall be the more happy to think the Falconbridge blood may persist through such clean manhood as your own. . . . Oh yes, George, I know. Jennifer has told me she is marrying you, and why, besides loving, she honours you. And so, my boy, I'm telling you I have cabled my agents in London to pay off the mortgages on your estates, to put Riderwood Manor into repair and fit it to receive its countess,—though not yet, I hope."

"Sir," said George, in choking voice. "Oh Gramps, you . . . I say, you know I . . . Oh thank God, here's Jennifer! Darling, say something . . . anything, before I snivel. . . . Oh curse it,—I am!"

"Dearest," she answered, bending above him, "this is just one more reason why I love you so frightfully much!"

"And Julius Fischer," said Old Anthony, grimly, "is still in hospital, I hear." Then he sighed deeply, rose with painful effort, staggered, sank down again, gasping. But Jennifer was beside him, her arm close about his feebleness, her little flask at his lips; while George started to an elbow, dismayed to see the old face show so pale, so haggard and ineffably weary.

"Thank you, my dear," said The Master, looking his gratitude; then, squaring his old shoulders, he sat up, resolute as ever, saying: "This poor, old body is wearing out, my children, but my mind, bless God, is strong and clear as ever . . . clearer. And to-day, George, Jennifer and I have arranged to get you married."

"Eh? . . . to-day?" exclaimed George. "Eureka! But, Jennifer, oh dash it all,—in these dam bandages!"

"Anyway and anyhow!" said Jennifer, kissing him.

CHAPTER XIII

RELATES HOW THE MASTER ACHIEVED

"Two more days, Sweetheart," said George, easing himself into his coat with the deft assistance of his wife, "just two more days and the job's done, my lady, the Dam completed and so forth! And what then?"

"Yes," sighed Jennifer, murmurous as he kissed her, "but oh I'll be glad when they're over, so much can happen in just two days."

"Can I come in, my lord?" cried Barbara, thumping on the door and entered gaily, forthwith. "Pray, how's the countess?" she laughed. "And Bill's just phoned up, George, to say you're to go down into camp, right now, Gramps wants you."

"Right-ho and eftsoons!" answered George. "I'm hencing this moment and— Hullo! hullo! D'you hear what I do?"

"No," said Jennifer.

"Not a thing!" answered Barbara.

"That's precisely it!" said George, clapping on his hat. "There's nothing to hear! The machines have stopped! Jennifer, stay here, yes and you, Barbara. There may be a spot of trouble and you girls are going to keep out of it. And that's definite, absolutely!" And away he strode, heedless of his wife's appeals not to over-tax his strength or take needless risks; for the air throbbed with a vague murmur afar, that swelled to the ominous hum of many angry voices, a growing clamour pierced now and then by fierce shouts and hoarse outcries.

And presently there met him O'Brien with tall Jansen and others of his chosen ten.
"The bhoys is out, sorr!"
"Ay, they bane yellin' for Fischer, boss."
"Sure enough, Mr. Rider, and there's durned fools telling 'em he's their friend, and how The Master's here to cut their pay, so all hell's broke loose—"
"Come on!" said George. "Let's try a crack at 'em!"
So on they sped until they beheld a great and riotous assemblage: and standing on an eminence above and surrounded by this wide sea of angry faces, uptossing arms and threatening fists, a solitary, old man leaning feebly on crutch-stick, one against a multitude that hooted, roared and clamoured.
"Holy Saint Michael!" exclaimed O'Brien. "Shall we thry to foight our ways to him, sorr?"
"No!" cried George, desperately, "No! Stand still and wait. Leave it to The Master. He's the only one can handle them,—if not . . . watch and be ready—watch!"
Mute and very still Old Anthony leaned there, surveying this riotous concourse with his lion's eyes, fronting this menace undismayed; while, above the tumult, voices of unseen agitators shouted all about him:
"We want Fischer!"
"Down with The Master! He's here to cut wages?"
"Don't let him speak, boys! Don't be fooled!"
And still the solitary, bowed old figure waited with a serene patience so unshakable that, little by little, the clamour subsided. Then slowly the old figure straightened, lifted one hand as if in benediction and, in voice clear and resonant, The Master spoke:
"Men of mine, because I am a very old man and feeble and you so many and strong, give me a hearing—"
At this, one or two voices began to hoot again and jeer, but were roared down and a deep voice cried:
"Fair's fair, boys! Let's hear him. Speak, Master!"

"Know then," continued Anthony, "that I have discharged Julius Fischer because he was a traitor to me and to you all. He was responsible for the deaths of some of you, therefore I have sent him to judgement. Proofs of this shall be shown to such as doubt my word. . . . Among you there are men of many nations who have come to this country to live free men,—because in our America we suffer no Tyrants, we want no dictators, we need no whips nor spurs to goad us to our duty. So I stand here,—not your taskmaster, bur rather as one of yourselves, a man to work and do his duty as he sees it. And so, friends all,—you workmen of America, you whose labours shall make our country so much the better for us and our children's children, I say to you, for their sakes and our own,—go back to your duty! Finish this great work on time and I promise you all, to every man and boy, a bounty according to his rating—" Shouts interrupted him, the dense crowd split asunder and a group of men came hurrying and foremost of them, Bill, and haled in the midst of them, a drooping, blood-stained shape of misery.

"It's Jake, boys!" cried a voice. "It's Fischer's jackal."

"He was all set to blow the Dam!" cried another.

"The Western overflow weir!" shouted a third. "What's for the skunk, boys?"

"Lynch . . . lynch him!" roared the swaying crowd. Now at this dreadful threat the doomed wretch broke from his captors and mad with terror came running to throw himself upon his knees before Old Anthony.

"Master . . ." he gasped. "Save me—!"

The furious crowd surged forward, but stepping before his wretched suppliant, Old Anthony faced this oncoming vengeance, and thus a missile intended for the cowering Jake, smote and staggered him; but Bill's strength upheld him as, with arms outstretched he strove to speak. . . . But now, at sight of this appealing gesture, beholding this silvery hair all blood bedabbled, revulsion came; back swayed the crowd, men shouted, they cheered and, crying upon The Master's name, caught up their abandoned tools. . . .

And presently the Titans were at work again.

CHAPTER XIV

VICTORY

"WELL, Ant, you've done it again! By heck, I'll say so, yessir!" quoth Mr. Tutt as they stood together arm in arm, gazing up at the mighty, man-made cliff that soared above them. "Yessir, you're successful now as you always were, Anthony Falconbridge."

"I wonder, Malachi," he answered, very wistfully, "I wonder if I truly am, indeed?"

"But why, sir?" questioned Bill, "you surely are successful, the Dam's finished and seven hours ahead of time!"

"Thank God, yes! But, my boy, what is true success? It is not achievement, nor wealth, nor power, for these may become a weariness. It is not honours or even fame . . . No, I dare to think Success is simply to live well loved and to die truly lamented."

They brought him where he might look down upon the completed work, this vast construction that one day would be a-brim and running over with life-giving water. And here seated, with old friends around him and loved relations close beside him, he glanced to the left on Bill and Barbara, to the right on George and his young wife and smiled very happily.

"*Nunc Dimittis!*" said he. "The work is done! A greater America! A coming generation better, perhaps, than mine! . . . Here soon, instead of agony and death, shall be happiness and life, and insomuch shall our America be richer. . . . This land our forefathers won from the wilderness! This America that by suffering has learned so much of late, shall find its soul again and live on fearlessly not for itself alone, but for

Humanity,—taking its place among the foremost nations at last and shouldering its responsibilities henceforth . . . an ever greater America!"

"Look!" cried Barbara, suddenly, "Look, Gramps, there is the first trickle of water! But only a trickle. For heaven's sake! Now how long will it take to fill?"

"Two years, about," answered Bill. "Then the Dam will discharge down those overflow weirs and the miracle will begin . . . grass first, and trees! Virgin soil to grow anything, pretty well, eh Master?"

"Yes," answered Old Anthony, "there shall be blessings of water . . . waters . . . of . . . life!" Once again the old voice was hushed, and this time for ever; though none were conscious of this until George touched his great-grandfather to find that, with the word, the soul of him had passed from life—to Life.

So died The Master, Anthony Three. But his indomitable spirit lives on in his children's children, and all true sons of the real America, to carry on the traditions of their ancestry from one generation to another, this imperishable, dauntless spirit that can lift their great country from weakness, through stress, to an ever mightier strength for the well-being and glory, not of themselves only, but of the whole, wide world.